The Curse of the Crocodile Queen

BY THE SAME AUTHOR

Mirazor (Matador, 2011)

The Curse
of the
Crocodile Queen

V. Peter Maslin

Copyright © 2024 V. Peter Maslin

The moral right of the author has been asserted.

Apart from any fair dealing for the purposes of research or private study, or criticism or review, as permitted under the Copyright, Designs and Patents Act 1988, this publication may only be reproduced, stored or transmitted, in any form or by any means, with the prior permission in writing of the publishers, or in the case of reprographic reproduction in accordance with the terms of licences issued by the Copyright Licensing Agency. Enquiries concerning reproduction outside those terms should be sent to the publishers.

This is a work of fiction. Names, characters, businesses, places, events and incidents are either the products of the author's imagination or used in a fictitious manner. Any resemblance to actual persons, living or dead, or actual events is purely coincidental.

Troubador Publishing Ltd
Unit E2 Airfield Business Park,
Harrison Road, Market Harborough,
Leicestershire LE16 7UL
Tel: 0116 279 2299
Email: books@troubador.co.uk
Web: www.troubador.co.uk

ISBN 978-1-80514-417-5

British Library Cataloguing in Publication Data.
A catalogue record for this book is available from the British Library.

Printed and bound by CPI Group (UK) Ltd, Croydon, CR0 4YY
Typeset in 11pt Aldine by Troubador Publishing Ltd, Leicester, UK

CONTENTS

1	Death at the Rose Tavern	1
2	Midnight Confidences	17
3	The Necropolis of Queen Mbembé	36
4	The Streets	55
5	Confessions	67
6	Captain Smalt and the *Sabrina Louise*	78
7	The Miasmic Vapours of the Isle of Dogs	97
8	Shades and Shadows	112
9	The *Sabrina Louise* is Transformed	128
10	The Ruins at Egypt Point	145
11	The Taking of the *Helga*	165
12	The Gold	178
13	In the Damnable Deptford Fog	191
14	A Midnight Visitation	208
15	The Creature Strikes Again	221
16	Mr Orzinga's Chamber of Curiosities	241
17	The Ceremony	261
18	The Horror at Graysons' Yard	277
19	Mischief at the Crow Hotel	292
20	Billy Falls Foul of the Law	307
21	Dastardly Deeds	326
22	The Hour of the Crocodile Queen	345

1

DEATH AT THE ROSE TAVERN

The river was choked with vessels of every description, from every far-flung corner of the Empire. Most were on their way up to Wapping, or the Upper Pool, but had been forced to anchor at Limehouse for the night, as the devilish fog had closed in.

It was *cold,* too, suddenly. *Weirdly* cold.

A tavern door clattered open on Thieves' Street and a solitary soul stumbled out. He had a dazed look about him. The bewildered look of a drunken sailor who'd forgotten which port he was in. Or which side of the world he was on. His old leather coat was coming apart at the seams. There were grisly shadows around his eyes and under his cheekbones. Ghostly shadows.

He didn't look well.

Several days' worth of grey stubble graced his chin.

He lingered in the glow of the establishment's windows for a moment or two, peering about and grunting to himself, as though he was trying to make his mind up about some matter of momentous importance.

An urgent need to empty his bladder was what, in actual fact, had brought Septimus Slim out into the night. He waddled into the filthy alleyway at the side of the building and moaned as he unbuttoned his breeches.

"Ooooohhh..."

His urine steamed as it gushed down the wall. Further up the alley, in the foggy dark, a couple were enjoying a noisy public congress. Despite the cold, and the various other inconveniences. The woman's ragged dress was up around her waist. She was shrieking insults at the man she was with. In several languages.

Septimus was dreamily, drunkenly impressed.

He admired talented people.

As he stood there, squinting into the gloom and squirming with relief, something suspiciously warm and wet started seeping up into his boots.

"Oh, damnation! Shit, shit, shit!"

He was standing in a pool of his own piss, he realised with disgust. Other people's too, almost certainly. He stood on tiptoe until he was done and then hurried out of the alley, splashing through more stinking puddles as he went. Both of his boots had holes in the bottom. He'd been meaning for weeks to get them repaired.

Septimus was impecunious. His debts were mounting by the day.

He buttoned himself up and went back inside.

The place was warm and thronged. The tavern's resident *chanteuse,* Harriet Wildfire, was up on the small stage, bellowing out one of her popular songs of love and loss and betrayal. She was dancing as she sang. Twirling around so the pink feathers of her costume flew out and showed off the sweaty flesh underneath. Her admirers whooped and shouted. At the end of the song she whirled about and shook her naked backside at the crowd – like an ecstatic Eve in the Garden of Eden.

It was her favourite trick. She did it most evenings. At least once.

"Hooo, hooo, hooo!" the idiots around the little stage howled.

Septimus chuckled at the familiar sight of Harriet's *derrière*. He was half in love with her.

Like everyone else in the place.

A heap of fine Newcastle coal, stolen from the local docks, very likely, was blazing in the big fireplace. Septimus found himself a seat close to the fire and stretched his legs out till his boots were almost touching the hot coals. He half-closed his eyes and listened, lazily, to the wash of voices around him. A group of women close by were discussing a recent murder. An Irish scullery-maid had been brutally killed, in the middle of the night, at an ale-house in nearby Ratcliffe.

It was the latest in a series of similar atrocities.

"Ah went in an' took a look for meself," a woman with a shrill voice was telling her companions. "She were in this little room, upstairs at the Black Dog. *Gawd...* it worra mess. I ain't never seen nuffink like it. *Blood* everywhere, all over the woles. *Drippin'* darn the woles, it was. I don't know 'ow they'll ever clean it orf. And the *smell*. Uugh! And she was such a *sweet* girl, so they say. What kind of a person would *do* somefink like that? *Eh?* He's gotta be a bloody madman, ain't he?"

Septimus listened with half an ear as his boots steamed. He knew about the killings. Everyone did. The previous day's edition of the *London Mercury* had carried a detailed report of the affair at the Black Dog. On its busy front page.

Someone had left a tattered copy of the journal in the public bog-house at Shipping Stairs. Septimus had perused it while he'd been sitting there in the stink, with the flies buzzing around his head and the river gurgling twenty feet below.

The Black Dog was a busy Ratcliffe alehouse, catering mostly to sailors. The body had been found in the servants' quarters, at dawn. The unfortunate girl had been killed in the small hours, it seemed. Nobody had seen or heard a thing. She'd been sleeping alone, that night, and had bolted the door of her tiny room. The other servants had been forced to break in, after they'd failed to rouse her. The room was in a state of disarray. Furniture had been thrown around. A mirror was broken.

There'd been a soot-fall. As though someone – *or something* – had come down the chimney. Though the chimney, they said, was hardly wide enough.

The devil himself would have struggled to get down it.

One of the resident girls brushed up behind Septimus. *"Hello, my sweet..."*

Septimus recognised the soft voice of Susie Kettle. He smiled as she kissed his ear. Susie hadn't been at the Rose Tavern all that long but Septimus had adored her from the moment he'd set eyes on her. She was slim and pretty, and strangely innocent, though she'd been sleeping on the streets until quite recently. Septimus had asked her to marry him. She'd told him that she would think about it.

They'd spent the night together, a couple of times.

She wriggled past him and squeezed into the space at his side. She was attired in a magnificent, shimmering red silk dress that he'd never seen before. It showed off her pale breasts and her narrow waist. Her shiny gold earrings were also new. They glittered in the smoky light as she brushed her hair back.

Septimus took a deep breath.

"You look... *angelic.* Is it a special occasion?"

Susie Kettle tittered.

"I'm going to sing. It was Harriet's idea. We've become quite good friends. She's thinking of leaving. With some fellow she's taken up with. A sea-captain. They've got plans. She's taught me a couple of her songs. Just one or two, to begin with. She knows *hundreds.* Most of them are filthy – you know what she's like. The ones I've learned, so far, are love songs. *I need the money,* Septimus. I don't want to be stuck in this place forever. Selling my favours. Like some common drab. It's *uncivilised.* They *throw* money at Harriet. *Golden guineas, even.* She makes a bloody fortune. Men come from all over the place. Just to see her."

"She's popular. It's true."

"She's fearless. I'm not half so brave. A drink would help, my love."

"Of course! Forgive me! I should have thought."

Septimus rose. A little unsteadily. He pushed his way through to the bar and ordered two good measures of French brandy. *The best they had.* The young Irish barmaid looked uncertain. Septimus had been drinking heavily for days. He hadn't paid a brass farthing on his account since the beginning of the month.

His reckoning already filled several pages in the black book. Madam O'Reilly would have to be consulted.

Septimus held his breath while his case was considered. But he needn't have worried. Madam O'Reilly glanced at the scribbled pages and nodded her approval, without even breaking off her conversation with the fellow she was with.

Madam O'Reilly *liked* Septimus.

He was a drunkard, but he had... *breeding*.

A dusty bottle was produced. Excellent French brandy was still finding its way to England. Despite the ongoing war. And the Channel blockade.

Septimus returned with two full glasses and a silly grin on his face. Susie Kettle kissed him, tenderly, on the lips.

"Thank you, kind sir!" she breathed. "Come and listen to me sing. Sit by the stage where I can see you! You could whistle and shout, perhaps, to encourage the rest of them. I'm scared of making a complete bloody fool of myself."

"That won't happen. You're *beautiful*. They'll adore you!"

She blushed, and smiled.

"I'll sing for you alone, Septimus! As though it was just us!" She mimed another kiss as she went off, clutching her glass.

Septimus got up and followed. He looked for a seat close to the stage but they were all taken. Confusedly, he wandered about, sipping the delicious brandy and looking for anywhere at all where he could sit down. His earlier seat had gone.

The big room was smoky and noisy. It was a busy night.

"Septimus! Thank God! I was hoping you'd be here!"

A familiar face emerged. It was Lachlan Malone. A local dealer in stolen coal, and other loot from the docks. Septimus had known the little Irishman for a while. They'd gone into business together. Selling French perfume. Door to door. Around the waterside. To the local whores, mostly. The perfume had been stolen from a Danish vessel that had stopped-off in London, for some unknown reason, on its way home from Marseilles to Copenhagen. One of the gang who'd actually lifted the stuff had been shot dead as they'd rowed off into the fog.

The Bow Street Runners were still looking for the other three.

"I'm so bloody glad to see you!" Lachlan whispered. *"I've had the most awful day!* I need to talk to somebody. Someone I can trust. *I've been robbed!* I'm ruined! *Dear God!* I need advice. *Come...* there's a table in the corner here."

Clutching his chest, as though he was in pain, he led Septimus over to a quiet corner by the front windows. It held a small table and a couple of empty chairs.

Condensation was dripping down the old leaded windows.

Septimus caught the bar-maid's eye and ordered two more brandies. A wretch with a black eye brought them over to the table.

Lachlan sighed as he picked up his full glass.

"You're a gentleman, Septimus! One of the few! *Dear God!* I needed this! I've had a *ghastly* day. I've been waiting for a, uh...*shipment* to arrive. *From over the water.* On a little brig. The *Sara*. She finally turned up, at Drunken Dock, earlier today. *Ten bloody days late!* Bad weather in the Channel. So they claimed."

"A shipment?"

"A cask of liquor. That's about all, really. But there was a *lot* more on the ship! As things turned out. Forty kegs of wine and *half a ton* of illegal silk! The Revenue men were waiting in the fog. They impounded the cargo and arrested the whole bloody crew. They could *swing*, the poor bastards. *There's no justice.*"

"What kind of liquor?"

"Something quite unusual. I came across it in Paris when I was over there, earlier this year. *Eau Sacré,* they call it. A bit like holy water! I tried some. Naturally. *It was most odd.* I had the *strangest* dreams. *Waking dreams.* I'd be lying there, in my room, minding my own business, and *fabulous* things would appear around me! Naked nymphs, bathing in pools of moonlight. Flying creatures. Devils and demons. Heaven knows what. *Heh, heh!* There's this new religious cult that's sprung up in France. *The Sign of the Crocodile Queen.* They use the *Eau Sacré* in their ceremonies."

"And you bought a *barrel* of it?"

"Well... a two-gallon cask. I met a fellow in the street. He arranged it all for me. My mother is over there, as you know. She was born in Paris. She met my Irish father in London but it never really worked out. They were chalk and cheese. In the end she went back home. She's quite settled over there now. She has a *very* decent little whorehouse in Montparnasse. To the south of the city. The cultists have constructed a *huge* temple, just around the corner from my mother's place. It took two years to build. *Le Temple des Rêves,* they call it. The Temple of Dreams. It's *huge.* It even has its own cemetery. The biggest in Paris. So they say."

"I thought they'd abolished religion. The revolutionaries."

"Officially, perhaps," Lachlan concurred, "though it seems to me that they're just creating new ones to take the place of the ones they've abolished. But... I had a *vision,* Septimus, as I stood there. In the shabby *rue d'Enfer.* In the Parisian drizzle. Staring up at that great, glittering, white building. Do you know what I saw?"

"I can't even guess. Pigeons?"

Lachlan shook his head and chuckled.

"Not *pigeons,* you fool. What I saw was... *money."*

He leaned closer.

"Just think! What does it *cost* to build a place like that? *Eh?* These people may be deluded, but they've got money coming out of their bloomin' ears! They're building a similar temple over here, now. In London. Over the river in Southwark. I thought I could sell the *Eau Sacré* to their English converts. At twice what I paid for it. *In little bottles.* I brought some samples over from Paris. But now, thanks to the interfering bloody Customs Service... *I've lost everything!* Damn them to hell!"

"Was your barrel marked? Was it clear what was in it?"

"Not really. Not at all, in fact. There were some heathenish symbols. Burned into the wood. The Revenue men would have had no idea what the stuff was. It didn't even *smell* particularly nice. They might have poured it straight into the river. Or fed it to the local pigs. It was a *stupid* idea, really. A moment of madness. I should have had more sense! I'm a Christian soul at heart, Septimus. A Catholic soul. I have my dear mother to thank for that. God bless her!"

"Is your father still alive?"

"He was hanged at Tyburn. Ten years ago. For stealing a leg of mutton."

"Oh, Jesus!"

Septimus could hear Susie Kettle singing, some distance away, at the other end of the room. She was struggling to make herself heard, above the usual late-night racket of the tavern. Septimus couldn't help but admire her courage.

If I could just make a little money, he thought, *I could pay for her to take singing lessons. She has a lovely voice. She just lacks confidence.*

Lachlan was still rambling on about his missing barrel.

"...at the place where the stuff is distilled. In Rouen."

Septimus tried his best to look sympathetic.

"You could get it back, I'm sure. It will be at the Customs House. They're not incorruptible. A golden guinea, in the right hands, can work wonders. But you can't go on like this, Lachlan. Trading with your French friends as though nothing has changed! We're at *war* with France. The charge would be treason if you were caught. *That's a capital offence.* There'd be no arguing. Just the bloody rope."

Lachlan pulled a face to show how little he cared.

"Baaahhh..."

He pushed his empty glass aside.

"Stealing a crust is a capital offence, these days. They're stringing 'em up every day, at Newgate. Poor bastards. Hungry men, most of 'em, without a penny to their name. Women, too, though the crowd don't like that so much. I've got no argument with the French. They're an inspiration to the world, if you ask me."

"But, uh..."

"Revolution is in the air, Septimus. Even here. *You can smell it!* In the bloody streets! London is full of troublemakers. From all over the world. I've been attending debates. At the Green Man, in Spitalfields. You should come and join us, one evening. You would enjoy it, I'm certain. Though they do insist on sobriety."

"I'll keep it in mind."

Susie had finished singing. There was some noisy clapping and shouting as she left the stage. Coins were being tossed. People were pressing around her.

Septimus waved and whistled but Susie was too far-off to notice.

As Septimus watched, a smartly-dressed, moustachioed stranger emerged from the crowd and embraced her. He was wearing a fine pair of leather riding-boots, a well-tailored top-coat and a silk shirt with embroidery and ruffles. Susie smiled. She seemed happy to see him. Septimus's heart sank slightly as the pair left together, arm-in-arm, by way of the gloomy corridor at the back of the stage.

It led to the rear rooms, and the stairs to the chambers above.

"Oh, well..." Septimus muttered to himself.

It was Susie's business. She was a free woman.

Lachlan was playing with his empty glass. Twirling it about with his fingers while he collected his thoughts. Septimus rescued it and took both glasses back to the bar to be refilled. He'd been drinking at the Rose Tavern for nearly six months. *Generally speaking,* they trusted him. He'd only let them down once, when he'd inadvertently paid his bill with fake silver shillings, but even then they'd been such good fakes that Madam O'Reilly had been able to pass them on fairly quickly.

"So... what do you think?" Lachlan asked him, when he returned.

"About what?"

"The *Eau Sacré*. It could still be good business. If I can get it back, that is. I'll make enquiries. I've still got some of the little bottles that I brought back myself. I could let you have some. For a few pence each. Would you be interested?"

Septimus shook his head.

"I've got no *funds,* Lachlan. Not a bloody farthing. I'm *utterly* on the rocks. My landlady is threatening to have me imprisoned for debt. If it wasn't for the kindness of Madam O'Reilly, I'd be starving. She lets me take breakfast here. A bit of bread and some coffee, that's about all, but... it keeps me alive."

"What about the money from the perfume?"

"All gone. What little there was. I'm not much good at hawking."

"You idiot! Why didn't you tell me? But, uh..."

Lachlan took a cautious look around.

"I've got other irons in the fire. Something else is coming

up! Some other business. I've had a letter. From a friend in the Low Countries. With some *most* interesting information. You'll hardly believe your ears! I've been meaning to speak to you. I've just been *so* bloody busy. *I'm going to need your help, Septimus.* We need to talk, but, uh... not here. Somewhere more private. *There'll be good money in it.* More than enough to get you back on your feet."

"What kind of business?"

"I'd prefer not to talk here. You'll understand my reticence when you hear what I've got to tell you. It's quite a story! I could come round to your lodgings, later. That might be better. You're still at the same place, I take it?"

"Sad to say."

"I'll call in. There's someone else I need to talk to but I won't be too long. An hour at the most. Will you be there? I'll give you a quiet knock."

"I'll be there. Wake me up if I'm snoring."

Lachlan nodded as he got to his feet. He seemed in a hurry to be off. Lachlan was *always* in a hurry. There were *always* people he needed to see. About one thing or another. Yellow fog wafted in from the street as he went out. The door slammed shut behind him. Septimus shrugged. He couldn't imagine what the mysterious business might be. Buying and selling purloined coal was the Irishman's usual line of work, but it was hardly a secret. The whole world knew it.

Septimus sat in the shadows for a while longer, as the tavern quietened and the candles were gradually extinguished. Susie Kettle didn't reappear. It seemed that she was going to be spending the remainder of the night with her new lover.

So that's who bought her the gold earrings, Septimus thought.

He'd looked like the type who could afford to throw money around.

"One more brandy, Septimus?" the bar-maid called.

Septimus signalled no. He'd had enough. He needed to go home. Home to the crumbling Crow Hotel – the verminous waterside hostelry that he'd been living in for the past six months. With luck there'd be food left out in the kitchen that he could steal. If he could creep in without waking the elderly night-watchman.

Madam O'Reilly had already retired for the night. She would be in her little parlour behind the bar, Septimus knew. Counting the takings.

The Rose Tavern's night-watchman was nowhere to be seen. He was usually on duty, at this hour. But no-one seemed particularly concerned.

The front door was already locked. A few lost souls were still drinking, at the tables. Harriet Wildfire had left earlier with a new man in tow. A tough-looking seafarer with a tarnished silver earring and an ugly scar down one side of his face.

A fellow you'd think twice about picking a fight with. Harriet's type. They'd looked well together.

Septimus struggled, sleepily, to his feet. He waved farewell to the girls at the bar. One of them brought a key to let him out, but before she was halfway to the door a colossal crash from the floor above stopped her in her tracks.

Everyone looked up. Open-mouthed.

Dust floated down. There was a brief, blood-curdling scream. Followed by inexplicable, muffled... *slurpings.*

And then, finally, the sound of running feet as someone fled.

Madam O'Reilly emerged from her quarters, dressed in her voluminous night-clothes and clutching a candle. She was shaking and gasping for breath. Her eyes were huge and luminous in the candlelight. Her face was deathly pale.

"For the love of God!" she shrieked. *"Don't just sit there! Do something! One of the girls could be hurt! Somebody get up there! For God's sake!"*

At last, somebody moved. A young foreign sailor – a scrawny Spaniard with gold earrings and oiled hair – sprang up and sprinted over to the rear door.

A blade appeared in his hand as he ducked through into the dark. Septimus followed. Leadenly. As though some evil was holding him back.

He'd hardly been aware, up to that point, of how intoxicated he was.

Chairs and tables were thrown around as more of the tavern's late-night customers came to their senses and joined the rush to the stairs. Septimus was dragged along with them. Past the ill-lit kitchen and up the twisting staircase.

It was Susie Kettle who'd screamed. He just knew it.

The mob slowed at the top of the stairs. Septimus pushed his way past. Susie's chamber door was wide open.

The knife-man went in first. With Septimus at his heels.

Fog was drifting in from the street outside. The window was smashed. The room was icily cold. It reeked of death. A guttering candle was the only source of light. Septimus put his hands to his face and stared in horror.

At the wrecked room...

And the ghastly remains of Susie Kettle. What was left of her.

The candle hissed in the cold air. A dog howled. Somewhere. Out in the night. Septimus swayed, drunkenly. He wanted to run but his legs had turned to jelly. His heart was thumping. The room was spinning.

He could hardly breathe.

The knife-man was cursing. In Spanish. There was a crucified Christ on the wall above the bed. A melancholy brass figure on a wooden cross, hanging from a rusty nail. It had been there when Susie had moved in. Left by an earlier tenant.

It was the last thing Septimus saw.

Before he passed out.

2

MIDNIGHT CONFIDENCES

Septimus groaned as he came back to his senses. A woman with sleepy, concerned eyes was holding him by the shoulders. She had broken teeth and smudged rouge on her cheeks. She reeked of some cheap perfume. He tried to pull himself away but the woman seemed determined to keep tight hold of him. She was dressed in a torn silk nightgown. Septimus had no idea who she was. He'd never seen her before.

For a bewildered moment, he barely knew where he was.

The cold air soon revived him. The mangled remains of Susie Kettle lay on the floor in front of him. Pale and still. Strangely bloodless. An assortment of spectators had squeezed themselves into the narrow doorway. They were peering in at the remains, as well as at Septimus, and the faded whore who was holding him.

He pushed the woman aside and struggled to his feet.

"You collapsed," she told him. *"We thought you was a goner."*

Septimus mumbled something. He wiped the dribbled spit from his chin and rubbed his eyes as he looked around. More candles had been brought into the room while he'd been unconscious. Blood was still trickling down the walls. Moths were fluttering around the candles. They'd come in through the broken window.

Susie's dressing-table mirror had also been smashed. Fragments of it were strewn across the floor. An empty perfume bottle lay by the body. It was a bottle that Septimus himself had given her. Part of the loot from the Danish ship.

"Bastards!" he muttered. *"Bastards!"*

Mercifully, the awful remains on the floor didn't look much at all like Susie Kettle. But... it was her. Septimus knew her well enough to be certain of the fact. He recognised her new earrings, and the red silk dress that she'd looked so lovely in.

Her hair, too, was unmistakeable. One of the other girls had helped her to dye it black, when she'd first arrived at the Rose Tavern, but the process hadn't gone so well. The dye had washed out, in no time at all. Her hair had gone back to its natural, striking, *slightly* unfashionable red. A few black streaks had remained.

They were still visible. In the fluttering candlelight.

A curious little mark behind her left ear caught Septimus's eye, as he stared. It was a tattoo, he realised. He edged closer, but all he could make out was a crude, vaguely serpent-like shape. A thing with wings. He scratched his head.

Whatever it was, he'd never noticed it before.

Madam O'Reilly appeared in the doorway. She took one look at the horrific scene in front of her and started screaming. Her mouth opened wide and a ghastly, terrible wail came out. Septimus covered his ears. He felt sick and dizzy.

With his coat pulled up around his head, he turned and fled.

The corridor outside was full of people. The regular girls and some of their bleary-eyed, drunken customers. All in various states of undress.

"Is Susie hurt?" one of the girls asked, as Septimus rushed by.

He blundered past without speaking. At the top of the stairs he missed his footing in the dark and crashed all the way to the bottom, flat on his back, banging his head on every step as he went down. He picked himself up and staggered to the back door. It was wide open. Cold fog was drifting in. Out of the night.

This, it seemed, was the way that Susie's killer had left the building.

He stumbled out into the back-alley and vomited. The fog crept around him. Like something alive. A ghostly dog appeared, out of nowhere. A hungry-looking, unhappy creature. At the sight of Septimus it lowered its head and snarled.

"Piss off!" Septimus snarled back. *"Go to hell!"*

The dog slunk off. It wasn't looking for a fight.

With no idea of where he was going, Septimus wiped the vomit from his chin and wandered off. The streets were mostly deserted. His only companions, out in the night, were of the four-legged variety. Dogs and cats. Rats and rooting pigs.

For two or three hours, he just walked. He crossed the Limehouse Cut and roamed down Narrow Street.

Into Ratcliffe. But, even here, in Sailor Town, there was hardly a soul around. The taverns and brothels had mostly closed for the night. The Golden Lion on Cut-Throat Lane was open for business, but Septimus had only ever been in there once or twice and he could hardly expect them to serve him a drink on trust. At this ungodly hour. They'd laugh in his face.

He walked straight past. Without even stopping to look in.

Eventually his legs started to ache and he turned back in the direction of his temporary accommodation. The Crow Hotel in Limehouse. It was a cheap place, on Zeelandia Street, close to Limehouse Bridge Dock. The front door was open all night, so you could always get in. Whatever time you got home.

He was almost sober by the time he got there. The cold air and the walking had cleared his head. An oil-lamp was lit in the entrance porch. It was a welcome sight. The night-watchman was awake, for once. He was reading something. By the light of a smoky candle. He glanced up as Septimus came in.

"A friend is waiting for you," he grunted. "Up in your room."

A friend? Septimus thought, worriedly. *At this hour?*

For a confused moment, he thought it might be Susie Kettle. But Susie was dead. It was a fact that had to be faced. Septimus couldn't imagine who might be visiting him. At this time of night. It wasn't as though he had many friends.

Then, with a weary sigh, he remembered Lachlan.

"You gave him my key?"

"Your door wasn't locked. You'd left it wide open."

"I'm a little forgetful, at times. Could I, uh... take something to drink? A drop of brandy, perhaps? Two glasses? You can add it to my reckoning. I won't let you down, sir. I'll be settling everything. *Very, very soon!* The gentleman upstairs has come to see me about an *extremely* promising new venture. I can't, uh..."

The watchman laughed.

"I don't know if you *have* a reckoning anymore, Mr Slim. There's a note in the ledger about you. If I remember rightly. Let me see..."

Officially, Septimus was no longer allowed to take food or drink at the Crow Hotel. They'd even barred him from bathing, or using the disgusting privy in the backyard. He'd become an unwelcome guest. The night-watchman was the only person in the place who treated Septimus with anything like Christian charity.

He was an old soldier. Like Septimus himself.

With a shrug, the old man shut the book and took Septimus through into the kitchen. He unlocked the cabinet where the liquor was kept and filled two greasy little cups with locally-made gin. Septimus thanked him. Glumly.

It's better than nothing, he told himself.

His chamber was up at the top of the building. Up several flights of creaking, dark stairs. His door was ajar when he eventually got there. He pushed it open.

Lachlan was sitting at the rickety table in the middle of the room. He was scribbling something. By candlelight. He turned, sleepily, as the door opened.

"*Septimus!* Dear God! *Where have you been?* I was getting worried."

"It's a long story. Here... I got you a drink."

"Thank you, my friend. Geneva?"

"It's all I could get. The old man downstairs took pity on me."

"I wondered where you'd got to," Lachlan said. He pushed the candles aside and put his cup down. "I even went back to the Rose Tavern to look for you, but the place was closed and shuttered. It seemed a little odd. Madam O'Reilly doesn't usually close so early. There was no-one around. The whole street was deserted. What happened? Was there a fight?"

Septimus didn't respond. He was still shocked. He felt cold and ill. He wasn't yet ready to talk about the events of the night. Lachlan had been drafting something, while he'd been waiting, on a pilfered sheet of Septimus's writing-paper. It was a map of the Thames Estuary, Septimus realised, as he leaned over the little Irishman's shoulder. Certain points on the Kent shore were marked with crosses and dotted lines. There was a crudely-drawn castle, with armed men at the battlements, and a blazing ship, half-sunk in the middle of the river.

"What are you proposing?" Septimus asked him. "I thought we were talking about a *business* deal. Not a bloody war. I don't want to fight anymore. I'm too old. Too sick. Too drunk. I've had enough of violence. *More than enough.*"

Lachlan looked horrified.

"No, no, no..." he protested.

He slid the drawing round so that Septimus could see it better.

"You've got the wrong idea. The burning ship was just an afterthought. If this affair goes well, there'll be no violence at all. What I'm proposing is a simple, straightforward robbery, out in the estuary. Nothing too complicated. It's a foreign vessel. Quite small. Five crew on board, at the very most. We'll tie up the crew, set them adrift in their own boat, and sail away with the goods. That's all there is to it.

"I've got *information,* Septimus. *Vital* information. The name of the ship. Times and dates. Intended route. Precise details of the cargo. Everything, in fact, that we could possibly need to know. It fell into my lap. *It's fate."*

Septimus perused the untidy drawing.

"What's on board?"

"Certain... *extremely valuable goods.* It will be worth your while, I promise. It's a sort of, uh... *secret shipment.* No-one else knows about it. *Only us.* We'll have our own vessel. A little cutter. Fast and manoeuvrable. Just what we need. She's down in Deptford at the moment. I've spoken to the captain already. He's a good man. A man of the world. He has *financial problems.* He needs the work."

Lachlan moved the candles closer and pointed to the map.

"There's a small inlet, *here,* on the Kent shore, opposite Canvey Island. It's well-hidden but it has good access, even at low tide. I've been down there already. That's where we'll transfer the cargo. *Roughly* a ton of it. In wooden boxes. We'll need to move it across onto our own ship. It won't take long. An hour at the most. Once we're done, we'll batten the hatches and sail home.

That's all there is to it, Septimus. A day's work. With good money at the end of it. *Very* good money."

"It's *piracy,* Lachlan. We'd swing if we got caught."

"We won't get caught. Believe me, Septimus. I've been working on the plan for several days. This is the first chance I've had to talk to you about it. The scribbled area here is the Hoo Peninsula. I haven't drawn it very well. It's mostly marshland. The creek, just here, is where we'll lie in wait. It's about forty miles downriver. We could be there and back in a day, with the right winds."

"And if the weather lets us down?"

"We'll be allowing ourselves plenty of time, of course. The headland that I've marked with a cross is called Egypt Point. There's an ancient, ruined manor house there. Hidden in the trees. That's going to be our base. It's a particularly desolate stretch of coast. Nobody will disturb us. It's perfect, for our purposes."

Septimus gulped the last of his gin and sat down.

"So... tell me more."

"Ha! I *knew* you'd be interested, once you'd got the gist of it. There isn't really so much more to tell. An *extremely* valuable cargo will be sailing past Egypt Point. In four days from now. It will be on a small Dutch ship, with almost no protection. There'll be a pistol or two on board, but that's about all."

"What's the cargo?"

"Something of considerable value. I don't want to give too much away, at this stage. If so much as a whisper leaked out, it could ruin everything. There'll be five of us in the gang. All trusted friends. Nobody else knows a thing. I've had you in mind all along, Septimus. You were a soldier, uh? Once upon a time."

"A long time ago."

"But it's *there*. In your head. You've got that experience."

"I could still shoot straight, I suppose. On a good day."

Septimus's hands were shaking. He felt dizzy, suddenly. His mouth still tasted of vomit. He went over to the wash-stand and splashed some filthy water onto his face, then crossed to the bed and sat on the edge with his head in his hands.

Lachlan stared at him.

"What is it? Are you ill?"

"*Uuuugh...*" Septimus moaned, through his hands.

He got up and opened his coal-scuttle. There was no coal in it. Just a wad of old newspapers. He pushed the papers aside and pulled out an odd-looking bottle.

"The bastards won't let me have coal anymore. Even in weather like this. I could freeze to death. They wouldn't care. They'd be glad to see the back of me."

He brought the bottle over into the light.

"I'd forgotten I had this. I bought it from a foreign sailor. A couple of nights ago. He was wandering about in the fog, talking to himself. I wished him a good night as I went past and he waved the bottle in my face. As though he was trying to sell it. '*Tree shillink!*' he shouted. In a thick accent. I had to laugh. I didn't even know what the stuff was. All I had in my pocket was thruppence-ha'penny. I offered him that and he accepted. I think he just wanted the price of a Ratcliffe whore."

"What is it?"

"Some sort of weird liquor. It's actually quite good.

Give me your cup. I was planning to save it. For a special occasion. I don't know what I had in mind, really, but it doesn't matter anymore. Everything has changed. There's been another murder, Lachlan. In Limehouse, this time. At the Rose Tavern. It happened after you left. That's why the place was closed, I suppose, when you went back."

"Oh, no! Please... no!"

"It was Susie. Susie Kettle."

Lachlan groaned. The blood drained from his face.

"Why didn't you tell me right away? You idiot! *For heaven's sakes!* I *knew* something was wrong. The moment you walked in. *For the love of God!* Are you sure it was Susie? Could there be a mistake? There's that other girl..."

"It was Susie. I saw the remains."

"Oh... *Jesus!* I'm to blame! *I'll burn in hell!* I brought her here. I met her in the street. She was homeless. She'd run away from some violent bastard of a husband. People had been taking advantage of her. She'd been selling herself. On street corners. She looked half-starved. I thought I was doing her a favour."

"You can't blame yourself. You did the right thing."

Lachlan wiped away a tear. He sipped the last dregs of his gin and pushed the empty cup across the table so that Septimus could refill it. The weird foreign liquor gurgled out of the bottle. It had a sweet, wild, *herbal* smell.

"Justice will be served," Lachlan growled, as he took his cup back. "You can be certain of that. Madam O'Reilly is well-connected. She knows the right people. She *has* to. In her line of work. The bastard who did this will be floating in the river by the end of the week. With his prick chopped off. A pistol-ball in his brain."

"If it *was* a man."

"Of course it was a man. It's *always* a man."

Septimus seemed less certain. He raised his cup.

"To our beloved Susie, uh?"

"To Susie."

They tipped their heads back and slugged the fiery stuff down.

"Ooof!" Lachlan gasped, as he wiped his mouth. "That's *good!"*

"Indeed," Septimus agreed. "I'd been hoping to share it with Susie, if the truth be told. I had plans. She spent the night here, a couple of times, but I was so bloody drunk, on both occasions. And now she's gone. The man she was with actually looked like quite a decent fellow. He didn't look like a killer."

"They never do. You saw him, then?"

"Briefly. From a distance. But I don't think he did it. He wasn't the sort. I walked around in the fog for hours, thinking about it. It *can't* have been him."

"How can you be so sure?"

"I don't *exactly* know. You'd understand, if you'd been there. There was something *odd* about the scene. Something *unnatural*. The remains didn't even *look* like Susie. Except for her clothes and her hair. There wasn't much else left. It was as though she'd been... *consumed*. A human being couldn't have done it. Some sort of *creature* is on the loose, if you ask me. A *predatory* creature. Like that twenty-foot python they found in Wapping Dock. Do you remember?"

"I remember the story," Lachlan admitted. "They had the bloody thing stuffed, after they'd killed it. It was on show for a while, at the Swan with Two Necks in Billingsgate. You could pay tuppence to go in and see it. I didn't get a chance, as things turned out. I was so busy, at the time. But you're barking up the wrong tree, Septimus. There have been *dozens* of these horrible murders, in recent weeks, and no mention at all, to my knowledge, of a *creature*. Somebody would have seen it, surely? How does it get in and out? Was there a chimney, in Susie's room?"

"The window was smashed. The mirror, too. There was broken glass..."

"*Oh, Lord!* But, even so... this man you saw needs to be found. He has questions to answer. Why did he run, if he has nothing to hide? Why did he not stay and talk? Any decent, civilised human-being would have done that."

"He was probably terrified. Do you want another drink?"

Lachlan plucked his watch from his waistcoat pocket.

"No, no, no. It's late. I really must go. Tomorrow is going to be an *extremely* busy day. So much has to be arranged. I'll need to make an early start."

Septimus pushed the cork back into the bottle. Lachlan sat quietly for a moment or two, and then got to his feet, with a deep sigh.

"What an appalling tragedy. We can talk about the, uh... *other business* tomorrow. The French cult. The interesting cargo. This isn't the right moment. Susie's funeral will need to be arranged. I'll speak to Madam O'Reilly in the morning. We can all contribute. You're penniless at the moment, I know, but that will soon be remedied. Harriet will want to help. She was Susie's best friend."

Septimus nodded.

"Until tomorrow then," Lachlan said. "I'll see you at the Rose Tavern. I'll buy you breakfast. Not too early. We're both in need of some sleep."

He lingered for a moment, with his hand on the doorknob.

"Just as a... final thought," he went on, a little hesitantly. "To set my mind at rest. I know it's not a good time to ask, but... are you, uh... *interested* in the other matter we discussed? Just as a possibility? There'll be good money in it. Enough to get you out of this flea-pit and into some decent lodgings. *Possibly* a great deal more than that. If things go well. What do you reckon?"

"Of *course* I'm interested. I'm *penniless*. The perfume business didn't really work out for me. I've given away more of the stuff than I've sold. I'm *drowning* in debt. My landlady is threatening to have me *imprisoned* if I don't start paying my bills. Mrs Lusardi. The uncaring bitch. I'm trying to drink less. That's where all the money goes. What *is* this mysterious cargo, anyway? Why are you being so coy about it? Is there something you don't want me to know?"

Lachlan opened the door and glanced out into the dark corridor. When he was certain that nobody was out there he pushed the door closed again.

With a quiet little click, it snapped shut.

"I'm just being cautious, Septimus. It's not that I don't trust you. You know that. It's just that... *so much is at stake.* We'll be sailing down to the old mansion house. The one I told you about. At Egypt Point. Out in the estuary. When the Dutch ship appears, we'll be lying in wait. We'll have the advantage of surprise."

"Yes, but... what's on board?"

"It's, uh..."

Lachlan left the door and sat down again.

"The stuff we all dream of Septimus. *Gold!* Almost a bloody ton of it. If my information is correct. *It belongs to the French cult I told you about.* This is why secrecy is so important. Nobody else knows about it. Only us."

"Which French cult?"

"The one I told you about earlier. *The Sign of the Crocodile Queen.* They're shipping some weird, uh... *religious artefacts* over here. From Ostend. For this heathen temple they're building in London. By a stroke of *damnable* good fortune, they've entrusted the task to an old Parisian friend of mine. A defrocked French naval officer. He has his own ship. A little trading-vessel. Illicitly acquired.

"When he realised what the cargo was, he sent his cabin-boy over on the next packet-boat, with an urgent letter for me. I sent the lad straight back with a reply. *Everything is arranged!* We'll be lying in wait, as they enter the Thames."

"Golden artefacts?"

"Exactly... manufactured in Paris, apparently, and then moved overland to Ostend. Because of the political situation. They were lucky to get away with it, if you ask me, but it seems they did. Fortunately for us. The vessel in question is a scruffy little Dutch coastal boat.

The *Helga*. My old associate, *Capitaine Clézio,* sent me a detailed list of what we can expect to find. When we open the hold."

"I'd be interested to see the list."

"I'll show it to you later. The most interesting item is a *ghastly heathen idol.* A statue of the Crocodile Queen. Intended for the new London temple. Clézio had actually seen the thing when he wrote to me. It's *pure gold,* he says. Over half a ton of it, in a strange wooden casket, covered in arcane symbols. The other items hadn't arrived, at the time he wrote, but his employers had told him to expect a *total lading* of about three tons. We don't know what else will be aboard. We'll find out in the fullness of time, but... there'll be *at least* half a ton of gold. Possibly more."

"Can we trust the information?"

"Of course! Clézio wouldn't mislead us. He's like a brother to me."

Septimus tapped the table while he thought about it.

"We'll need to be well-armed. This won't be like stealing coal from the bloody docks. They'll have mercenaries on board. *Professionals.* Europe is awash with soldiers for hire. There'll be a couple, at least. Along with the ship's crew."

"Possibly. Clézio thinks they'll be depending more on secrecy. It's just the way they prefer to do things. They don't trust outsiders. My plan is that we'll approach them in our own craft – disguised as customs officers. Clézio will know it's us, of course. We'll order them to heave-to, for a routine inspection of their documents. Once we're aboard, we'll produce our pistols, tie the crew up below decks and help ourselves to the cargo. It shouldn't take long. What do you think?"

"*Uuuuhh...*"

Septimus wasn't really sure what he thought. The idea sounded simple enough. It wouldn't go so well if they were caught. The authorities would feel duty-bound to make an example of them. He closed his eyes and scratched his nose while he thought about it. In his mind's eye, he could already see the newspaper reports.

The inky headlines...

LIMEHOUSE PIRATES HANGED, AT EXECUTION DOCK!

At the *very least,* they'd be transported. To New South Wales. Though, if they got away with it, they'd be in clover.

"*So...*" he asked. "What are your terms? Equal shares?"

Lachlan nodded.

"That goes without saying. Minus a few expenses. Nothing you won't agree to. The boat has to be arranged. The weapons and so on. We don't have a lot of time. There'll be five of us in the gang. All good men. I'll arrange a meeting."

"Just tell me when."

"I'll let you know. I'll see you in the morning. At the tavern. Not a *word* to anyone else, uh? The only other person who knows *anything* is Harriet. This new fellow of hers is involved. He came along at just the right time. *It's fate.*"

The candles hissed and smoked as Lachlan got to his feet.

"There'll be Susie's funeral to think of, too," he said. "Sadly, but it will have to be faced. We could arrange things now, I suppose, and buy her a headstone later. Something grand. I wouldn't want to see her in a pauper's grave. She was one of us. Do you know anything about her family? I never thought to ask."

Septimus shook his head.

"She was brought up in the Foundling Hospital. That's all she knew. She had a tiny piece of red ribbon that her mother had left with her at the hospital. The mothers leave such tokens, apparently, so they'll know their own child if they ever change their minds and go back – but Susie's mother never went back."

"Oh, dear Lord..." Lachlan sighed.

"We could have a monument built," Septimus suggested. "If this enterprise of yours goes well. In the churchyard at Saint Anne's. Something *really* grand. With Susie's name carved in gold and some biblical words below. An angel or two on top, perhaps. With folded wings. Keeping watch. She would like that, I think."

"You're right. Of course."

Lachlan crossed himself as he went over to the door.

"Get some sleep, uh? We can talk things over tomorrow."

"I'll see you at the tavern."

The floorboards outside creaked as Lachlan departed. Septimus got up and locked the door. Looking back, he was relieved that the Irishman had come. It wasn't just the business of the gold and the prospect of earning some money. It was the thought of what he might have done, if he'd had to spend that hour alone.

He moved the candles over to his bedside and stretched out, as comfortably as he could, on the filthy mattress. Mice were scratching, behind the wainscoting. An enormous, ghostly cockroach was wriggling up the wall, at one side of the window.

Septimus watched its slow progress, with a slight feeling of disgust. Of all the Lord's creatures, cockroaches were his least favourite. Up at the top, the ghastly thing stopped and sniffed around a bit, before crawling all the way back down.

"Uuuugh..."

With a groan, he blew out the candles and pulled his blanket up over his head.

Just moments later, as he drifted off into shallow sleep, a quiet little 'bump' from somewhere in the room brought him suddenly and disturbingly back to his senses.

He raised his head and peered out into the darkness.

Something had collided with his table. By the sound of it.

Mrs Lusardi's diabolical cats would creep into his room sometimes, when he'd come home drunk and left the door half open. But on this particular occasion, he was certain that he'd locked it. The key was still in the lock, he felt sure.

Worriedly, he stared into the gloom. *Something* was there. It was moving in the dark. He could *feel* it. His flesh tingled as he sensed the presence of Susie Kettle. It was very strong, as though she was close by and trying to get his attention.

"*Susie?*" he whispered.

There was no response.

Light rain, tapping against the window, was the only sound.

3

THE NECROPOLIS OF QUEEN MBEMBÉ

It was still raining when Septimus woke again. Water from a broken gutter was splashing down outside. He felt he'd slept well, for a change. Sometimes he didn't sleep at all. Slowly, the events of the night before came back to him. Susie's murder. Lachlan's late-night visit. The business of the gold.

Someone was banging on his door. *Thump, thump, thump!*

"Mr Slim!" a female voice shouted. "Mr Slim! We have to talk!"

It was Mrs Lusardi, the elderly widow who ran the place.

Thump, thump!

"What do you want?" he shouted back. "It's the middle of the bloody night!"

"It's the middle of the *morning!* Open this door!"

Septimus dragged himself out of bed and stumbled across the floor. As usual, he'd slept in his clothes. He unlocked the door and held it slightly open, with his foot against it so she couldn't push her way in. He could see her outside, in her widow's weeds, peering in at him, narrow-eyed, through the gap.

"It *smells* in there," she said.

"It's my boots. I stood in some dog-shit. What do you want?"

"What I *want,* Mr Slim, is some *money.* I've not had a *ha'penny* from you for nearly four weeks. I haven't even *seen* you for a fortnight. You come home drunk, night after night, annoying the other guests. People have complained. *And* you steal food from the kitchen. *I know it's you.* I've had reports. I'm a decent, Christian woman, as I'm sure you know – but *I won't be taken advantage of.* If you can't pay, you'll have to go. That's my final word. *Do you understand?*"

"My dear lady... *of course.* Please don't shout. *It's quite unnecessary.* If you could just bear with me for... *a day or two longer.* A week at the most. No more than that. I have money coming. From overseas. *A substantial amount.*"

He smiled and tried to look trustworthy. Mrs Lusardi was unimpressed.

"You can stay until the end of the week. After that – you will have to go. This is an *hotel,* Mr Slim. Not a charitable institution. Your room is seven shillings a week, in case you've forgotten. I'm giving you until Sunday. Is that clear?"

With a final glare, she turned and trotted off down the corridor. Septimus watched her retreating. At the top of the stairs she looked back and wagged one of her skeletal fingers at him. Like a hag-witch casting a curse.

"Sunday!"

Septimus slammed the door. Overall, he felt relieved.

She was giving him three more days. With luck he'd have a little money by then.

He prowled the room, grunting and scratching, while he thought things over. The Crow Hotel was infested with fleas. They were spread by the resident cats. Mrs Lusardi had a weakness for small furry creatures. She bought half-rotten horsemeat for them and left it out on filthy tin plates by the back door. Septimus would have eaten the stuff himself, sometimes, if he'd had any way of cooking it.

It was mid-morning. So she'd said. Septimus had promised to meet Lachlan Malone at the Rose Tavern. Susie's funeral had to be arranged.

Mercifully, there was no-one around when he got downstairs. He could hear the scullery-maids gossiping in the kitchen. As quietly as he could, he crept across the freshly-scrubbed, shiny-wet tiles of the hall and let himself out.

Zeelandia Street was a muddy morass after the night's rain. Heavy carts were splashing by, loaded with coal and other goods from the local wharves.

He picked his way between the fetid puddles, as best he could. His boots were still leaking. For the sake of his health and general well-being, he took a circuitous route to Thieves' Street. Along the driest pavements he could find.

Lachlan was waiting for him at the tavern. He glanced up and waved as Septimus came in. The big room was pleasantly warm. A few of the local hackney coachmen were sitting around the fire, smoking their long pipes and talking.

"I've spoken to Madam O'Reilly," Lachlan said, as

Septimus joined him at the corner table. "I told her that we were ready to help, in any way we could, with Susie's funeral, but we're too late, it seems. Everything has been arranged. Priests from the Sign of the Crocodile Queen took the body. Early this morning. It was *completely* unexpected. Susie had been attending their services. *Apparently.*"

"*Eh?*"

"So they claimed. They've taken her to Southwark."

"*To Southwark?*"

"That's where this new temple of theirs is. The Temple of Dreams."

"*But... what about us? Don't we get a say in the matter?*"

"It seems not. Madam O'Reilly is quite distressed. The bastards took her by surprise, she says. The hearse was outside when she opened the front door this morning. The priests were attired in sinister black cloaks, with pointed hoods that hid their faces. They claimed that Susie had been initiated into the cult, and that the Southwark cemetery is where she would wish to be interred. The *Necropolis,* they call it. Madam O'Reilly protested, of course, but they simply refused to listen."

"*No, no!*" Septimus spluttered. "This can't be right. It's clearly a mistake. A case of, uh... *mistaken identity.* They must have got the wrong address. The wrong Rose Tavern. The wrong Susie! It's the only *possible* explanation!"

"I don't know. They gave her full name, Madam O'Reilly says. Mistress Susan Kettle. They even knew how old she was. Twenty three. I didn't know that. The bastards knew everything about her. So it appears.

Somebody is going to have to go down there, Septimus. To this heathen bone-yard. To make sure that things are being done properly. To get her out, if we can, and bring her back home."

"Where is it, exactly?"

"Barnaby Street. I know a couple of Irish lads who've been working there. Masons, from Sligo. It covers a *vast* area. So they tell me. Twenty acres, or so. They're building stone crypts. In the French style. *Thousands of 'em!*"

"Are they expecting the Apocalypse?"

"I wouldn't be surprised. London seems to be full of people who're expecting the End of Days. Crazy old men, mostly. Waving their battered Bibles on street corners and ranting to anyone who'll stop and listen. The Necropolis is already in use, apparently. Despite the ongoing building-work. They're excavating shafts and tunnels. There have been some *dreadful* accidents. Explosions. Roof-falls. Workers have died. *Hundreds* of the poor bastards! The widows get nothing."

"Why would they be digging tunnels? In a *cemetery?*"

Lachlan shrugged.

"Don't ask me. *Drainage,* perhaps. Who knows?"

Madam O'Reilly appeared with a jug of coffee and some cups. She looked distressed and tearful. Septimus pulled another chair across for her.

"There's no bread today," she apologised, as she sat down. "The bakery has run out of flour. *Again!* I've sent one of the girls out to see what she can find."

"Did Susie say anything to you?" Septimus asked. "About this French cult?"

Madam O'Reilly wiped her eyes with the cloth she was carrying.

"Very little. She'd attended some sort of ceremony. In Wapping. A couple of days ago. Somebody had given her an invitation. She went with a friend of hers. A girl from the Star. In Ratcliffe. I didn't think much about it, at the time. I don't bully the girls. They come and go as they please. They're like my own daughters. We're *family*. We look after each other. She just laughed, when I asked her about the ceremony. As far as I could tell she hadn't taken it very seriously."

"That's the way she was," Septimus agreed. "Light-hearted."

Madam O'Reilly looked perplexed, suddenly.

"What I don't understand is – *how did they know she was dead?* Those ghastly hooded priests? How did they find out? So soon? I'm surprised they even knew who she was. Do they keep a record of every lost soul who comes their way?"

"They must keep a register of some sort."

"But... London is a *huge* city. The biggest in the world, so they say. How did they find us? Susie must have given this as her address, I suppose. The Rose Tavern, Limehouse. The ceremony she attended was at the old Gaiety Theatre in Wapping. It's been closed for years. They made her drink some sort of *potion*. It was disgusting, she said. When she'd swallowed it they gave her the money."

Septimus blinked. He wasn't sure if he'd misheard.
"The money?"

"Twenty shillings. In silver. They give it to everyone

who turns up. So I'm told. A goodly sum, eh? For five minutes of your time. The difference between life and death for a good many, I should think. Susie spent it on clothes. That's where she got that lovely silk dress. The one she was wearing. In her final hours. It came from an old clothes shop in Shadwell. She was *so* pleased with it."

Remembering the dress seemed to quite overwhelm Madam O'Reilly. Tears rolled from her eyes. Her immense breasts shook as she sobbed.

"Susie was such a *lovely* girl. She could have found herself a good husband, if she'd had a mind to. I only ever tried to help her. She was half-starved, when she turned up at my door. This madman needs to be caught, before he strikes again. As far as I know, we're the only people who have actually *seen* him. At close quarters. A pair of Bow Street officers came round this morning. I described him. As best I could. The waxed moustache. The expensive riding-boots. He was *high-class.*"

"We shouldn't jump to conclusions," Septimus advised her. "I also got a good look at him. I don't think he did it. He wasn't the type. How *could* he have torn her apart, like that, in the two minutes it took us to get up there? The remains were barely recognisable. It looked as though some predatory creature had *fed* on her."

Madam O'Reilly moaned and crossed herself.

"I'm in agreement with Madam O'Reilly," Lachlan broke in. "It simply *had* to be him. Who else was there? *Nobody.* He needs to be brought to justice."

Septimus shrugged. He hardly knew what to think. Madam O'Reilly wiped her tears and went off to deal with some of her other customers. The coachmen around the fire were shouting for more beer. A group of bedraggled-looking young women had come in off the street. Waterside ladies. They wanted coffee, with a drop of something harder and a warm place to sit for an hour or two.

"We could go to Southwark right now," Septimus suggested. "One of these hackney-coachmen might take us down there, if we asked. We could pay later."

"I wouldn't think so," Lachlan cautioned. "They don't give credit."

He lowered his voice.

"I can't go right now. I've got to see Harriet. This new fellow of hers, the one with the facial scars and the earrings, is a master mariner with his own vessel. A little cargo cutter. Whitby-built. Small and fast. All being well, we're going to use it on the day. It's exactly what we need! It's down in Deptford, at the moment. At anchor in the river. Harriet is going to take me down there. When she gets here. I've got to talk things over with the skipper. Why don't you join us?"

"I'd prefer to go to Southwark, to be truthful," Septimus confessed. "It's not so far. I can walk. We need to get Susie *out* of that awful place. Out of the hands of those heathens. Before it's too late. Before she's six feet under, and lost to us."

"You're right, of course," Lachlan agreed. "I should've..."

The front door flew open as he spoke and Harriet rushed in. Breathless and panting as though she'd been running. She brushed her loose hair back and smiled as she crossed the room. No-one had told her the tragic news. It was clear to see.

"Forgive me, good sirs!" she apologised as she crossed the room. *"I'm late, I know!* The river was busy. I spent the night in Deptford with my handsome new lover. *Captain Smalt!* We were late in rising and then I had to wait nearly an hour for a bloody boat. It's foggy, out on the river, and then there were..."

She stopped in mid-sentence.

"What's wrong? Why all the sad faces?"

No-one spoke. No-one knew quite what to say. Madam O'Reilly broke off her business with the hackney-coachmen and came back over to the corner-table.

"Come and take some coffee," she told Harriet. "In my parlour. It's more private, there. We can talk more quietly. Something rather terrible happened. Late last night. After you'd left. I was up half the night and then we had unexpected callers. At the crack of dawn. Before I'd even collected my wits. I should have told them to piss off. I desperately wish that I had, but..."

"What callers? What are you talking about?"

Harriet turned pale. She gasped and pressed her fingers to her lips, as though she'd already guessed. As though she'd read it in Madam O'Reilly's eyes and didn't need to be told. Without a backward glance, she followed Madam O'Reilly across the half-empty room and through into the back. To Madam O'Reilly's private quarters.

"Dear God!" Lachlan muttered. "Harriet won't take this well. She'll be in need of a drink. She's a sensitive soul. Behind that tough front she has. I'll just have to sit and wait. You may as well go to Southwark, Septimus. I'll get everyone together this evening. *There's work to be done.* We don't have much time."

"Harriet won't let you down."

Lachlan nodded. He'd known Harriet for years.

Septimus noticed some unattended food as he was leaving. On a table by the door. A half-empty tankard of ale and a plate of steaming, hot pie. The pie had already been cut into several pieces. The only sign of the person who'd ordered it was a greasy coat, slung over the back of a chair. No-one was watching. As far as he could tell. He sidled close, grabbed a slice of the pie and rushed for the door.

Outside in the street he took a first bite of his prize. It was mutton, or quite possibly goat, baked in a thick, soft pastry. The warm gravy ran down his chin as he chewed. He raised his eyes to heaven and gave thanks to the angels above.

"It's the last time, I promise!"

I won't need to live like this anymore, he told himself. *This business of Lachlan's will change everything. If all goes well, I'll buy a hot meal for every poor soul in the parish. With a pint of ale and a drop of brandy to follow. I could feed the five thousand – if there's as much gold as Lachlan reckons. I'll buy myself a bloody house. And a carriage. Set myself up as a gentleman. Somewhere up in the north, perhaps. Where nobody knows me. It will be a new beginning.*

He washed his hands, when he was done, at a public pump.

The hot pie had restored his spirits. He'd hardly eaten a thing, the day before. He ambled down Narrow Street, to Shadwell, and the Ratcliffe Highway. The roads were crowded and muddy. There were people in rags, sleeping in doorways. Carts and carriages. Rattling by. London was a busy city, these days. Septimus had forgotten how busy it was. Or how badly it smelled. He'd been abroad for years.

Since his return, he'd hardly been out of Limehouse.

He trudged across London Bridge. Half-lost in thought. The old houses on the bridge had been removed, long ago, but Septimus still had vague memories of them. From childhood visits to London with his father. At the southern end of the bridge he turned left. On to Tooley Street. He'd spent his first night back in England here. At the Swan Inn. Six months earlier. It felt more like a thousand years.

He wasn't *exactly* sure where the Temple of Dreams was. He didn't know Southwark well, though he'd passed through, occasionally. At one time or another.

It was a densely-populated area. A warren of stinking manufactories and smoky lanes. The smells came from the numerous slaughterhouses and tanneries.

The local people got used to it, he guessed, as he walked.

A pack of dogs followed him down a filthy alleyway. He picked up a piece of brick to show them that he was ready for a fight. The dogs bared their teeth and snarled as they retreated. An old man came into view. An elderly pauper in a raggedy coat. His moth-eaten periwig had seen better days. He was dragging a reluctant billy-goat along behind him, by a rope affixed to its horns.

Septimus hailed him.

"Could you direct me to the, uh... *Temple of Dreams,* good sir?"

"To the... *what?*"

"The Temple of Dreams. A heathen edifice. Newly-constructed. I'm actually looking for the attached burial-ground. The *Necropolis,* I believe they call it."

"And why, sir, if I may ask, would you be looking for this awful place?"

"Well... I just am. Why, sir, would you want to know?"

The goat-man spat into a patch of nettles at his side. The goat was already chewing the nettles. It seemed impervious to the stings.

"I thought for a moment that you might be one of *them,*" the old man said. "But something tells me that you're not. You don't have that dead look in your eyes. I have to tell you though – you're wasting your time. They won't let you in. There are guards on the gate, day and night. Servants of the so-called *Crocodile Queen.*"

He spat again.

"Even if you got in, you might never get out again. The place is *cursed.* It's haunted. People disappear into the mysterious bloody mists. *Hundreds* of masons and day-labourers have been working there. They get well-paid for a couple of days. Then they vanish. Like will-o'-the-wisps. Nobody ever sees them again."

"Doesn't anybody go looking for them?"

"Of course they do. Wives, sons, brothers. They try to evade the guards but they invariably get caught. You have to be *initiated* before you can get in there. You have to drink some vile concoction. I forget what it's called. They even pay you for your trouble, if you're brave enough to try it. I wouldn't recommend it."

"My girl is in there," Septimus told him. "My beloved. She took their damned money. Twenty shillings, I believe, was the price. But then she was *horribly murdered.* Late last night, at the Rose Tavern in Limehouse. A Sign of the Crocodile Queen wagon came round this morning and took her remains away."

"Jesus..."

The goat-man's face softened.

"Why didn't you tell me that in the first place? We are brothers in tragedy, my friend. My own dear wife was taken, in remarkably similar circumstances. She attended a ceremony. Two days later she was struck by a speeding carriage on Bank Side. The carriage didn't stop. It appeared at the time to have been a dreadful accident. She died instantly. So they told me. We brought her home on a cart. At dawn the next day, a couple of those hooded priests turned up at my door. They offered to make all the necessary arrangements, at no cost whatsoever to myself. It was hard to resist such a generous offer. They took her away in a shimmering black hearse. The horses were beautifully turned-out. It seemed a fine affair, but..."

He stepped closer and gripped Septimus's arm.

"I don't know what the bastards have done with her!" They wouldn't let me pass when I turned up at the front gate with flowers for the grave. They refused to even speak to me. I borrowed a pick-axe, the following day, and crept in with a gang of workmen, in the pre-dawn dark. By some miracle, I got away with it. I've been back several times since. As yet, I've found nothing. *The tombs are empty!"*

"It's a huge place, by all accounts."

"It's an *evil* place, my friend. You *feel* it, the moment

you walk in. The fog never seems to clear. It's dammed hard to find your way around. There are deep shafts, with stairs going down, underneath some of the larger crypts. No-one seems to know what their purpose is. The men who dug them have all disappeared."

"How very odd."

The goat-man shrugged.

Septimus had heard enough. He hardly knew what to believe. "How do I get there from here?" he asked.

"Turn left at the end of this lane. It's not very far. You'll see the Temple of Dreams as you get closer. It's impossible to miss. There's nothing else like it around here. The entrance to the Necropolis is on Barnaby Street. The gates will be open but there'll be crocodile priests on guard. *Be cautious, eh?* Some of those 'priests' carry loaded pistols. Underneath their robes! *Don't say I didn't warn you!*"

He pulled his goat out of the nettles and resumed his journey.

"Thank you, kind sir!" Septimus called after him.

"They won't let you in!" the old man shouted. "Believe me! I *know!*"

He adjusted his ancient periwig and trudged off, with his bleating companion in tow. Septimus set off in the opposite direction. There was a brewery, of some sort, at the end of the lane, and a narrow passageway that led out onto a busy road.

This was Barnaby Street, Septimus realised, as he stepped out into the dust and noise. As he glanced about, he caught his first glimpse of the Temple of Dreams. A stray beam of sunlight had broken through the clouds.

The temple's marble dome was weirdly aglow. From a distance, it looked... *almost alive.*

Septimus gawped.

The place was *huge*. It had an odd, *alien* look about it. As though it been brought from elsewhere and reconstructed, brick by brick, in London. Septimus was reminded of a mysterious ruin he'd once come across. Out in the Indian jungle. In his army days. Even the Bengali sepoys in his patrol hadn't known what it was, or what its original purpose might have been. A 'house of djinns', they'd called it.

The Temple of Dreams had that same air of mystery. It didn't, somehow... quite *belong*.

Septimus wandered closer. The temple stood on raised ground, he realised, as he walked. From out in the street it appeared to be *floating*. In a lake of mist.

The front gates of the Necropolis were wide open. There were priests on guard, as the goat-man had predicted. Their faces were barely visible, under their pointed hoods. Beyond the gates, all Septimus could see was a solid wall of fog.

The guards stepped aside as a shiny black hearse raced out. A solitary crocodile priest was at the reins, whip in hand. The horses snorted and shook their magnificent heads as they clattered out into Barnaby Street. A passing hackney-coach was forced to swerve, to avoid a collision. The coachman spat and cursed.

"Damn you to hell! You godless son of a whore!"

Septimus chuckled. At the same moment, a curious spectacle caught his eye. A pair of young women had thrown a ladder up against the perimeter wall. They'd been hiding in the bushes, a short distance away from the gates. One of them was steadying the ladder while the other tried to shin over the high brickwork.

She almost succeeded, but then one of the guards turned.

"Stop! Get down, now, or you'll be shot!"

He produced a pistol and took aim. The women abandoned the scheme and fled. They weren't fools. The guards hurried along to the spot and pulled the ladder down. Septimus grabbed his chance. While the guards were busy with the rotten old ladder, he ambled over to the gates and walked straight through.

Nobody challenged him.

The fog folded around him as he entered. It was *cold*, inside the walls. He shivered, and pulled his coat more tightly around himself. It felt as though he'd strayed through an invisible barrier, into a slightly different world.

Dim shapes flitted past.

"Hello?" he called out.

There was no response. Only the sound of his own breath. As far as he could tell, he was completely alone. It was weirdly quiet. The ground underfoot was rough and rubble-strewn. A ghostly shape loomed in front of him. It was a stone vault, he realised, as he got closer. Weather-beaten and decayed. As though it had stood there for a thousand years. There were similar structures all around him, he realised, as the fog moved. Crumbling, cobwebbed, ancient tombs.

It made no sense. *Nothing here was old.* Until recently, there'd been nothing here at all. So he'd been told. Only wasteland, and long-abandoned clay-pits.

He crept up to the front of the vault and shook the rusty door. It was locked.

A hideous stone gargoyle peered down at him from the pediment. It looked nothing like a crocodile and even less like a queen, but Septimus knew straightaway what the thing was. He'd seen something like it before, as a tiny blue mark on Susie Kettle's neck. In the waxy candlelight of her chamber. On the night she'd died.

Skeins of old spider-web trailed between the tombs. He pulled the stuff away to clear a path for himself. Before long he was completely lost. He thought that he was probably walking around in circles. Everything looked the same, in the cold fog. Muffled sounds reached him. Footsteps. From close by. Nervously, he stopped and listened. He was worried that they might just shoot him dead, without a second thought, if they came across him unexpectedly.

"Who's there?" he called.

No-one responded. A little while later, after countless false turns, he found himself on a paved road. It led to a decayed archway, and a further set of gates.

This was the inner line of the Necropolis's defences, he surmised as he got closer.

Hooded figures were watching him, from the other side.

"Who are you?" one of them screeched. *"How did you get in here?"*

Septimus sauntered up to the barricade.

"I'm looking for a friend," he snarled. "A young woman by the name of Susan Kettle. Recently deceased. She was brought here this morning by your people. So I've been

told. *Where is she?* What have you done with her, you evil bastards?"

He pushed his face up to the rusty ironwork of the gates and peered through at the black-draped, motionless priests. They stared silently back at him.

He cursed and kicked the gate.

"Are you all deaf?" he yelled. *"Have you had your tongues cut out?"*

The one who had spoken first stepped forward. Two luminous slits, like the eyes of a snake, flickered in the darkness underneath his hood.

"Return to your parish, sir," he told Septimus. "Wherever that may be. You cannot just walk in here. There are *procedures* which must be followed. You must drink the sacred secretions of the Crocodile Queen, and be cleansed of sin."

"Cleansed of sin?" Septimus spluttered.

He sneered, threateningly, through the gaps in the ironwork.

"Don't talk to me about sin, you gutless little rat! I could teach you a thing or two about that, believe me! What have you done with Susie Kettle? Open this bloody gate and we'll talk it over. Like men! Who do you people think you are?"

The crocodile priest retreated into the safety of the fog.

"This is *private property,*" he hissed. "If you don't leave *immediately,* I'll have you shot. You're a trespasser. The law is on my side. Leave!"

"God Almighty..."

Septimus shook the heavy gate. He knew when he was beaten. The Necropolis stank of lies and death. He had no desire to join the army of lost souls who'd gone in there and never come out again. It was time to go.

With his hands in his pockets he turned and strolled away. A variety of entertaining insults crossed his mind as he left, but he kept them to himself.

We have to get Susie moved, he told himself. *Whatever it takes.*

The paved road he was on led all the way back to the place where he'd come in. Nobody else bothered him. The Barnaby Street guards seemed unsurprised to see him come wandering out of the fog. As though they'd been informed.

The gates slammed noisily shut behind him as he went out.

Mysteriously – *illogically* – the hellish fog stopped at the gates.

Out in the real world, the sun was shining.

4

THE STREETS

Beggars and whores importuned Septimus as he walked back towards the river. A skinny young woman with ticks in her hair offered him the full enjoyment of her person, as she daintily put it, for a shilling and a pint of wine.

Septimus declined the offer and walked on.

He would have *given* her a shilling, if he'd had one to give.

It was early afternoon, now. He was in no particular hurry. He lingered on the riverbank for a while, by Bull Stairs, watching the passing boats and enjoying the magnificent views of the City on the other side. It was a scene he'd often dreamed of, in the long years of his exile. He could see Ermine House, in the distance.

The great house looked peaceable enough, in the afternoon mist.

The last time Septimus had seen the place had been on the night, two decades earlier, when Lord Blackthorpe's hired bullies had dragged him up out of the cellars, half-dead, and flung him into the back of a filthy little cart. It was a fate he'd brought upon himself, he'd had to admit, when he'd looked back, in later years. But he really hadn't deserved the *merciless* thrashing the bastards had given him.

Everybody made mistakes.

He'd assumed that he was on his final ride, as the horrible little cart had rattled through the empty streets. But instead of taking him to the river and hurling him in, as he'd expected, the gang had taken him to a wharf in Wapping and hauled him aboard a mysterious vessel that was making ready to sail. He'd ended up on the other side of the world, several weeks later. Half-starved, but still alive.

Lord Blackthorpe had also left the country, Septimus had since found out. Blackthorpe had gone to Jamaica, to take charge of the family sugar business. He was a foul-tempered, unpredictable, rapacious man. His wife, Lady Constance, came from an equally rich, landed family, but the marriage hadn't worked out. The pair had lived separate lives, right from the start, at opposite ends of the vast house.

Septimus had been in their employ. As a liveried footman. After his army days. He'd been close to Lady Constance. A little *too* close, as things had turned out. He'd been caught with his breeches down, in his lady's chamber.

The consequences had been fairly appalling.

He still had the scars.

An urge to take a look at the old place came upon him.

It wasn't so far. He crossed the river by way of Blackfriars Bridge and made his way towards the Strand, through a tangle of alleys and smoky streets.

Twenty years had gone by since he'd last passed this

way. Nothing looked the same. So much had changed. The Fleet Ditch had been covered over. Taverns he half-remembered had been pulled down, or had taken new names.

The Strand itself was much as he remembered it. There were new buildings, here and there. He crossed to the north side and sauntered along the busy pavement. Slowly, the great house came into view. He peered across at it, through the mist and smoke. The place had been almost new when he'd last seen it. It looked *older* now. Older and grimier. Weeds were growing out of the soot-stained stonework.

"Jesus!" he murmured.

Some of the upper windows were open but there were no other signs of life. The gates were not locked, as far as he could tell. No-one was in sight. He could have walked straight in. Across the courtyard. Up the steps to the front entrance.

Though not in the clothes he was wearing.

He would need to come back. After the business at Egypt Point. Septimus wasn't exactly sure what a ton of gold would be worth, or what his own share of the proceeds might be. All he knew for certain was – *it would be a lot of money.*

Enough to change everything.

An outbreak of shouting and jeering interrupted his thoughts. A trio of high-class whores were being harassed by a group of uniformed constables, not far from where Septimus was standing. The women clearly saw themselves as socially superior to the officers. A crowd was gathering. It was a free show.

Septimus roamed off. The day was almost done. The sun was going down. He still had to walk all the way back to Limehouse. Lachlan was planning to get the whole gang together that evening. At the Rose Tavern. The Dutch ship was doubtless already at sea. Things had to be arranged. There wasn't much time.

He trudged east, along Fleet Street and Watling Street, to the Tower and the familiar precincts beyond. In the dusky gloom of Swan Alley, Smithfield, he stopped for a moment to extract a stone from one of his boots. Wearily, he perched on the edge of a horse-trough and yanked the offending boot off. A plump woman with bits of straw in her hair watched from a nearby doorway as he shook the stone out.

"You alright, my darling?" she called. "No need to be lonely 'ere, you know, sweetheart. You look like a man who knows 'ow to look after a woman. Eh? Ha, ha, ha! Come and 'ave a drink wiv me and my friends, you won't regret it."

"I'm a Methodist minister, madam," Septimus informed her.

"Oh, yeah? Ha!! Pull me other leg, it's got bells on! Ha, ha!!! I ain't never seen a Methodist minister with 'oles in the bottom of 'is boots, sitting on a bloody 'orse-trough and looking like he ain't eaten nuffink for a bloody week!"

Septimus shrugged. "There's a first time for everything."

The woman shrieked and went back inside to tell her friends about Septimus. He'd stopped outside the local gin-shop, it seemed. Uproarious laughter came from the interior as the woman told her tale.

He pulled his boot back on and hurried off into the gloom.

On Ratcliffe Highway a group of well-dressed women were handing out curious little printed cards to anyone they could persuade to take one. The group were devotees of the Crocodile Queen, Septimus realised as he got closer. The cards were invitations to a heathen ceremony that was going to take place in Wapping, later that evening. He took one, out of curiosity, as he hurried past.

This was how they'd snared Susie, he guessed, as he glanced at the card. It promised the holder a payment of twenty shillings. Just for turning up. Susie, he knew, would have found such an offer hard to resist. She'd been so determined to better herself. To shake off her sorrowful past and start anew.

Maybe she'd already had her eye on that lovely red dress, he mused. He pocketed the card and continued on his way.

The Highway was unusually busy. Overloaded carts and carriages were thundering by. Bartholomew Fair had just finished. The roadsides were crowded with peddlers, pickpockets, gypsy fortune-tellers and weary revellers who'd spent every penny they had and were going to have to walk all the way home.

Smoke from a thousand tottering chimney-pots hung over the scene. Fog was creeping in from the marshes, fields and graveyards. Goats and pigs were rooting in heaps of waste. Lamps were being lit, though it was not yet fully dark.

A solitary figure on the far side of the road caught Septimus's eye. It was a young man, standing very still as the world rushed past him. He was leaned against the front wall of a rotting old house. The upper stories of the place were jettied-out over the street, in the antique style. The kid was lurking, like a wraith, in the crepuscular shadows below. He had a thin clay pipe in his mouth but didn't appear to be smoking. The pipe wasn't even lit, as far as Septimus could tell.

Septimus was intrigued. He lingered for a moment, and watched.

Whatever he was up to, the youth had chosen a good place to position himself. He had a thin, pale, pointed face. He was wrapped in a thick old top-coat, with the collars pulled up around his ears. As though he was feeling the cold.

A Chinese gentleman came into view. A prosperous merchant, by the look of him. A number of Chinese traders had settled in the Ratcliffe area, of late. British sea-captains would turn to them for advice about the politics and trading-conditions of the Orient. Chinese sailors who'd washed-up in London would approach them for help with lodgings, language, female company, familiar foodstuffs, and so on.

Everything was available, if you knew where to ask.

The Chinese merchant had his hair tied back in a slim, oiled pigtail. A bunch of keys and a small leather pouch hung from a cord at his waist. The pouch was half hidden in the folds of his robe, but was swaying into plain view as he hurried along.

Another man, a secretary, by the look of him, was following a few steps behind his master, with a loosely-tied bundle of papers and documents under his arm.

Septimus observed, interestedly, from the other side of the road.

They're good at business, these people, he thought. *Damnably good! It's in their blood. We could learn a lot from them. I should have invested my savings in silk. Or opium. Instead of Lachlan's bloody perfume. I could have been...*

At that precise moment, something exploded, in an alleyway right next to where the mischievous-looking youth was standing. The entire street shook. Dust and smoke poured out from the alley. Screaming people and frightened horses ran about in circles as they tried to escape the smoke and the flying debris. In the chaos, somebody bumped head-first into the Chinese merchant. Simultaneously, the pale-faced youth reappeared. A blade flashed and the money-pouch was gone.

It was all over in a moment. Septimus glimpsed the thief as he ran off. A young woman in a pink bonnet was standing on the pavement nearby, looking tearful and distressed. The youth shoved her aside as he fled. No-one else noticed, in the confusion, but Septimus distinctly saw the pouch change hands again. Quick as a flash, the girl had palmed it and pushed it down the front of her dress.

"I'll be damned..." Septimus muttered, as the girl, too, slipped away.

He couldn't help but chuckle. It had been neatly done.

"Thief! Thief! Stopper him!" the victim screamed.

He pointed, this way and that, but it was already too late.

Nobody had been seriously hurt but a heavy wagon had rolled over and it was going to take some time to calm the horses and clear the road. The local constables arrived as the wagon was being righted but there was little they could do. The guilty party had vanished. Nobody had actually seen him, as far as the constables could make out. The dust and smoke had hidden everything.

Septimus had seen him but he didn't feel inclined to talk. The victim had lost his valuables but the kid would lose his life if he was caught. He'd be dangling from the Newgate gallows before the week was out. Food for the crows.

"*This ain't the first time!*" an enraged woman shrieked. Into Septimus's ear. "*The brainless, thieving bastard!* He broke all the bloody windas. Didn't he? Darn Ellington Street. *Just last week!* It's a bloody miracle that he ain't already *killed* somebody, if you arsk me. Wiv luck, he'll blow *'imself* up, before too bloody long!"

"It would be poetical justice," Septimus agreed.

The woman laughed, nastily. She wasn't the forgiving sort.

Septimus wiped the dust off his coat and went on his way. It was getting late. He was supposed to be meeting Lachlan's gang. In a room at the Rose Tavern.

A lamplighter went by. With his ladder. Ratcliffe was badly-lit, at night, but there were lamps here and there. On the busier streets. The temperature was dropping. Dramatically. The fog was getting thicker. Septimus's legs were starting to fail him, after all the miles he'd walked. He stopped to rest, for a moment.

Outside the Bell and Crown Inn. On Broad Street.

A delicious smell of cooking was coming from the inn's kitchen. Dinner was being prepared, it seemed. For the fortunate few. Septimus moaned. All he'd eaten all day had been the stolen pie. He was feeling a little weak at the knees.

A movement caught his eye. Further up the street. A curious figure emerged from the shadows of an alley. A well-dressed fellow in a peculiar hat.

There was a street-lamp directly above him. A feeble light. The man's face was hidden in the shadow of his hat, but Septimus could *just about* make out his tied-back hair and his neatly-trimmed, pointed beard. The clothes he was wearing looked expensive. Expensive enough to get him garrotted, in Sailor Town, at this time of night. He wasn't wearing a sword but Septimus didn't doubt that he'd be carrying a pistol. Somewhere about his person. Underneath his fine clothes.

Who in the world is he? Septimus wondered.

He looked like a foreigner. A Dutchman perhaps. Of the better sort. When he eventually moved off, Septimus crept out of his hiding-place and followed. He wasn't exactly sure why. *Something* about the man looked familiar. The distinctive hat made him easy to follow. It was a large, black, silk hat, with a wide brim.

At a leisurely pace, as though he'd come out to enjoy the night air, the fellow sauntered through the notorious Ratcliffe streets. He was heading south. Towards Ratcliffe Cross Stairs. At the site of the old cross he turned east, onto Narrow Street. Septimus followed, at a safe distance. He could just about see the big hat, up ahead, in the fog. Carts and carriages were rattling by. The waterside was still busy, at this early-evening hour. The pavements were crowded with hawkers, evening strollers, sailors-ashore and ladies of the town. A stall selling cure-all potions and lucky charms caught Septimus's eye as he hurried along. Tucked in among the boxes, bones and bottles were several small, gleaming, brass effigies of the Crocodile Queen.

Their red eyes looked weirdly alive in the lantern-light. Septimus stopped and stared.

"How much are those things?" he asked the stallholder.

"A shillin' apiece, sir. They 'ave... *magical powers.*"

He held one up so that Septimus could see it better. Septimus shuddered.

"I'll, uh... need to think about it," he mumbled.

The fellow he'd been following had in the meantime disappeared. The fog had swallowed him. With a shrug, Septimus abandoned the chase. He trudged up towards Thieves' Street, panting as he went. It had been a hard day. He'd soon forgotten all about the character he'd been stalking. Then he turned a corner and there the fellow was, again, just a stone's throw away, on the other side of the road.

If it hadn't been for the hat, Septimus would have hardly noticed him. He was standing very still, in the unlit porch of an ale-house. Septimus shrank back into the shadows he'd just emerged from. The man appeared to be waiting for something, or someone. His eyes were oddly, *mysteriously* luminous.

The eyes of the devil himself, Septimus thought.

A shiny black carriage, pulled by a team of handsome black horses, creaked out of the fog and pulled to a stop outside the ale-house. The driver climbed down and held the door open while the man in the hat strode over to the conveyance.

Septimus watched. From the shadows.

The man climbed into the carriage. As he pulled the door shut he turned, suddenly, and looked directly at Septimus. As though he could see in the dark.

As though he'd known all along that Septimus was there.

"*Damnation!*" Septimus muttered.

His heart thumped against his ribcage. For an indecently long moment, the luminous eyes stayed fixed on him. Septimus pressed himself back against a damp wall. Finally, the malevolent eyes turned away. The carriage door slammed shut.

The driver cracked his whip and the ghostly equipage jingled off.

With a sigh of relief, Septimus hurried on up the road.

"*Who in the name of hell was that?*" he asked himself.

It was a face he'd seen before, *somewhere,* but he couldn't for the life of him think where. Years of immoderate drinking had blunted Septimus's mind and blurred his memories. He was trying to give up the habit, with some success. For several weeks now he hadn't drunk before noon. Having no money had helped.

Evenings were more difficult because he didn't know what else to do, but he rarely drank more than a pint or two of brandy, washed down with a few beers, and the odd drop of wine, if he was in friendly company and his credit would run to it.

Afterwards he would stay up late in his room, working on his memoirs.

He'd already written several foolscap pages. Vivid recollections would come to him, out of nowhere, in the small hours. Memories of India. Of Saint-Domingue, in the French West Indies, where he'd lived for many years. Names and smells and faces would float up to the surface of his mind, in the lonely lost midnight.

For the moment he couldn't think who the man in the big hat was, but it would come to him, sooner or later, he felt sure. As the world turned.

5

CONFESSIONS

Septimus pressed on. Through the thickening fog. Stopping every now and then to be sure of where he was. He was fearful of falling into the dock. It was a frequent occurrence, on nights like this. People simply disappeared, never to be seen again.

"Septimus!" someone called as he approached Thieves' Street.

It was Harriet Wildfire. He'd rushed past without recognising her, in the fog. She was wearing a shabby old coat that didn't seem to fit her very well. He guessed that she'd borrowed it from one of the other girls. They had the habit of wearing each other's clothes. Her hair was tied up in a loose bun, with long black ribbons that hung down her back. She was in mourning, he realised.

"Harriet! Forgive me! I didn't see you. This *nightmarish* bloody weather! It's getting worse by the day, I swear. I'm on my way to see Lachlan, about this, uh... *affair* he's arranging. The matter we're not supposed to mention. I'm a little late. There was a disturbance on Ratcliffe Highway. Are you not working?"

She made a wry face and shrugged.

"Not tonight. It wouldn't be right, after all that's happened. I'm going in anyway, just for the company. I had an appointment earlier, with a priest. It's become a once-a-week thing. I've been doing it for several weeks."

Septimus struggled to conceal his astonishment.

"Are you, uh... receiving instruction?"

She giggled.

"Good Lord, no! Nothing like that. It's more a discreet sort of... *business* arrangement. Somebody had told him about my famous arse and he wanted to see it for himself. Being a man of the cloth, he didn't feel able to come and see me perform at the tavern. Instead, he sent me a note. We made an arrangement to meet in private at my lodgings. Now he comes round once a week, at the same time. I take all my clothes off and walk around a bit for a few minutes while he watches. We don't engage in any conversation, beyond the usual pleasantries. When he's ready to go he thanks me, very politely, and takes his leave. He gives me a guinea. I can't complain. It pays the rent."

"*Heh, heh, heh!*" Septimus chuckled.

"It doesn't hurt anybody. He probably begs the forgiveness of the Almighty when he gets home, the poor sod. I have the feeling that he might want to try caning, eventually. The clergy tend to like that, in my experience, though to be completely honest I'm happy with our present arrangement. I hope to be going away, in any case, before too long. To warmer climes."

"You're leaving London?"

"Hopefully. If things go well. This business of Lachlan's, uh? I don't know much about it, obviously, but it sounds very promising. It's going to make us all rich, Lachlan reckons. This new man of mine, Captain Smalt, is very much involved. You'll meet him, this evening. He's a good man. You can trust him."

"That's good to know."

"From what I've heard, things are going to happen very quickly. We could have the money in no time at all. Within days. Everything has been arranged, so Lachlan says. Captain Smalt – Tobias – wants to take me abroad. That's our plan. We'll start a new life together. Just the two of us. In sunnier climes."

"It sounds good to me."

They were walking past a row of decrepit handcarts that had been chained together at the side of the dock. Harriet pulled Septimus aside.

"Let's sit for five minutes, Septimus. The world can wait. It's peaceful out here. In the bloody fog. It's so damned noisy in the tavern. Madam O'Reilly prefers it that way. *Noise is money,* she likes to say. *Ha!* She told me about last night. *Dear God!* I've been crying all day. I probably look a complete mess. I'd been teaching Susie to sing. She had a good voice. She just lacked confidence. What about you, Septimus? You were fond of each other, I know, the pair of you."

She sat down, on one of the carts. Septimus joined her.

"I've been walking around all day," he confessed. "Turning things over in my mind. Trying to make sense of it all. Susie was in my room last night, I swear. Her ghost, that is. Her presence was very strong. *As though she wanted to tell me something.* And then this morning those weird bloody *priests* turned up and took her away. To their ghastly bone-yard in Southwark. I went down there earlier."

"Have they buried her?"

"Who knows? The bastards threw me out. They weren't very friendly. We almost came to blows. They threatened to shoot me if I didn't leave. That's the kind of people they are. There's something *extremely* odd about this whole business, Harriet. The Southwark cemetery is downright bizarre. The *'Necropolis',* they call it. The City of the Dead. But it's not *real.* It's a sham. *No-one* is buried there, if you ask me. I intend to go again, but in secret, next time. By moonlight."

Harriet nodded. She seemed to understand.

"Were you actually there, when Susie was killed?"

"I was downstairs. Susie had retired to her chamber with a fellow I'd never seen before. I was a little drunk. As usual. Three sheets to the wind, as they say. I could hardly stand up. I'd been drinking for hours. Today I've not taken a drop. I don't have a farthing to my name. That obviously helps. But..."

He shook his head and sighed.

"I could have saved her life. If I'd been a bit quicker on my feet. The thought has been tormenting me all day. I was a soldier, once, you know. Captain Slim. Light Dragoons. At your service! I don't often talk about it, but it's a fact."

"Really?"

"I wouldn't lie to you, Harriet. I got discharged. Drunkenness on duty. Gambling. Financial problems. Family problems. It was a difficult time. I went overseas, in the end. Signed up with the East India Company. The *Honourable* East India Company, as it styles itself. 'John Company', we men called it. They weren't too choosy. They'd take anybody. They even let me keep my rank."

"I had no idea."

"It was a long time ago. I was in Bengal. We didn't do much fighting while I was there, as things turned out. It was too bloody hot. We just marched up and down and did musket drills, to impress the natives. I went down with malaria. In Calcutta. Nearly died. They sent me home, in the end. I never went back."

"It's the climate. So they say."

"Possibly. Don't get me wrong. I loved India. The malaria was just bad luck. It was fate, I suppose. *Karma,* they call it. I came back penniless. In desperation, I entered service. At Ermine House. With the Blackthorpes. I was a liveried footman. It wasn't all that different from being in the bloody army."

"You were at Ermine House? On the Strand? *Heavens above!* That's one of the grandest houses in London! I've walked past it, many a time. They say that Lady Blackthorpe lives there alone, now. His Lordship ran off with an actress."

"So they say. I've heard the same rumours."

"What was it like? Working there?"

"Well... I couldn't complain. They fed us and paid us. Lady Constance was a very decent woman. Lord Blackthorpe was away most of the time, even in those days. The estate stewards ran the place. The Blackthorpe family have substantial interests overseas. Sugar and slavery. That's where their wealth comes from.

Blackthorpe himself was a complete bastard, if you want to know the truth. He collected things. Horses. Oil paintings. Stuffed animals. Other people's wives."

"The British aristocracy, eh? God bless 'em."

"Indeed. Lachlan hopes to see the guillotine set up. On Tower Hill."

"Ha, ha, ha!" Harriet giggled.

"I wouldn't be averse to seeing Lord Blackthorpe's head roll, I must confess. He's the worst of the worst. Believe me. I didn't see him often, to be truthful, while I was at the house. He was permanently absent. He only spoke to me once, face to face, in the whole time I was there. One unforgettable night. The worst night of my entire life. I remember his eyes. There was something almost... *satanic* about them. *Something I've never seen in the eyes of another human being."*

Septimus gasped, suddenly, and put his hands to his face.

"Oh, my God! Of course! Of course!"

"What is it?" Harriet asked worriedly.

"I think I've just *seen* him. *Isaiah bloody Blackthorpe.* The devil himself. I was outside the Bell and Crown Inn, on Broad Street, resting my legs, when I noticed this odd character nearby, under a light. He looked strangely familiar. I followed him for a while. At the time I couldn't think who he was. He was dressed like a French pimp, but... *those eyes!* Dear Lord! It was *him*. I'd stake my life on it."

"In Ratcliffe? Are you sure? When did you last see him?"

"A good many years ago. Twenty, at least. On that

fateful night. The one I mentioned. I was chained to a wall at the time. In a ghastly, damp cellar. Strung up by my toes. Like a pig for the slaughter. The bastard was screaming vile insults at me while I hung there, upside down. I thought it was the end."

Harriet shifted a little closer.

"You weren't exactly on the best of terms, then?"

"That's putting it mildly. I never saw him again. After that night. As things turned out. Luckily for me, I suppose. I've never talked about it before. It's been bottled up. For all these years. God knows what the odious bastard was doing in Ratcliffe. Of all places. Whoring, perhaps. He went off in a very fine carriage."

Harriet was looking increasingly perplexed.

"What had you actually done, to upset him so?"

"Oh... it's a tragic tale. The truth is I'd got to know Lady Constance quite well while I'd been at the house. A little too well, you might say. She was lonely. We took to each other, somehow. I was a handsome enough young fellow, in those days. We had an *affaire*. As the French say. A brief one. We were caught. *Inflagrante*. Almost. That's how I came to be strung up by my toes. In the bloody cellars."

Harriet's eyes widened.

"You were fucking Lady Blackthorpe?"

"Well... you could put it like that, I suppose. Lord Blackthorpe was away. As far as we knew he was in the West Indies. Looking after his business interests. Sugar, mostly. Tobacco. There were plantations in Jamaica, and elsewhere. We hadn't seen him for months. The marriage was a sham. Lady Constance and I became friendly, and then... you know how it goes. One thing led to another."

"I'll be damned. You dark horse."

"I'd even started sleeping in her chamber. That's how stupid I was."

"What happened? Did he just burst in? While you were, uh..."

"It wasn't quite like that. There was a fire. In one of the kitchens. In the small hours. The house was full of smoke and screaming people. I'd slipped out of my lady's chamber, as fast as I could, the moment the commotion had started. All I had on was an undershirt. I was carrying the rest of my garments. Unhappily – unluckily – somebody saw me. A little Irish girl. One of the lower servants. I offered her a golden guinea to keep her mouth shut but she wouldn't take it. She had religious principles. The word spread quicker than the fire. The steward had me arrested. At gunpoint. They dragged me downstairs and locked me up."

"At least they didn't shoot you."

"It might have been better if they had. Lord Blackthorpe turned up at dawn. *Out of nowhere.* We didn't even know he was in the *country,* let alone in London. As far as we knew, he was thousands of miles away. On the other side of the world."

"And the house was on fire?"

"The fire wasn't so serious. They extinguished it fairly quickly. I was locked in a filthy cellar. Blackthorpe came down to take a look at me. It was an eerie scene. I was terrified. There was hardly any light. It was an old cold-room, of some sort. It had a rusty iron gate.

He peered in at me through the gate and wished me a good morning. Polite as you like. Then he went off to take breakfast and a pair of hired ruffians took his place. They beat me half to death with a pick-axe handle. At some point in the proceedings they stripped me naked and chained me to the bloody wall. I hung there all day. Bleeding and dazed. Several hours later they came back and gave me another dose of the same medicine. This time Blackthorpe came and watched. He enjoyed it a lot more than I did, I would imagine."

"But you survived."

"By some miracle. I was unconscious for what seemed like hours. It was pitch-black when I came to my senses again. I wasn't *entirely* sure that I was still in the Land of the Living, though the pain felt real enough. The pain and the cold. I could hear water dripping and the rats scampering about. Then a pair of strange men turned up with an oil-lamp and a bunch of keys. It took them forever and a day to get the door open. They lifted me down from the wall and carried me out to the stables at the back of the house. Next thing I knew I was in a little cart, rattling through the empty streets. They took me to Wapping Dock and put me on a ship. I was barely conscious. I hardly knew what was happening."

"Who were they?"

"I never found out. They were well-spoken. I couldn't really see their faces, in the dark. They advised me that I should behave myself and keep my mouth shut, if I knew what was good for me. And that I could never, *ever* return to England."

"But you didn't listen. Clearly."

"No! *Ha, ha, ha!* I never do. Even so, it took me twenty years to work up the courage. I'll tell you the whole story, one day, Harriet. Not right now. It would take all night. I'm hoping to publish my memoirs. I've already written a few pages. I won't directly mention the Blackthorpes, of course. It would be improper."

"Did Lord Blackthorpe recognise you?"

"I don't think he did. I doubt that he even remembers me. My rescuers probably told him that I was dead. Whoever they were. In Blackthorpe's eyes I was a person of no consequence. A faceless bloody servant. Part of the furniture."

Some foreign sailors wandered by. Dutchmen. They shouted something to Harriet as they went past, in their own language. It sounded friendly enough.

Harriet smiled and waved. She was used to the attention of men.

"Let's get inside, Septimus," she said. "It's getting *cold* out here. I've never known such strange weather. It's hardly autumn yet. There was a *huge* storm of hailstones the other night. The streets were white-over. It was quite odd."

They strolled down Thieves' Street in silence. Picking their way past the piled horse-shit and the rooting pigs. The racket of the tavern reached their ears as they got closer. The familiar sound of an early-evening crowd. There were whorehouses aplenty on the Limehouse waterfront, but Madam O'Reilly's Rose Tavern was by far the most famous. Sailors from every part of the world knew the place.

To Septimus, it had come to feel like home.

He held the door for Harriet and followed her inside.

Her admirers cheered as she walked in. She waved and smiled, though she wasn't thinking of performing.

She pecked Septimus on the cheek and went through into the back.

To the dismal little dressing-room at the back of the stage that the girls retreated to when they wanted to be alone. Or to talk, privately, with their friends.

The main rooms were busy and noisy. Life was going on as normal. So it seemed. Despite Susie's death. Nothing much had changed. It was hard to believe that that there'd been a gruesome murder. Less than twenty-four hours before.

Septimus himself could hardly believe that Susie was gone.

Was it really her? he asked himself as he pushed his way through the crowd. *That mangled corpse in her room? Could it have been some hideous, evil trick?*

He was beginning to wish that he'd taken a closer look at Susie's mortal remains. Before he'd rushed away. *Something wasn't right.* He just knew it. The priests at the Necropolis had been withholding something. They hadn't wanted him there. They didn't want *anyone* there. *Unless they'd drunk the ghastly Eau Sacré.*

He pushed the confused thoughts out of his mind.

For the moment, he just needed to find Lachlan.

6

CAPTAIN SMALT AND THE
SABRINA LOUISE

The tavern was full of foreign sailors, enjoying an evening ashore. The luckier ones had money in their pockets. Money they *desperately* needed to spend. A grinning Dutchman bought Septimus a brandy, for no reason at all. He was just ecstatically drunk and happy. He slapped Septimus on the back when the business was done, before rushing off to rejoin his shipmates and the girls they were with.

Septimus downed the brandy in one go. It was the first time in weeks that he'd gone through a whole day without a drink. He felt quite proud of himself.

With the empty glass in hand, he roamed the crowded room, in search of Lachlan.

Worryingly, the Irishman was nowhere to be seen. He wasn't at his usual table. There were people in one of the private booths, talking in whispers behind a tattered curtain, but Septimus couldn't quite make out who they were.

As he stood there, wondering what to do, the curtain flew back and Madam O'Reilly emerged, in the company of an ancient, rather auspicious-looking Chinese gentleman. Madam O'Reilly was trying to persuade her companion to stay a while longer and perhaps enjoy the company of one of the girls, but he had other, more pressing matters to attend to, it seemed. He bowed politely as he departed.

Madam O'Reilly caught sight of Septimus.

"Septimus! Here you are! Mr Malone has been looking for you."

She took hold of Septimus's arm and pulled him closer.

"That was my friend Mr Lee. He lives on Cooper Street. Near the Half Moon. I get my laudanum from him. Most weeks. *For my legs.* And for the girls, too. When they need it. Without Mr Lee, I don't know how we'd manage."

Septimus nodded. Mr Lee was an apothecary, it appeared.

"He'd heard the awful news," Madam O'Reilly whispered. "About Susie. I've tried my best to keep it quiet, but... you know how it is. You can't stop people talking. There may be more than one killer, Mr Lee says. He's come across this kind of thing before. Out in the East. In China. A *secret society* of assassins may be committing these terrible crimes. *Opium fiends.* Dabblers in dark magic. They lose all control, sometimes. *Evil spirits* take hold of them."

Septimus shook his head.

"No, no, no. He's completely wrong, Madam O'Reilly. I'm certain of it. Susie wasn't killed by a madman. Or even a mad woman. Those *awful* injuries she suffered could

only have been caused by some sort of... *vile creature*. She hardly had time to scream. The thing must have come in through the window. It could still be out there. *Creeping around in the fog!* Looking for its next victim."

Madam O'Reilly groaned, and shuddered.

"*Dear God!* I hardly know what to think anymore. We're living in such *strange* times. Even the weather is changing! It's so bloody *cold*. Not to mention these *horrible* fogs. Food prices are going up by the day! People are starving in the streets. The price of coal has doubled. *In just three months!* If it wasn't for decent, Christian souls like Mr Malone we'd all be freezing to death! And now there's a killer on the loose. Human or otherwise. Where will it all end?"

"I only wish I knew. Where *is* Mr Malone, by the way? I was supposed to meet him here. We have some, uh... *important business* to discuss."

"Ah! Forgive me! I forgot. He left this for you."

She extracted a folded note from her cleavage and passed it to Septimus. It was addressed, in Lachlan's unmistakable, feverish handwriting, to 'Septimus Slim, Esquire, at the Rose Tavern'. It had been crudely sealed, with some sort of glue. Septimus held it up to his nose. It had the ghastly smell of rabbit-skin glue, with a tantalising whiff of Madam O'Reilly's perfume mixed in.

He thanked her and took it over to the fireplace. There were candles on the mantelshelf and an ancient mirror that reflected light out into the room.

A silver coin dropped out as he tore the letter open.

'*Come as soon as you get this!*' he read. '*Our ship is a little cargo-cutter, the Sabrina Louise. We're at anchor in the river, just off Creyke's Wharf, near the Naval Dockyard. Take a boat. A shilling piece enclosed in case you're short of funds. It should be enough. Burn this letter when you've read it!'*

There was no signature. Just a scribbled map showing the location of Creyke's Wharf, in case Septimus didn't know the place. It was about a mile down-river, on the Deptford side. Roughly opposite the night-soil dock.

Septimus retrieved the shilling and consigned the note to the flames.

He pocketed the coin and hurried off.

It was a short walk from Thieves' Street to Limehouse Hole Stairs. A solitary waterman was in attendance when Septimus got there. He was squatting in the stern of his boat with a greasy cloak over his shoulders and a clay pipe in his mouth.

The pipe glowed through the murk as its owner drew on it.

"Creyke's Wharf, Deptford?" Septimus shouted.

"That'll be one and a tanner. At this time o' night."

"Uh... I can only give you a shilling."

"You can give me one and six, or swim. It's up to you."

"Oh... well."

With a shrug, Septimus climbed aboard. It seemed pointless to argue. He'd actually found a sixpence while he'd been walking around, that afternoon. He'd been planning to spend it on food, but fate – as usual – was not on his side.

He didn't talk much to the boatman on the way downriver. It seemed wise to keep his mouth shut. What Lachlan was proposing was no petty crime. It was an act of organised piracy. River piracy. They'd face the rope, if they were caught.

A notorious gang of coal-pirates had been strung up at York, just two weeks previously, after they'd been caught by the navy. Somewhere up the East Coast.

The waterman grumbled and cursed as he sculled through the fog. Past long lines of anchored ships. The tide was on the ebb. It took a while to find the vessel they were looking for, when they finally reached Deptford. Then, at last, they came up under a low-lit stern and there was the name, in gilded letters that glinted, uncannily, through the drifting fog. *'Sabrina Louise, Whitby.'*

She was sitting low in the water. A stove-pipe was smoking, aft.

Septimus paid the boatman and clambered up over the gunnel as the fellow rowed off. An ugly black dog rattled its chains and snarled at the new arrival.

A hatch opened. Yellow light flooded out.

"*Septimus?*"

Lachlan's grinning head emerged from the hatch.

"Don't worry about the dog. He wouldn't hurt a fly. *Thank God you've got here!* I was worried that you might have had second thoughts. Or had some sort of dreadful accident. There was a riot in Westminster. Apparently. Earlier today. Several people were shot dead. By the army. *Innocent citizens!* Protesting about the food shortages. Come on down! Did you have enough for the boat?"

"Just. He charged me a shilling and sixpence. The thieving bastard. You could sail to the Indies and back, for less than that, in the old days."

"Ha, ha! Things have changed, my friend. Sadly."

The ship was rocking, gently, on the ebb. Septimus followed Lachlan down into the smoky saloon, where the rest of the gang were waiting. A swaying oil-lamp hung above a greasy table. There were already several empty bottles on the table.

The men grunted and nodded as Septimus joined them.

An old iron stove was aglow in the galley, astern. The skipper's sleeping-quarters were at the forward end of the cabin, behind a half-drawn curtain.

A painted scene on the bulkhead above the bed caught Septimus's eye as he glanced about. It showed a pair of naked women, locked in a sweaty embrace with their legs intertwined and their tongues in each other's mouths. There were similar scenes in other places. Septimus's jaw dropped slightly as he took it all in.

It wasn't at all what he'd expected.

His fellow conspirators cackled and snorted. Brandy glugged from a bottle as they refilled their cups and glasses and filled another one for Septimus.

Lachlan chuckled as he passed Septimus his drink.

"They're *damnably* good, eh? A change from the usual. Bowls of fruit and all that. This is my good friend Septimus Slim, everyone. He's an old soldier. *Captain Slim.* No less. Light Dragoons. *Just the man we need.* He can use a cutlass and shoot straight. He's been abroad for the best part of twenty years. Exile in the Americas. Don't ask me what he did. He doesn't like to talk about it."

The men laughed. Septimus had seen them all before. At one time or another. In the local taverns. The scar-faced master of the *Sabrina Louise* was the new fellow in Harriet Wildfire's life. He was a tough-looking seafarer with sun bleached hair. Tied back in a horse's tail. A silver trinket in the shape of a dolphin dangled from his left ear. His other ear had, at some point, been cut clean off.

Over the table from the captain was another familiar face. The gunpowder enthusiast from the Ratcliffe Highway was sitting in the smoky light looking almost indecently pleased with himself. As though he'd had a *most* satisfactory day.

He'd dusted himself off since Septimus had last seen him.

It was a small world.

"This fine young fellow is Billy Moon," Lachlan said, nodding towards the lad. "I've known Billy since he was knee-high to a donkey. His dear mother, bless her soul, made me promise that I'd look after him when she was gone. Billy's young but he's quick-thinking and reliable. I'd trust him with my life. He can use a musket, too. We'll have at least two with us, on the day. *Excellent* pieces, both of 'em."

Billy Moon reached across and shook Septimus's hand.

"Two muskets?" Septimus asked. "Is that all we're taking?"

"We've got pistols, too, obviously," Lachlan said, slightly aggrieved. "And a blunderbuss that you could bring an armoured elephant down with. It should be enough. We've got a full keg of powder. An *ample* supply of balls and wadding. Enough to start a small war. If we were so inclined. We'll be well-armed."

An older man stirred. In the shadows at the end of the table. He leaned forward into the lamplight. Septimus had hardly noticed him. Up to that point. He had faded tattoos on the back of his hands and an impressive mouthful of gold teeth that glittered in the sudden light as he smiled.

"Our great advantage will be that of *surprise*," he informed Septimus. "They won't be expecting trouble. Not in the Thames Estuary. On a busy morning. In broad daylight. We could *ram the bastards,* in any case. If they don't behave."

"Not that we'd want to," Lachlan added hurriedly. "It would be too much of a bloody risk. We could *sink* 'em. The prize would be lost. This is Mr Serocoal, by the way, Septimus. One of my oldest and dearest friends. Mr Serocoal trained as a goldsmith, in his youth, but then – somewhere along the tangled path of life – he became a coiner. One of the best in London. His golden guineas are almost as good as the real thing. They have *real gold* in them. Even more importantly, Mr Serocoal *knows* people. Useful people. If everything goes to plan, we'll be selling the bulk of our haul to one of Mr Serocoal's old acquaintances. A goldsmith in the City."

Septimus nodded, a little distractedly. A painting at the opposite side of the cabin had caught his eye. It showed a beautiful, brown-skinned, naked woman, floating contentedly at the bottom of a sunlit lagoon. Bubbles were streaming up from various parts of her anatomy. A strange, soft, pink creature was holding her in its long tentacles. The woman appeared to be engaged in a peculiar sexual act with a *giant jellyfish*. The artistry was impressive. It was a minor masterpiece.

Lachlan giggled when he realised what Septimus was staring at. "What do you think, Septimus? They're *good*, eh?"

"They're, uh... *unusual*. They'd be worth a bob or two. In certain quarters."

The one-eared captain guffawed and poured himself another drink.

"Do you think so? *Ha!* My ex-wife painted them. The beautiful Katarina. She had a taste for other women, if you know what I mean. It was the way she was. A pretty ankle could turn her head. She copied these things from prints. There are shops in Drury Lane where you can buy such things. It kept her out of mischief. We were together for ten years, the two of us. The times we had! I can hardly tell you."

He sighed as he picked up his cup.

"But then she turned against me, for some reason. The ungrateful bitch. Women, eh? There's just no accounting for them. She jumped ship. In St. Peter Port. I'd been ashore for a week. Drunk as a rat in a barrel. I hardly knew where I was. I thought I was in bloody China. *Heh, heh!* When I finally sobered up and got back to the ship, she'd gone. She'd taken all her clothes. And all my savings. Every last farthing. I've never seen her since. Heaven only knows where she went."

The bottles on the table were all empty. The captain went aft and selected another from a well-stocked locker. He blew the dust off it with a grin.

"*Women!*" he complained, as he sat down again.

"They've been the bane of my life, I swear. But now I've met the incomparable Harriet and all that has changed. I could have had a thousand wives, like some ancient Sheik of Araby, and the whole damned lot of them *put together* wouldn't have measured up to Harriet. *Ha, ha!* We plan on leaving the country. When this present business is done. We'll provision the ship and head south. It should be possible. Despite the bloody war."

"Where do you plan to go?" Septimus asked.

"Malta. All being well. Do you know it?"

"No."

"I was in Valetta three years ago. That's the capital, and the main port. I took a certain English lord out there. He had to leave the country in a hurry. The usual thing. *Gambling debts.* Valetta is a splendid city. They have these drinking dens. Deep underground. In stone cellars. Even in the summer heat, they stay cool. Most people speak a little French. A little English. They're *traders.*"

Lachlan replenished everyone's cups.

"To business, uh? This is Captain Smalt, Septimus. Tobias, to his intimates. Harriet introduced us when I happened to mention that I was looking for a little vessel of some sort. It was Divine Providence. The holy angels are on our side in this venture. I just *know* it. I feel it in my bones. Everything is falling into place."

"You may be right. Let's, uh... go over the details again."

Captain Smalt cleared the table and rolled out a musty chart.

"What we have here, Septimus," he explained, "is the 1792 Trinity House chart of the Thames Estuary. An *excellent* piece of work. I know these waters like the back of my hand, but, just this once, I thought we needed a chart. The Dutch ship will be coming up along the coast. We'll be lying in wait *here,* at Egypt Point. Lachlan has told you about the old manor house, I think. That will be our base. It's not shown on the chart. I've marked the exact position with a cross."

Septimus perused the chart, in the swaying lamplight.

"The house is an overgrown ruin," Smalt went on. "All that's left are the old walls. It's barely visible, from out on the river. At low tide, there's nothing to see at all. Just miles of mud. Dotted with little islands and old wrecks. It's a *haunted* place. The nearest village is several miles away. Over the marshes. I've landed brandy at the old house. More than once. Over the years. There's a little creek. Close to the ruins. Hidden among the trees. Even at low water we can slide in and out. I've done it before. On many a moonlit night."

"What do you reckon, Septimus?" Lachlan asked.

"Can we actually see the river, from the ruins?"

"There's an old watchtower. Attached to the house. We've got a picture of it, somewhere. We'll be keeping watch, from the tower. When the Dutch boat shows up we'll sail straight out and intercept her. We'll haul up the flags and pennants of the British Customs Service and order her to heave-to. Once we're aboard, we'll overpower the unsuspecting crew and tie them up below decks. The biggest job will be transferring the cargo. That will take a bit of time. An hour, at least."

"How big is this ship?"

"Quite small, as I understand. It's a little Dutch brig."

"And the crew? What happens to them?"

"We'll just leave them adrift. Or run them aground. That might be better. They'll free themselves eventually, no doubt, but... we'll be long gone."

Septimus helped himself to another brandy.

"You got the information from an old friend, uh?"

"The skipper of the Dutch ship. *Capitaine Clézio*. A Frenchman. He was a French naval officer, until quite recently. I met him at my mother's *maison,* in Montparnasse. Several years ago. But then he had to leave France. During the revolution. He had some problems. *Misappropriation of funds.* That kind of thing. I don't know the exact details. He was in danger of losing his head."

Septimus nodded, understandingly.

"And he's in Ostend, right now?"

"In the harbour at Ostend. Unless he's already sailed, of course. The golden statue was already at the port when he wrote to me. It was manufactured in Paris, he says, and then hauled overland to the Netherlands, to avoid the Channel blockade, and so on. It's in a huge, carved wooden box. Clézio's vessel is a nondescript little Dutch coastal boat, the *Helga*. He probably bought it with the money he stole."

"Can we trust him?"

"Absolutely. He's a perfect gentleman. Agents for the cult offered him the job a few weeks ago. They needed to ship their heathen artefacts *discreetly,* for obvious reasons. They're *devil worshippers.* It's not to everybody's taste."

Captain Smalt poured everyone another drink. Septimus had already consumed half a pint of brandy. His feelings about the scheme were improving as the bottles emptied. The ship was creaking quietly. The cabin was warm.

"So – the *Helga's* captain is on *our* side, uh? He's a bloody Judas."

Lachlan grinned happily.

"That's the beauty of it. When Clézio found out what the cargo was, he could hardly believe his ears. That's when he contacted me. Weather permitting, the *Helga* will reach Egypt Point in exactly three days' time. Early in the morning."

"What else will be on the ship?"

"Furnishings for the new temple. Chairs. Candlesticks. Golden ornaments. *Heaven-knows-what.* Clézio sent me a list but I couldn't make much sense of it. Some of it was in French. Some in Dutch. The golden statue is the most important thing. As long as we get that, I'll be happy. It's *enormous.* About twelve feet high, as I understand. We'll have to break it up, somehow. Into manageable pieces. We'll take a heavy axe with us. *Altogether* – there could be a ton of gold on board."

"Jesus!" Septimus murmured. *"Really?"*

"That was Clézio's estimate. From what he'd seen of it."

"What will it be worth?"

"About three-hundred thousand. British pounds. So Mr Serocoal reckons. If there *is* a ton. That's on the open market, of course. We'll be lucky to make half that, but... we could still walk away with thirty thousand each. *No mean sum!"*

Septimus whistled. The other men laughed.

"So... when do we sail?"

Lachlan rolled-up the Trinity House chart.

"As soon as we can. The ship needs a bit of attention. Some new cordage. She's got to have that shiny *look* of a Revenue Service boat. We'll get the work done tomorrow and leave the next morning. It will take us all day to get downriver."

"What about the firearms? Where are they?"

"Safely stowed. Up in the fo'c'sle. With the dog."

"Are they all in good order?"

Lachlan nodded.

"We fired 'em all, yesterday. Me and young Billy. Billy downed a pigeon. With one of the muskets. *At fifty yards!* We had it for dinner. The pistols are all in good order. We've got *boxes* of ammunition. *Hopefully...* it won't be needed."

He tapped the tabletop. For luck.

"It's going to go well. I just *know* it."

"I'm inclined to agree," Smalt said. "What could possibly go wrong? We'll get the ship cleaned-up. I'll provision the galley and put the dog ashore. I don't want to take him with us. A Customs Service boat wouldn't have a dog aboard."

He produced another bottle from the locker. The men conversed quietly about this and that as they drank. About the weather and the price of gold. About crime and politics, smuggling, women, war and revolution.

About how they were going to spend the money.

Billy was also thinking of seeing the world.

"How do you create the explosions?" Septimus asked him.

"*Uh?*"

"I saw you at work. On Ratcliffe Highway. Earlier today. I was mightily impressed. It was quite a show. It will pay you to move on, though. People are getting sick of you breaking their windows. It wouldn't go well, if you got caught."

Billy looked embarrassed. *Almost* contrite.

"I try to choose a different place each time. They've been pasting my picture up in the streets. I don't really care, Mr Septimus. I can say goodbye to all that, now. Thank God! It's a disgusting way to make a living. It ruins your clothes."

"How much did you take from that unfortunate Chinese gentleman?"

"Eight guineas. Just over. There are costs involved, obviously. It takes two or three of us to make it work. I couldn't do it alone. An old naval gunner makes the grenades for me. The fuses are just cotton wadding, soaked in lamp-oil. My girl, Esther, gives me a sign when a suitable-looking cully comes along. I light the fuse and get into position, and... *bang!* Off it goes."

"Heh, heh, heh!"

Captain Smalt laughed as he refilled Billy's cup.

"We're saving you from a life of crime, young man. From an appointment with the hangman, even, by the sound of it. You'll be a gentleman from now on. A man-about-town. You'll be able to make something of yourself."

The *Sabrina Louise* rolled as another vessel passed by, out in the night. The lantern squeaked as it swung. Septimus felt curiously at home in the smoky cabin. He'd spent long stretches of his life at sea, for one reason or another. Through no choice of his own, mostly. It was just the way things had turned out.

"Did you find Susie?" Lachlan asked him. "At the Necropolis?"

"No. Sad to say. I found the Necropolis. It's a peculiar bloody place. Cold and strange. I crept in and wondered about for a while. But then a gang of those so-called bloody *priests* caught me and threw me out. They seemed to know straight away that I wasn't one of their people. I don't know how they knew."

"They must use secret signs. Like the Freemasons."

"Perhaps. They were *damned* unfriendly. I didn't like the place. It didn't *feel* right. Something about it was just *wrong*. There were no trees. No flowers. No birds. Just row after row of silent, decaying tombs and crypts. Festooned with cobwebs and shrouded in fog. The tombs look ancient, as though they've been there for centuries, but... it's all *false*. Some kind of bloody sorcery. They've *made* it look old. They only acquired the land six months ago. So I've been told."

"What was there before?" Mr Serocoal asked.

"It was common-land, apparently. Local people used it."

"So how did these heathen bastards get hold of it?"

"Nobody seems to know."

Mr Serocoal pretended to spit.

"Isn't that just bloody typical? The poor have no rights. As usual."

"I will go again. As soon as I can. We need to get Susie out of there. We could have her reinterred. In the old churchyard at St. Anne's. She'd be at peace there,

I think. She was a Christian soul. At heart. It's hard to believe that she's gone, to be truthful. I'll speak to the church-warden. When we get back."

Lachlan sighed, and nodded.

"Did you see the new temple, while you were there?"

"Only from a distance. Through the mist and smoke. The building work looked almost finished. I couldn't get close. They wouldn't let me pass."

"The uncivilised bastards," Captain Smalt muttered.

He held a bottle up to the light, to see what was left in it.

"Does she really exist, do you think?" he asked, a little nervously, as he trickled the last drops from the bottle into his cup. "This ghastly creature? The Crocodile Queen? Have these lunatics awoken some ancient fiend? A sleeping fiend, from the fiery depths of hell? Was it the smell of blood, perhaps, that drew her to Paris?"

"Heaven forfend!" Lachlan protested.

"I'm just speculating."

"This is how they prey on people. *Little by little,* you get sucked in. Before you know where you are, you're done. *It's a moon-struck bloody cult.* One of the *many* that sprang up in Paris, as Madame Guillotine did her dreadful work. This particular cult has *money.* So it seems. But it won't last. *People aren't stupid."*

"You're probably right," Captain Smalt agreed.

"I *am* right," Lachlan insisted. "I'm *absolutely* right."

The other men laughed, quietly.

"The gold is all we need to worry about," Mr Serocoal said. "For the moment, at least. Gold is gold. It's a lovely metal that happens to be worth a lot of money. We can worry about the Crocodile Queen later. While we're melting her down."

Septimus joined in the merry laughter. He gulped his brandy.

"I need to be on my way," he said. "Can I get a boat? From hereabouts?"

"Billy will take you over the river," Lachlan told him. "In the ship's boat. There'll be wherries at the King's Arms. It's always busy there. I'm going to stay aboard. Overnight. With Billy and Mr Serocoal. We're taking the ship into Deptford Creek. First thing tomorrow. For the repairs. Friends of the captain have agreed to do the work. At short notice. We haven't yet agreed on a price."

"Do they know why we're doing it?"

"Absolutely not. It's *essential* that we keep all of this to ourselves. We'll turn up out of the blue, lift the gold, and vanish into the bloody mist. Like ghosts."

Mr Serocoal leaned forward and caught Septimus's eye.

"The theft won't even be *reported,*" he said, with a grin that showed off his magnificent gold teeth. "That's the beauty of it. This cargo is being brought into the country *illegally.* They're *smuggling* it in. Or hoping to. The loss will upset them, no doubt, but they'll get over it. They're *swimming* in money. What they've spent on building the Temple of Dreams would have fed the poor of London for a hundred years. Or more. By the end of the month, all of this will be ancient history."

Lachlan nodded.

"And we'll be long-gone. With our ill-gotten gains."

Septimus swayed, a little uncertainly, as he got to his feet.

"I might just walk home. I'll think things over, while I'm walking."

"You can't walk from here, you fool," Lachlan reminded him. "We're in the middle of the bloody river. Billy will row you over to the King's Arms. You could walk from there I suppose, if you really have to. Take one of the pistols. The Millwall Road isn't safe at night. We don't want to lose you to footpads. That would be calamitous. *Heh, heh!* I'll see you tomorrow. At the tavern!"

7

THE MIASMIC VAPOURS OF
THE ISLE OF DOGS

It didn't take Billy long to scull across to the King's Arms. Despite the fog and the rows of anchored ships. The noise of the place served as a beacon. A fight was going on. A chorus of drunks were singing Irish songs, in the godless English dark.

The boat slid up onto the foreshore mud. It was low tide. Wherrymen were still touting for business, as Lachlan had predicted. Lanterns and muffled shouts advertised their presence. Septimus ignored them as he paddled ashore.

He wanted to walk. He waved farewell to Billy, from the steps.

Septimus had no idea what time it was. He hadn't thought to ask. He guessed that it was well past midnight, but it wouldn't take him all that long to walk to Limehouse. As long as he kept out of trouble. The Millwall Road was a notorious haunt of thieves and cut-throats. It was bad enough in broad daylight.

He'd forgotten to take the pistol from Billy, but he wasn't too worried.

He was gloriously drunk. Too drunk to care.

The riverside path was hard to make out, in the gloom. Somewhere up ahead was the inlet where the night-soil boats loaded their stinking cargoes. Shit Creek, the locals called it. Septimus could already smell it. The rickety wooden bridge that crossed it had been put up as a temporary measure while the new dock was being dug. But then the war with France had broken out and funds for a more permanent structure had been withdrawn, or diverted to the war-effort. The middle section of the wooden bridge opened, to let the night-soil barges in and out.

It took Septimus half an hour to reach the bridge. He'd walked this way once or twice before, but never at night, and never in such thick fog. He climbed the steps on the south side and stumbled out onto the slippery planks of the central span. The flimsy bridge creaked under his weight. The smell of Thames mud and sewage rose around him. It was abominably dark. All he could see, beyond the rusty wheels and chains of the bridge's opening mechanism, was the ghastly, malefic fog.

The stench, on this occasion, wasn't so bad. It was almost bearable.

Are the shit-ships all out at sea? he wondered.

It seemed quite possible. He peered around to make sure that nobody was following him. There were frequent murders in the area. It was that kind of place.

As far as he could tell he was completely alone. All he could hear, beside the sound of his own movements, was the creaking of the bridge and the quiet murmur of the waters below. With a sigh of relief, he set off again.

A ghostly shape streaked past him. He lost his footing as he jerked away from it. For a terrible moment, he thought he was going over the side.

"*FUCK!*" he screamed, as he landed, with a crash, flat on his back.

An enormous rat scampered off. Septimus lay where he'd fallen, rubbing his bloodied head and staring up into the hellish dark. He was almost disappointed that he *hadn't* gone over the edge and drowned. It would have solved all his problems.

"Damn you, King George! You mad bastard!"

The shit-dock had been the King's idea. It was one of the many Great Projects that the Hanoverian monarch had set in motion. Parliament had even debated the idea of calling it the King George Dock, though this proposal had eventually been decided against. On grounds of good taste. The dock had been part of a scheme to clean up the Thames. Some of the ordure was dumped at sea. The great bulk of it was sold as fertiliser and spread onto farmland, around the coasts of Kent and Essex.

"Damn the whole fucking lot of you!" Septimus raged, from where he lay. *"You bewigged bastards! If it wasn't for your wars and whores and sewage... I'd be at home in my bed. Not lying here on this stupid bloody bridge! Damn you all!"*

Septimus was tired and hungry. He was also ridiculously drunk. More so than he'd realised when he'd left the ship. When he tried to get back to his feet he found that he couldn't. His legs were refusing to obey orders. He closed his eyes and tried to make himself more comfortable. There appeared to be no-one else about. Apart from the stragglers at the King's Arms he hadn't seen another soul.

Lord Blackthorpe came back into his thoughts. Blackthorpe had been a familiar figure at the court. At one time. Septimus had respected the aristocracy, in those days. But then the bastards had all ganged up on him. It was *nothing whatsoever* to do with the fact that he'd been bedding Lord Blackthorpe's wife.

It was because... *he wasn't of their class.*

Lady Constance was alone now. So he'd heard. He imagined her pale, distraught figure, roaming the moonlit corridors of Ermine House, while her vile husband cavorted in the sun with his innumerable mistresses and concubines.

There was no justice.

The sound of approaching footsteps caught Septimus's attention. Quiet footsteps. Muffled by the fog. Someone else was coming up onto the bridge.

Whoever the owner of the feet was, he didn't sound dangerous. He was grunting and wheezing like a worn-out old nag as he climbed the steps.

"Who's there?" Septimus shouted.

"Septimus?"

A familiar face emerged from the gloom.

"Lachlan? For heaven's sakes! What are you doing here? I thought you were going to sleep on the ship. With the others. Is something wrong?"

"No, no, no. Nothing like that. I was just worried about you. You didn't take the pistol. I'd given it to Billy but Billy forgot to give it to you. He shouted after you but you'd already gone. I thought I'd try and catch you.

To make sure you got home in one piece. We don't want to lose you. What are you doing here? You can't sleep here. You could topple into the bloody creek and drown."

"I slipped. Couldn't get up again. I'm just... *slightly* pickled."

"*Ha, ha!* You're not the only one. Smalt was looking a bit groggy when I left. I threw a blanket over him. Mr Serocoal was hardly conscious. Billy was alright. He always is. Billy's the sort who can drink all night and still be fresh as a daisy the next morning. He was just born that way. Attila will keep an eye on things."

"Attila?"

"Smalt's dog."

"Ah."

Septimus dragged himself up into a sitting position.

"You've organised this business well, Lachlan. They're a good bunch. The kind of people you know you can trust. It's an excellent vessel and the skipper's *exactly* the man we need. I liked him. Billy's a good lad. Mr Serocoal, too."

"True. I've known Billy since he was a babe-in-arms. His mother was a decent, god-fearing woman. She died young. Sadly. Consumption. Mr Serocoal is an old friend. I met him in Newgate Prison. *Many* years ago. He got us both out. Mr Serocoal was always good at that sort of thing. He has *connections.*"

"What sort of connections?"

"With the affluent classes. Land-owners. Speculators. Lords and Ladies. Mr Serocoal is well-known. In those circles. He's the man they turn to when they're up to their ears in shit. You wouldn't believe some of the stories he's told me, over the years. You get some bloody duchess who's gambled away her husband's entire fortune and wants to sell some jewellery that doesn't even belong to her. Mr Serocoal is *discreet.* He can arrange such things. He doesn't take advantage."

Septimus nodded. He looked thoughtful, suddenly.

"Mr Serocoal could perhaps assist me. There's something important I have to do. I need to get into Ermine House. On the Strand. Do you know the place?"

"Ermine House? Of course I know it. Who doesn't?"

"I was a servant there. A footman. To the Blackthorpe's. Many years ago. It's the reason I had to leave the country. I've never talked about it much, I know."

"You've never talked about it *at all.* I didn't like to ask."

"I was, uh... caught between the sheets with Lady Blackthorpe."

Lachlan nearly slipped off the bridge.

"Mother of God! You're pulling my leg, surely?"

"It's the truth. I've tried to erase it from my memory, but then... I was talking to Harriet earlier and the whole stupid story came tumbling out. It was youthful madness. I was caught in the act with the beautiful Lady Constance. I paid for it. Believe me. They beat me half to death and put me on a ship. To the other side of the world. They left me for dead. On a tiny island in the middle of nowhere."

"Where?"

"Off the coast of Venezuela, though I only found that out later. At the time I had no bloody idea where I was. We'd been at sea for weeks. I'd been chained-up.

Below decks. Sleeping in my own filth. They took me ashore in a boat. Dragged me up the beach and left me. In leg-irons, with my hands tied behind my back and a piece of rag in my mouth. I could hear the bastards laughing as they rowed off."

"They just left you there?"

"That's about the size of it. In the steaming sand. With the surf splashing up around me. They were just following orders, I suppose. It was nothing personal."

"But, even so..."

Lachlan grimaced. He was clearly shocked.

"And you want to return to the scene of your crime? Have you taken leave of your senses? They'd skin you alive if they caught you again. I think we need to get you home. C'mon. Give me your hand. Let's go. We both need our beds."

Septimus chuckled as Lachlan pulled him up.

"I'll tell you the rest of the story one day. It gets better as it goes along."

"It couldn't get much worse. I'm surprised you survived."

Cautiously, Lachlan led Septimus over the creaking bridge and down the other side. They still had a way to go. Septimus talked about his days as a footman as they walked. The cold fog swirled around them. Like something alive.

"We could burgle Ermine House," Lachlan suggested. "If we could get in. Have you ever thought of it? It would serve them right, after the way they treated you. You *know* the place. It's a huge house. It must be *stuffed* with valuables."

"Yes, but..."

Septimus didn't seem to like the idea much.

"It wouldn't be easy. The place is a fortress. The watchmen are armed."

"It might be worth thinking about."

"A lad got in through the drains, once," Septimus admitted. "He took some silver spoons. They caught him. He was strung up, the poor bastard."

"Oh, Lord..."

Lachlan muttered a quiet prayer and crossed himself.

It was getting cold, out in the night. The Limehouse waterfront was fogbound and silent. The men lingered, for a moment, at the end of Dock Street. Septimus was almost home. Lachlan lived in Poplar. He still had some way to go.

"Do you think the tavern might be open?" Septimus asked. "We could take another drink. I'm almost sober again. Cold air has that effect on me."

"I wouldn't think so. God knows what time it is. I left my pocket-watch on the ship. *Nowhere* around here will be open. We'd have to walk up to Ratcliffe. Go *home*, Septimus. Get some sleep. Tomorrow will be another busy day."

Another thought seemed to strike him as he turned to leave. He fished in his pockets and pulled out two tiny green bottles. They had wax seals and unreadable labels. Septimus wasn't sure what they were. They looked vaguely dangerous.

"This will get you off into the Land of Nod, Septimus. I meant to give these to Smalt, but then I somehow forgot. This is genuine *Eau Sacré,* from France. They were giving it out in the streets, one day, in Paris. It was the Crocodile Queen's birthday or something. I didn't exactly grasp what the occasion was. They gave me a few of these bottles. I tried it, naturally. It's what inspired me to buy the barrel I had sent over. The one that got bloody stolen. Try it when you get home. You'll sleep the sleep of the dead, I promise. You'll feel like a new man in the morning."

Septimus took the bottles. He looked uncertain.

"Are you sure that it's, uh... safe?"

"Of course. It's just alcohol. With weird herbs. Eldritch herbs and a dash of opium. It has that familiar, musty taste. A thimbleful of it knocked me out, the first time I tried it. I slept for bloody hours. I had some *very* strange dreams."

With a shrug, Septimus pocketed the bottles. Lachlan shouted something about breakfast as he disappeared into the fog. The words were lost. Septimus sighed. His own lodgings were close by. At the Crow Hotel. On Zeelandia Street.

A monstrous cat darted out as he opened the front door. One of Mrs Lusardi's familiars. The night-watchman was snoring, noisily. In his ill-lit alcove. His toothless mouth was hanging open. The candle at his side had almost guttered out. Anybody could have walked in off the street and stolen anything they'd liked.

If there'd been anything in the place worth stealing.

While the night-watchman snored, Septimus tiptoed through into the kitchen. The cats and the cockroaches had been there before him but under an upturned dish he found a piece of dry bread and a greasy cooked sausage. He closed the door quietly behind him and crept upstairs with his haul. He was desperately hungry.

In the privacy of his chamber he lit a candle and laid his little collection out on the table. The tiny bottles glowed in the candlelight. *They looked almost alive.* He picked one up and examined it while he ate.

The label was hard to read. He held it closer to the candle flame. The fancy lettering at the top just said *'Eau Sacré'*. Underneath was an engraved image of the Crocodile Queen with her scaly wings outstretched and a shining disc on top of her head that appeared to be the sun. The background was a field of stars.

The print below was so small he could hardly see it.

'Sécrétions Authentiques de la Reine Crocodile', he made out. *'100% Pure'*.

"Uh?" he grunted.

Lachlan hadn't said anything about *secretions*.

He broke the seal and levered the cork out with his pocket knife. The smell of the stuff reminded him of something but he wasn't sure what.

There was only a mouthful or two in the bottle. He downed it all in one go.

"*Uuugh!*" he moaned.

The taste wasn't *entirely* unpleasant.

He opened the second bottle and emptied that one, too, squirming once again as the contents went down. While he caught his breath and cursed he took another look at the label. Some tiny print, right down at the bottom, caught his eye.

'Approuvé par le Grand Haut Pontieff', he read.

The signature underneath didn't reveal much. It was barely legible. Septimus squinted at it. He was curious to know who the 'Grand High Pontieff' might be.

The scrawled shapes writhed in the candlelight.

"Eh?" he gasped, as he suddenly made sense of them.

The bottle slid from his fingers.

'Isaiah Blackthorpe' was what the spidery scrawl said. Septimus retrieved the bottle and looked again. There was no mistaking it. The Grand High Priest of the Sign of the Crocodile Queen was... *Lord Blackthorpe.* He'd omitted his noble title, on this occasion, but it had to be him. There was only one Isaiah Blackthorpe.

"Good God in Heaven!" Septimus whispered.

It explained where the money was coming from. The Blackthorpe estates. Lady Caroline's inheritance. Caribbean sugar. The slave trade. It also went some way towards explaining what Blackthorpe was doing in London. Wandering about dressed like a French pimp. With a coach and four at his disposal.

What it didn't explain at all was – *to what purpose?*

Septimus stumbled over to his bed and sat on the edge with his head in his hands. The taste of the *Eau Sacré* still lingered on his tongue. There was something horribly familiar about it. He wasn't sure what. He felt dizzy and feverish. His ill-lit chamber appeared to be spinning around him, as though it had come adrift from the rest of the building and was floating, weirdly, in the night.

Susie Kettle came into his mind. Susie had also drunk the *Eau Sacré,* he recalled. The crocodile priests had given her twenty shillings and she'd bought a beautiful red dress with it. She'd looked so happy, in her shiny new silk dress and her gold earrings. It was the way he wanted to remember her. The fact that she'd gone off with another man didn't seem to matter so much anymore.

She was the best girl I ever knew, he told himself.

The candle extinguished itself, suddenly. A cold draught was blowing in from the window. There were several broken panes. Septimus could hear somebody shouting outside. Some inebriated lost soul was howling his many complaints to the Lord Above as he stumbled home through the foggy Limehouse night.

"*Uuuugh...*" Septimus moaned.

The door to his room creaked. He hadn't closed it properly when he'd come in. One of the devilish cats had pushed its way through. There was a quiet 'thump' as the cat jumped up onto the table. Its mysterious feline eyes glowed through the dark. It was staring, wildly, at something that Septimus couldn't see.

"What's the matter with you?" Septimus asked it.

He often talked to the cats, in the lonely night hours, though he didn't really like them coming into his room. They were unhealthy, and crawling with fleas.

"I'm just a *little* drunk," he told it. "Nothing to worry about."

In actual fact, he felt extremely unwell. The temperature in the room had dropped. It was *cold*. Things appeared to be moving in the shadows. Unnatural, shapeless things. The cat had left the door open as it had come in and the door was now swaying, rhythmically... open and closed... open and closed.

As though the room was breathing.

Has that madman Lachlan poisoned me? Septimus thought, worriedly.

The furniture was losing its grip on the floor. Powerful, unknown forces seemed to be at work. The wash-stand gurgled as it floated up towards the ceiling. A ghostly flotsam of small articles – cups, spoons, glasses, corks and tiny pieces of torn-up paper – was already bobbing about in the gloom above.

The window was rattling. As Septimus watched, the lower sash rose, noisily. A moment later, as he stared in horror, it slammed shut again. Fragments of broken glass tinkled down into the dark yard outside.

The wall where the wash-stand had once stood was *dissolving.* Golden light was bubbling through from the Other Side.

A naked woman appeared, floating, mysteriously, in the light.

It was Susie Kettle.

Her lovely red hair was billowing out behind her. In the divine wind. She looked happier, somehow, than she'd ever been in real life. And more beautiful.

As though all care and sorrow had been cleansed from her soul.

Perfumed mists swirled about her. Her jewels sparkled.

Septimus shrank away in terror. He wriggled backwards. Over his filthy mattress. Until his head hit the wainscoting and he could go no further. Susie drew closer. He shivered as she reached down towards him. Out of the light.

He wasn't sure if he was dreaming. Or if he'd just gone completely mad.

He'd heard of things like this happening to heavy drinkers. Though he hadn't really drunk *that* much. Just a pint or two of rough brandy. And the *Eau Sacré*.

"*Fear not, my dearest,*" Susie whispered. "*This is no time for fear. I am still yours. Nothing has changed between us. This light you see, all around, is the light of the New World. The Golden World of Queen Mbembé. Soon you will join me here. We will be as one, you and I. Do you not desire me, still?*"

Septimus stared. Her beauty was quite extraordinary. There was no denying it. She was a little plumper, perhaps. As though she'd been eating well. In the Golden World. And taking better care of herself. Her skin was aglow.

The air filled, suddenly, with the sweet aroma of the scent he'd given her.

'Hungary Water', it was called. For some odd reason. It had been her favourite.

"*What do you want?*" he breathed.

"To be with you again, my love," she told him. "*Here, in the light!* You have tasted the *Eau Sacré*. Now you must attend the ceremony! Use your invitation! Claim your twenty shillings! Spend it as you wish, my dearest. Get some good food. Have a drink or two! Find yourself a woman for the night. After that – fate will take its inevitable course! We will be together once again. You and I. *Together forever!* In the Blessed Light of Queen Mbembé! *Come... come closer!*"

She floated down, as though she intended to embrace him.

"NO!!!" Septimus screamed.

He threw off the grimy blanket he was hiding under and tried to crawl away. In the same instant, he seemed to wake up. The ghostly light fizzled out. Susie Kettle vanished. The hellish noises ceased. The room stopped spinning.

He groaned.

"Oh... Jesus!"

Cold light was creeping in from the world outside. It was almost dawn. Cocks were already crowing. As his eyes adjusted to the twilight he got up and inspected his chamber. The furniture was all back where it was supposed to be. The cat had disappeared. The door was half-open. He went over and slammed it shut.

I have to get out of here, he thought. *Before I go completely mad! As soon as we've got the money, I'll find a better place. In a better part of town. A nice, clean house in one of the newer streets. A place without cockroaches. Or ghosts.*

8

SHADES AND SHADOWS

Hailstones were clattering down when Septimus woke again. The racket had woken him. Wearily, he dragged himself out of bed and hobbled over to the window.

Lumps of ice the size of door-knobs were tumbling from the heavens.

Glistening, icy heaps were piling up, in the early light.

The low buildings behind the hotel were already half-buried.

"What on earth is going on?" he asked himself as he peered out. "This is London, for heaven's sakes! *Not the North Pole!* Has the world gone mad?"

He limped over to the wash-stand and examined his face in the mirror. There was an ugly bruise on his forehead and a nasty gash down one of his cheeks. It looked as though he'd been in a fight, but he had no recollection of it. While he was inspecting his wounds he remembered the awful dream he'd had.

After he'd drunk the *Eau Sacré*.

It was just a nightmare, he reasoned. *A ghastly, stupid dream.*

Though it had seemed real enough, at the time.

A dead spider was floating in his washing-bowl, with its legs stretched out as though it had expired from the sheer effort of trying to stay afloat.

He fished the little corpse out and threw it away.

It was early morning. About half-past six, he guessed. Going by the light.

He could revisit the Necropolis, he realised. If he moved quickly enough. The crocodile priests would be out and about, but they'd be half-asleep, like everyone else, at this early hour. He could still be back in time to meet Lachlan.

There was a heartening smell of coffee in the air when he got downstairs. The night-watchman was at his desk, in the candlelight, with his nose in a copy of the *Weekly Advertiser*. He peered, sleepily, at Septimus. Over the top of his spectacles.

"You're an early bird, for once," he observed. "Are you ill?"

"The storm woke me. The hailstones. The noise was enough to waken the dead. The ice is piled high. I've never seen anything quite like it. We didn't have weather like this in my day, I swear. Not at this time of year. *Not ever*, in fact."

"In your day? And when exactly was that? If I may be so bold."

"Well, I've, uh... *been away*. My affairs took me overseas."

"*Heh, heh, heh!*"

The old man sniggered as he folded his newspaper.

"Somebody stole my breakfast. Was it you? You thieving bastard!"

"Good God! *No!* How can you even *think* such a thing? *Please!* I've just this very moment risen from my bed! Is that, uh... *coffee* I can smell? Could I perchance... take a small cup? You can put it on my account. I'll be paying everything I owe. *Very soon!* You have my word – as a gentleman – on that."

"You don't *have* an account anymore, Mr Slim! You're *persona non grata,* these days. As I understand. I'm surprised to see you here at all. I thought you'd gone. Find yourself a chair. I'll get you some coffee. No-one else is awake yet."

Septimus dragged a chair over. From the parlour.

"There was another foul murder," the watchman went on, as he returned with the coffee. "In the middle of the night. Just a few houses away. At the corner."

He put two small cups down and pushed one across to Septimus.

"I'd dozed off. Suddenly I woke up. People were screaming and shouting. Out in the street. It was a horrible, cold night. Thick fog. I didn't go out. One of the neighbours came by later and told me what had happened. Some poor devil had been slain. In his bed! *Dear God!* We're no longer safe in our own beds!"

"Indeed."

Septimus gulped his coffee. He was eager to be off.

"Who was the victim?"

"A local coal-heaver. A lodger in one of those rowdy places down the street. The ones with a dozen people in every room. Irish, mostly. A few foreigners. He was a drinker, they say. Had a wife back in Ireland. He'd been here for years."

"What about yourself? Have you been in this place awhile?"

"Forty years. Since I left the army. This was a *fine establishment* in those days, Mr Slim. The *aristocracy* used to stay here. Lords and ladies. They'd stay for a few nights. Sometimes longer. When they returned from Europe. But things have changed. Sadly. The *world* has changed. There's a French countess here at the moment but she has no bloody manners. She looks down her nose at everybody and speaks French to the kitchen maids. You've probably met her."

Septimus grunted and nodded. He'd passed her on the stairs, once or twice. She'd looked down her nose at him, too. But the countess had clearly come down in the world. The present-day Crow Hotel was a flea-pit, by anybody's standards.

He thanked the watchman for the coffee and left. The Necropolis was several miles away, on the other side of the river, but Septimus was going to have to walk. Unfortunately. It was his only option. He didn't have the price of a hackney-coach.

Zeelandia Street was uncannily quiet. It was early, still. The hailstones had mostly melted. Patches of fog still lingered, in the chilly air. A ghostly black hearse was standing unattended in the fog, at the bottom end of the street. The black horses snorted quietly as Septimus approached. Their breath steamed.

The hearse was identical in every respect to the one that Septimus had seen coming out of the Necropolis gates, the day before. This one had clearly come for the remains of the murdered coal-heaver. Once again, the crocodile priests had learned of the outrage before the corpse was even cold. Or so it appeared.

There was no-one about. The driver was nowhere to be seen.

Septimus stopped and took a closer look at the lugubrious vehicle. It was beetle-black, with ecclesiastical carvings and purple curtains that hid the interior from public view. It looked alien and odd. In the dismal dawn light.

A quiet splashing sound caught Septimus's ear.

Someone was pissing, behind a nearby wall.

While the driver attended to nature's call, Septimus investigated further. He raised the purple curtain and peered into the gloomy back. A rough wooden coffin filled half the space. There was room enough for a second carcass, alongside.

Without stopping to think, he climbed up and wriggled in.

The driver cursed and spat as he finished his business. Septimus held his breath as the follow re-crossed the street and clambered up onto the hearse's box.

Then, with a crack of the whip, they were off, and on their way.

What devilish good luck! Septimus thought to himself.

He pulled the curtain back as they bounced along, so he could see what route the driver was taking. It was a rough ride, but he could hardly complain.

The city was coming to life as the sun rose. Filthy smoke from various grim manufactories half-choked him as they raced through Ratcliffe. Further west, in Shadwell, gypsy families were brewing tea over fires at the side of the road.

Septimus's back and shoulders were soon aching. In an attempt to make himself more comfortable he pushed the horrible coffin a little further over to the side. It gave him a bit more space, though it didn't stop the constant shaking and lurching of the cart, or make the planks he was lying on any softer.

Blood began oozing from the base of the coffin. It was a crudely-made thing. With a shudder, he edged himself away from the spreading pool. He wondered who the poor sod in the box was, but he wasn't at all tempted to prise it open and take a look. Whoever the bastard was, he was beyond help. However you looked at it.

Nobody was ever going to see him again.

The hearse slowed, suddenly, on the approach to Tower Hill. Septimus heard barked commands and the sound of marching feet. Through the gap in the curtains he glimpsed a red military coat and the gilded hilt of an extremely expensive cutlass. An officer's weapon. Soldiers from the Tower were blocking the road, he realised. They were questioning the hearse-driver. About his reasons for being there.

Damn! Septimus thought. *I should have closed the bloody curtain.*

It was too late now. He tried not to breathe as the soldiers milled about. Gravel had been strewn over the road for some reason. Perhaps by the artillery. To help with the movement of heavy guns. The city had been on edge for weeks. There had been riots. In a dozen different parishes. Food riots. Anti-taxation riots. Anti-royalist riots. Government buildings had been ransacked and burned.

The stones crunched as the soldiery moved about.

A hand reached in and raised the curtain. Septimus rolled his eyes back and tried his best to look dead. It wasn't hard. His head was throbbing, from the hammering he'd taken during the journey. He'd only had an hour's sleep.

The officer peered in at Septimus's sickly, contorted face.

"Who's this in the back?" he shouted to the hearse-driver.

"A murder victim. From Limehouse."

"Uuugh..." the officer grunted. He poked Septimus in the side.

"Some poxy piece of shit," he informed his companions. "A foreign sailor, by the look of 'im. Not been dead long. I can't even see a wound. God... *he stinks!"*

The curtain dropped and the hearse was allowed on its way.

Septimus held his breath as they started moving again. His blood was pounding in his ears. As they rolled down into Thames Street he gave up the pretence and started breathing again. His lungs filled with smoky London air.

Ignorant bastards! he fumed, silently. *A poxy piece of shit? How dare they? They're a bloody disgrace. They have no respect for the dead.*

He pushed himself up onto one elbow and peeped out.

London Bridge was in sight. Nobody was collecting tolls, as they'd done in the old days. The toll-booth at the end of the bridge was boarded-up and covered with advertising bills for prize fights, lotteries and Italian circuses.

People and conveyances were streaming across. Even at this hour.

The hearse-driver whipped his horses on.

A wagon with a broken wheel was causing delays at the southern end of the bridge. Septimus peered out. Through the funereal curtains. The city was waking up. Early-morning chimneys were belching black smoke. Damp bedding was being hung from windows. A servant-girl outside a tavern caught sight of Septimus's ghostly face as he went past and almost dropped the pail she was carrying.

As Septimus had hoped, the corpse was being delivered to the Necropolis.

The hearse slowed as it neared the gates.

In the back, Septimus got ready to jump.

He tugged the curtains open, and leaned out.

"Pssst...!"

A quiet whistle caught his attention. A figure appeared from the shadows. *It was the goat-man.* The very soul who'd warned Septimus that the crocodile priests wouldn't let him in. That they wouldn't let *anybody* in. Except their own.

The goat-man was gesturing, urgently.

"Jump!" he hissed.

In the circumstances, Septimus thought it best to heed the advice. He took a deep breath, braced himself, and jumped. The hearse raced on, through the open gates and into the consuming fog beyond. In the blink of an eye it was gone.

Septimus picked himself up and hobbled over to where the old man was.

"What are you doing here?" he whispered.

"The same thing as you, I would imagine. I'm looking for my departed wife. I thought I was dreaming when I saw your face. Staring out of that bloody hearse. I've been in there all night. You can't go in now. It's far too dangerous. There are crocodile priests everywhere. We need to get away from here. Follow me!"

He adjusted his ancient periwig and set off. With Septimus in pursuit.

"Where are we going, exactly?"

"We'll walk up to the Swan Inn. We can talk privately there. It's a busy place. You can get a good breakfast for a few pence. With *excellent* coffee."

"Oh, uh..."

Septimus fumbled in his pockets.

"I seem to have... mislaid my purse."

"No matter. I have a bob or two upon me. We need to talk, sir. *I've seen things.* In that ghastly city of the dead. *Unspeakable things.* Things that... *nobody in their right mind would believe.* You've been in there yourself, I'm guessing. You might understand. *I broke into one of those bloody vaults.* In the middle of the bloody night. The bastards nearly caught me. Luck was on my side, as it turned out, but only just. What's your name, good sir? If you don't mind me asking."

"Slim, sir. Septimus to my friends. And yours, good sir?"

"Withers. Ebenezer Withers. It's a pleasure to meet you, sir."

It took them half an hour to stroll up to the Swan Inn. Septimus knew the place. Very slightly. It was a busy coaching-inn, on Tooley Street, close to London Bridge.

Regular coaches to the south coast plied from the inner courtyard. Septimus had spent a pleasant night there. Six months previously. His first night back in England. It had cost him five shillings and sixpence, with supper and a bottle of brandy included. The very next morning he'd taken a boat downriver to Limehouse, where decent accommodation could be had for thruppence a night.

Or so he'd been told. His room at the Crow Hotel was actually a shilling a night – with additional charges for food, coal, alcohol, bedding, water – and anything else that came into their heads while they were penning the bills.

The Swan Inn was an elegant old building with timber framing and soot-stained stucco-work on the upper parts. It had stood there since 1692, a sign on the front wall proclaimed. Even at this early hour it was busy. A yellow-painted *Flyer* from one of the Kent ports was discharging sleepy passengers in the main courtyard.

Trunks and sacks were being passed down from the coach's roof.

The sweating horses were being led off to the stables.

Ebenezer Withers led Septimus through the courtyard and down some well-scrubbed steps to the basement dining-room. A fire was blazing at one end of the room. Porters and coachmen were enjoying flagons of ale at the fireside. In happier times the goat-man might well have joined them. But not today.

He took Septimus over to a quiet corner.

"So..." Septimus asked, as they sat down. "What exactly did you find?"

"*Appalling* things, Mr Slim. Forgive me, while I

collect my thoughts. I hardly know where to begin. I was in there all night. *In the Necropolis.* Alone in the fog. I'd climbed over the wall. Just after midnight. There was no-one around. As far as I could tell. I hid for a while, and then – *I broke into one of the vaults."*

"Really?"

"Truly. It wasn't easy. I'd brought along everything I thought I would need. A few tools. Some candles. A tinderbox. I had no idea of what I might find. I was expecting rotting corpses and crumbling old coffins. It took me half the night to break through the bloody door. It was solid iron, half an inch thick, with a massive, corroded lock. My plan was to pick the lock but I couldn't do it, as things turned out. The mechanism was *extremely* complicated. In the end I resorted to sheer brute force. I hammered an old chisel into the lock. Through the keyhole. It took a while, but then, just as I was about to give up, the bloody door opened."

"I'll be damned. You clever devil."

"Stupid might be a better word. I'd made a lot of noise but I was fairly sure that the fog would have muffled it. I lit a candle when I got inside, and pulled the door closed behind me. Against all my expectations – *there was nothing in there.* It was empty. Dusty and cobwebbed, but completely empty. There was a shaft, at one end, with stairs going down into the dark. Strange sounds were coming up from below. I had no idea what I'd stumbled into."

"And you went down?"

"With some trepidation. I could see curious, twinkling lights, way down below. Having got that far,

I felt that it was my duty to keep going. The light got stronger as I went down. Water was dripping all around me. The stairs were rotten. The air was foul. The stench of decay was appalling. Almost overwhelming."

"They've obviously dug down below the water table."

"It would seem so," the goat-man agreed. "They may be using steam pumps. That would explain the mysterious sounds. What I found at the bottom of the shaft, though, was beyond belief. I hardly know where to start. It was a scene from a nightmare. A hellish nightmare. I came out into a sort of *domed chamber.* Misty light was coming down from somewhere above. I couldn't make out the exact source. Tunnels led off, in several directions. It was *horribly* cold."

"What was in the tunnels?" Septimus asked him. "I'd heard that they were digging tunnels. To be truthful, I hadn't really believed it. It made no sense."

"This is where the nightmare begins. The, uh..."

He fell silent as a serving-wench appeared with food for them. Fresh bread. Still warm from the oven. Butter, in a little dish. Coffee in a china pot. Septimus's mouth watered as she put the food down and poured the coffee.

"I don't often eat so well," he confessed, as the wench went off.

"My pleasure," the goat-man said. "I still haven't told you what I saw."

"So... what did you see?"

The goat-man took a deep breath.

"The *living dead,* Mr Slim. Down in those dreadful tunnels. *Creatures from hell.* Row after row of them. An *army* of dead souls. Lined up like waxworks in the ghastly dark. My blood ran cold. *I thought I was seeing things.* Their skin was grey. They had cadaverous faces and long yellow teeth. Their eyes were slightly luminous. They were *watching* me, I swear. As though... *from beyond the grave.*"

"God in heaven!" Septimus spluttered.

He stared worriedly at the old man.

"You hadn't... by chance... *drunk* anything?"

"No, no. I swear. Not a drop. I stood there like an utter fool for some time. Frozen to the spot. With my mouth hanging open. Gawping. I almost collapsed. *I almost died of fright.* Then a sudden noise distracted me. It brought me back to my senses. I tried to hide, as best I could, as whatever it was got closer."

He poured some sugar into his coffee.

"A sort of metal cart appeared. From one of the tunnels. The wheels were squeaking. One of those heathen priests was pushing it. There was a half-human corpse on top of it. On a marble slab. *It had scaly skin.* Like some sort of bloody serpent. Purple smoke was streaming out of it. *As though its insides were on fire.*"

"Uuugh..."

Septimus was starting to feel a little nauseous.

"The bloody thing was *putrid,*" Ebenezer Withers went on. "I almost retched at the stench. That's what did it for me. The crocodile priest heard me grunting. He whirled round and looked straight at me. I could see the yellow slits of his eyes. Under his hood. He screamed at me. In some foreign tongue. I just went for him. *What else could I do?* I smacked him in the mouth, *hard as I bloody could,* and ran for it. It was a good move, as it turned out. He fell over the cart and cracked his head. He was out cold. For a moment or two. Then all hell broke loose."

"How on earth did you get away?"

The goat-man shrugged.

"God knows. More of the bastards were appearing. I could hear them shouting. Shots were being fired. Pistol balls were whistling past me, in the shaft. By some miracle, I got out. I'd left a ladder. Hidden. Near the perimeter wall. Mercifully, they hadn't found it. I'd just climbed out into Barnaby Street when I saw you. In the back of that bloody hearse. I could hardly believe my eyes."

"We were *both* lucky. By the sound of things."

Septimus scratched his head as he tried to make sense of it all.

"First of all – we need to inform the authorities."

"But *which* authorities, Mr Slim? Who is going to believe us?"

He glanced about. Worriedly.

"The whole bloody business is horrifying. *It makes no sense.* Where did those hideous *things* in the tunnels come from? They looked as though they'd been *pickled*. How did they die? This is what troubles me. The Necropolis wasn't even *there,* six months ago. It was just empty land. Common land. We all used it."

"The bodies could have been brought from elsewhere," Septimus suggested. "Some of the old graveyards in the city are full to overflowing. There's been talk of digging them up and moving the remains. The smell has become a problem. In certain areas. London is such a big city, these days. It's *immense.* And people do die. Sadly. Hundreds every day, I should think. From one thing or another."

"But they don't normally end up in icy tunnels underneath Southwark. With scaly skin and yellow eyes and smoke coming out of their arseholes. *It's an abomination.* A sin against Christendom. Against everything we hold dear."

Septimus grunted. He couldn't disagree.

"You didn't find your wife, I take it?"

"I wasn't in there long enough. Those scarecrows in the tunnels didn't look like *people* at all. *They were all the same.* They had no *sex.* No character. You couldn't really tell them apart. They didn't have *hair.* Some of them might have had feathers. I'm not sure. It was hard to tell. In the ghastly dark."

"Does your wife ever, uh... *appear* to you? In the small hours?"

Ebenezer Withers froze. The crust he was holding fell from his fingers.

"How did you know that?"

"My late girl, Susie, has been *haunting* me. I hardly know what she wants. She appeared in my chamber, again, last night. Like some wandering lost soul. Adrift in the beyond. *Wanting me to join her.* There was a cat in the room. I'd left the door open and the silly creature had wandered in. *Even the cat saw her.* Its fur was up on end. It was *petrified.* Susie was stark naked. She was *floating.* Up above. In a pool of light. *Unearthly light.* I was as scared as the bloody cat."

"It was perhaps just a dream. A bad dream."

"I'm not so sure. It seemed utterly real, at the time. I'd drunk something. A friend had given it to me. To help me sleep. A sort of... *tincture.* In a little bottle. Imported from France. *Secretions of the bloody Crocodile*

Queen. Apparently. Dissolved in alcohol. *Eau Sacré,* they call it. Have you come across it?"

"Of course. It's everywhere, these days. Gypsy women are hawking the stuff on street corners. As a sort of nostrum. A cure for all ills. I tried it myself. Once or twice. After my wife's death. For the same reason as you, I suppose. I wasn't sleeping well. It didn't help. Not really. Things went from bad to worse."

He called the serving-wench over and settled the bill.

"I'll have to be getting along, Mr Slim. I need to get some rest. It's been a long night. We should meet again though, you and I. You're a *gentleman.* You're *educated.* Together, we could take a stand. You could *write* something. *Uh?* For the newspapers. What do you think? People need to be *told.* Before it's too late."

"You're right, of course. *Something* has to be done."

They agreed to meet again, as they strolled out through the busy yard.

The Swan Inn was Ebenezer Withers' regular haunt, of an evening.

Septimus explained that he was going to be out of town for a day or two, but that he'd return as soon as he could. The goat-man's story had shocked him. He hardly knew what to make of it. He wasn't *entirely* sure that he believed it.

It was so damned strange.

The men embraced, like old friends, as they parted company.

Septimus swore that he'd be back. Very soon.

Afterwards, he repaired to the Crow Hotel and slept for a while.

9

THE *SABRINA LOUISE* IS TRANSFORMED

It was still light when Septimus woke again. He wasn't sure what time it was. He'd slept quite deeply. His small room, up at the back of the hotel, was fairly quiet in the afternoons. Nobody bothered him. Most of his neighbours were out.

Doing whatever they did, in the daylight hours.

Something had been pushed under his door, he noticed, as he glanced about. Sleepily, he wondered what it might be, though he didn't really care. For a while he didn't bother getting up. He'd been half-expecting another angry blast from Mrs Lusardi. A final warning. Official notice that she was having the bailiffs brought round to throw him out. He wasn't particularly worried. By the end of the week, if things went to plan, he was going to have enough money to buy the awful place, and the rest of the street as well, if the fancy took him.

When he eventually dragged himself out of bed and picked up the folded note he realised straight away that it was actually from Lachlan. The madcap, scrawled handwriting was unmistakable. Mrs Lusardi, for all her faults, had a fine hand.

Septimus had received several angry *communiqués* from her while he'd been at the hotel, complaining about his snoring, or his habit of coming home drunk in the middle of the night in the company of low-class whores. Every one of her epistles had been as beautifully-penned as an edict from the Pope himself.

He took the note over to the window, where the light was better.

'Where in the world are you?' he eventually made out. *'Your door is locked! I've tried knocking. I've tried asking. The servant-girls downstairs won't even speak to me. There's been a change of plan. WE'RE SAILING TONIGHT! I'll meet you at the Rose Tavern. AT SIX O'CLOCK! Don't be late! We'll be away for two or three days. Bring whatever you think you'll need! I'll be waiting. L.M.'*

For some reason, they were leaving a day earlier than planned.

Septimus pulled out his ancient haversack and stuffed a few things into it. Along with his cleanest shirt and a half-presentable pair of breeches he put in a few sheets of writing-paper, a quill pen and a supply of ink in a little stoneware bottle.

I could work on my memoirs, he thought. *If we happen to get stuck out at Egypt Point for days on end. Waiting for this Dutch ship to arrive.*

He'd already written several pages. About his early years, mostly.

Lachlan was waiting. Impatiently. In the fog outside the tavern. "Where have you *been?*" he wailed, as Septimus appeared.

"I was in bed. You should have knocked louder."

"In bed? In the middle of the bloody afternoon?"

"You advised us to get plenty of rest. I had a bad night, to be truthful. A *terrible* night. I rose at dawn and went to the Necropolis again. Susie is still so much on my mind. I've learned things, Lachlan, about that place. It's worse than it looks. Worse than anything we've heard. Something *dark* is going on there."

"We can talk about it later."

He noticed Septimus's haversack.

"You've brought your things, uh? Let's be on our way. They're waiting for us. Down in Deptford. Smalt wants to leave on the evening tide. If possible. The work on the ship didn't take so long. She's been scrubbed and scraped. Polished and painted. Partially re-rigged. You won't believe your eyes. She'll pass for a Customs Service boat. *Easily.* I've done a deal. We're going to pay for the work later. In a week or two. When we've got the money. Are you ready?"

"Let's go. I haven't brought much. A few essentials. A change of clothes. Some writing materials. I thought it would give me something to do if the other ship gets delayed, for any reason. Adverse tides. Bad weather. Whatever."

"That won't happen. Clézio knows his business. We'll be back in Deptford in a couple of days. With a cargo of gold! *God willing!* I was also up early. I went to Morning Mass. For the first time in months. At St. Cecilia's in Wapping. I prayed for good fortune. I promised to give money to the church. To the poor of the parish. To the Foundling Hospital. To my ex-wife. Wherever she may be. I didn't want to leave anything to chance. We need the holy angels on our side."

"Let's hope they heard you. Up there in the heavens."

"They hear everything, Septimus. *Every last whisper.*"

The sun was going down. There was a fiery glow in the western sky. Gulls and crows were squabbling over scraps in the darkening streets. Fog was gathering over the river, as the daylight faded. Septimus told Lachlan *some* of what he'd heard from the goat-man, as they hurried along the waterfront.

About the Necropolis, and the haunted tunnels below.

He didn't go into too much detail. For a host of reasons. Septimus felt that he should find out more, before he started spreading the story around. It wasn't so much that he didn't believe it. It was just that... *it made no sense.*

Lachlan, in any case, had more important things on his mind.

They took a wherry to Deptford. From Limehouse Hole Stairs. As night fell. Over the crowded Thames. The *Sabrina Louise* had been moved to a ship-breaking yard in Deptford Creek. This was where the improvements had been carried out.

The journey took nearly an hour, though it was only a couple of miles. The fog was getting worse. A few big vessels were still trying to make their way up to the Pool. On the evening tide. Hundreds more lay at anchor, in mid-stream.

Lachlan got the boatman to drop them at the creek mouth.

"We can walk from here," he told Septimus, as the fellow sculled off into the gloom. "The less people know about our business, the better. I didn't like the look of that bastard. He looked the sort who'd sell his own mother to Arab slavers. For the price of a drink. Or five minutes with a poxy Ratcliffe whore."

"It's a tough life, I would think. Working the river."

"It's a tough life *whatever* you do, Septimus. Unless you're one of the lucky few. Born with a silver spoon in your mouth. Servants at your beck and call. Income from estates. Valuables in the vaults and brass in the bank. Even then, nothing is guaranteed. Take yourself, for instance. You've *suffered.*"

"I wasn't born into money. I'm the son of a country parson."

"But you're *educated*. You just made some bad decisions."

"You could say that."

"No matter. Another week and we'll be pigs in clover. We've *already* got a buyer for the gold. Thanks to Mr Serocoal. All we have to do is go and collect the stuff. *Providence is on our side.* It will be a new start, Septimus. We'll be trotting around in our own shiny carriages. Before the month is out. Looking down our noses at the riff-raff in the streets. The very people we ourselves once were."

Septimus chuckled.

It was an enticing prospect.

The tide was already on the turn. Night had set in by the time they reached the ship. There was a busy-looking tavern, and some tumbledown houses, at the mouth of a muddy inlet. Old vessels lay, half-wrecked, in the mud. The *Sabrina Louise* was tied-up at a ramshackle wooden jetty. Behind some trees.

"So..." Lachlan asked. "What do you reckon?"

He stepped back while Septimus took a look.

The ship was uncannily aglow. Moths, and a host of other insects, large and small, were swarming in the foggy air around her. She was lit-up like the Royal Barge on the King's birthday. A multitude of smoky oil-lamps dangled from the rigging. The shipwrights had only just finished work, by the look of things. Their tools and paint-pots were still on the jetty, waiting to be taken away.

"I'll be damned..." Septimus murmured. "I'm impressed! I wasn't sure what to expect. You've *transformed* the old wreck! She really does look the part, now. A little wide in the beam, perhaps, for a Customs Service boat, but... who's going to notice? It's a minor detail. Everything else is bloody perfect."

"We've got all the correct flags and pennants," Lachlan told him. "Billy got hold of them. He's got friends in the naval dockyard. The *Helga's* crew won't have much time to weigh things up. As we approach. We'll run up the signal flags, hail them, board them, and tie them up. At gunpoint. If necessary. It will all be over in five minutes. They'll be half-asleep, anyway. After a long night at sea."

"Is the ship ready to sail?"

"Just about. The supplies are all loaded. Enough food and drink to last a fortnight. We won't starve. I've saved the old cordage. We'll use it to tie the Dutch crew up. I've even got a forged warrant that authorises us to search foreign ships in British waters. Mr Serocoal's handiwork! In case they're in a mood to argue."

Billy was up in the rigging. Taking down the lamps.

Lachlan led Septimus aboard. The captain and Mr Serocoal were down below. Trying on the uniforms. Mr Serocoal had selected an officer's top-coat from the heap on the table, along with a tricorn hat. The outfit rather suited the old rogue.

"One of these should fit you, Septimus," Lachlan said. "I bought a few. Old navy coats with brass buttons. All fairly clean. From a place in Ratcliffe. Try one on, when you're ready. You can't wear that old leather thing. You look like a bloody footpad! We need to create a good impression, as we come up alongside the *Helga.*"

"And then what? We all just jump aboard?"

"Mr Serocoal and I will board first, I think. Waving the warrant. You and Billy can cover us, *discreetly,* from a safe distance. With the muskets."

"And then?"

"As soon as we're safely aboard we'll produce our pistols and take the ship over. We'll tie the crew up. There'll only be four or five of them. They'll hardly know what's happening. Once we're in control we'll tow the *Helga* into the shallows and move the cargo across onto the *Sabrina Louise.* It shouldn't take long. By the end of the day, all being well, we'll be back here in Deptford. Celebrating!"

They took a drink, for luck, before leaving. Billy joined them.

Lachlan lowered his head and murmured a few words.

"May the holy angels look down on us, and keep us safe."
"Amen to that," Billy added, as they raised their glasses.
The ship rolled. Ominously.

"So..." Smalt said. "That's it! Let's go! Billy is going to crew for me. He's a good lad. He knows what's needed. The two of us can handle her, in the river. There's not much of a wind but it's blowing in the right direction. We could be at Egypt Point by dawn. If all goes well. That will give us a day in hand. We'll be ready and waiting. Well-fed and well-prepared. When the *Helga* finally appears."

The ship's dog howled, horribly, from the shore, as Billy took in the lines. The beast had been left in the care of the local tavern-keeper. For a night or two. The tavern served as Smalt's London address, but the dog wasn't often left there alone. This was one of the rare occasions when he'd had to watch from the shore as the *Sabrina Louise* slid off into the dark. En route for heaven-knows-where.

Billy raised the mainsail as they edged out of the creek. Into the foggy river. Smalt shouted orders, from the wheel. The *Sabrina Louise* was a fairly small vessel. She was a typical Whitby cutter, with a cargo-hold amidships and a poky cabin in the stern. The *Sabrina Louise's* cabin had been extended. *Slightly.* Into the after-part of the hold. To create more space for the captain and his concubines.

She was fast and manoeuvrable – as the captain had promised.

Billy seemed quite at home on deck. He knew the ropes. He'd worked on the river as a ten-year-old. For pennies and crusts. Helping his unfortunate mother feed half-a-dozen hungry children. A brood of which Billy was the only survivor. He'd grown up with a sense of destiny. And a nose for well-stuffed purses.

Greasy fog was drifting in off the Isle of Dogs.

The river was lined with ghostly, anchored vessels.

Moonlight was dripping from their yards, and their high sterns. It was weirdly quiet.

The *Sabrina Louise* rolled, sweetly, as she ploughed on, through the night. Fog-bells were sounding, here and there, but the fog was not, as yet, impeding the gang's progress. Septimus settled himself on the afterdeck. Among the piled ropes.

It was warmer below, but he was enjoying the night air.

Lachlan joined him. He passed Septimus a bottle.

"I've brought my flask," he said. "We won't die of thirst. There are more bottles in the galley. Enough to keep us going for a week. Smalt prefers to abstain, when he's at the helm. You need your wits about you, he says. On nights like this. Billy's sharing a pipe with Mr Serocoal. Up in the bow. God knows what they're smoking. Opium, I rather suspect. Billy has been picking up bad habits, of late."

"He needs a serious talking-to. Can I see the firearms?"

"Tomorrow, uh? When it gets light. We've got plenty of time. I acquired a couple of blades, too. From a pawnbroker I know. Naval cutlasses. Fine-looking weapons. I've got them on loan. They've got to go back, when we're done."

"That's good thinking. You can't always rely on a pistol, in a mêlée on a ship's deck. All it takes is a misfire and you're dead. These people might be armed to the teeth. We really don't know. It could turn into a bloodbath."

Lachlan squirmed.

"Let's hope not."

The lights of Greenwich went by, to starboard. Spray splashed up over the cutter's bow as the wind picked-up. Billy and Mr Serocoal had to move further aft, to avoid a soaking. Captain Smalt was humming quietly to himself, at the wheel.

Septimus stared out into the foggy dark.

"It's good to be back," he said. "Back home."

Lachlan took another swig from his flask.

"Where *were* you? Actually? For all those lost years? If you don't mind me asking. I can't help but be curious. You were away for a long time. You didn't spend twenty years alone, surely? On that island. The one they left you on. Those heartless bastards. Like Robinson Crusoe, eh? *Heh, heh!* Is that how it was?"

"No, no. It *felt* like twenty years, at the time, but it was actually just months. Six months and twelve days. I kept a tally. Crusoe was lucky. Have you read the book? He had supplies. I had nothing. No food. No tools. Nothing to wear but a few rags. It wasn't easy. I could well have died. I was resigned to my fate."

"But you survived. Somehow."

"Well... I was young. That helped. It was the end of the rainy season when they put me ashore. There was always water. *Somewhere.* In nooks and crannies. That kept me going. For the first few days. I didn't even know where I was, at the time. I knew we'd been sailing south. By the growing heat. Then, one day, there was a lot of noise on deck and I guessed that we'd arrived. I heard the anchors go in. Nobody told me anything. They dragged me up out of the filthy hole I'd been kept in, threw me in a boat and took me ashore. Like they were discharging cargo."

"No word of explanation?"

"Not a bloody word. I had a rag stuffed in my mouth. My feet were chained. My hands were tied behind my back. I could hardly see, in the sudden light. When we reached the shore they just pushed me out of the boat and left me. On the beach. In the blazing sun. With the surf coming up around me. And that was it."

"*Jesus!*"

"It could have been worse. Where there's life, there's hope. I freed my hands fairly quickly but it took me days to get the bloody leg-irons off. I hammered at the links with heavy stones. For days on end. I was lucky not to get eaten alive. The island was infested with tropical snakes and starving rats. There were creatures that crawled up out of the sea at night, in search of food. Disgusting things. *Gloopers,* I called them. From the noise they made as they came up the beach."

"What were they?"

"Heaven knows. I learned to avoid them. I was able to move around, once I'd got the chains off. The island was tiny, I soon found out. You could walk all the way around it in a day. But there was water, as I say, and food, of one sort or another. Birds. Crabs. Fish. Fruit. I managed to start a fire. After about a month of trying. Looking back, I think I could have survived for years."

"But you didn't have to, eh?"

"Fate had other things in store for me."

"You were rescued?"

"In a manner of speaking. I was picked up by a gang of Venezuelan pirates. They'd seen the smoke from my fire as they were sailing past. I was skin and bones by that time. Hair halfway down to my waist and a beard like an Old Testament prophet. Luckily for me they decided I was the funniest thing they'd ever seen. If I'd been Spanish they'd have quite likely fed me to the sharks, but they had a lot of respect for English pirates and I think they thought I was one. They took me aboard their ship. Fed me. Clothed me. Treated me like one of their own. I could hardly complain. When they eventually sailed, I went with 'em."

"What language did they speak?"

"Local tribal languages. Some Spanish. There were a couple of ex-slaves among them who'd learned English and French on the plantations. We were a polyglot bunch. We taught each other words as we went along."

Lachlan chuckled. He pulled out his flask and took another slug of whatever he'd got in it. It was a battered old thing. Silver-plated and well-used. Its original owner was probably still missing it.

"You've had an interesting life, Septimus."

"You could say that. I still have nightmares. After all this time. I spent three years with those mad bastards. Drinking and fighting. Homeward-bound Spanish ships were our main target. Every now and then we'd come across real treasure. The kind that takes your breath away. *Barrels* of bloody gold. Silver crucifixes set with precious stones. It was an education. Believe me. I'll probably burn in hell. My only consolation is that I won't be alone. I'll be among friends."

He paused for a moment as he cast his mind back.

"In the end, I walked. One fateful night. We'd been laid-up, for nearly a month, in a little creek on the outskirts of Maracaibo. Catching our breath. The ship was being cleaned and caulked. I had money. Enough to last me for years. Gold pieces, sewn into the lining of my coat. Some precious stones. I was well-prepared. I went out drinking with my pirate *amigos,* one night. In Maracaibo. It was quite a place, in those days. At some point in the night I went upstairs with a fat old whore. Maria, she called herself. She was so drunk she could hardly stand. When we got into the room she passed out. It was a feverishly hot night. The window was wide open. I sat and watched the old woman snoring for a while. Then I went over to the window, took a quick look out, and jumped. It was a long way down but the Good Lord was on my side. Just for once. There wasn't too much damage. A few cuts and bruises. I picked myself up and walked. Didn't look back."

"Where did you go?"

"I headed north. Over the mountains. Walking from town to town. Bought myself a pistol. Several weeks later, I reached the port of Santa Marta. The only place I could get a passage to was Saint-Domingue. So that's where I went."

"One of the sugar islands?"

"Indeed. The richest of them all. Sugar and coffee. It's a French colony, nowadays. A *restless* place. Home to *thousands* of rebellious African slaves who are fighting to make it their own land. *Officially* they are no longer slaves. The revolutionaries in Paris abolished slavery. By decree. The plantation owners are still resisting, but... the deed is done. The Africans are not fools. They completely understand the principles of the revolution. *Liberté. Égalité. Fraternité.* You can't really argue with that. There are no sub-clauses. No excuses."

Lachlan shook a fist in the air.

"Vive la France! So... how long did you stay? In Saint-Domingue?"

"Donkey's years. It became my home. I had my ill-gotten riches. I could afford to live quite well. I met a woman in Port-au-Prince. The lovely Rozalita."

He sighed, at the memory.

"Have you travelled much yourself, Lachlan? Besides France?"

"Hardly at all. I got as far as Avignon, once, with a Parisian whore I used to know. A fine young woman. She married into money, I believe, and became a bit of a lady, with a chateau and a title. Such things happen, sometimes, in France."

"You'd like Saint-Domingue. It's a French colony, as I say. I might have stayed forever, but... the slaves' revolt changed everything. It had to happen. Things had to change. The plantation owners were bastards. We were fairly safe, in Port-au-Prince. We could have ridden out the storm. But then..."

He gave another long sigh.

"The lovely Rozalita walked out on me. She took all the money she could find. Ran off with a French coffee-trader. God knows where they went. I never saw her again. Luckily I'd hidden some of my tainted gold away. In case the house ever got robbed. It hurt my feelings, though. I took it quite badly."

Lachlan shrugged, sympathetically.

"Women, eh?"

"I was half to blame. We'd both been drinking heavily. You could buy a gallon of rum for a few sous. In Port-au-Prince. Fine, dark rum. I stopped eating, after she'd left. I just drank. It helped. Then one day I woke up and realised that everything was gone. Every last *centime*. I was on the rocks."

"What did you do?"

"I sold things. Odds and ends from the house. But there wasn't really much to sell. In the end – out of desperation – I joined the French navy. As a marine."

"You dark horse. You've never mentioned any of this before."

"Well... you know how it is. We got recalled to France, shortly afterwards. Plans were being made for the invasion of England. Which put me in a difficult position, obviously. Happily, I got shot in the leg while we were crossing the Atlantic. In a little skirmish we had with an English frigate. The wound wasn't so serious as it turned out, but it was the end of my naval career. I could barely move, for the bloody pain. I got discharged. Three weeks later. In La Rochelle."

"Did they pay you off?"

"They treated me well. I got extra pay. As a wounded hero. I stayed in the port for nearly six months while my leg healed. Then I set out for home. In the middle of last winter. That *appalling* bloody winter. I walked all the way across France. To Boulogne. It took me several weeks. In the snow. The harbour was frozen-over when I finally got to Boulogne. *Nothing* was moving. The packet-services had been suspended, in any case, because of the war. In the end a friendly fisherman brought me over from Dieppe, in the middle of the night. I came ashore in Pevensey Bay. At three o'clock in the morning. Like Duke William. In 1066."

"Ha, ha, ha!"

Lachlan took another swig from his flask. Septimus tossed his own empty bottle over the side. The cutter was rolling. Spray was coming up over the gunnels. Mr Serocoal had gone below. Billy was dozing. Flat on his back. On the cargo hatch. Captain Smalt seemed content enough, at the wheel.

"We'll need to make ourselves scarce," Lachlan confided. "Once we've got the money. The crocodile priests are going to be aggrieved. Obviously. About losing their golden idol. It's probably not even insured. And then there's the war. The French invasion could come at any time. That's the way things are looking. There'll be *weeks* of mayhem. *We could lose everything.* Everything we've worked for."

"It won't happen," Septimus assured him. "The French are not ready."

"It *could* happen," Lachlan insisted. "Many people would welcome it. I've been attending meetings of the London Corresponding Society. At the Green Man in Spitalfields. A small number of us get together, in an upstairs room, on Thursday evenings. We're *inspired* by the example of the French. By the lofty ideals of the revolution. We see no reason why one man should be seen as more deserving than another. Why the poor should go hungry while the rich get fat. The French have made mistakes, it can't be denied, but they are *essentially* on the right path."

Septimus scratched himself. Thoughtfully.

"There have been injustices."

On his trek across France, in the middle of that awful winter, Septimus had met several dispossessed aristocrats, tramping the roads in beggars' rags without a sou to their name. He'd shared a bottle of rough wine with one or two of them, by a little fire at the roadside, as the snow had come down. They'd seemed no different to ordinary men. Or women. He'd felt some sympathy for the poor bastards.

"What about your religious principles?"

Lachlan looked hurt.

"Septimus! *Please!* What about them? Our Redeemer Himself would be supporting the revolution, I'm certain. Were He here among us. At this troubled time. I've got nothing against rich people – *fundamentally.* The whole point of this present enterprise is to make a little money. *God knows,* we've earned it."

"Do you reckon?"

"It's *a fact,* Septimus. It's *indisputable.*"

Lachlan had a way of rationalising things. They were on their way to commit an act of armed piracy. A crime they'd undoubtedly hang for if they got caught. But in Lachlan's eyes it wasn't a crime at all. It was a noble act.

A *righteous* act.

10

THE RUINS AT EGYPT POINT

Septimus was moaning in his sleep. His arms and legs twitched as he relived old battles and argued the night away with long-dead friends. The fiery Rozalita hurled a table across the room and stormed out of his life. For the millionth time. Naked Amazonian devil-women swarmed through the streets and *plazas* of Maracaibo, cursing the *conquistadors* and the blue-eyed English pigs who dealt in slaves.

"*NO!!!*" Septimus screamed, as the women turned on him.

A sudden swell picked the *Sabrina Louise* up and rolled her halfway over onto her side. Pots and pans clattered down from the galley shelves. Septimus clung to the straw mattress he'd been sleeping on as both he and it slid down the near-vertical slope of the cabin floor. He woke up with a groan as he hit the side-timbers.

"*Uuugh!*"

Cold morning light was streaming in through the hatch. Mr Serocoal was in the galley, trying to light the stove. Lachlan was collecting up the scattered pots.

"Where are we?" Septimus asked, sleepily.

"Just past Gravesend," Lachlan told him. "We're almost there. Another hour, Smalt reckons. It's a misty morning. A ship-o'-the-line just cut straight across our bow. The *Glorious Revenge,* on her way up-river. Arrogant bastards. They have no bloody manners. Their bow-wave nearly tipped us over."

"What time is it?"

"I'm not exactly sure. I've mislaid my pocket-watch. It's early. Just after dawn. We're making good progress. Everything is going to plan. Touch wood."

Septimus stowed his bedding and went up on deck to take the air. The ship was scudding along, under full sail. Smalt was still at the wheel. He was looking just a *little* weary. Billy was up in the rigging, adjusting a slack rope. It was high water. There were dozens of other vessels in sight. Most were heading up-river. Against the wind. On their way up to the Pool, or one of the new docks.

"Have you not slept?" Septimus asked the captain.

"I'm used to it. I'll catch up later."

Smoke was soon billowing from the galley stove-pipe. Lachlan brought up some breakfast. Bread and coffee. Hungry gulls screeched overhead.

Talk turned to the guns. One of the muskets was brought up, for Septimus's perusal. He grunted approvingly as he examined it.

"It looks good."

"Do you want to try firing it?" Lachlan asked him.

"There's no point in wasting powder. We know they work. You've bought well. This is a cavalry carbine. A murderous bloody thing, at close range."

"The other musket came from the East India Company stores. One of Billy's nefarious friends acquired it for us. We'll get rid of it, as soon as we're done. We've got the blunderbuss, as well, don't forget. And several pistols. *Hopefully,* we won't need to use them. *Deception* is going to be our main weapon."

Septimus nodded.

"What about this forged warrant you've got?"

"Would you like to see it?"

"I'd be interested to take a look."

Lachlan went down and got the document. The instrument that *purportedly* authorised him to search foreign vessels in the Thames. It had been bound into a fancy old leather wallet. The sort that lawyers used. To give it some substance.

'In the Name of His Britannic Majesty, King George III of England, Scotland, Ireland, Wales and France...' Septimus read. Vague references to the rest of the Empire followed. The thing appeared to have been penned in some haste, and then carelessly blotted, to render it even more unreadable. There was vague mention of the *'Course of the Thames',* and the *'Exigencies of the Current Conflict'.*

A red wax Admiralty seal, the size of a small dinner plate, gave the document a magnificent aura of authority. It was signed by the 'Deputy Minister of War'.

"Good God!" Septimus spluttered.

He passed it back.

"You made the bloody thing yourselves?"

"Well..."

Lachlan looked embarrassed.

"Mr Serocoal made the seal and did the actual writing. The vellum came from a book-binder in St. Paul's Churchyard. We just made it up as we went along. It's not perfect, I know, but... it's the best we could do. I would have preferred to have had it printed, but I couldn't take the risk. The chances are we won't even need it."

"It looks fine to me," Septimus assured him. "At a glance, it would convince anyone. But it will have to go into the galley stove, the *moment* the job is done. Along with the flags and uniforms. Even the charts. *Anything* that could hang us."

"We'll burn everything. Don't worry about that."

They were almost out in the estuary. Close in to the Kent coast. In shallow water, strewn with old wrecks. There was fog inland. Over the Kent marshes. The captain surveyed the coast with a brass telescope as they edged ever closer.

"We're almost there," he said. "Do you see those trees? Directly up ahead? That's Egypt Point. The old manor house is hidden. Behind the trees. It's not the easiest place in the world to get to, but... that's part of its charm. We're already scraping the bottom. At low tide, in this part of the river, all you can see is mud. Mile after mile of mud. There are channels, but you have to know where they are."

Billy took soundings as they sailed in.

"There's a hidden inlet," Smalt went on. "You'll see it in a minute. I've landed brandy here. More than once. Over the years. I know the area well."

Startled crows flocked up from the overhanging trees as the *Sabrina Louise* slid into the muddy creek.

Low branches brushed against the cutter's rigging, and scraped her newly-painted bulwarks. The rotting remains of an old landing-stage came into view. Billy jumped ashore with a rope and pulled the ship in.

Septimus glanced about, worriedly. It wasn't what he'd expected.

"So... where is the house?" he asked.

"It's well-hidden," Smalt explained. "Not much of it is left, to be completely honest. You'll see what I mean when we get up there. The roof and the upper floors have all gone. The watchtower is completely overgrown. You could walk straight past it without even realising it was there. *Nobody* comes out here anymore. The nearest village is a dozen miles away. On the other side of the marshes."

"How did you ever find the place?"

"It was pure fate. A local smuggler told me about it. I met him in a tavern in Rochester. A good few years ago. We did some uh... *business* together. *Come!* Let's get ashore. I'll show you the house. Watch your step on the old planks."

He led the way. Through the trees and up a twisting path. Septimus and the rest of the gang followed. In single file. It was oddly quiet. There was no birdsong.

Steps led up to a gap in an old wall. Ivy and cobwebs trailed down from an ancient stone lintel. This, by the look of things, had been the old house's principal entrance. The columns that had once flanked it lay, toppled, in the undergrowth.

Little was left of the place. Trees had taken root inside the walls.

"It would have been a grand residence, in its day, no doubt," the captain mused as he climbed the steps. "Though it's hard to imagine why they chose to build out here. In this remote bloody place. There's no accounting for people's tastes, eh? The watchtower was probably added later, during one of the Dutch wars. It's in poor condition, now, but you can still see all the way across to Canvey Island, from up at the top. Come inside! I'll show you around. Not that there's much to see."

He brushed the ivy aside and stepped through.

"STOP!!! RIGHT WHERE YOU ARE!!!" someone shouted.

Smalt stopped, right where he was. Septimus crept up behind him. A scared-looking young man was standing in the ruins, straight up ahead. His clothes were in tatters. He was pointing a fully-cocked pistol at the captain. The weapon was shaking. *Dangerously.* Lachlan edged forward. He stared open-mouthed at the trembling pistol and the quivering, terrified figure that was holding it.

"Who *are* you people?" the youth shouted.

"Who are *you*, good sir?" Lachlan asked, in return.

"Is that any of your damned business?"

"Well, uh..." Lachlan shrugged. He took a cautious step closer.

The gun swung in Lachlan's direction.

"Stay away from me, you bastard!"

Lachlan spluttered. The young man pulled the trigger.

B-O-O-M!!! Smoke and flame streamed from the weapon's muzzle. It had been badly loaded. It kicked up as it fired. The ball whistled, harmlessly, over the top of Lachlan's head. For a horrible moment, the youth's contorted visage was hidden in the smoke. Lachlan didn't move a muscle. He just stood there, with his arms limp at his sides and a slightly astonished look on his face.

Billy Moon was the first to react. He rushed at the would-be assassin and kicked his feet out from under him, then for good measure walloped him again, in the side of the head, as he dropped. Septimus joined Billy and helped him subdue the struggling, angry youngster. They sat on top of him, to hold him still.

"Get some rope!" Billy shouted.

Mr Serocoal went off to find some rope. He returned with some of the *Sabrina Louise's* old cordage, which they'd kept to tie up the crew of the *Helga*. Billy bound the kid's hands and feet. To stop him wriggling they pulled him up and lashed him to one of the young trees that had taken root in the crumbling floor.

He hung his head and whimpered.

"What's your name, lad?" Septimus asked him.

"Spiker, sir."

"Spiker who?"

"Spiker Pettigrew, sir."

"Why are you so unfriendly? We haven't done anything to hurt you."

"I thought you were a press gang."

"*A press gang?* God in heaven! Do we *look* like a press gang?"

"I saw you sail in. I thought you'd come looking for me."

Septimus sighed. Bewilderedly. Mr Serocoal picked

up the discharged pistol and examined it. The gang milled about, in front of their captive, staring at his torn clothes, his tearful face and his thin limbs. He was unshaven and barefoot.

Lachlan glowered at him.

"You could have *killed* me! *You stupid bastard!* Jesus! I swear I've never felt so close to the Golden Gates! *Thank God you're a bad shot!* That's all I can say. We're not a bloody *press gang*. We're just innocent citizens, going about our lawful business. Where did you get that gun from? It looks expensive."

Spiker Pettigrew gave a tearful little shrug.

"It's a long story. I stole it from a drunken marine. In Dover. I'm a simple soul, sir. A farmer's lad from the Isle of Grain. I was impressed into the Royal Navy. A year ago. To my great misfortune. I'd been in Rochester with my father. We'd taken some beasts to market and then stayed in the town overnight. They dragged me out of a tavern. Feet first. I was too drunk to save myself. I woke up the next morning on the *Scourge of the Seas.* On my way to the East Indies. It was the Law of the Land, they said. A chance to serve King and Country."

Mr Serocoal groaned and spat.

"Damn them! The bastards! May they rot in hell!"

"They made a sailor out of me, I suppose, but it wasn't of my choosing."

"So... what brought you *here?*" Septimus asked him.

"I jumped ship. We were in the Channel. On our way home. So we thought. But then a rumour went round, below decks, that we'd got new orders. That we were sailing straight on. To Denmark or Russia. A party of us were sent ashore. In Dover. To pick up supplies and freshwater. It took longer than expected. The marines they'd sent with us got drunker and drunker as the day went on. They even picked up a couple of women. In a tavern. We'd been at sea for months. You know how it is. Suddenly, I saw my chance. Without really thinking about it, I lifted the officer's pistol and ran. Like the bloody wind. Over the hills and far away. It was a stupid thing to do. But... by the Grace of God, I got away with it."

"You didn't even get paid off? After a year at sea?"

"I thought I could sell the pistol. It's a *very* fine piece."

Septimus caught Lachlan's eye. Lachlan shrugged.

"Untie him, Billy. I think he's learned his lesson. We could even offer him some work. A chance to earn a bob or two. He's a sailor, after all. It would be an extra pair of hands. See if you can find him a change of clothes. Bring a bucket of water while you're at it. And some soap. He looks in need of a wash."

While Billy untied the new recruit Lachlan and Septimus took a first look at the crumbling watchtower. It was an overgrown, brick-built structure. Thirty or forty feet high. A low doorway, half-hidden under a thicket of ivy and weeds, was the only entrance. The rotting remains of an old door hung, askew, in the opening.

Lachlan squinted up at the high parapet.

"We'll need to have somebody up there from the crack of dawn. The *Helga* might not arrive till noon, but we can't take any chances. She might turn up early. I'll give Billy the job. He's got excellent eyesight. He won't let us down."

The door creaked as Septimus pushed his way

through. The interior stank of damp. It was piled high with dead leaves. Stone steps led up to the higher levels.

As he glanced about...*something moved.* In the shadows above.

A tiny stone skittered down. *Tippety-Tap!*

Someone was up there. Out of sight. In the gloom.

He stepped back, warily.

"Show yourself!" he shouted. *"Whoever you are!"*

For a moment nothing happened. Then the shadows moved, again, and a young woman emerged. A scruffy wench in a ragged dress and an old shawl. She had untidy black hair, cropped short, and fierce, dark, sullen eyes.

Septimus moaned. This was *another* complication.

He didn't need to ask who she was. It was plain to see.

This was Spiker Pettigrew's girl.

"Come on down, mistress!" he called, softly. "We intend you no harm, I swear. Spiker is outside. He's perfectly safe. The gunshot you heard was an accident. A *misunderstanding,* you might say. We're all friends now. *Come!* Take my hand!"

Without a word, she raised the hem of her dress and picked her way down the greasy steps. She was a little older than Spiker. Cleverer, too, Septimus rather thought, as he studied her mistrustful face. She looked like a woman who'd seen something of the world – and hadn't thought much of it.

Lachlan groaned as Septimus led her out into the daylight.

"God in heaven!" he screeched. *"Who is this?"*

He was clearly horrified. His plans hadn't included any provision for women. The possibility hadn't even crossed his mind. It hadn't crossed *anyone's* mind.

Spiker was squatting on the ground, nursing his bruises.

"This is my *fiancé*," he said. "Mulu."

"*Mulu?*"

"Her real name is Melissa but she prefers Mulu. It's what her grandmother used to call her. We met on the road, while I was walking up from Dover. We're going to start a new life together. In London. If we ever *get* to London, that is."

Lachlan sighed.

"You're going to need *money* to start a new life in London," he told Spiker. "I'm taking it that you don't have any. You can't live *anywhere,* these days, without money. I speak from bitter experience, believe me. But... we could offer you some work. Just for a day or two. As a sailor. If you'd be interested. We'll pay you well, for your trouble. *And...* I'll buy the pistol off you. How does that sound?"

"Well, uh..."

Spiker wiped his bloodied nose. He seemed a little nonplussed.

"I want *at least* four guineas for the pistol. It's an *excellent* piece."

"Whatever you say. I'm not going to argue. We'll have to pay you in gold, by weight. I hope that's acceptable. Any pawnbroker will take it off you. We could recommend someone. Mr Serocoal will advise you. He's expert in such matters."

Mr Serocoal nodded, as though to confirm this.

"If you're willing to crew for us, young man," Lachlan went on. "Just for the one day, tomorrow – I'll pay you what you would have got for your *entire year* on the *Scourge of the Seas*. What do you say to that? I could hardly be more generous."

Spiker glanced around while he considered this astounding proposal. The anguish in his eyes melted away. Bewilderment took its place. For a moment. Then – enlightenment. He looked up at his new comrades and chuckled.

"You're smugglers, eh? I should have known."

"Not exactly... *smugglers*," Lachlan corrected him. *"Thieves* might be a better word, but I don't want to give you the wrong impression. We're decent, God-fearing folk. The valuables in question belong to a *heathenish foreign cult*. You'll come across it, quite likely, when you get to London. Are you Church of Rome, Spiker?"

"Uh... no. Does it make a difference?"

"No, no, no! Of course not! You're a Christian soul. That's the important thing. You're also a bag of bones. *Dear Lord!* What have you been eating?"

"We've been living off the land. It hasn't been easy."

"We can remedy that. We've got food in the galley. You'll need your strength for tomorrow. You can help Billy on deck. It will be a hectic day. I'll explain things to you later. Would a fire be permissible, Captain? Could we make some coffee?"

Smalt sniffed the air. He seemed uncertain.

"If we can keep the smoke down. There's an old stove round the back. I spent a week here last winter.

With my Rochester friends. The coldest bloody week in the history of the world. The river froze! We kept a fire going, day and night, on that occasion. Nobody bothered us. A small blaze wouldn't hurt, I suppose."

The stove in the back was a rusting heap with a broken chimney. Lachlan thought it best to wait until nightfall before lighting it. As a compromise, they rekindled the smaller stove on the ship. There was no shortage of fuel. The ruins were littered with bits of broken furniture and timber from the collapsed roof.

Septimus pulled out a rotten old leather armchair and sat down in it. It was surprisingly comfortable. He was tempted to keep it and take it home. Mr Serocoal was exploring the tower. He shouted something, from the top. About the view.

Lachlan grinned and waved back.

"We could have somebody up there through the night," Septimus suggested. "Keeping watch. It's the perfect place for a look-out. *Anybody* could turn up and take us by surprise. We've already picked up two complete strangers."

"What else could we do?" Lachlan protested. "Throw 'em in the bloody river? I'm not too concerned. They seem a decent pair. I've offered them a *damnably* good deal. They're not fools. They understand. Spiker's a naval deserter. He'd be facing the noose if he was caught. They could set up house together with the money we're offering. Start a little business, even. We'll drop them off somewhere. On the way back. Gravesend, perhaps. Give 'em the gold and send 'em on their way. With our blessings. They'll be as happy as larks. I don't foresee any problems."

"They'll certainly remember us."

Spiker and Mulu were talking. Quietly. Some distance away.

"What about tomorrow?" Septimus asked. "While we're occupied? Out on the river? What do we do with Mulu? We can hardly take her with us."

"She'll have to stay ashore. That's all there is to it. She won't do anything stupid. They're *penniless,* let's face it. They've probably not eaten for days. I could give them two or three ounces of gold. *More,* if they behave well. It's hardly going to hurt us. What would Spiker have earned, do you suppose, for his year at sea?"

"I'm not really sure. We could ask him. Smalt might know."

"It makes no damned difference, really. We'll have nearly a ton of gold, if Clézio has got his facts right. I'll give 'em enough to live on for a year or two. To live *comfortably.* Even in London. We'll be their saviours. They won't betray us."

"You're probably right," Septimus agreed. "The pistol is a lucky find. It looks a good weapon. *Expensive.* Worth *double* what he's asking for it, I'd think."

"Who knows? It *fires,* we know that! If Spiker had been a better shot you'd be digging a hole for me now and trying to think of some suitable words."

"Ha, ha, ha! It was an accident. He just panicked."

"I don't think he'd ever fired a gun before. He looked as shocked as me when the bloody thing went off. I felt the wind as the ball whistled over my head. *Jesus!* He'll be a good man on deck, though. We just need to get him cleaned up a bit."

Billy brought some food up for the pair. Bread and cheese, with fresh-brewed coffee. They fell on it like hungry animals. Mulu had hardly spoken a word since they'd found her in the tower. She seemed moody and resentful. Towards Lachlan, especially. *As though she didn't like the look of him.* For some reason. Spiker, with his naval training, was easier to deal with. He was used to following orders.

Later in the day, as the light began to fail, the gang moved into what had once been the old house's main kitchen. Little was left of it. The roof was gone. The pots and plates were all smashed. Billy got a fire going, in the rusty stove. Captain Smalt brought some candles over from the ship. And a bottle or two. In his gentlemanly way he offered the first glass to Mulu. The ghost of a smile crossed her face.

Lachlan found a shaky chair for her and wiped it clean.

With some reluctance, she took a seat. In front of the fire. Her dark eyes glittered, sulkily, in the candlelight.

Lachlan dragged another chair over and sat at her side.

"My dear lady..." he pleaded. "You're not making this easy. *I'm trying to help!* We didn't expect to find a woman in this remote place, but, as you're here..."

Mulu scowled as she drained her glass.

Captain Smalt refilled it for her.

"...I want to do the *right thing,*" Lachlan continued. *"For both of you.* If things go well, on the morrow – as we hope they will – *we are going to make a little money.* A shilling or two. If you get my meaning. We could offer you a share of the proceeds. *In exchange for your friendly cooperation.* Do you understand?"

A cunning glint entered Mulu's eyes. She understood perfectly.

An owl hooted. Out in the night.

"How much?"

"I can't say, as yet. I'll know better tomorrow. Enough to change your lives, certainly. I'm a man of my word. I won't let you down. All I ask is that you *behave* yourselves and do as you're told. For the next day or two. Can we agree on that?"

Mulu shrugged.

"For two days, then."

Lachlan nodded wearily. A deal, of sorts, it seemed, was done. Captain Smalt uncorked another bottle.

"What brought you to this godforsaken place?" he asked Mulu.

"Chance..." she said. "Spiker grew up in these parts. We were looking for somewhere to hide. We thought the navy might still be looking for him. They'd hang him from the yards, the evil bastards. Without a second thought."

Spiker was sitting on the cracked tiles at Mulu's feet. Despite his year on the high seas, he was a timid country boy at heart. A victim of politics. Of cruel fate.

"Where do you actually hail from, lad?" Septimus asked him.

"Hogg's Marsh. On the Isle of Grain. We were tenant farmers. My father took to the drink. While I was away at sea. He disappeared. The neighbours think he perished. Out on the marshes. My mother died many years ago. I've got a married sister in London. She's a laundress. In Moor Fields. At a place called Man in the Moon Yard. That's where we plan to go. When things have settled down."

"We could take you with us when we sail," Lachlan offered. "If that would suit you. We could take you as far as Woolwich. Mulu could help in the galley."

By way of a response, Mulu spat into the fire.

Septimus decided to sleep on dry land. He lugged his mattress up from the ship and rolled it out in an old pantry at the very back of the building.

He could see a few pale stars, through what was left of the roof.

Billy and the captain returned to the ship. Lachlan stayed ashore. To keep an eye on Spiker and Mulu. Mr Serocoal was going to take the night watch.

The revised plan was that Mr Serocoal would keep Mulu company the next day. Spiker, the trained sailor, would take Mr Serocoal's place on the ship.

A malefic moon rose over the ruins as the night air cooled. Owls were hunting, in the surrounding woodland. Their cries echoed off the ancient walls.

Septimus pulled his blanket up over his ears.

For the first half of the night he slept like a bag of old bones. The ruined walls could have toppled down around him and he would hardly have noticed. But then, at some ungodly, ghostly hour, he woke with a start and a wail of terror.

Someone, or *something,* had poked him in the ribs.

"*Uh?*" he grunted.

He peered about. It was uncannily cold. Inexplicable *scraping* sounds were coming from the darkness around him. The cold stones underneath his mattress were *moving*. The *walls* were moving. In the hidden depths below, the foundations were groaning. Septimus's heart raced. Something – he knew not what – was tugging at his blanket. When he tried to raise himself he found that he couldn't move. An unearthly force was holding him down. He could barely breathe.

Sniggering demons swarmed in the ghastly, haunted dark. He moaned. He screamed and howled, at the top of his voice, but no-one came to help.

Then, in an instant, as though by decree, the demons vanished.

Golden light flooded into the little room. Susie Kettle appeared, overhead, in a swirl of luminous mist. Her angelic wings flapped, softly, in the perfumed air.

"Septimus!" she cooed. *"My dearest! My sweetest! I come to warn you! Abandon this ill-fated enterprise, while there is yet time! Save yourself! Walk away! Join me, my darling! Here in the light! The ineffable light of Queen Mbembé. You must partake of the Sacred Secretions! One more time! Under the guidance of one who is properly trained in the mysteries!"*

"No-o-o-o-o-o!" Septimus moaned. *"Go to hell!"*

"Open your eyes! Am I not the woman you loved?"

She was naked. Septimus tried his best not to look.

"Leave me alone, damn you!"

With a shrug, she extended her immense wings and drifted away. An army of cackling fiends appeared in her wake. They had tangled hair and scaly grey skin. Like the living corpses in the Necropolis that Ebenezer Withers had stumbled upon.

Their eyes were clouded and bloodshot. Like the eyes of old drinkers. There was something horribly familiar about them, Septimus realised.

They looked weirdly like... *himself.*

They bared their yellow teeth and slithered towards him.

He screamed... and screamed... and screamed.

"SEPTIMUS!" someone shouted.

"Uhh?"

Something scampered over Septimus's blanket as he came to his senses. He glimpsed a hungry-looking rat as it scurried off. Moonlight was creeping in, through the ruined roof. Someone was standing in the doorway. A familiar figure.

"Lachlan?"

"You were shouting in your sleep, you mad bastard."

"Oh... *sorry.* I was having a bad dream. A bloody nightmare."

"It sounded like it. What were you dreaming about?"

"I hardly know. I've already forgotten."

"It's this bloody place. *It's haunted.* I swear. I left half-a-dozen candles burning in the kitchen when I went to sleep. *They've all blown out.* Every last one. *But there's no wind.* Not a breath. Just thinking about it gives me the shivers."

"Somebody must have extinguished them. Mulu, perhaps."

"Perhaps. But I'll be glad to get out of here. With luck the *Helga* will turn up early. By midday we could be on our way home. With a ton of gold in our possession. *Half a ton* at the very least, but even then I wouldn't complain.

We'll celebrate later. At the end of the day. When we get back to Deptford."

"Uh, huh."

"Get some sleep, Septimus. We'll need our wits about us tomorrow."

"Let's just hope it goes well, eh?"

"It will. This is our *destiny,* my friend. Sleep well."

"I'll do my best."

11

THE TAKING OF THE *HELGA*

It was late morning when the ship finally appeared. Lachlan had been prowling the ruins since before dawn. The gang were ready. The guns were loaded. The weather was perfect, with a light south-easterly wind. It had been misty at daybreak but the mist had cleared, through the morning, as the wind had strengthened.

Lachlan had purloined Mr Serocoal's silver-gilt pocket watch. He'd just consulted it, for the hundredth time, when a shout came from the tower. Billy had been up there for hours, scanning the waterway with Smalt's telescope.

"It's them!" Billy shouted. *"Come and take a look!"*

Lachlan rushed to the tower and clattered up the stone steps. The sun had disappeared into a bank of cloud but you could still see for miles. The tide was on its way out. Countless ships were visible, from the tower-top. There was an out-bound Indiaman in mid-stream, a multitude of smaller craft and a fleet of Newcastle colliers, on their way home, in ballast. Along with several shit-ships.

Over to the east, about two miles off, a scruffy-looking little foreign brig was ploughing through the inshore shallows. Under reduced sail. Close in the Kent coast, as though she was politely giving way to the larger vessels in the channel.

Feverishly, Lachlan adjusted the telescope.

"Yes!" he yelled. *"It's her! Let's get moving!"*

He hurried back down the steps with Billy at his heels. Septimus and Smalt were in the kitchen with Spiker and Mulu. Spiker had been telling tales of his time at sea. He'd been in the Far East, but had never been allowed off the ship.

"It's the *Helga,* alright!" Lachlan told them. *"No doubt about it!* I could even see the name on her bow. This is it, eh? Clézio has done his bit. *Exactly as he promised.* The cunning bastard. It's up to us, now. They'll reach us in about half an hour, I should think. At the rate they're going. We'll let them pass by and then go after them. I don't want to arouse their suspicions. We need to be cautious."

"How many on deck?" Septimus asked.

"I could see two or three. That's all. There could be more below."

"As long as we're not outnumbered."

The *Sabrina Louise* was ready to sail. Everything was prepared.

Mulu watched, uneasily, from the shore, as the cutter slid out, through the trees. Spiker's naval experience had been on a big square-rigger, but he soon had the hang of the smaller ship. He grinned as the sails filled. It was like old times.

They pulled on the uniforms. As Mr Serocoal was staying ashore, Lachlan gave Spiker the tricorn hat. It fitted him perfectly and seemed to rather please him. The navy had never treated him so well. He gave Lachlan a respectful salute.

Inch by inch, they crept up on the wallowing *Helga*.

She was a decrepit-looking little Dutch coastal boat, moving at the speed of a drunken donkey and rolling so badly she looked in grave danger of sinking.

Captain Smalt studied her through the telescope.

"What a bloody wreck," he murmured. "They haven't noticed us, yet."

Lachlan handed out the guns.

"Keep them well-hidden. We'll only use them if we have to."

While Billy was hauling up the flags and pennants, something in the sky above caught Septimus's eye. A moving shadow. Some way off. Under the clouds.

He pointed.

"What in the world is that? Up there. In the eastern sky…"

Whatever it was, it was moving at considerable speed and growing larger as it got closer. An eerie twilight fell as the spreading shadow consumed the sun.

"Oh, Jesus…" Lachlan whispered.

"It's coming for us!" Billy yelled. *"Get down!"*

The darkness thickened. Weird lightning flickered around the ship. Icy blasts tore at the sails. Septimus grabbed the rigging and clung on for dear life. He could see *something,* in the gloom above, but he couldn't make out what it was.

It appeared to be… *a creature.* Of some sort.

"It looks like…"

He couldn't finish the sentence. It didn't look like... *anything*.

The *Sabrina Louise* was pitching wildly. The decks were awash. Septimus heard the slow beat of the creature's wings as it came down. Through the inky dark. Like a thing from hell. He glimpsed its murderous, gleaming, blood-red eyes.

"*God help us!*" Lachlan screamed. "*Shoot* the bloody thing, somebody! Before it sinks us! BILLY! The muskets! *Jesus!* Why has it picked on *us?* For God's sake! *Septimus!* Don't just stand there gawping! *Do something!*"

Septimus cocked his pistol but couldn't see a clear target. All he could make out were shadows and shifting shapes. The yawing of the ship wasn't helping.

Then, suddenly, the shades parted. A repulsive head appeared. Directly above. Septimus took aim. BADOOM!!! He aimed for the creature's eyes but missed. The ball went through one of its horrible, slapping wings. Yellow slime splattered down onto the *Sabrina Louise's* deck. The creature shrieked. It retreated and circled, as though it was planning a new attack. From a different direction.

Its evil eyes glimmered, through the murk.

"*Forget the pistol!*" Lachlan shouted. "*Get the big guns!*"

The larger guns were under a sheet, in the stern. Hidden from sight. Ready for use. If needed. Septimus uncovered the cavalry carbine, then changed his mind and grabbed the blunderbuss instead. It was a huge, heavy weapon. They'd loaded it with a variety of pistol balls, stones, old nails and bits of rusty wire.

He braced himself as the fiery eyes bore down.

As the creature closed in, he pulled the trigger.

The explosion was deafening. Ten yards of flame poured from the gun's great muzzle. Septimus was hurled back against the heaving, wet afterdeck.

The creature exploded. In mid-air.

The grotesque head, with most of its brains blown out, crashed on to the foredeck. At Billy's feet. Its jaws were still moving. Noxious slime was bubbling out of its nostrils. Billy stared, wide-eyed, as the abomination wriggled towards him.

"Billy!" Smalt yelled. *"Don't move! I'm coming!"*

He rushed forward and kicked the awful thing over the side. The yellow slime splashed up his legs as he waded through it. His stockings and breeches were smoking when he got back to the wheel. His good leather shoes were ruined.

"What is this stuff?" he howled. *"It's creeping up my bloody legs!"*

"Don't touch it," Septimus advised. "It might be dangerous."

"Don't *touch* it? *For heaven's sake!* I'm *covered* in it!"

Despite all the horror, no-one had been seriously hurt. The pernicious mists were clearing. Spiker was up aloft. The ship itself appeared undamaged.

"Lord above!" Lachlan spluttered. "What *was* that thing? Why did it pick on us? Of all the ships in sight? It came straight for us! Out of nowhere! Like a cat after a bloody rat! *It could have sunk us!* Thank God we brought the guns!"

"It won't be troubling anyone else," Smalt observed, sourly. "Whatever the damn thing was. Its guts are all over the bloody ship. We'll have to clean up later. This isn't the moment. The *Helga* is straight up ahead. We're almost upon her."

Lachlan took a quick look through the telescope.

"I can't see Clézio," he said worriedly. "Just those bloody crocodile priests. *Lord, save us!* Four or five of them. By the look of it. All in pointed black hoods. *Jesus!* The very sight turns my stomach. One of 'em is at the tiller. The others appear to be swabbing the decks. This horrible slime must have hit them, too."

"All the better," Smalt said. "Let's do it! Let's go!"

The Customs Service flags were still fluttering, at the mast-head.

Smalt found a speaking-trumpet. Lachlan raised it.

"BRITISH CUSTOMS SERVICE!" he bawled. "HEAVE TO!"

The crocodile priests stopped whatever it was they were doing and stared across at the *Sabrina Louise*. It was impossible to tell what they were thinking.

"*Customs Service!*" Lachlan shouted, again. "*As a foreign-flagged vessel, you require a permit to enter the Thames! At this time! I have the documents! Right here! We are coming alongside! It will take two minutes! No more!*"

There was no response at all from the other ship.

"What's their game?" Lachlan muttered. "Where is Captain Clézio? Why are they staring at us like that? Do they not understand plain English?"

While Lachlan dithered, a raffish-looking character emerged from the *Helga's* stern cabin. He was wearing knee-high boots and a thick sea-coat with a fur collar. He'd lost his left eye, at some point in his evidently interesting life. A leather patch covered the empty socket. He had several pistols pushed into his belt and another one at the ready in his right hand. He conferred urgently with the crocodile priests.

"Who the fuck is this?" Lachlan whispered.

"It's not Clézio, then, I take it?" Septimus asked.

"Good God, no! Clézio is... *respectable."*

The crocodile priests were muttering and pointing. The man with the missing eye narrowed his good eye and peered across at Lachlan, through the rising spray.

"A Prussian mercenary, perhaps," Septimus suggested. "He doesn't look particularly friendly, whoever he is. He's armed. We'll need to be cautious."

"Damn them!" Lachlan mumbled. "So... let's, uh..."

There was a sudden explosion. From the bow. BOOM!!! It was Billy. He'd taken matters into his own hands. Smoke streamed from the long musket. Over on the *Helga,* the raffish man-at-arms shuddered and clutched his chest. A blood-red stain began spreading down the front of his silk shirt. As the ship rolled, he toppled forward and dropped. Into the rushing river. In the blink of an eye he was gone.

Lachlan turned pale.

"Billy..." he groaned.

This wasn't the way things were supposed to go. Bloodshed wasn't part of the plan. Billy was young and impetuous. He didn't understand.

But there was no turning back. The deed was done.

The crocodile priests were already returning fire, with pistols they'd pulled out from under their robes. While Billy reloaded, Septimus grabbed the other musket and despatched the first priest he saw. The man's hood flew off as he dropped.

He had a gaping, toothless mouth. Grey skin, and yellow eyes. *Unnatural eyes...* Septimus thought, as he reloaded the carbine. Someone screamed, up in the rigging of the *Sabrina Louise*.

It was Spiker. He howled as he fell. He hit the river with an almighty splash and struggled for a moment as the eddying water pulled him down. Septimus cursed. Spiker hadn't stood a chance. He hadn't even been armed.

Despite the chaos, and the thickening smoke, Lachlan managed to shoot dead the *Helga's* steersman. With a lucky shot. The hooded figure fell to the deck.

Septimus shot another, as the two ships hit, broadside-on, with a crash of breaking spars. An odd silence followed. The only sound was the rush of the river.

A ghostly shape slithered up over the Dutch brig's stern.

It was Billy Moon. Dripping wet. With a blade in his mouth.

Like an avenging angel, he despatched two more of the cowering priests.

The last one alive leapt overboard.

With a triumphant whoop, Billy dropped the brig's mainsail.

"*For pity's sake!*" Lachlan muttered, as Billy heaved the grim corpses over the side. "*Why didn't they just do as they were told?* The stupid bastards! We could have settled everything. *Peaceably and amicably.* If they'd just *cooperated*.

I'm worried about the noise and smoke. We could have drawn attention to ourselves."

There were several other vessels in sight.

"They're all a fair way off," Septimus reasoned. "They won't want to get involved. But where is Captain Clézio? He was supposed to be in charge."

"They must have left him in Ostend. Perhaps they didn't trust him. Who knows? Let's just hope that the bloody gold is there. After all this horror. We need to get a tow-line onto the *Helga*. It shouldn't take us long to shift the cargo."

"Somebody will have to explain things to Mulu," Septimus pointed out, as the dead crocodile priests splashed, like bundles of old rags, into the Thames. "It won't be easy. She'll be inconsolable. She'll never forgive us."

"But..."

Lachlan stared out over the muddy river.

"Spiker could have swum ashore. It's only half a mile."

"I saw him hit the water. He didn't come up again."

"Oh, dear Lord..."

"We'll have to take care of Mulu. We owe the lad that. At the very least. We can't just give her a few shillings and bid her farewell. She's alone in the world, now."

"You're right – *of course,*" Lachlan agreed. "We'll take her with us when we sail. She could stay with me, I suppose. In Poplar. For a day or two. Until we've got the money. We'll give her a fair share. We'll have to talk things over with her."

They got a line on to the *Helga*. Lachlan and Septimus

boarded the little brig and took a quick look around. The cargo hatch was partly open, at the after end.

A piece of old canvas had been thrown across it.

Curious whimpering sounds were coming up from below. Septimus pulled the canvas back and peered down into the malodorous dark of the vessel's hold.

He was unprepared for the horrific scene that met his gaze.

"For the love of God!"

Daylight filtered in as he rolled back the covering. An emaciated, naked man came into view. He'd been strung up to the filthy rear bulkhead by his wrists. He was blinking in the sudden light. As though he'd been in the dark for days.

Lachlan stepped up to the hatch and looked in.

"Oh, no! Please! No..."

"Who is it?" Septimus asked.

"It's *Clézio*. Who else? *What have they done?* Those fiends! They must have got wind of the plot. Somehow. Perhaps he got drunk and blabbed. He has a weakness for the drink. It's been the ruin of him. They've beaten him half to death. By the look of it. *Dear God!* Those *unspeakable,* heathen bastards!"

Septimus dragged back the rest of the old tarpaulin.

"Let's get him out. Up into the fresh air."

They were approaching the concealed inlet at Egypt Point. While Lachlan fretted, Septimus climbed down into the *Helga's* hold. He glanced about as he reached the bottom. Glimmers of gold were visible. Everywhere he looked.

Despite the setbacks, it seemed that all was not lost.

As gently as they could, they cut Captain Clézio's lashings and hauled him up into the daylight. There wasn't much they could do for him, at that moment, beyond offering comfort and cleaning off the filth he was covered in. Septimus held him while Lachlan poured buckets of malodorous Thames water over him.

"*Jabbja...jajja...*" the captain gurgled.

"What happened?" Lachlan asked him. "How did you get into this state?"

"*Bhurff...*"

Clézio moaned. Yellow slime dribbled from his mouth. He stared blankly at his rescuers, as though he had no idea who they were, or why they were throwing cold water over him. Lachlan tried to calm him, as they sluiced him down.

"You're safe now, *mon ami*," he told him. "You're among friends. I don't know what those evil bastards have done to you, but it's all over now. We'll take care of you. We'll get you the best medical treatment that money can buy. You'll soon be back on your feet. We're going to be *rich,* my friend. *Just as we planned.* Money will be no object. Whatever it takes, you will have it. That's a solemn promise."

Clezio whimpered.

"*Jazha-jazha...*" he croaked.

The *Helga's* decks and hatches were still strewn with disgusting bits and pieces of the flying creature's anatomy. Septimus had to be careful where he stood.

Some of the larger pieces weren't even properly

dead. The scattered lumps were wriggling towards each other – as *though they were trying to reunite.*

An entire foot, with twitching claws, was slithering along the deck. It was heading aft. Towards the stern. Lachlan retreated as the awful thing got closer.

He flung a wooden bucket at it but the foot just kept on coming.

"Septimus!" he screamed. *"Do something! Shoot it!"*

But Septimus wasn't armed. The weapons were all on the other ship.

The foot was heading towards Captain Clézio.

Clézio gibbered as it approached.

"Jajajaja...jaja..."

Septimus lunged at the thing with a boathook but it did no good. The claws were already snapping at Clézio's toes. The *capitaine* howled in terror as he fought the thing off. He staggered aft and jumped overboard. The foot followed.

It *shrieked* as it flew through the air.

"God in heaven!" Septimus gasped.

He rushed to the stern and looked down. Clézio was being tossed about in a whirlpool of yellow foam. His outlines were becoming blurred. Soon they could hardly see him at all. There was nothing anybody could do. It was the end.

Captain Smalt was trying his best to bring the two vessels in alongside each other. He was in need of Billy's help, but Billy was momentarily distracted. While Smalt shouted and cursed, Billy joined the other men at the brig's stern-rail.

He stared, bewilderedly, at the foaming yellow water.

"For the love of God!" he breathed. *"What is it?"*

Lachlan muttered something, in biblical Latin, and crossed himself.

"It's Captain Clézio," he said. *"He's dissolving."*

12

THE GOLD

The two ships were soon tied-up, side by side in the muddy creek. The *Helga* had grounded as they'd towed her in, but it hardly mattered. She was well-hidden, under the overhanging trees, and fairly close to where Smalt had wanted to put her.

Mulu was waiting. At the front entrance of the ruins. Mr Serocoal had been making coffee. There was a rich smell of it in the air. Mulu watched anxiously as the gang came ashore. One by one. The only person missing was Spiker.

A solitary tear trickled down Mulu's cheek.

Lachlan hobbled up the steps. He stopped in front of her and hung his head. As though he didn't know what to say. As though there was nothing he *could* say.

Mulu slapped him, noisily and hard, across the face. *"You bastard!"* she screamed. *"Where is he?"*

Lachlan mumbled some hopeless words of apology. He blamed the Fates. The tides. The flying creature. The Tower of Babel. The priests of the Crocodile Queen and their evil practices. Mulu screamed and screamed. Lachlan closed his eyes and covered his ears. He tried to explain. He had no idea of how things had gone so horribly wrong. People hadn't *listened*. Things... *hadn't gone to plan.*

Mulu spat in his face.

Septimus pushed the Irishman out of the way.

"It wasn't his fault," he told Mulu. "It wasn't *anybody's* fault. It was a tragic accident. We lost *two* good men. Spiker – and the captain of the other ship. An old friend of Lachlan's. Spiker was up in the rigging when the bastards suddenly opened fire on us. I don't think they even *meant* to shoot him. The ships were rolling. Quite heavily. In mid-river. *It happened so fast.* One minute he was there. The next he was gone. There was *nothing* we could have done to save him."

Mulu sobbed. Septimus felt shabby and ashamed.

"Get some rest," he advised her. "None of us slept well. We'll be on our way quite soon. In an hour or so. Our business here is just about done. We'll take you with us, of course. If you want to come. We can't just leave you. You can stay with us. In London. At least until we get the money. We'll make sure that you're well provided for. Spiker would have expected no less of us."

"The money?"

She spat again.

"I wouldn't touch the *dregs* of your *filthy money!* I'm not some penny ha'penny bloody whore! Whatever you may think! *You* can go to London. You can go to the bloody *moon,* for all I care! Spiker will come back. *I know him better than you do!* Do you really think I'd go *anywhere* with you *deceitful bastards?* Do you take me for a fool? *Why should I believe a bloody word?"*

She stormed off. In a flood of tears. Septimus wiped the spit from his face and watched her go. There was nothing more he could do. He felt unclean. He hadn't had a drink all day. The yellow slime had soaked through into his boots, despite the torn pages from the *Advertiser* he'd stuffed the holes with.

He desperately needed a bath and a change of clothes.

After that he needed to get drunk. For at least a month.

In the meantime there was work to be done. His fellow thieves were already at work in the *Helga's* hold. They'd torn off the brig's hatch-coverings and were laughing and shouting as they hurled things around, down below.

Smalt was up on deck. He grinned as Septimus climbed aboard.

"*Come and look, Septimus!* It's all there! *Just as promised!* Clézio wasn't exaggerating. *Quite the opposite!* I can hardly believe my bloody eyes! It's a *crime* that he won't get his share. The poor devil. *Come!* Come and take a look!"

Septimus crossed the deck and peered down. Billy and Mr Serocoal were busy in the gloom below. Billy was moving the loose straw that had been thrown in to conceal the cargo. The air was full of dust. Strange objects were emerging.

An immense wooden casket filled the centre of the hold. Its outer surfaces were covered in weird, arcane carvings. It looked... *unimaginably old.*

Loops of rusty chain held it shut.

Lachlan watched from the deck as Billy cleared away the straw.

"Break it open!" Lachlan shouted. *"Use the axe!"*

"Is that wise?" Septimus asked. "It could be worth good money."

"We can't take it with us. It's too big. We couldn't sell it, in any case. Who would want it? Look at those *ghastly* carvings. We'll burn it. It's for the best."

He leaned down.

"Just do it, Billy! Take the axe to it!"

They stepped back as Billy went to work. He smashed the corroded chains and forced open the heavy lid. It fell back with a crash. Dust poured up.

"Oh... Lord, save us!" Lachlan murmured.

The golden statue lay on its back in the great casket. It was bigger than they'd imagined. Billy pulled away some of the rags it was wrapped in. A golden head appeared. A *reptilian* head. Its red eyes glowed, ominously, through the dust.

Lachlan shuddered.

"Dear God! Were people actually going to *worship* this... *abomination?* In this day and age? *In London?* A golden woman with a crocodile's head? She's quite shapely, I suppose, in her way, but... *uugh!* Look at those *hideous* teeth!"

Septimus shrugged.

"There's no accounting for people's tastes, eh?"

"But this is *England.* We're civilised people."

"So they say. Sometimes I wonder."

"Yes, but..."

Lachlan's thoughts were turning to more pressing matters.

"Those red stones in the eyes must be rubies. A fair little pile of 'em. They're quite pretty, eh? I know a jeweller who'll take them off us. They'll be worth a few guineas. We could give them to Mulu, perhaps. She could have some earrings made. It would suit her. The gold is our only concern, really. It's hard to guess how much there is. At *least* half a ton. By the look of it. Clézio reckoned a ton, in total. We won't know for certain until we've got it home and weighed it."

Billy was still tearing off the statue's wrappings.

"Don't bother with that, lad!" Lachlan shouted. "We don't have time. Get chopping! Try and get the head off. That will give us an idea of how solid she is."

They'd borrowed the axe from the ship-breakers' yard in Deptford. It was a crude, heavy tool. Freshly sharpened. Billy half-severed the statue's golden neck with his first stroke. The horrible head *screeched* – weirdly – as it toppled back.

Billy froze. The axe fell from his hands.

The statue was *moving*. Its red eyes were evilly aglow. One of its golden arms rose, suddenly. In the dusty gloaming. A quivering finger pointed at Billy.

"Jesus!" he screamed. *"The bloody thing's alive!"*

He recovered the axe and took another swing at the half-severed head. The body twitched and jerked. As though it was trying to get to its feet. Strange sounds came out of it. Clicks and whirrs. Gasps and groans. Then, finally – as though all the fight had gone out of it – it crashed back into the great casket and fell silent.

The onlookers stared in horror.

Lachlan was the first to speak.

"Mother of God!" he muttered. *"Is the bloody thing dead?"*

Septimus laughed, as the truth dawned on him.

"It's an *automaton*. A piece of mechanical trickery. There must be a clockwork engine, of some sort, somewhere inside it. That's why they had it made in France, I'll wager. There are workshops in Paris that specialise in such things. You can buy them over here. In London. If you're rich enough. I saw a mechanical monkey, once, that played the piano. In my servant days. It could play hundreds of tunes. You just had to turn a wheel, on the back, and off it would go."

Lachlan sighed. With evident relief.

Billy seemed less sure. He studied the smashed head, warily. "What's the bloody point?"

"To impress the simple folk who turn up to their ceremonies," Septimus suggested. "That would be my guess. They give 'em the *Eau Sacré,* and then dazzle them with something like this. The living goddess! Ten feet high! With limbs that move! You can imagine the scene. Even we were fooled. Just for a moment."

"You can say that again," Billy grumbled.

"Damn the bastards!" Lachlan spat. *"Let's get back to work!"*

Billy returned to his task. With renewed vigour. Smalt and Mr Serocoal moved the glittering pieces over to the other ship. Septimus went below to help Billy. The clockwork engine tumbled out as they ripped open the torso. As Septimus had surmised, the thing was of French manufacture. It was beautifully-made. A brass plate bore the makers' name – *Berliau Frères, 48 rue Galande, Paris.*

Billy thought they could sell it to a clockmaker, but

Lachlan was against the idea. It was a fine thing but it was... *too unusual.* Too easily identifiable. After a brief debate, they hauled it up onto the deck and pushed it over the side.

It sank like a stone. Never to be seen again.

All that remained were the statue's golden wings – which had been removed and stowed separately – and a pile of wooden boxes in the forward part of the hold.

While Septimus and Mr Serocoal dealt with the wings, Billy went to work on the boxes. One by one, they splintered under the axe. More gold tumbled out.

Joyful, shimmering heaps of it.

There were orbs and sceptres, bowls and bells. Incense burners, medallions, candlesticks and golden chains. Along with other, even more curious things. The most surprising find was an immense golden throne that had been dismantled and shipped as parts, in separate boxes. An elegant rosewood case, rather like a lady's jewellery box, contained all the screws and pegs needed to reassemble the thing.

Lachlan came down and took a look at it.

"Who do you suppose it was for?" Billy asked. "The Crocodile Queen?"

Lachlan looked aghast.

"Billy! *Please!* There *is* no bloody Crocodile Queen! It's a fairytale!"

All that was left in the *Helga's* hold, when the giant throne had been lifted out, were the broken boxes, the ancient, ghastly casket, with its heathen carvings, and a huge pile of dusty straw. The gold had all been moved to the *Sabrina Louise.*

The job was done. It had taken two hours.

They took a final look around, in case they'd missed anything.

Mr Serocoal found a shapely golden toe, in among the debris.

He blew the dust off it and held it up into the light.

"Just look at that!" he whispered. "Is it not beautiful?"

"It's only a bloody toe!" Lachlan snapped.

"I wasn't thinking of the toe. Not exactly. Though it is rather lovely. The people who created this monstrous thing were *masters of their craft.* Heaven knows what the bloody thing must have cost. It hardly bears thinking about. The quality of the *metal itself,* though, is what I'm alluding to. Look at the colour! Look at the way it takes the light! It's South American, I would guess. *Pure gold.* Looted from ancient temples by the *conquistadors.* We'll get a good price for it."

"What about the other items?" Lachlan asked him. "The candlesticks and so on. Is it all of the same quality? Can you tell just by looking at it?"

"It looks fine to me. Mostly pure gold, I'd say. Even that huge bloody throne. Most gold is alloyed, these days. In Europe, at least. Ours is just as the Good Lord made it. As far as I can tell. It will need to be assayed, of course, at some point, but I don't foresee any problems. I could turn one of those ugly candlesticks into coin, perhaps, when we get back to London. It would give us some ready cash. Some golden guineas, uh? Enough to keep us going. We don't need to starve."

Lachlan nodded in agreement.

"How long will it take, do you think? Until we get paid?"

"Not long. A week at the most. *Everything is arranged.* All we have to do is deliver the stuff. The gentleman we're dealing with is *very* well connected. He's an old friend. A City goldsmith. I've known him all my life. He won't let us down."

A troubled look crossed Lachlan's face.

"Will he be able to take it all? It's a *huge* bloody amount. We won't know *exactly* how much until we've weighed it, but... there could *well* be a ton. Maybe a little less. Maybe *more.* We'll need to be paid in Bank of England notes. Payment on delivery. Mr Serocoal can check the notes while we're counting them."

"He won't bat an eyelid," Mr Serocoal promised. "He understands. I've told him that there could be as much as a ton. Obviously I didn't tell him the whole story. Just the general outlines. He was curious, naturally, but he understood the need for discretion. We discussed the matter of payment, at some length, over a brandy or two, earlier in the week. He assured me that he could get the money at fairly short notice. Within forty-eight hours. Once we've agreed on a price."

"How soon can we see him?"

"Tomorrow. He's expecting us."

"Where does he live?"

"Just off Poland Street. Near the old Pantheon Theatre. You'll like him. He's a man of property and a gentleman, but, uh... *our* sort of gentleman. A rogue in a powdered wig. He's got *history,* if you get my meaning."

Lachlan smiled. After all the horrors of the day, things seemed to be finally going well. The gold was securely stowed on the *Sabrina Louise.* Smalt and Billy were already at work, battening the hatches. The ship was about ready to sail

"Where's Mulu?" Lachlan asked. "I'd almost forgotten about her."

"She's sleeping, I think," Septimus said. "I told her to get some rest while we moved the cargo. She's grief-stricken. Understandably. This has been a terrible day for her. She blames us for Spiker's death. I tried to explain things to her but she refused to listen. She doesn't want anything more to do with us, but we can't just leave her here. We can't just abandon her. It wouldn't be right. The *least* we can do is take her to London. We could arrange a service of remembrance, perhaps, for Spiker. At one of the local churches. Just the few of us. It would be the decent thing to do. She might appreciate that. I'll go and rouse her."

While Smalt fretted about the state of the tide, Septimus went in search of the grieving Mulu. He was slightly concerned that she might have run off. Into the marshes. It would be a nuisance. A complication. She knew too much. Even their names. They'd have to stay until they found her. However long it took.

"*Mulu!*" he called, as he went up the steps.

There was no response. The ruins were silent.

"*Mulu!*" he called again.

A herring-gull skittered up into the mist as he entered the ruined kitchen. The bird had been picking over the scraps the gang had discarded when the call to action had come. Crusts and crumbs. Thrown aside without a thought.

Nothing had been moved. The stove was still smoking.

A quiet moan caught Septimus's ear. It had come

from a tiny pantry at the back of the room. Mulu hadn't gone far. He tiptoed across and looked in.

She was lying on her back in a heap of rags and straw. Her face was deathly pale. Her lips were slightly parted. She wasn't moving. As far as Septimus could tell, she wasn't even breathing. He knelt down and grabbed her by the shoulder.

"Mulu! For heaven's sakes! Wake up!"

The little room stank. She and Spiker had been sleeping there for weeks, by the look of things. They'd collected a few homely items. An earthenware jug with some dead roses in it. From who-knows-where. A faded image of the Virgin Mary, speckled with mould. This latter hung from the wall, just above Mulu's head.

She was alive. Her body was warm. Her heart was beating, though only just. Septimus pulled her up to a sitting position and shook her. She grunted in protest.

He caught a whiff of her breath and groaned.

"God help us!" he muttered. *"What have you been drinking?"*

Her mouth moved. Meaningless sounds came out. For a ghastly moment Septimus thought that she was going to vomit but then her head fell forward and she began to sob. She tried to tell him something but the words wouldn't come.

An empty stoneware beer bottle lay in the straw nearby. The kind that brewers used, throughout the land. Septimus picked it up and sniffed it. What he smelled wasn't beer. It was cheap gin. Half-hidden in the straw he found several more, similar bottles. All of them empty. The corks were scattered about.

"Mulu! *Dear God!* You're worse than me! *For heaven's sakes!* Where did you *find* this stuff? I thought you'd been living on rats and nettles. You and young Spiker. But you had the mothers' ruin, for comfort, eh? When the nights got cold."

Mulu whispered, in what sounded like some kind of accord.

"Let's get you out into the fresh air."

She was still only half-conscious. Septimus wrapped her in her shabby shawl and got her to her feet. She mumbled, sleepily, as he led her down to the ship.

He carried her aboard.

The tide was turning. The *Sabrina Louise* was rocking, gently, in the rising water. Septimus dropped Mulu onto the deck, with her back propped against the swaying mast. She opened her eyes and peered around, with the dazed look of someone waking from sleep. It seemed to dawn on her that she was no longer in her own bed. She pulled her shawl tighter and muttered to herself.

Her expression changed as Lachlan came in sight.

"You!" she snarled. *"You bastard! I'll have your guts!"*

Lachlan covered his ears.

"Take her below, Septimus," he pleaded. "Put her in Smalt's bunk. Just for the moment. It's the only comfortable berth. We can talk later. When we've all had time to think. Hopefully she'll calm down. Let's get the ropes off and get out of here! I don't want to spend another second in this terrible place."

They set fire to the *Helga* as they sailed out. Mr Serocoal tossed a blazing copy of the *Weekly Enquirer* into the Dutch brig's straw-filled, open hold.

The flames spread quickly. In no time at all, the whole ship was ablaze.

"Praise the Lord!" Lachlan murmured. *"The job is done!"*

Smoke and flames poured up from the burning vessel as the *Sabrina Louise* put out into the river. It was a spectacular sight. They hadn't expected the little brig to burn so quickly. The flames were soon hidden, behind the trees, but the smoke was hard to miss. It was rising, almost vertically, for a hundred feet or more, before levelling off and slowly dispersing. In a light, south-easterly wind.

"That smoke is going to attract attention," Septimus observed.

Lachlan shrugged.

"I don't think we need to worry. It could be anything. A burning barn. A haystack. *Who knows?* Nobody is going to come running. Not out here. They wouldn't find much, even if they did. By nightfall, there'll be nothing left."

13

IN THE DAMNABLE DEPTFORD FOG

The smoke was still visible, half an hour later. If anything, it was getting thicker. The *Sabrina Louise* was some distance away by this time, on the far side of the river. Close in to the Essex shore and making good headway, in the light wind.

Smalt was at the helm, as usual. Billy was at work on deck.

As they reached the Lower Hope a sudden mysterious flash lit up the river. It was followed, a moment later, by the 'thump' of a colossal explosion.

Screaming seagulls flocked up from the mudflats. Fiery debris streamed up from the burning ship. Blazing fragments floated down, like fallen stars from the heavens. The gulls keened and wailed. Like lost souls.

Lachlan gawped up at the circling gulls and the smoke-filled sky.

"Mother of God!" he spluttered. *"What was that?"*

Septimus poked his ringing ears while he thought about it.

"It will have woken the locals up, eh? Whatever it was. That was quite a bang! It must have been heard for miles around. *Jesus!* Those bastards must have had gunpowder aboard! Half a ton of it, by the sound of things. *Enough to start a small war!* We should have searched the whole ship. I didn't think of it. *Stupidly!* They'd come prepared for a fight. That's why they didn't stop when we ordered them to. They were *expecting* trouble. *They were ready for us!*"

"It looks that way," Lachlan agreed. "*Clézio!* The poor devil! They must have beaten it out of him. We all saw the state he was in. He was *deranged*. God only knows what they'd done to him. At least we made them pay. For their sins. Clézio will be among the holy angels, now. In the Abode of the Blessed. Those murderous heathens will be exactly where they deserve to be. In the pits of hell!"

"*Uh, huh...*"

Septimus couldn't help thinking that the unfortunate *capitaine* had, to some extent at least, brought about his own downfall. Spiker had suffered a much greater injustice. Fate had conspired against the lad for no apparent reason at all. A merry hour in a Rochester tavern had changed the entire course of his young life.

There was no accounting for the fickle cruelty of it.

The smoke disappeared astern as they tacked south, towards Gravesend. The river was busy. A thousand other vessels were making their way upstream. On the tide. Bigger vessels like the vast East Indiamen dominated the river, at times like this, though smaller craft like the *Sabrina Louise* had certain advantages.

They were more manoeuvrable – and much less noticeable.

A pair of Newcastle colliers had been detained by His Majesty's Customs at Gravesend. The officers paid no attention at all to the innocent-looking *Sabrina Louise* as she slipped quietly past, in mid-stream.

Smalt grinned. They were fairly safe, from this point on. Lachlan gave thanks to the Lord.

Septimus was still just a *little* worried.

"Who *else* might have been told?" he asked. "Beside those idiots on the *Helga?* Letters could have been sent. From Ostend. The Bow Street Runners might already be looking for us! They could be *waiting* for us. In Deptford."

Lachlan seemed more sanguine. He shook his head.

"That's unlikely. Clézio knew very little about us. He only knew me as Lachlan. As far as I know. I've used a few different names. Over the years. Though he knew my mother. In Paris. She still calls herself Madame Malone. He could have put two and two together, I suppose. It's not impossible."

"You can't be the only Lachlan Malone in London. There must be dozens of 'em. It's a good Irish name. Most of the navvies on the new dock schemes are Irish. Some of 'em are *sure* to be Malones. At least a few will be your namesakes."

"But not all as well-known as me. I've been in trouble since the day I was born. I've been accused of every crime in the book. Theft. Fraud. Drunkenness. Conspiracy. Sedition. I was innocent, most of the time, it goes without saying. But... you know how it is. It's difficult to shed a reputation, once you've got one. We should get out of England, Septimus. *As soon as we bloody can.* We'll have the money before the month is out. Within days, Mr Serocoal reckons."

"But... *to where?* Are you decided?"

"America. I've got a cousin in New York. We can take Mulu with us."

"Mulu might have her own plans. She doesn't hold us in particularly high esteem at the moment. *Understandably.* She'd happily see us hang."

"She'll come to her senses. Once she's sobered up."

"Let's hope so. My own dream would be to take Lady Constance. My old lover. She's living alone, now. So I've heard. In that vast, cold house. With a few servants and no support at all from her mad husband. I'm sure I could persuade her. If I could just get to see her. We were *close.* She and I. For a short while."

"You'll have *money,*" Lachlan pointed out. "That always helps. Enough to live on. She wouldn't need to take in laundry. Far from it. You could have a grand residence. A carriage or two. New friends. I've never been quite so lucky with women, myself. I've got a pair of half-wild Irish country girls living in my house at the moment. Distant relatives, on my father's side, but I don't plan on taking them with me. Drinking and fighting are the only things they're any good at."

It was still daylight. Dried-out, late-summer gorse bushes dotted the river banks. Trees and meadows lay beyond. Tiny villages went by as they sailed on. Windmills and church spires. Bedraggled barges, at rotting wharves.

Familiar scenes. Little by little, the gang started to relax.

It was time for a celebratory drink. There was just

one full bottle left in the galley. Mr Serocoal went down and got it as they passed Purfleet. Mulu was still asleep. As far as he could tell. Behind the frayed curtain that concealed Smalt's bunk. It seemed best to leave her where she was. For the moment.

Serocoal uncorked the brandy and filled five cups. The men laughed and joked as they drank. The horrors of the morning were all but forgotten. They were already starting to feel like men of means. The *Sabrina Louise* was ballasted with almost a ton of pure gold. Legitimately acquired. So they felt.

All that remained was to collect the money.

Excitedly, they discussed what the haul might be worth, on the assumption that they had *approximately* three-quarters of a ton. Gold had risen in price since the conflict with the French had broken out. The official rate was close to ten pounds an ounce, but *stolen* gold was only worth what you could get for it.

Septimus hardly cared. He just wanted to go home.

Mist hung over the marshes as they rounded the Isle of Dogs.

A murky red glow in the western sky was all that was left of the day.

Deptford Creek was already hidden in fog. Flares had been lit, at the mouth of the creek, for the benefit of mariners. Billy lowered the little cutter's sails as they slipped down towards their berth at the ship-breaking yard.

Fog cloaked the waterside trees. Smalt's dog leapt aboard as Billy secured the mooring-lines. He raced around the deck, whimpering and wagging his tail.

Smalt grabbed him and gave him a friendly hug.

"He knows I always come back!"

"It's good to *be* back!" Lachlan breathed. "The London fog has never smelled so good, I swear! What a bloody day, uh? It could have been worse, I suppose. We can weigh the gold in the morning. It won't take long. I found some scales. The sort that market-traders use. At the local tavern. The landlord didn't bat an eyelid when I asked if we could borrow them. I told him that we're weighing turnips. *Ha!* Once we've got a figure we can go and talk to the goldsmith."

"Who's going to stay aboard?" Septimus asked.

"You may as well go home, Septimus. Sleep in your own bed, eh? We're all in need of a good night's sleep. The gold is safe. The dog's on deck. The guns have all been reloaded. Billy can keep an eye on things, overnight. Captain Smalt looks exhausted. He's been at the wheel for hours. There's Mulu to think of, too. *What are we going to do with Mulu?* For heaven's sakes?"

Nobody had a ready answer. Nobody quite knew.

Billy was happy to stay aboard. Along with the captain and Mr Serocoal. The old coiner wanted to start weighing the gold at first light. With Billy's help.

Lachlan, on balance, decided to head home.

"The Irish girls will be wondering where I am. I didn't tell them anything. Couldn't risk it. Their tongues are too loose. I could take Mulu with me, I suppose. If she'd consent. We have a spare bed. You, too, Septimus. If you want to come."

"I should go back to my lodgings. I've been away for nearly three days. My landlady will be thinking that I've left without paying. We're not *exactly* the best of friends. She'll be hoping that I've been *garrotted*. Down some stinking alleyway."

"Perhaps *you* could take Mulu home? To the Crow Hotel. Just for tonight. She might agree to that. *Tomorrow...* we can talk things over. Hopefully."

Mulu had barely spoken a word since they'd brought her aboard, several hours earlier. They'd heard her moaning in her sleep, once or twice. Lachlan didn't want her to roam off on her own. He wasn't *quite* sure whose side she was on. He was secretly terrified that she might betray them to the Bow Street Magistrates, or – even worse – to the ghoulish, ghastly prelates of the Sign of the Crocodile Queen.

For better or worse, the unpredictable Mulu had to be confronted. Lachlan led the way. Septimus followed him down. The cramped saloon didn't smell any better. It was urgently in need of an airing. Mulu was in Smalt's curtained-off bunk at the forward end. They could hear her moving around as they approached.

She was awake. By the sound of things.

"Bring the lantern!" Lachlan whispered.

Septimus unhooked the lamp and brought it forward. He could see Mulu. Just. Through the frayed holes in the curtain. She appeared to be decently dressed.

"Mademoiselle?" Lachlan called, softly. "Can we, uh... *talk?"*

Silence ensued. Mulu, it seemed, was in no mood to talk.

Septimus pulled the curtain back.

She was sitting in the middle of Smalt's bunk with a greasy blanket draped around her shoulders. She blinked in the sudden lamplight, then turned and stared, with some surprise, at the Sapphic nudes on the bulkhead behind her.

Lachlan edged a little closer. Mulu pretended not to see him.

"I'll be leaving, now," she said, sulkily, to no-one in particular. "You can't keep me here. *You have no right.* I'm not some *chattel.* I'm not for sale."

"Of course..." Lachlan agreed. *"The only thing is..."*

"You murdering bastard!" she snarled. "The only thing is *what?* Who are you to tell me what I can and cannot do? What do you think I am? Some piece of shit you can push around like you just bought me at a bloody horse-fair? *Eh?* You think you can drag me on to your disgusting boat and take me anywhere you like? Well... we'll soon see about that. *You can think again!"*

She flung the blanket aside. As though she was preparing to leave.

"Wait..." Lachlan pleaded. An apologetic tone came into his voice. *"Mulu...* my *dear* lady. Listen to me. *Please!* For just a moment. You're mistaking my intentions. *I'm trying to do the right thing.* For once in my hopeless bloody life. It's been a terrible day, I know. *For all of us.* I've also lost a friend."

Mulu's ferocious black eyes turned towards him.

"We've *all* suffered," Lachlan went on. "But we want to make things right, as best we can. Despite the terrible events of the day, we're quite wealthy men, now. Do you understand? There's a great *heap* of stolen gold on the other side of this very bulkhead, just behind your pretty head. Part of it is yours. We've all agreed. We can't bring Spiker back but we want to treat you fairly."

"Huh!" she sneered.

"We'll all *hang* if we get caught," he continued. "We'd be a public spectacle at the Newgate gallows. Brief entertainment for a crowd of fools. Understandably, we're hoping for a better outcome. That's why we *had* to bring you with us. I'd give my own worthless life, I swear, if it would bring Spiker back, but he's gone to a place beyond the comprehension of mortal men. He's with our Gracious Lord, now. In the incomparable company of saints and angels."

She stared blankly at him for a moment, and then giggled.

"You're a Catholic."

"Indeed. Yourself?"

"I'm an unbeliever."

Lachlan looked shocked. He poked his ears.

"What faith were you brought up in?"

"What's that got to do with you? *You nosy bastard!* When are you going to get to the point? You think you can buy my silence. That's what all this *shilly-shallying* is about, is it not? You're a *thief!* Good sir. For all your grand talk."

"You misconstrue me, mistress," Lachlan protested. "I'm not some *common footpad*. I'm a believer in the Rights of Man. In truth and justice. *Liberté. Égalité. Fraternité.* What I'm offering you is a *fair share* in the proceeds of our enterprise. *A small bloody fortune.* Do you understand? We can discuss the exact details later. You'll be *rich*. If things go well. As we hope they will. *Think about it!* You'll be able to go anywhere you wish. Travel the world. Buy a house. Employ servants. It will take a week, roughly speaking, to have the gold valued and changed into coin of the realm. Until then, I'd like you to come and stay with me. If you would do me that honour. Just for a week. I have a house in Poplar. It's not far."

"You expect me to live at your bloody house?"

"Just for a week."

"And then I get paid, uh?"

"Exactly. It will take a few days, as I say. *Hopefully* no more than a week. What about you, Septimus? You could join us. Mulu trusts you. You're English. You speak nicely. You don't have to go back to that hole you're living in. There's plenty of room at the house. You could stay. We'd enjoy your company."

Septimus shrugged.

"Why not?"

Mulu was less convinced.

"I'm not for sale!" she spat, suddenly. "What do you take me for? Some Drury Lane drab? You can *keep* your filthy money! I don't need it!"

She slipped off the bed and made a dash for the companion ladder. Septimus got there first and stood by the ladder, momentarily blocking her path. Mulu hissed and cursed. When he didn't move she slapped him, hard, across the face.

Septimus closed his eyes and rubbed his stinging cheek.

"Mulu..." he groaned. "Why can't you just *listen,* for once? We're not trying to take advantage of you. It's just that....*we haven't known you for very long.* If you were to talk to the, uh... Runners... or to *anyone at all,* really, you'd be putting a rope around our necks. *We're not bad people.* We're not *murderers.* Spiker's death was a terrible accident. Just as Lachlan said. You've got hold of the

wrong end of the stick. We're just... *decent, honest men.* Trying to make a little money."

"You have a damned peculiar way of going about it."

"Well... these are hard times. Life isn't easy. Not for anyone. Unless you're one of the lucky few. We all do things that we later regret. But we're doing our best to put things right. As Lachlan tried to explain – we have a quantity of gold aboard. A *considerable* quantity. Dubiously acquired, it's true. From an unsavoury French cult. We have a buyer. Everything is arranged. All we have to do is deliver the stuff and get paid. Until then, we'd like you to stay with us. Just for a few days. I'll *personally* look after you and defend your honour. You have my word."

A flicker of a smile crossed Mulu's face. Septimus and Mr Serocoal were the only members of the gang she seemed particularly inclined to trust.

She glanced around at the mess in the *Sabrina Louise's* saloon cabin.

"You want me to live in this stinking hell-hole for a *week?*"

Lachlan rejoined the conversation.

"*No, no, no...*" he insisted. "Not *here*. I have a house, as I say. In Poplar. Not so far from here. I rent it from a local dairyman. You can have your own room, with a comfortable bed. You won't be alone. There are other women in the house. Good-hearted Irish girls. We'll take good care of you. I promise."

"And then what?"

"And then... when the time comes, we'll give you the money. After that you can do whatever you like. You're a free woman, as you rightly point out. We'll help you, of course, in any way we can. We owe you that. You could come to America with us. Why not? It's worth thinking about. A new life, uh? In a new land."

Mulu sat down again. She looked thoughtful.

"How much?"

"I can't say right now. Not *precisely*. It depends on what we can get. It's *business*. We should know tomorrow. Obviously we have a rough idea. We'll be selling the haul for a lot less than its real worth, but even so..."

Lachlan paused and scratched his chin. As though he was thinking.

"Thousands of pounds."

"Each?"

"Uh, huh."

Mulu's eyes widened. She pulled off one of her shoes and scratched her foot while she weighed the idea up. Cold fog was creeping in through the hatch above.

"For one week, then," she said, finally. "I will stay at your house for a week. Then I get the money and I keep my mouth shut. I agree."

Lachlan nodded wearily. Mulu was hard work.

"That's all settled, then. Let's be on our way. We're all tired. We'll use the ship's boat. Billy can row us up to Limehouse Hole. What about you, Septimus? Are you joining us? The boat won't take the four of us. We'll have to wait for you in Limehouse. Unless I draw you a map. To show you where the house is."

Septimus was re-hanging the lamp. In its usual place. Mulu watched him, through narrowed eyes.

"He doesn't have to come," she said. "I can defend

my own honour. I've had enough practice in my time, believe me. I'm going to take you people at your word. What have I got to lose? I've already lost everything. Your friend looks like a man who has a woman waiting. Somewhere. Am I not right? You can always tell. *It's in their eyes.* They can't hide it. However bloody hard they try."

Septimus didn't respond. Mulu was perceptive, on the whole, but on this particular occasion she'd misread the signs. Septimus just wanted to sleep in his own bed. The only woman who might be thinking of him was Mrs Lusardi.

She would be hoping that he was gone for good.

He nodded.

"I'll go home. I'll hail a wherry. From the creek-mouth."

Lachlan looked relieved. He was eager to be off. There was work to be done, the next day. He cast a covert wink in Septimus's direction as Mulu ascended the ladder. Smalt went out to help with the ship's boat. There was a noisy splash as it hit the water, then muffled shouts and the creak of oars as Billy rowed away.

"This *damnable* fog," Smalt grumbled, as he came back down. "It's getting worse by the day. Billy will be fine. He knows what he's about. His father was a waterman. So he says. He's got river-water in his blood. Sadly, I've got nothing to offer you, my friends. The galley is bare. Give me a couple of minutes. I'll get something from the tavern. A bottle and some food, eh? We don't need to starve. They usually have something. In the kitchen. I'll see what I can get."

"Stay aboard, Septimus!" Mr Serocoal suggested as

the captain left. "It's late. You don't have to go. Have a drink with us. Eat something."

"I need to move. I've left things in my chamber. My books and papers. My landlady has been threatening to throw me out. I'm just a *little* behind with the rent. My absence will have been noted. She'll be thinking that I've been locked-up. Or murdered. Preferably the latter. We're not the best of friends."

"Where are you living?"

"The Crow Hotel. In Limehouse."

"*Ah!* Mrs Lusardi! *Gloria!* I knew her. In the old days. Her husband took poison. Poor soul. I haven't seen her for years. She was quite a girl, in her day."

"She's still quite a girl."

"*Ha, ha, ha!*"

Mr Serocoal's gold teeth flashed in the lamplight.

"Our troubles are all but over, Septimus. I'll get the scales brought round at the crack of dawn. We'll do the work down in the hold. Out of sight. It shouldn't take long. Once we know what we've got we'll go and see my old friend Mr Orzinga."

"He's going to have to find a lot of money. Very quickly."

"It will be fine. He has *connections.* If you know what I mean. In *banking* and so on. He's a Freemason. Westminster Lodge. That's the sort of circles he moves in. I've known him all my life. I've been dealing with him for a *long* time."

"What kind of dealings?"

"Well... you know. Passing things on. Bits and bobs that have come my way. Not just gold. He *collects* things.

Antiquities and curios. He'll probably show you his collection, while we're there. He's enormously proud of it. I've acted as a sort of... *middleman* for him. Over the years. He doesn't like getting his hands dirty. He has his reputation as a gentleman to think of. I've frequently procured gold for him. The proceeds of country-house robberies and coach hold-ups. I would melt the items down and pass the gold on. With false bills-of-sale. Small amounts, generally. An ounce here. An ounce there. Nothing on this scale."

"Does he have any idea of what we've got?"

"A fair idea. I told him *roughly* half a ton. *Possibly* more. Just to get his reaction. He didn't even blink. He says he can raise the money. He'll just need a day or two. He won't let us down. I could see the interest in his eyes when I first broached the matter with him. The flicker of greed! He *wants* this gold. It's going to be bloody good business for him. He'll probably re-sell it. In Antwerp. In six months' time. For twice what he paid us for it. But that's just the way the world works. We can't really complain. We're damned lucky to have a buyer."

Septimus gave a philosophical shrug.

"What are your own plans, Mr Serocoal? America?"

"My wife is averse to sea-travel, unfortunately. We may just pack our things and move to the English countryside. I've got a place in mind. A fortified manor house with a hundred acres. Near St. Albans. I came across it quite by chance. I've already made enquiries. You could come and visit, Septimus. Once we're settled. The place has forty rooms. So I'm told. I'd get lonely, I think, if no-one came."

"You'll have to give me the address."

Captain Smalt had returned. With food and drink.

"You, too, Captain," Mr Serocoal said. "You'll be most welcome."

"We'll need to keep in touch," the captain agreed. "There's no pleasure like chewing the cud with old friends. Glass in hand! Remembering the old days! I plan to sail south, with the divine Harriet, but we'll be coming back, I'm quite sure. Harriet will miss London. It's her spiritual home. What about you, Septimus?"

"I'm still undecided. I have some, uh... *unfinished business.* An affair of the heart, you might say. If I can resolve things I'll sail to New York with Lachlan. We could take Billy with us. The lad might find his feet, in a new land. Mulu, too. Why not? The further we all are from London, the better, it seems to me."

The men grunted in agreement. Septimus rose to his feet.

"I'll have to be getting along. It will take me a while to get home. Could one of you lend me a shilling? For the boat? I didn't think to ask Lachlan."

Mr Serocoal pulled out a couple of tarnished old shillings.

"They're genuine! Don't worry. Try the tavern, as you go by. Some of the local boatmen drink in there. Some of them seem to *live* in there. One of 'em will row you home, I'm sure. Even at this hour. I'll try and stamp a few golden guineas tomorrow. We're hardly paupers! We don't need to suffer."

Septimus wished the men a good night and clambered out into the fog. The dog snarled as he appeared on deck.

It was chewing a bloody piece of bone.

Even for the dog, things were looking up.

The tavern was still busy. Septimus could hear the racket of the place the moment he got ashore. A drunken fight was in progress. Furniture was being hurled around. By the sound of things. A woman was screaming. At the top of her voice. Septimus walked straight past. There were some stairs at the mouth of the creek where he thought he'd be able to hail a boat. Despite the fog and the late hour.

It was close to midnight.

His only ambition was to get home.

And sleep...

14

A MIDNIGHT VISITATION

Zeelandia Street was deserted. It was uncannily quiet. All Septimus could hear as he trudged up the street was the sound of his own feet. The fog was so thick he could barely see where he was. The Crow Hotel, when he finally got there, looked ruinous and abandoned. The lamp in the entrance porch was unlit.

Candles were burning in the front hall. One of the greasy kitchen wenches was mopping the floor, in the smoky light. She sneered, evilly, at Septimus.

The night-watchman was nowhere to be seen.

He's probably out in the yard, Septimus thought. *On a call of nature.*

Wearily, he ascended the stairs. A lighted candle had been left out on the first-floor landing – for the benefit of the establishment's *more desirable* guests.

The cheaper rooms were higher up. On the top floors.

Septimus pilfered the candle and took it up with him.

Cunning eyes followed his progress. *Feline eyes.* Weirdly aglow in the moving candlelight. Mrs Lusardi's familiars *owned* the place at night.

Septimus's chamber, as far as he could tell, was exactly as he'd left it. Nothing had been moved. He dropped his haversack and put the stolen candle down on the table. He was tired and hungry, but... *elated,* too. Things on the whole had gone better than he'd expected. He was relieved to be still alive. The gold was safely stowed. On the *Sabrina Louise.* In Deptford Creek. It wasn't a dream.

He'd seen it with his own eyes. He'd touched it and smelled it.

We bloody did it... he thought.

Two innocent men had died, even so, he reminded himself. As well as the entire crew of the other ship, though it was all they deserved, after their atrocious treatment of the unfortunate *capitaine.* The poor bastard had lost his wits.

The flying creature had then finished him off. Or so it had seemed. The yellow slime had dissolved his flesh. The severed foot had chased him over the side. Septimus had no idea of what the flying creature could have been. He'd never before seen anything like it. Except in nightmares. And in curious old books.

He pushed the troubled thoughts out of his mind.

There was nothing to eat in his room and it didn't seem a good moment to go poking around downstairs. The wench in the hall would no doubt have reported his reappearance. To the authorities. There was no telling what they might do if they caught him in the kitchen. Stealing food. It hardly bore thinking about.

Mercifully, he *did* have something to drink. The foreign liquor. He hadn't touched it since the night of Susie's death. There was still some of it left.

He rooted the heavy bottle out and poured himself a glass.

"*Aaaahhh...*" he moaned, as the first delectable mouthful went down.

It was just what his body needed. He sat in the candlelight while he drank. His chamber smelled of damp and dust and loneliness. It was cold and empty, but the stolen candle gave off a little warmth and the magical foreign liquor did the rest.

Before long the entire cosmos was spinning. Slowly and majestically. The way it sometimes did, late at night, when he'd been drinking. Owls and lost cats howled in the blackness outside. Mice scuttled in the wainscoting. Like restless ghosts.

Septimus dragged his boots off.

"*I'm going to be rich!*" he confided to the shadows. "*Dear Lord!* Who would ever have thought it? I'm *already* rich. *Arguably.* All we have to do is collect the bloody money. It will be a new beginning. I'll be starting afresh."

The bottle was all-too-soon empty. He sat in the candlelight for a while. Half-lost in dreams. Then, with a sigh, he crossed to his bed and clambered in. Sleep took him very quickly. For an hour or more he slept like a stone. When he woke again – disturbed by some sound – he wasn't *immediately* sure where he was. Inexplicable creaks and groans were coming out of the dark. His bed seemed to be *moving*. For a moment he thought he was back on the ship. But then – he remembered walking home. Through the midnight fog. And creeping upstairs.

He peered out from under his blankets.

Something was tapping at the window.

Tat-a-tat! Tat! Tat! Tat!

It was hail, he realised, as he came to his senses.

Once again, unholy ice was tumbling from the heavens.

"Lord, save us!" he muttered.

A luminous twist of smoke was floating in the gloom above his table. He'd forgotten to snuff the candle. It had almost burned out. He stared sleepily at the waxy smoke and the tiny flame below. As he watched, *something moved,* in the darkness beyond the flame. A ghostly presence. Its garments rustled as it turned.

Septimus's heart pounded.

"Uh?" he grunted. *"What the...?"*

He pushed himself up. And froze.

"Susie?"

Susie Kettle was sitting in one of his chairs. He hadn't noticed her. She'd been sitting so still. Her hair was unpinned. Eldritch light was flickering in the gloom around her. *Ghostly light.* She was wearing the same, beautiful, red silk dress that she'd worn on the night of her murder, but she looked... *different.*

Her skin was misty grey. Her eyes were golden and luminous.

"Susie? *Dear God!* Is it really you? Am I dreaming?"

"Does it matter? *I am here.* Is that not enough? I have broken all the rules to do this. To see you again. I may be punished. *I am changing, Septimus.* The process is almost complete. I am slipping away. From the world we once shared. Queen Mbembé is growing in power. As each day passes. As more souls are drawn towards her ineffable light. The Final Reckoning is at hand. As prophesied.

In the ancient texts. I tried to communicate with you at Egypt Point, but I couldn't get your attention. You were preoccupied. Your mind was on other things."

"The *gold* was the only thing on my mind! That monstrous effigy of your new mistress. She *squealed,* horribly, when we chopped her ugly head off!"

"I know all that, Septimus. I see everything, now. From on high. *I am trying to save you!* From the consequences of your actions. *Join me!* My darling. Here in the light! *Redeem yourself!* Take my hand! *We will be together forever..."*

Her golden eyes shone, like alchemical charms, through the murk.

She extended a grey hand, as though to claim him.

Septimus shrank back against his lumpy mattress.

"No-o-o-o-o!!!" he wailed. "I *loved* you, Susie! *I swear!* I love you still! There *is* no-one else! *Only you!* But, obviously... *our situation has changed!"*

"Ha, ha, ha!" she laughed.

She was floating, now. High up, among fiery clouds.

"I'm not the only woman you've lied to, Septimus. There have been *so many* of us. *So many lies.* There was that pretty whore in Calcutta, for instance."

"Zaira! My God! Is she still alive?"

"Very much so. And then there was that other woman. In Port-au-Prince. The one who ran off with all your money. Another wounded soul."

"Rozalita. The beautiful Rozalita."

"Yes. She died, sadly. Barely a year later. From alcohol poisoning. That's what she spent your money on. Black rum. The last word she ever spoke was your name. *Septimuso!* A whispered word in the tropical night. The French soldier she was with didn't know what she meant, and she was too drunk to explain."

"Oh, Jesus..."

Septimus wasn't sure what point Susie Kettle was trying to make. He was starting to wish that she'd go away and leave him alone. He was shivering. The room was horrendously cold, suddenly. He felt sick and dizzy.

Her silk dress fluttered up as she floated above him. A fleeting glimpse of her thighs inflamed him. The old heartache returned. The impossible longing. He stumbled to his feet with the feeling that he, too, might fly. If he just tried hard enough. All it took was willpower, he told himself. He reached up towards her.

"No!" she screamed.

She extended her seraphic wings and hovered. Out of reach.

"Not now, my love! It cannot be! *You are not yet one of the immortals!* The days of humanity are numbered, Septimus. Soon all the lands of the Earth will be laid to waste. The moon and stars will be extinguished. Fire and flood will obliterate the great cities of the world. I came here to warn you. *Look..."*

She pointed to the crumbling wall behind Septimus's washing-stand. The one she'd burst through on her last visit. Once again, the wall began to dissolve.

A ravaged landscape appeared. Winged creatures were circling, high up, in a blood-red, fiery sky. Smoke was rising from a distant mountain range. As though the mountains themselves were on fire. On the plain below, a mysterious, dark wave was forming. It was spreading out over the landscape. Like a primordial flood. As it edged closer, Septimus realised that it was, in fact, *an army*. A multitude of ghostly, identical forms. Grey shades, in pointed hoods that concealed their faces.

"What are they?" Septimus whispered.

"The numberless dead. No earthly power will prevail against them. Once they are set loose. Their new bodies are already stirring. Underground. In the depths of the earth. The darkness, I fear, will not hold them for much longer."

Septimus groaned and gripped his nose as the dreadful stink of death rose up around him. The scene filled his entire field of vision. As though he was looking down from the top of an impossibly high tower. The sky all around was dotted with ghastly, fire-breathing creatures. Like the one he'd shot down at Egypt Point.

They were circling. Hungrily. Like vultures.

The grey army halted, suddenly. The left and right flanks drew apart. A spectral vehicle appeared. A shimmering black coach. In the shape of a beetle. Drawn by a hundred black horses. Dust streamed up from the beasts' hooves.

The equipage thundered to a halt.

A low moan rose from the assembled multitude.

"Behold – our master!" Susie Kettle murmured.

Septimus's ancient foe stepped down from the conveyance. Hermetic signs sparkled in the folds of his cloak as he turned towards Septimus. His face was hidden. There was *nothing* inside the pointed hood, as far as Septimus could see.

Only darkness.

Septimus had seen enough. He stepped back... and fell. *Down and down.* When he eventually landed, lifetimes later, he found himself back in his own bed.

His relief was short-lived.

The Grand High Pontieff was standing in the moonlight at his feet.

"Uuuuugh..." Septimus moaned.

He stared up in horror at the faceless figure. When he tried to wriggle away he found himself unable to move. An unearthly force was pushing him down.

Pinning him to the bed. The black-robed apparition moved closer. Silently, with skeletal fingers, it pulled back its ghastly hood and revealed its awful face.

The murderous visage of Isaiah Blackthorpe!

Septimus shivered in terror as the great lord reached into the folds of his cloak and pulled out a sinister-looking chirurgical instrument. A glass vessel in a shiny metal frame, with levers and wheels, valves made of imported French rubber and a sharp point at one end. The kind of thing that horse-doctors used to impregnate inexperienced mares. Septimus whimpered. He tried again to move but he couldn't fight the evil force that was holding him. He was as helpless as a corpse. The glass bulb of the instrument was full of bubbling, freshly-secreted *Eau Sacré*.

With a hideous laugh, Lord Blackthorpe stepped forward and plunged the pointed end of the instrument into Septimus's guts. He pushed and pushed. *Deeper and deeper.* The *Eau Sacré* gushed out and flooded into every part of Septimus's being. It gurgled in his brain and spurted from his ears. Blackthorpe giggled. He pulled the terrible contrivance out and waved it, triumphantly, in the cold air.

An audience of ghouls applauded, from the shadows.

Septimus moaned and wailed. He summoned all his strength and kicked out at Lord Blackthorpe. He rattled his bed against the floor in the hope that *somebody* would hear, and come to his rescue. But no-one heard. No-one came.

In a final attempt to save himself, he opened his mouth and screamed. Loud enough to waken the dead.

"Aaaaaaaaaaaahhhhhhhh!!!"

Instantly, everything changed. Lord Blackthorpe vanished. There was a sudden commotion in the corridor outside. Doors were opening. Floorboards were squeaking. Septimus could hear people muttering and cursing.

He wasn't *quite* sure what was going on.

"Mr Slim!" somebody shouted. *"Mr Slim!"*

It was Mrs Lusardi. Septimus was still shaking. He was *cold*. He didn't particularly want to talk to anybody. The candle on his table had burned out. He could barely see a thing. Spit was dribbling out of his mouth and running down his chin. A horrible, icy pool of it had soaked into his mattress. Somebody was banging on his door. He put his hands over his ears to shut out the awful noise.

"Mr Slim!"

"Uuugh?" Septimus grunted.

The door-knob rattled. Mrs Lusardi's shrunken apple of a face appeared as the door creaked open. She was clutching a candle. Septimus had evidently not locked the door when he'd come in. Mrs Lusardi raised the candle and peered into the room. When she'd made sure that it was safe she pushed the door wide open and marched through. She was attired in a sleeping-bonnet, and the pink woollen dressing-gown that she donned when troublesome guests brought her out at night.

Her nose twitched as she peered around.

"It *smells* in here," she said. "Do you *always* sleep in your clothes?"

"*Uuuh...*"

More faces appeared. Some of Septimus's neighbours had come in to take a look at him. He didn't recognise any of them. Septimus rarely encountered his fellow lodgers. He didn't think much of the specimens in his doorway. They looked like the kind of people who would jeer at condemned men on their way to the gallows, or throw dead cats at petty criminals in the stocks.

He glowered at them from his bed.

Mrs Lusardi made a brief tour of inspection. Her candle fluttered and smoked as she poked around. Her nose wrinkled disapprovingly as she peered into the chamber's dusty corners and sniffed the unwholesome air.

"Why were you making all that noise?" she asked him. "Are you intoxicated? *Have you gone quite mad?* We thought someone was trying to *murder* you. One of your drunken friends, perhaps. I was on the point of sending Podo out to bring the constables. *It's three in the morning.* In case you hadn't noticed."

Podo? Septimus thought, confusedly. *Who's Podo?*

She had a bad-tempered little dog that pissed in

the corridors and stole things from people's rooms. It didn't like Septimus much. If it saw him coming it would retreat and growl – from a safe distance. It had even bitten him, once. He'd come to think that it didn't like the slightly odd, decayed smell of his leather coat.

He smirked at the thought of little Podo, scampering bravely off into the night to raise the alarm, and summon the constables.

Surely not, he thought. *It must be the old man downstairs.*

Mrs Lusardi glared at him.

"I'm glad you find this amusing, Mr Slim, but... *I do not,* I'm afraid. We simply cannot continue like this. My patience is quite exhausted. I'm a reasonable woman, as you well know, but... *I will not be taken advantage of.* My late husband, were he still alive, would have thrown you out long ago. You haven't paid your rent for weeks. We haven't even *seen* you for several days. I can only presume that you were too drunk to find your way back from wherever you've been. Either that or you've been locked-up somewhere. Which wouldn't surprise me in the slightest."

"My dear lady..."

"I am *not* your *dear lady,* Mr Slim. I want you *out.* That's all there is to it. This dreadful screaming, at all hours, is simply... *the final straw.* You can stay until morning, I suppose. If you must. Until midday, let's say. It would be *unchristian* of me to throw you out right now. But... *by midday,* at the latest, I want you *gone.* Do we understand each other? Just take your things and leave. Is that quite clear?"

She raised the candle and looked around.

"If you *have* any things, that is."

"It was just a dream," Septimus protested. "A dreadful dream."

He tried his best to look contrite.

"A nightmare. I'm an old soldier. I fought for King and country. For the British Empire. And the East India Company. *In the malarial swamps of Bengal.* In the steaming jungle. I still carry the scars. I still have the dreams. It doesn't happen often. If you could just bear with me, madam. *For another day or two.* I have money on its way. I can recompense you. For the inconvenience."

"*Tomorrow,* Mr Slim. That's my final word. If you can pay your dues we can talk things over. Otherwise, you'll have to find yourself some new lodgings. For the moment – I'll bid you goodnight. Or good morning. As the case may be. *Please* don't make any more noise. As things stand, I'll expect you to be gone by midday. *At the very latest.* I will need to have this chamber *thoroughly cleaned.*"

Septimus's loathsome neighbours were still lurking in the doorway. Mrs Lusardi pushed past them and departed, tut-tutting furiously as she went. Septimus got up and slammed the door. Silence returned as the little crowd dispersed.

He sat on the edge of the bed and scratched himself. In the dark.

Was it just a dream? he asked himself. *Or am I really going mad?*

He didn't *desperately* care whether Mrs Lusardi threw him out or not. Lachlan had offered to put him up. For a day or two. Until they'd been paid. It would be a cruel irony, even so, he told himself, to be evicted from his flea-ridden Limehouse lodgings, when he was so close to becoming as rich as a bloody lord.

The idea of America was growing on him.

A new life in New York.

With a weary sigh, he climbed back into bed.

Just one more week, he thought, *and I'll be free.*

15

THE CREATURE STRIKES AGAIN

It was daylight when Septimus woke. He didn't feel good. He hadn't slept well. Somebody was sweeping the floorboards outside his room. One of the sullen servant girls, he guessed. The wretch was banging her broom against the bottom of his door, as though she was under orders to make as much noise as possible.

"Damnable women!" he muttered.

Mrs Lusardi had given him until noon to pay his bill, he recalled, as the events of the night came back to him. He wasn't sure how long he'd slept. It was early morning, as far as he could make out. Going by the light. He still had time to find the money. It was hardly a fortune. A couple of guineas. He could borrow it.

He lay in bed for a while. Listening to the familiar sounds of morning. The calls and cries of milkmen and coalmen. Barrow-boys and fire-ash collectors.

Smoke was puffing from a chimney in the yard.

The water boiler was in use, it seemed. The luckier guests would be enjoying their morning ablutions. In the privacy of their chambers. Septimus was forbidden this convenience. He'd been washing as best he could in horse-troughs and rainwater butts, but on this particular morning he was in desperate need of a bath.

The carnage at Egypt Point had left him feeling soiled.

He searched his pockets and found a few small coins. A sixpenny piece he'd forgotten he had, and some change from the two shillings that Mr Serocoal had given him, the night before. Almost enough, in fact, for an hour at the Cable Street bath-house, but he didn't have time for that. He would have to face the servants.

There was a glorious smell of coffee in the air when he got downstairs. It was coming from the main parlour. Septimus took a sneaky look, in the hope that he could filch a cup, but... it wasn't to be. Several splendid-looking fellows in powdered wigs were at the table, enjoying a cooked breakfast. Ships' officers, by the look of them. The Crow Hotel catered for such types. As well as for general travellers. The cook herself was serving the food. Mrs Lusardi was notably absent. Septimus thought that she'd probably slept late, after all the merriment of the night.

He crept down the hall and peered into the kitchen. The only person in sight was one of the grimy urchins who stoked the boiler, out in the backyard.

"Is, uh... hot water available, boy?" Septimus asked him.

"Not t' you, sir. I *'as orders*. You don't live 'ere no more."

"I'm allowed to stay until midday, as a matter of fact. Mrs Lusardi and I have come to an amicable agreement. You are clearly not well-informed. I'll take two buckets, if you would be so kind. You can't deny me *water*, for

God's sake. It's not as though it *costs* you anything. It falls from the bloody heavens. Like mercy."

A cunning look stole across the lad's face.

"But this ain't *any* old water, sir. It's been *purified*. By the Limehouse Water Company. And then there's the cost o' the *coal* to be thought of. You'll 'ave to pay in advance, sir. Two shillin'. I'll be in *serious* trouble if I get caught."

"Two shillings! You conniving little bastard! That's daylight robbery! I'll give you sixpence. Not a penny more. What do you say? Do we have a deal?"

"For that you only get 'arf a bucket."

"Damn you to hell! I'll be in my chamber. You can bring it up."

He handed over the sixpence. It wasn't the end of the world. Mr Serocoal was hoping to strike a few golden guineas, later in the day. If he could find the time. He was going to melt down one of the candlesticks. From the cargo. The coins would be easy to pass. In the waterside taverns. They'd be as good as the real thing.

The bucket was barely half-full when it eventually arrived, but Septimus could hardly complain. He gave the lad another penny. For his trouble. The water was brown and smelly – despite the best efforts of the Limehouse Water Company – but it was hot. Septimus pulled all his clothes off, for the first time in weeks, and scrubbed himself down with a lump of hard soap and a piece of old rag.

He redressed in the cleanest clothes he could find and tidied his hair in front of the mirror. It felt good to be clean again. They were to meet the goldsmith, that afternoon, at his residence. Three of them would go, it had been decided. Septimus, Lachlan, and Mr Serocoal. Lachlan had stressed the need to look respectable.

The goldsmith wasn't some common rogue.

He was a *gentleman*. With connections to the highest in the land.

Septimus locked his door as he left and pocketed the key.

Numerous official pronouncements had been pasted-up, overnight, on the local walls, he noticed, as he hurried round to Thieves' Street. New taxes were to be levied, to finance the escalating war with France. Hawkers and other casual traders were to be licensed. From now on, they would have to pay *ten shillings a year* for the privilege of erecting their booths and stalls on the public pavements.

It was a sorry idea, Septimus thought as he walked. Most of the ill-fated souls in that line of work were poor and illiterate. The only thing the new law would bring about would be an increase in the prison population. And more starving families.

On Claypit Lane, down by the river, elegantly-dressed devotees of the Crocodile Queen were handing out invitations to one of their satanic ceremonies.

Septimus already had one. He quickened his step with the intention of hurrying past, but then, to his astonishment, he recognised one of the women.

It was Lady Henrietta de Vere. Septimus could hardly believe his eyes. He hadn't seen her for at least twenty years. He stopped and stared. Lady de Vere had been a regular guest at Ermine House, during Septimus's time there. She'd been a famous beauty. Notorious for her *risqué* relationships, and her reckless gambling.

Septimus had only ever exchanged polite words with her, in his capacity as a footman, but he'd suspected that she'd known all about his secret *affaire*.

She'd had a curious, pensive way of watching him. Sometimes.

Across a busy room, perhaps. When she thought he wasn't looking.

Septimus wasn't entirely surprised that Lady de Vere had become involved with the mysterious Sign of the Crocodile Queen. She'd always been just a *tiny* bit odd. What *did* surprise him was how *young* she looked. How little she'd changed. Over the years. Even the hat she was wearing – a huge, black, lacy thing – was entirely in character. As he stared, she turned, suddenly, and caught his eye.

"My good man..." she called out, invitingly.

She raised a gloved hand and waved. Septimus got ready to run. He wasn't sure if she'd recognised him. It seemed unlikely. After so long.

Lady de Vere stepped closer.

"Don't be alarmed, good sir! We are not seeking your vote, or the contents of your purse. Our only concern is your health and well-being! Have you by chance heard of Queen Mbembé, the Goddess of Good Fortune and Prosperity?"

"Uuuhh..."

"You have?"

"I may have 'eard, uh... *mention*."

"Then this, good sir, is a *golden opportunity* to find

out more! All we ask is a *moment of your time.* It will be to your advantage, I promise you. There will be a *public ceremony,* this very evening, in the parish of Wapping. At the ..."

She stopped, suddenly, and stared intently at Septimus.

"Have I not met you before, somewhere?"

"Oi think not, ma'am," Septimus mumbled.

Her eyes narrowed.

"I must be mistaken. For a moment, I was reminded of someone."

With a sigh, she handed him one of the printed cards.

"Take it, sir, if you would be so kind. It is an invitation to this evening's proceedings. At the Gaiety Theatre in Wapping. *Please do attend!* You will receive *twenty shillings.* Just for coming! *Twenty silver shillings!* There is a handbill, too. If you would like one. Are you literate? Can you read?"

Of course I can bloody read, Septimus thought, irritably.

He caught her eye, fleetingly. It was so *very* strange to see her again. He was sorely tempted to confess who he was and ask for news of Lady Constance. But he decided against it. The ghastly Lord Blackthorpe had been one of Lady de Vere's many lovers. Despite her good looks, and her smiles, he didn't really trust her. '

"Thank 'ee kindly," he grunted, as he hurried off.

"Be sure to come!" she called after him.

Septimus didn't respond. The encounter had shaken him. Memories of his days at Ermine House flooded back. He couldn't think when he'd last seen Lady de Vere. It would have been at some ball, or banquet, he imagined. The house would have been full of people. He would have been on duty. With the other footmen.

He glanced back, from the end of the street. The curiously ageless Lady de Vere had already accosted another passer-by. The fellow was scrutinising the card she'd given him. He seemed bemused. Twenty shillings was a considerable sum.

Septimus, too, was a little bewildered. He examined his own card as he walked. He had two of them, now. He was vaguely wondering if he might be able to claim a double payment. *Forty shillings!* It would be more money than he'd seen for a while. Enough to appease Mrs Lusardi and still have a ha'penny or two left over. The affair was to take place at the old Gaiety Theatre in Wapping. Septimus was tempted to attend. It wasn't far. He could be there and back in an hour.

He wondered if they'd expect him to drink the *Eau Sacré* again. Before they'd give him the money. He'd been having peculiar dreams, since his first encounter with the stuff. Though it didn't seem to have done him any great harm otherwise.

For twenty shillings I'd drink rat-piss, he thought.

He unfolded the handbill she'd given him. It was poorly printed, on rough paper. There was an apocalyptic engraved scene at the top of the sheet, with burning buildings, skulls, bones, flooded cities and rotting corpses. The Crocodile Queen was floating serenely above it all, with her immense, magnificent wings outstretched.

It looked like an advertisement for fire insurance.

The text was a noisy tirade about the End of the World. The godless cities of Europe and America, it claimed, would soon be laid to waste by Fire, Flood and Plague. There would be no more Drinking and Whoring. No more Dancing, Gambling and Making Merry. *All that was over.* Only the Crocodile Queen offered Hope and Salvation. To those brave enough to partake of her *mystic secretions.*

Septimus screwed the bill up and tossed it into a nearby pile of horse-shit.

He'd heard it all before. Toothless old men were preaching hell-fire and damnation on every street-corner in London. Generally speaking they were expecting the world to end at midnight on the last day of the century. The end of December, 1799.

Which at least gave mankind another few years of drinking and whoring.

The prophets of The Sign seemed less optimistic.

The handbill didn't give a specific date for the end of everything but the urgent tone suggested that it wasn't far off. A few days, *at the very most,* the thunderous black print seemed to be saying, and that would be it. *Finis.*

"What nonsense," Septimus muttered, under his breath.

He spat into a puddle. He didn't believe a word.

The world around him looked solid enough. People were going about their business, as usual. Pigs were foraging in the muddy streets. The air was warming, just a little, as the night-fog cleared. Carts and carriages were clattering past.

On top of all that, Septimus was about to become rich.

Lachlan was waiting for him. At the tavern.

"Am I late?" Septimus asked.

"Not at all. Sit yourself down. We still have to wait for Mr Serocoal. He should be on his way. Everything is in hand. Billy was here, earlier."

He dropped his voice. There were other people within earshot.

"The news is good," he whispered. "Billy and Mr Serocoal have been up since before dawn, weighing the gold. There's *almost* a bloody ton, Billy says. Eighteen hundredweight, just over. Not *quite* a ton, but damned close. I'm enormously relieved. I didn't sleep well. I was worried that the final figure was going to be much lower. But I needn't have worried. Clézio's estimate was *just about* right. We're going to *prosper*, Septimus. The five of us. I've been doing the sums, in my head, while I've been sitting here. We'll have a few small bills to pay. For the weapons, mostly, and the work that was done on the ship. It won't be much. *The rest is all ours.* Every last bloody penny."

"There were other costs," Septimus pointed out. "I'm thinking of the loss of life. Clézio and young Spiker. The poor bastards. Spiker was just an innocent lad."

"Of course..."

Lachlan hung his head.

"We can't bring 'em back. What's done is done. Sadly. Mulu is still angry. We've talked a bit. She understands, I think. Deep down. I've promised to light candles. In remembrance. As soon as I can. At the Church of Our Lady of the Assumption and St. Gregory. For their heavenly souls. Spiker's share of the proceeds will go to Mulu, of course. I think we've all agreed on that.

Clézio's case is more difficult. He had a Dutch wife. As I understand. In Ostend. The trouble is, he had other wives. In other ports. He once told me that he had thirty or forty children, scattered around northern France and the Low Countries. I could put advertisements in the local newspapers, I suppose, reporting his untimely death and asking his dependents to get in touch with me. Here in England."

"Would that be wise? A thousand screaming women might turn up, all claiming to be widows of the late *Capitaine Clézio*. How could we prove otherwise?"

"Heh, heh! You're right, of course. I hadn't thought of it. People are so damned dishonest, these days. The simplest solution, I suppose, would be to track down his most recent wife and leave it at that. It would salve my conscience. I could take the packet-boat over to Ostend. If the French haven't closed the port."

Madam O'Reilly came over with some coffee and freshly-made bread. Her enormous breasts slipped out of her bodice as she leaned over the table. Septimus pretended not to notice. She giggled as she readjusted her underclothes.

"Welcome back, gentlemen! I've missed you! You've had... *things to attend to.* I know. Harriet whispered in my ear. All went well, I trust?"

"Tolerably well," Lachlan assured her.

"I'm not one to pry," she responded, with a sly wink.

"Has it been peaceful?" Lachlan asked. "In our absence?"

"Hardly. Quite the opposite, in fact. There was another murder. On the night you left. A dreadful affair.

I'm surprised you haven't heard. The story was even in the newspapers. Everybody has been talking about it. It seems that you were right all along, Septimus. These crimes are not the work of some solitary lunatic. There's a *creature* on the loose. *A blood-sucking serpent!*"

Septimus almost choked on his coffee.

"Really?"

Madam O'Reilly pulled another chair across and sat down.

"It's shocking news, I know, but it does appear to be true. The creature has actually been *seen*. In confused circumstances, it has to be said, but, even so..."

"What happened?"

"Another poor soul was killed. Just down the street. At the Fox and Duck. A short while after midnight. On the day you left. It was a foggy night, as you probably remember. *Cold, too.* We'd bolted all the doors. Back and front. So that nobody could get in without knocking. I'd even locked the upstairs windows."

"Who was the victim?"

"A serving-wench at the Fox and Duck. A lovely girl, by all accounts. She was in bed with her friend, one of the other wenches, when the attack took place. The other girl escaped. That's how we know. *She saw the bloody thing!*"

"But she survived? This other girl?"

"By some miracle. We took her in. The poor child had fled in terror. She'd run all the way out into the street. Stark naked. Out into the cold fog. Screaming and shouting and hammering on every bloody door she came to."

Madam O'Reilly refilled the men's cups. The coffee was still hot.

"We'd been busy, that evening. You know how it is, sometimes. The place was still packed. We'd heard the screams, obviously. I opened the front door and went out. With some of the men. The girl heard us calling and ran towards us. She was shaking like a leaf. She was absolutely terrified. We brought her inside."

"What did she say?"

"Very little, at first. She just whimpered and moaned. I sat her down by the fire and got her some brandy. One of the girls found her a blanket. She was half frozen. We couldn't get much sense at all out of her. She was in such a state."

"Understandably, uh?"

"But then... as the brandy took effect, she began to talk. She and her friend had been in bed together, she told us. At the end of a long day. They seem to have been maids-of-all-work. Forced to share a cot in a poky attic room. *'It was a serpent!'* she wailed. *'A creature from the pits of hell! It burst through the bloody wall!'* Somehow, she'd managed to crawl away. Her friend was less lucky."

"Dear Lord..." Septimus murmured. "So... this is what killed Susie, eh? It's plain to see. It struck at close to midnight, in both cases. *It's a creature of the night.* I've heard of such things. You were wise to lock the windows. There could be more of them out there. In the fog. *Dozens of them.* We just don't know."

"Septimus... please!" Madam O'Reilly protested.

She mopped her face with the cloth she was carrying.

"Did the girl say anything more?" Septimus asked.

"Eventually. We found her some clothes and got her warmed-up a bit. I gave her a drop of laudanum. Just a drop. I keep a bottle in my parlour. For my legs. Some drunken idiots from the Fox and Duck were out in the street. Screaming and shouting and calling for the watch. We took the poor girl upstairs. For her own safety. You know how it is. It didn't look good. She could have been arrested."

"What was her name?"

"Isabella. She was Italian. The girl who died was Irish. The pair had been asleep in bed. They'd been up since before dawn. Lighting fires and emptying chamber-pots. Isabella had woken when the room had started shaking. She'd thought at first that it was an earthquake. They have them, apparently, in the place she's from. Then the wall behind her *exploded* as the creature burst through. It was *hideous,* she said. With red eyes and fiery breath. The night air filled with blood as the ghastly thing gorged on her friend. Isabella thought it was the end. *For both of them.* But then, somehow, while the creature was at its evil work, she unbolted the chamber door and got out. She just ran. For her life. Screaming as she went."

"Dear God! How *big* was this thing? Do we know?"

"It appears to have been enormous. I think she only saw it for a second or two before she ran. It had rows of pointed teeth, she said. And... *tentacles."*

"Tentacles? You mean, like, uh... *an octopus?"*

"I think that's what she meant. Her English wasn't so good. Little was left of the poor soul who died, I learned later. The remains were barely recognisable. It all happened very quickly, by the sound of things. A small mercy, I suppose."

"Uh, huh..."

Septimus rubbed his eyes and scratched his head.

"Where is she now? This Italian girl?"

"I sent her away. Out of London. To Norwich. She'd been in service up there when she first came to England. So she said. She thought her old employers might take her back. It seemed for the best. I bought her a ticket and put her on the morning coach. With a few shillings in her pocket. It would have been *far* too dangerous for her to stay in Limehouse. Those half-wits from the Fox and Duck would have had her burned at the stake. They were *convinced* that she'd done it."

"It must have looked that way. To a late-night crowd of drunks. Was there any connection with the, uh... *French cult?* Do you happen to know? Was either girl involved? It seems to have been a factor in all these killings. Susie's included."

Madam O'Reilly's brow creased.

"I don't really know. I hardly knew the girl. We'd passed the time of day, occasionally, out in the street. I believe she was from County Cork. Though a pair of those disgusting hooded *priests* came for the body, early the next morning, now you mention it. The hearse appeared at the crack o' dawn. I'd been up all night with Isabella. She was in a terrible state. I was afraid to leave her alone."

"So – what time did the hearse come?"

"Around first light. It must have been about half past six. I went out to get some milk, from the dairy down the road. I saw them bringing the dead girl out. They'd nailed her into a rough wooden box, the poor soul. As though her life was worth nothing. I lit a candle for her. Later in the day, at St. Cecilia's. It was all I could do, really. I said a few prayers. I was more concerned for Isabella."

Lachlan had stopped listening. He was scribbling something in the little book he carried around with him. Lachlan was a rationalist. He still believed that the man with the waxed moustache had killed Susie Kettle. The other murders didn't particularly interest him. They weren't *personal*. They were just stories.

Septimus was puzzling about something else.

"How did those so-called bloody priests *know* about this latest murder?" he asked. "How did they know where to come? It makes no sense. The same thing happened on the night Susie died. On that occasion, too, they turned up at dawn to collect the body. Nobody had *asked* them to come. And then *another* unfortunate girl is killed, days later, on the same street, and once again – in the grey dawn light – a Sign of the Crocodile Queen hearse turns up to collect the remains. *How did they know?* How *could* they know? Who told them? A ghost? A little bird?"

Lachlan shrugged and folded his pocket-book.

"Bad news travels fast," he suggested.

"Indeed, but..."

Madam O'Reilly got to her feet. Other customers were trying to get her attention. She hurried off, clutching a tin tray and the empty coffee-pot.

"What bloody nonsense!" Lachlan muttered, when she'd gone. "She means well, of course, but... a *human being* is committing these terrible crimes. *A man*. A man possessed by the devil, quite clearly, but a *man*, nonetheless. Not some bloody *creature*. Crawling around

in the small hours. In search of female flesh. *For heaven's sakes!* I heard the whole story earlier. From one the girls. With even more gory details. It's just gossip! *They make it up as they go along.*"

"But..."

"*No, no, no!* Madam O'Reilly is just repeating what she's been told. You know what they're like, these waterside girls. They *drink* to excess. They don't *eat* properly. They consume *weird concoctions,* for the pox and whatever else happens to be ailing them. *They talk nonsense!* Susie was different. She was a good hearted, decent, respectable girl. Some of them are quite mad. Sadly."

"Susie was... *barely recognisable!*" Septimus snapped. "*I saw her!* In case you've forgotten. *What was left of her.* I was drunk at the time, I can't deny, but...*I know what I saw!* It was... *inexplicable.* It was not human work. *Something* is out there! Some ghastly, murderous creature! *Or a whole army of the bloody things!* They come out at night, it seems, and then return to their holes when the sun comes up. Out in the marshes, perhaps. Or in ruined buildings."

Lachlan shuddered.

"I don't know. You may be right. There was that creature we shot down. Out in the estuary. What was that? I've never seen anything like it."

"Me neither," Septimus agreed. "But that thing was *huge.* It was the size of a bloody house. We need to be looking for something smaller. Something that can squeeze through tiny holes and down chimneys. A *worm* of some kind."

"*Oh, fuck...*"

The very mention of *worms* seemed to upset Lachlan.

"We should get away," he whispered. "As soon as we're able. Why not? We could have the money by the end of the week. We could sail to New York, from Falmouth. It would mean a long coach-ride, down to Cornwall. Four days, at least, but it would get us out of London. You could take this woman of yours. Lady Constance. I might take Mulu. I feel responsible for her welfare."

"How is she?"

"The same. Bad-tempered. We're *almost* on speaking terms."

"Uh, huh."

The tavern windows had steamed-up again. It was another cold day. That whole year had been dull and wintery. Snow had fallen in mid-summer. Falls of giant hailstones had become a regular occurrence. The ice would sometimes lie on the ground for days, without melting. The harvest had failed, for the third year in a row. Food prices had risen. *Dramatically.* A loaf of bread could cost a week's wages – for a working man. Every day that went by brought more beggars out onto the streets. More sad-eyed, rickety children. More bedraggled hawkers, gypsy fortune-tellers, syphilitic whores and old soldiers with missing limbs.

The awful murders could hardly have come at a worse time.

Lachlan wiped one of the windows and peered out. He reached into one of his waistcoat pockets and extracted his timepiece. It was nearly noon.

"Mr Serocoal is late. It's not like him. We need to be on our way. He'd stayed behind to re-weigh some of the smaller items. Apparently. I don't know why. We don't have to worry about every last little scrap. That can be done later."

"Mr Serocoal knows what he's doing."

"He's almost too fastidious. At times. But you're right, of course. We'd be lost without him. He knows what he's doing. *Disposing* of the gold would have been a bloody nightmare, without Mr Serocoal's experience. And his connections."

"At what time is the goldsmith expecting us?"

"Early afternoon. But he's miles away. On the other side of the city. It will take us a while to get there. We'll take a few samples with us. Bits and pieces. To give him a rough idea of what we've got. The three of us will go. You and me and Mr Serocoal. That seems best. We can't all go. I'm a little scared of being *robbed*. You hear such stories, these days. Only last week an elderly furrier was held up at gun-point, on Ludgate Hill, by a gang of street-thieves. He lost five *hundred pounds*. So he claimed. *In banknotes*. Nobody came to his aid, though somebody threw a chamber-pot full of piss over the robbers' heads as they ran off. From a window above. Harriet told me the story."

"What kind of a fool would carry *five hundred pounds* around on his person?" Septimus asked. "He was probably exaggerating. To impress his friends."

"Perhaps so. But we do need to be cautious."

"We should have brought one of the pistols."

"Mr Serocoal might have thought of it. Hopefully the need won't arise. We don't particularly *look* like rich men. Far from it! Though you've cleaned yourself up a bit Septimus, I'm glad to see. I didn't like to mention it! This fellow we're going to see is... *of the quality.* As I understand. He has friends in high places. *Very* high places. His bloody servants will probably look down their noses at us."

Septimus chuckled.

"Let's hope not. Speaking of money... could you, uh... possibly let me have some? In advance? Just a small amount to keep me going? I'm *slightly* behind with my rent. The way they're treating me, at my lodgings, is utterly despicable."

"I came prepared," Lachlan told him. "I knew you were in need."

He pulled out a folded banknote and pushed it across the table. A crisp-looking Bank of England five-pound note. Septimus examined it. A little warily.

"Is it real?"

"As far as I know. It looks real enough. I don't think you need to worry. We did... *a bit of business.*" He dropped his voice. "With a pawnbroker in Wapping. A friend of Billy's. One of those revolting candlesticks. Mr Serocoal melted it down. Mulu has been pestering me for money. God knows what she wants it for! She's got everything she could possibly need. For the moment, at least. Food and drink. A roof over her head. A comfortable bed. The Irish girls are looking after her."

"Is she recovering?"

"Hard to tell. She still blames me for Spiker's death. If she needs anything, she tells the Irish girls and they pass the message on. She decided this morning that she wants a *dressing-table.* Not just *any* old dressing-table. One of those expensive French ones with candleholders at both sides and several mirrors so you can see your face from different angles. I told her that I could have one made in Paris, *especially for her,* but that it might take a little time, the way things are."

Lachlan consulted his pocket-watch again. He was eager to be off. It was a fair way to Poland Street. The goldsmith would be wondering where they'd got to.

Septimus thought of ordering some food, now that he had the wherewithal, but while he was weighing the idea up the street door flew open and Mr Serocoal came in. He grinned and waved as he crossed the room. He was carrying a grimy little wooden box with a leather handle. A tradesman's box. At a glance he could have passed for an itinerant rat-catcher, on his way to deal with an infestation.

He gave a conspiratorial wink as he put the box down.

"I've got the, uh... *goods,*" he said. "Are you gentlemen ready?"

"Ready as we'll ever be," Lachlan grumbled.

"I'm a little late, I know! But we don't need to panic. I've got a boatman waiting. Just down the street. At Limehouse Dock. An accommodating fellow. He's going to take us up to Black Lion Stairs. We can almost walk from there."

Lachlan took a deep breath, to calm himself.

"Let's go! Before this accommodating fellow changes his mind."

16

MR ORZINGA'S
CHAMBER OF CURIOSITIES

Madam O'Reilly was talking to someone at the bar. She waved to the men as they went out. A sudden guilty thought crossed Septimus's mind. He hurried back and handed Madam O'Reilly the five-pound note that Lachlan had just given him.

"It should cover what I owe," he told her, apologetically.

"It's a sight *more* than what you owe, my darlin'," she assured him.

She slipped the note into her perfumed cleavage.

Septimus kissed her hand.

"You can give me the change later."

Madam O'Reilly tittered. She had a soft spot for Septimus, though she'd never been *quite* sure what to make of him. Susie Kettle had been fond of him.

The other men had waited, outside.

"There'll be plenty more where that came from, don't worry," Mr Serocoal told Septimus. He'd noticed the chivalrous gesture. "We're going to have money coming out of our ears! Out of our bloody *arses*. We weighed the gold, this morning. Me and Billy. Every last piece. Down in the ship's hold. There's *almost* a bloody ton. Eighteen hundredweight and five pounds. Give or take an ounce or two. I've never *seen* so much bloody gold! It's going to change everything. We're going to be rich!"

"What will it be worth? In rough terms?"

"Hard to say, exactly. Enough to put a smile on our faces."

"What can we expect?"

"Well, uh... I've got a figure in mind, obviously."

Mr Serocoal shooed away a muddy pig that was blocking the path.

"The official price, last time I checked, was nine pounds twelve shillings an ounce. I consulted Lloyd's List. At a coffee house in Cheapside. The price may well have risen since then. It's been rising steadily for weeks. Mr Orzinga will have sent his footman round to the Exchange. First thing this morning. To gain the latest intelligence. *Stolen* gold is obviously going to be worth a lot less. Half the going rate, typically. It's hard to be exact. The *size* of our haul will also be a factor. It's such a huge quantity. Even so, I'm hoping for a good price. I'm expecting a final offer of... *something like...* a hundred and fifty thousand. Pounds."

"Jesus!" Septimus spluttered.

"Thirty thousand each," Mr Serocoal added. "No mean sum."

"Are you sure we can trust this fellow?" Septimus asked.

"Mr Orzinga? *Absolutely.* I've known him all my life! He's like my own flesh and blood. We were apprenticed to the same master goldsmith, as boys. My own career went a little awry. Sadly. I was locked up for stealing gold-dust. On my twelfth birthday! Mercifully, they didn't hang me, but I spent two years in the Marshalsea. I was lucky not to starve to death. Orzinga, on the other hand, got *rich* from stealing. The lucky devil. It's just the way things go, sometimes. They gave him the Order of the Garter, or some such bloody thing."

Lachlan shrugged.

"*Fate,* huh? There's simply no accounting for it."

The accommodating boatman was waiting, at the mouth of the dock. Slippery steps led down to the water. The journey up-river took nearly an hour. The men didn't talk much as the riverside scenery slid by. The wharfs and warehouses.

Ermine House was largely hidden in mist. All that could be seen from the river were the high garden walls and the vague outlines of the roofs and towers beyond. Wooden scaffolding still covered one side of the East Tower. There was no sign of any work being done. The great house had a ghostly, abandoned look.

The trio disembarked at Black Lion Stairs and took a hackney-coach to Poland Street. Mr Orzinga's residence was in a hidden courtyard behind the old Pantheon Theatre. Several grand houses overlooked the quiet court. Mr Orzinga's was the grandest of all. Marble steps led up to an imposing front entrance.

"This is it," Mr Serocoal said. "This is the place."

Septimus gawped up at the building's immense frontage.

"He lives well. *For a goldsmith.* It's a bloody palace!"

"They all live well. Gold is a good business to be

in. Mr Orzinga has done better than most, it has to be said. He's more of a *merchant,* these days. Buying and selling. He has family connections in Rotterdam and Antwerp. That's where our gold will probably end up. In six months' time. If the bloody French don't ruin everything. They've already taken Flanders. So people are saying."

"How long has he lived here?"

"A good few years. He didn't always live so well. I've seen him getting richer and richer, as the years have gone by. He has friends in high places, now. In *very* high places. He arranges loans for luckless lords and flighty duchesses. Helps them out with their gambling debts. He's hobnobbing with the highest in the land."

"The bloody house must have cost a fortune."

"I hope he hasn't despaired of us. We're just a *little* late."

The front door had a brass knocker. In the shape of a Chinese dragon. Mr Serocoal mounted the marble steps and knocked. Immediately, the door opened. A liveried black footman appeared. He stepped aside, politely, to let the men in.

"The master is expecting you, sirs. We were getting worried."

The entrance hall was spacious and quiet. There were marble statues. On plinths. The floor, too, was marble. The air smelled of rosewater and wax polish.

It was the odour of affluence. Septimus recognised it instantly – though it had been a while since he'd last come across it. The manservant tapped on a half-open door.

"The, uh...*gentlemen* are here, sir," he announced.

"*At last!*" someone responded, from within. "Well, don't just stand there! Pulling silly faces! Send 'em in! Bring us something to drink, while you're at it, Joseph. Something suitable to the occasion. The *special brandy*, I rather think."

The goldsmith rose to his feet as the men entered. He was a jovial-looking character in a powdered wig. Red-faced and well-attired. Clearly affuent.

It was a handsome room with panelled walls. Daylight was flooding in through two huge, high windows. There were Dutch oil-paintings on the walls and a glass-fronted bookcase stuffed with leather-bound volumes. An ornate French clock was ticking on the mantel of a magnificent marble fireplace.

"Pray, be seated, my friends!" the goldsmith beseeched his guests. "We'll sit by the fire. It's not so warm. Even in the bloody house. Introductions would be in order, I think, Mr Serocoal. Then we'll enjoy a drink while we talk things over."

Mr Serocoal presented his fellow-thieves.

"This, sir, is Mr Lachlan Malone. One of my dearest friends. The guiding spirit of our enterprise. A gentleman. *Of sorts*. And this is Mr Septimus Slim. *Captain Slim*. Soldier of the King. Retired. Septimus has been our, uh... *military adviser*, you might say. We've brought a few small pieces along with us. To give you an idea of what we've got. Random samples. From a *considerable* pile."

Mr Orzinga smiled as he shook the men's hands.

"Welcome to my abode, gentlemen! Mr Serocoal has given me a few facts, of course, and outlined what is on offer. A *substantial quantity* of pure gold. I'm intrigued, I must confess. You appear to have accomplished a damnable piece of devilry. A crime of, uh... *heroic proportions,* one might say. But there have been no reports. Not in the newspapers. Not in the gentlemen's clubs or the coffee houses. Not anywhere! *Not even whispers.* It's perplexing. *Heh, heh!* But I won't pry. The least I know, the better, I would imagine. Mr Serocoal has assured me that the gold is untraceable, and I accept that. Mr Serocoal's word is good enough for me."

The manservant returned with a crystal decanter and some small glasses. He filled the glasses, passed them around, and left, closing the door as he went out.

"What we have here, sirs, is an *exceptionally* fine cognac," Mr Orzinga said, proudly, raising his glass as he spoke. "From the cellars of Buckingham House, no less! A gift from the King himself. I made a small contribution to the Military Requisition Budget. It pays to be patriotic, in times of war. This was my reward. Enough good French brandy to bathe in for a year. *Ha!* But... let's get down to business. Let's see what you've brought me. In that curious-looking box."

Mr Serocoal opened the battered little box he'd brought with him. He pulled out a cloth bag and tipped the contents out onto a low table. An assortment of gold fragments fell out. Torn pieces, from various parts of the *Helga's* strange cargo.

They glowed, prettily, in the soft light.

"Pure gold, all of it, to the best of my knowledge," Mr Serocoal affirmed.

"Aaahh..."

Mr Orzinga picked up one of the fragments and examined it. He took a piece of black stone from a box at his side and stroked the fragment against it, nodding as he studied the resulting mark. All was well, it appeared.

"It looks fine. I didn't expect otherwise. The touchstone doesn't lie, as they say. It appears to be pure gold. I can assay it later. It's beautiful. From the New World, I would guess. Peruvian, perhaps. I can *feel* the bloody history in it. The only question now is – how much have you got? The figure of half a ton was mentioned, last time we spoke. With the possibility of a fair bit more."

"As things have turned out, I was underestimating," Mr Serocoal told him. "I was being over-cautious. Force of habit. You'll need to weigh it yourself, of course, but... by my reckoning we have eighteen hundredweight and five pounds. In total. Just over two thousand and twenty pounds. I was using a borrowed balance. To save time. A hoary old thing, but that's a *fairly* accurate figure. It won't be so far off. Two thousand and twenty pounds. That's what we have. Nearly a ton."

A long silence ensued. The coals in the fireplace glowed. The ornate clock on the mantel above ticked quietly. Mr Orzinga closed his eyes and scratched his nose as he ran the figures through his mind. Mr Serocoal picked up the crystal decanter and poured everyone another measure of the King's brandy.

"I could take it all," Mr Orzinga announced, finally. "Assuming of course that we can agree on terms. It's a *considerable* quantity. The price of gold is high at the moment. Because of the war and the fear of invasion.

The market price is close to ten pounds an ounce. As I'm sure you know. But this is *purloined* gold. As I understand. There's a *hideous* amount of risk involved. I will need to borrow the money. At a *murderously* high rate of interest. The gold will need to be moved abroad. Mr Serocoal and I discussed these issues earlier. In the circumstances, the *most* I could afford to pay would be four pounds an ounce."

Mr Serocoal looked shocked.

"I was hoping for five. That's what the pawnbrokers are offering."

"Of course. But you couldn't sell a quantity like this to a pawnbroker. Or a local fence. It would take you *forever* to get rid of it. One small piece at a time. I'm lifting that burden from your shoulders, gentlemen. I'm taking all the risk. The price could fall. We just don't know. The French could relinquish their military ambitions. That would change everything. I could lose a bloody fortune. It would ruin me. But... as it's you, Mr Serocoal... in respect of our long friendship..."

The goldsmith took a deep breath and held it.

"I could go up to... let's say... four pounds and five shillings. A *substantial* increase. That would give you a total of... what? Have you got a pencil?"

Lachlan took out his trusty pocket-book and did the arithmetic, on one of the end-papers, with the stub of pencil he kept in the book. It took him ten minutes.

"A hundred and thirty-seven thousand pounds. Roughly."

"A tidy sum, eh? How does it sound?"

Mr Serocoal interrogated the others with a quick glance. He nodded.

"It's *most* acceptable, my friend. We understand your concerns. It's a generous offer. You won't regret it. The price will continue to rise. For at least another year. All that remains is to arrange delivery. We will need to be paid on the nail, of course. Once you've weighed the gold. And confirmed the quality."

"I'll have the money brought to the house. It will take a day or two. I'll be paying in Bank of England notes. How soon can you deliver the goods?"

"The day after tomorrow?"

"I can have the money by then. Early afternoon, let's say."

He shook Mr Serocoal's hand. The deal was done. As an afterthought he shook Septimus's hand, too, and then Lachlan's. Lachlan smirked.

Mr Orzinga poured everyone another brandy.

"How do you intend to, uh, *move* the gold?" he asked Lachlan.

"I've acquired some old tea crates," Lachlan told him. "Heavy old China Tea boxes. Solid old things. They still smell of tea. We'll have everything ready by tomorrow. I'll hire a wagon. We can do the heavy work ourselves. The lifting and loading. The wagoner won't suspect anything. If he asks, I'll tell him to mind his own bloody business. I could tell him that we're tea-traders, I suppose."

"Tell him that you're delivering crockery," Mr Orzinga suggested. "That might be better. You'll need to be armed, even so. Loaded pistols. Underneath your topcoats. It's *always* best. On top of that, you'll need a carriage. For your journey home. There's a stables down the street where you could probably arrange something. I'm thinking of your own safety. It's a *huge* amount of money."

More brandy was brought.

Mr Orzinga seemed to be enjoying the occasion.

"Would you care to see my collection of curiosities, Mr Slim?" he asked. "Mr Serocoal knows it well. He has procured some fine pieces for me, over the years. I keep them hidden away. Down below. This house has extensive cellars. I had one of them bricked-up when I first moved in. Come! Let me show you!"

He got to his feet and crossed the room.

A gaudy oil-painting of nymphs at their toilette decorated the rear wall. Mr Orzinga slid the work aside and pressed a concealed catch. Septimus chuckled as a section of the panelling slid open. He'd seen secret chambers before.

Stone steps led down. Something in the gloom overhead caught Septimus's eye as he descended. A recess in the brickwork contained what looked, at first sight, like the dried-out remains of a dead rat. On closer inspection he realised that it was, in fact... *a severed human hand.* A ghastly, shrunken, desiccated relic.

"Jesus!" he muttered. *"What in the world...?"*

Mr Orzinga glanced up. From the bottom of the steps.

"It's a *main de gloire,*" he said.

"A what?"

"A *main de gloire*. A 'hand of glory', uh? In plain English. It's an old tradition. *From the dark arts.* It protects my property. This particular hand was cut from the body of the axe-murderer, John Wallace.

After the bastard was hanged. At Tyburn Crossroads. It cost me twenty guineas! A travelling magician installed it for me. A mysterious Turk. I met him at a house of ill-repute. In Covent Garden. The hocus-pocus took a whole bloody day, but it seems to have been effective. We've had no trouble with intruders. It was a worthwhile investment."

Septimus shuddered.

Mr Orzinga chuckled, at the sight of Septimus's face. "Mr Slim! *Please!* Don't worry! *You're my guest!*"

A candle was burning in the chamber below. As though Mr Orzinga had been down there earlier and had expected to return. The cellar was surprisingly large. It was brick-built, with a vaulted ceiling. There was a slight whiff of damp in the air.

Wondrous things appeared as Mr Orzinga lit more candles. Ivory figures peered out from glass cabinets. Golden ornaments glowed, in the smoky gloom. Chinese vases glittered. A mysterious, hawk-headed demon, carved from a single, immense block of black stone, stood on a low plinth at the end of the chamber.

Septimus gasped as he caught sight of the thing. Mr Orzinga moved one of the candleholders closer.

"It's a sight to behold, uh? Egyptian, I believe. One of the ancient deities of that land. A French army officer brought it to London, several years ago. He tried to sell it to King George, but the Queen didn't like it. She thought it satanic. I acquired it for a pittance. It has a strange beauty. Would you not agree?"

Septimus hesitated. He could see the Queen's point of view.

"The workmanship is extraordinary."

"Indeed! The ancient peoples were superior to us, in so many ways. If you ask me. It's hard to deny, sometimes. *Staggering* things are unearthed. Take *this,* for instance. This little bowl. I acquired it recently. From an old friend."

He lifted the piece down and passed it to Septimus.

"It's silver. Heavily tarnished. I will have it cleaned, eventually. It was found in a bog in Denmark. Some fellow brought it to London. The figures on the sides appear to be the ancient Norse gods. Thor and Odin and all the rest. The pagan pantheon. We still call the days of the week after them. After all this time."

Mr Orzinga noticed Septimus's empty glass. He opened a cupboard and took out another bottle of the King's brandy, while Septimus perused the little bowl.

"It's *repoussé* work," the goldsmith told him. "Hammered out from behind. By a master craftsman. God only knows how such a lovely thing ended up in a bog."

Lachlan and Mr Serocoal were admiring some old Spanish coins. While he refilled everyone's glasses, Mr Orzinga pointed out more of his favourite pieces.

"This *lovely* silver hairpin came from a plague-pit. The marble woman with no arms was found in the Thames mud. Underneath London Bridge! She's almost certainly Roman. From a memorial of some sort. A rich man's wife."

Septimus put the silver bowl back in place. Another curiosity had caught his eye. An ancient-looking wooden boat with rows of small figures on deck. Traces of red paint and gilding were still visible on the carved hull. Nothing was left of the rigging and sails. The wooden figures appeared to be oarsmen, though the oars themselves had disappeared. Only a wide steering-oar remained. At the stern.

"This, too, is Egyptian," Mr Orzinga explained. "It's a Ship of the Dead. As I understand. For the final journey of the soul, over the River of the Underworld, to the Land of the Immortals. It appears to have come from a *very* ancient tomb."

"Where did you get it?" Septimus asked him.

"A wild-eyed madman in rags brought it to my door. Late one night. Someone had told him that I might be interested in such a thing. Heaven knows where *he'd* acquired it. It's clearly authentic. I gave him five shillings for it."

Lachlan caught Septimus's eye. Things were looking up. At last. They could start to relax. The worst was over. The hard times. They were drinking the King's brandy! In a secret chamber piled high with glittering treasures!

"What do you think, Mr Slim?" Mr Orzinga asked.

"I'm at a loss for words, sir. The only comparable collection I ever saw was at Ermine House. On the Strand. Many years ago. I was briefly in the employ of Lord Blackthorpe. Your own collection – if I may say so – is *immeasurably* superior."

Mr Orzinga's face changed.

"*Lord Blackthorpe?* That *despicable* man? Forgive me, Mr Slim. The very mention of that *ghastly* name makes my blood run cold. I had the misfortune to make his acquaintance. In my younger years. I was fool enough to be deceived by him. Those dazzling interiors at Ermine House were *my* handiwork. My assistants and I were there for *months*. There were *acres* of gilding in the bloody place. Not to mention the chandeliers. The mirrors. The golden door-knobs. It was the first job of that kind I'd ever taken on. *And the last.* You will remember it, no doubt?"

"It was *magnificent* work, sir. I remember it well."

"The evil bastard never paid me. He gave me a *pitiful* amount in advance, and then disputed the bill when the work was done. He almost ruined me."

"That's the kind of man he is."

"It was a lesson in life. When I threatened him with legal action he sent me a life-sized portrait of his young wife. The young Lady Constance. As *compensation*. As he laughingly called it. He had it conveyed to my residence on a fishmonger's cart. With musicians in attendance. So the whole of London could enjoy the jest! I still have it, as a matter of fact. It's in the library, upstairs. 'A Portrait of Lady Constance Blackthorpe', by Sir Joshua Reynolds. In oils. Signed by the artist."

Septimus's eyes widened.

"You have a portrait of Lady Blackthorpe?"

"By chance. The *young* Lady Blackthorpe. It was painted, *oh...* twenty-five years ago, I suppose. At the time of her marriage. I've tried to sell it, from time to time, without any success. The family are not *particularly* well thought of, these days. Nobody wants it. Would you be interested, Mr Slim? You must have known her ladyship. I've never met her, but I'm told that the picture is a perfect likeness."

"Well, I, uh..."

"Come and take a look. It's a fine piece of work."

Mr Orzinga extinguished the candles and led the men back upstairs.

Septimus caught another glimpse of the shrunken *main de gloire,* in its dusty dark recess, as he re-ascended the steps. He shivered and looked away.

"I never saw Lord Blackthorpe again, as things turned out," Mr Orzinga went on. "He moved abroad, I believe. To the West Indies. Lady Constance has lived alone in that vast, bleak house, for God knows how many years. It's a tragic story."

He re-secured the secret door and ushered the men out into the hall. The library was at the back of the house. It was an untidy room, crammed from floor to ceiling with old books, paintings, prints and ornaments. The single window looked out onto a walled garden, with rose bushes. Septimus barely noticed these details.

All he had eyes for was the portrait of Lady Constance.

As Mr Orzinga had intimated, it was close to life-size. It showed Lady Constance, in a beautiful, mauve silk dress, with pearls at her neck. She was seated in a purple armchair with turquoise cushions. The fingers of her right hand were pressed against her cheek. She looked thoughtful and pensive, as though sitting for Sir Joshua had given her time to think and dream. Septimus was transfixed.

"I'll be damned," he muttered.

"I've taken good care of it," Mr Orzinga assured him.

"How much would I, uh... need to pay for it?"

"Oh..."

The goldsmith took a long deep breath while he considered.

"In the circumstances, Mr Slim, I would let you have it for a hundred guineas. A *trifling* sum, obviously, in the light of our other business. Sir Joshua is deceased now, as you probably know. His work is going up in value by the day. It will be a good investment. I'm quite sure. What do you think? Are you tempted?"

"I'll take it," Septimus said.

He'd never seen the picture before. Or heard the bizarre tale that went with it. The price seemed reasonable enough. The thing was clearly a masterpiece. He had no idea of what he was going to do with it. He could hardly hang it in his filthy room at the Crow Hotel, and he still had no definite plans for the future.

If I could just get to see Lady Constance, he told himself. *It would change everything. I'll have money! We could go away together. Start a new life! In America! We could take the painting with us. As a reminder of the old times.*

Lachlan was getting restless. He was eager to be off.

"It's been a memorable day, sir," he told Mr Orzinga. "A *most* memorable day, but... there's still work to be done. The gold needs to be securely boxed. We'll make the delivery on Thursday. As agreed. I'll hire a cart for the day. I'll tell the carter that we're delivering crockery. As you suggested. It makes perfect sense. We could be here by noon. Depending on the weather and the state of the roads. Early afternoon, let's say. If that would suit you. It's hard to be precise."

"Any time after midday," Mr Orzinga said. "I'll have the money by then. You can bring the cart right up to the front steps. No-one will remark on it. I have things delivered all the time. *All kinds of odd things.* My neighbours are quite used to it. As long as the boxes are well-fastened. So nothing can fall out."

"I'll make sure of it," Lachlan promised. "They're good, solid boxes. We've got some old sail-cloth, too, that we're going to line them with. To keep things in place. It will be a big load. Thirty or forty boxes. All quite heavy."

"You'll have to bring them in yourselves. For the sake of appearances. It shouldn't take too long. We'll do the actual business in the drawing-room. You gentlemen can count the money while my manservant and I deal with the gold."

Mr Orzinga himself accompanied the men to the front door. He shook their hands, at the top of the steps, as they left.

"Until Thursday!" he called after them. "Be cautious, uh? Don't get too drunk! Be careful who you talk to! Let me know if any problems arise!"

The thieves trudged off. Tightening their topcoats as they went. It was late afternoon. The light was already fading. Evening shadows were stealing in.

"So... that's it," Mr Serocoal said, with a shrug, as they departed the little square and turned south into Poland Street. "It didn't go so badly. He was straight with us. As I knew he would be. It's a *bloody* good price. What do you think?"

"I was hoping for more," Lachlan admitted, "but I didn't want to interfere."

"I'm glad you didn't. He wouldn't have gone higher. I could see it in his eyes. That was his limit. But we can hardly complain. He's taking everything we've got. For a good price. And we get paid in two days' time. What more could we ask?"

"It's a good deal," Septimus agreed. "Though he'll probably double his money when he sells the gold on. In Antwerp. Or wherever. *Jesus!* No wonder he can afford to live so well. I take my hat off to him, to be quite honest."

"He won't let us down," Mr Serocoal said. "That's the important thing. The money will be there. Exactly as promised. He'll have raised it from one of his banker friends. We'll need something to carry it in. A travelling-trunk, I suppose. Perhaps even *two* trunks. I'm not really sure. I've never *seen* so much money!"

Lachlan laughed.

"One should be enough. It's paper money. What was that final figure again? A hundred and thirty-seven thousand? *Dear Lord!* Who would ever have believed it? We'll take it straight down to Deptford, I think, and share it out on the ship. We can have a celebratory drink at the same time. We've certainly earned it. Mulu can join us. I still don't know how much to give her. What do you think? She's not stupid. By any means. She must have a fair idea of what the gold is worth."

"Have you discussed it with her?" Septimus asked.

"We're still not, uh... *entirely* on speaking terms. The Irish girls are acting as her ambassadors. She doesn't think much of my house. It's not what she expected. The room we've given her is too small. It smells. The window won't open. The bed has fleas. She can't get comfortable in it. The linen isn't up to her standards. For a woman without a farthing to her name, she has some *very* grand ideas."

Septimus chuckled.

"She'll see sense, eventually. We're the only friends she's got."

"Try telling that to Mulu. She has friends everywhere. So she says. Women she met in Newgate prison, mostly. Whores and thieves and drunkards."

"Mulu was in Newgate? What on earth for?"

"Horse-stealing. Apparently. There's more to Mulu than meets the eye. She's a woman with a past. If I'd known how difficult she was going to be, I would have left her behind. At Egypt Point. She's worse than a bloody wife."

"Ha, ha, ha! We did the right thing. We couldn't have left her behind. It would have been *uncivilised.* What are we going to do though, when it comes to a parting of the ways? We can't just turf her out into the night. With a fortune in banknotes stuffed down the front of her dress. *God only knows what trouble she might get into.* She could send us *all* to the bloody gallows."

"Indeed..."

Lachlan hung his head and sighed.

"You're right, of course. I'm going to have to sit down and have a serious talk with her. She's a loose cannon. Good-looking! You'll be surprised when you see her. She's cleaned-up well. The Irish girls have been looking after her. Perhaps *you* could talk to her, Septimus. We can't just give her the money and bid her a fond farewell. It's true. *Anything* could happen. She could fall in with the wrong sort of people. We'd never forgive ourselves. Not everybody is as honest and decent as us."

"You could take her to America. To New York."

"I'll suggest it. If she'll listen. She might laugh in my face."

"It's worth asking."

"I'll broach the subject with her. Over a drink, perhaps."

17

THE CEREMONY

The men walked back to Black Lion Stairs and took a boat downriver, in the thickening fog. They dropped Septimus at Limehouse as they passed by, on their way to Deptford. Lachlan had given Septimus some more money. To pay his dues at the Crow Hotel. The gang's financial worries were over. So they thought.

All that remained was to deliver the goods.

Gold coins clinked in Septimus's coat pockets as he crept into his lodgings.

He wasn't expecting much of a welcome. Happily, his return went unnoticed. Mrs Lusardi was in the kitchen, berating the dim scullery wenches about something they had or hadn't done. Her little dog was yapping, nastily, in the background.

Septimus slunk past. His door was wide open, when he got upstairs.

Everything he owned had been flung out into the corridor.

There it all was. His books. His papers. Numerous empty bottles. His haversack. His dirty clothes. A rusty razor. A grimy piece of dried-out soap.

Wearily, he lugged it all back inside. The room had been cleaned, in his absence. The floor had been swept and scrubbed. An unfamiliar, flowery scent hung in the air. It wasn't *entirely* unpleasant. There was a jug of clean water on his washing-stand, and a fresh lump of soap. The chamber-pot underneath his bed had been emptied. They'd even *washed* it. It looked clean enough to eat out of.

Whoever had cleaned the chamber had left a key behind. It had a cardboard tag, with a scrawled number on it. Septimus used it to lock the door as he departed.

He pocketed the new key and went back downstairs.

Mrs Lusardi had finished harassing the lower servants. She was sitting at the desk, now, leafing through one of the mysterious ledgers. She glanced round as Septimus appeared. Her face paled at the sight of him. Her lips quivered.

"*Mr Slim...*"

The dread name floated, like an ancient curse, in the cold air. Before she had time to say another word, Septimus pulled a handful of coins from his coat pocket and slapped them down. Golden guineas and silver shillings. Plus a few coppers.

He'd counted it, most carefully, up in his room.

"There it is, madam. *Every penny I owe.* I can only apologise for the late payment. *It won't happen again.* I promise. My situation is improving."

Mrs Lusardi stared, distractedly, at Septimus and the unexpected pile of coins. She spluttered. Septimus had clearly taken her by surprise. Her little dog growled, threateningly, from the half-open kitchen door. It had never much liked Septimus.

While Mrs Lusardi struggled with her conscience, Septimus fled.

"I may be late back," he apprised her as he left. "But don't be concerned. Mr Podo will let me in. We're old soldiers, he and I. *Comrades in arms.* Almost."

He rushed out. Down the wet stone steps. Into the evening fog.

Just one more day, he thought.

For reasons he couldn't have explained, even to himself, Septimus had decided to attend the French cult's ghastly ceremony. In Wapping. The invitation card that Lady de Vere had given him was still in his coat pocket. The fact that Lady de Vere was involved had intrigued him. The woman he remembered, from his time at Ermine House, was no fool. She was a rich, attractive, intelligent, independent woman. She had no need of such nonsense. So Septimus told himself.

Despite having the price of a hackney-carriage, or a boat, on his person, he decided to walk to Wapping. It wasn't so far, and he wanted to eat, along the way.

He stopped at a crowded tavern in Ratcliffe and ordered pigeon pie, with roasted potatoes and a bottle of brandy. The place was in a passageway off Broad Street. He sat on his own in a corner, turning things over in his mind while he ate.

There was much to think about. In just two days' time he was going to be rich. *Ridiculously rich.* Thanks to Lachlan. The idea of leaving England was growing on him. With Lady Constance at his side, if he could persuade her.

London no longer felt safe. They couldn't afford to

be complacent. There was always the *tiny* possibility that somebody would betray them.

And then there were the murders. The horrific, nightly murders.

And the ongoing war.

The French were planning to cross the Channel in hot-air balloons, according to a report Septimus had read in the *Weekly Examiner.* Local militias were being set up, in Kent and Sussex, to support the regular army when the invasion came.

At the same time, taverns and ale-houses in the capital were brimming with enthusiastic revolutionists who could hardly *wait* for the French forces to arrive.

"*Vite, vite, citoyens! Dépêchez-vous!*" they would shout, as the beer flowed.

Even Lachlan, who had been in Paris at the time of the Terror and had seen *Madame Guillotine* at work in the streets, was of this persuasion. Septimus was less sure.

All he really wanted was a quiet life.

He drained the last dregs from his bottle and resumed his journey.

It was still half an hour's walk to Wapping. He vaguely remembered the Gaiety Theatre. It had been famous, in its day, for rowdy shows with half-naked dancing-girls, singers of *risqué* songs, magicians, performing animals, fireworks and anything else that would bring people in. Septimus had spent the odd evening there, in the distant past, with a friendly street-girl he'd known. The place had been derelict for years, so he'd heard. After a huge fire. The building had had no fire insurance and the owners had been unable, or unwilling, to pay for the repairs.

The doors were still closed when he got there. A crowd had gathered in the darkness outside. The people who'd turned up were mainly from the lower classes. The London poor. Their clothes were shabby. A good few of them were drunk.

They were clutching their printed invitation cards and discussing their reasons for being there. The main reason – unsurprisingly – was the money.

"For twenty shillin', I'd sell me soul to the Prince o' Darkness 'imself," a toothless old hag cackled.

"I doubt if he'd want it, you silly old cow," somebody shouted.

The crowd laughed. The old woman laughed along with them.

Despite the gloom, and the thickening fog, Septimus could see signs of the fire damage that had caused the theatre to close. The brickwork was soot-stained and black. Windows had been boarded-over. Parts of the roof had fallen in.

The moon came out. For a moment. An ancient sign came to life. *'The Best Show in Town!'* it proclaimed. In ghostly letters. High up on the old facade.

The crowd moved back as a handsome carriage rolled into the street. Fog swirled around it as it drew to a halt. The horses' sweating flanks steamed in the light from the vehicle's lamps. Septimus recognised the conveyance as the one he'd seen Lord Blackthorpe getting into, just days ago, in the equally dismal environs of Limehouse Dock. He hadn't recognised the bastard, at the time.

On that occasion Septimus had been alone. Now he was one among many. A face in a crowd. He edged closer for a better look. Lamps were being lit. Inside the building. A phalanx of crocodile priests emerged. They pushed the crowd back as the Grand High Pontieff stepped down from his carriage. Blackthorpe's face was hidden under the hood of his robe, but Septimus had no doubt at all that it was him.

He could almost *smell* him.

"This is a moment to remember!" an old man at Septimus's side murmured. He gripped Septimus's arm. "A moment of destiny! *Of liberation!* We will be raised up! *And reborn!* We happy few. *In the eternal light of Queen Mbembé.*"

"Is that a fact?" Septimus asked him, worriedly.

"Do you doubt it, my friend? *I have seen the light!* We will be *together forever,* we chosen ones! *In the everlasting day that is about to dawn!*"

Septimus freed himself from the old man's grasp. He'd heard more than enough of such nonsense, lately. From one place or another. *Together forever...* the old man had proclaimed. Susie's ghost had whispered the selfsame words.

Over and over. In the haunted midnight at the Crow Hotel. Septimus shivered.

The night air felt colder, suddenly.

Hooded priests escorted the Grand High Pontieff into the derelict theatre. The show was about to start. Flaming torches had been lit, at either side of the entrance doors. The flames hissed, like the fires of hell, in the fog.

The crowd surged forward as the doors opened. Septimus jostled his way in with the rest of them. He sniffed the foul air as he went in. *The building was a burned-out ruin.* No attempt at all had been made to clean the place up.

It *stank*. Like a public shit-house.

Candles were burning, here and there, in the dark. Dusty cobwebs trailed down from the ceilings. Evil-looking rats scurried through the shadows.

It was a scene from a nightmare. Septimus was tempted to turn and leave. He didn't *desperately* need the twenty shillings. He didn't need to be there at all. But curiosity got the better of him. He wanted to hear his old enemy speak.

The crowd shoved him along. Into the gloomy auditorium.

A dusty crystal chandelier hung above the stage. A row of faceless crocodile priests stood in line below. In the smoky glow of a thousand candles.

Like soldiers on parade, Septimus thought.

There were exactly twelve of them, he realised. He was reminded of a picture from his childhood. A coloured engraving of the Last Supper that had hung in his father's study. He'd been rather fond of it. It was a picture that told a story.

Perfumed smoke was coiling up from ornate brass incense burners at the sides of the stage. It wasn't doing much to improve the smell of the place.

Septimus hid himself in the dark at the back of the hall.

Little was left of the theatre he remembered. The gaudy decorations had all gone. The painted scenes on the walls. The gilded plasterwork. All that remained was a sooty ruin with holes in the roof and a pervasive stink of damp.

A gong sounded. *B-O-O-O-M...*

Blackthorpe emerged, like a ghost, out of the smoke. He raised his arms to silence the crowd.

"In the name of Queen Mbembé," he hissed. *"I bid you welcome!* Ye seekers after truth! You have come from far and wide to be here, I know, but you will not be disappointed. Tonight, you will taste... *the Elixir of Immortality!* The gates of the Imponderable Beyond will be opened unto you! The lies and deceits of the world will be cleansed from your weary souls! The loads will be lifted from your shoulders! In the blink of an eye... *you will be raised up!* Out of this ghoulish darkness! Into the perfect light of Her Celestial Majesty Queen Mbembé – *the Crocodile Queen!"*

Smoke from the incense burners swirled around him.

"Let the proceedings commence!"

His silken robe sparkled in the light as he moved.

The pointed hood concealed his face. The voice was Lord Blackthorpe's but the man Septimus remembered had never had such... *presence.* He'd been rich, arrogant, and casually cruel, but these were common enough traits in a man of his class. The wealth had come from sugar and slavery. The arrogance was inbred. Deep inside he'd been a pathetic weakling. The lowest of his servants had known it.

Something had clearly changed.

Smoke from the incense burners was accumulating in the air above the stage. Candlelight from the great chandelier glowed through it. One of the crocodile priests was shaking a string of tiny bells tied to a stick. The *tish, tish, tish* of the little bells was having an odd, soporific effect on the audience. Septimus included. He was finding it hard to keep his eyes open. He was reminded of an extraordinary display of magic he'd once seen. Half a lifetime ago. In the native quarter of Calcutta. On that occasion, too, there'd been a tiny, tinkling bell in the background.

He'd given the magician twenty paise.

"*Tonight,* good citizens, you will be *cleansed and regenerated!*" the Grand High Pontieff informed his audience. "Your dull lives will be *transformed.* Your days of poverty and ignorance are over. Your deepest desires will be fulfilled. *You will have palaces! Fine clothes! Food and wine! Golden goblets! Jewelled ornaments!* You will be lifted up! *In the celestial light of Queen Mbembé!*"

The audience muttered their drowsy approval.

The shadow under Blackthorpe's pointed hood was as black and empty as midnight in the pits of hell. He raised his head, suddenly, and looked out.

Two slits of cold, yellow light appeared.

In the ghastly void where his face should have been.

Septimus squirmed and moaned.

"*Uuugh...*"

He remembered the nightmare he'd woken from. In the small hours.

"In a moment," Lord Blackthorpe continued, "the magical ceremony will commence. One by one, you will step up and partake of the *Eau Sacré.* The sacred secretions of Her Perfect Majesty, Queen Mbembé.

But first, before we begin... *the aetherial presence must be summoned.* Prepare yourselves!"

"*Uh?*" Septimus muttered.

Once again, he was tempted to turn and leave. Before things got any worse.

He hadn't expected to be so scared. This wasn't *at all* the Lord Blackthorpe he remembered. Though he wasn't *entirely* surprised. There'd been books on magic, and magical practice, in Blackthorpe's study at Ermine House. They'd been kept in a locked cabinet, but Septimus had found it open one day, when no-one had been around. With some surprise, he'd perused the titles of the ancient volumes and wondered what on *earth* the mad bastard was doing with them. Though he hadn't really cared. With a shrug he'd walked away and forgotten all about them.

Until this moment.

The tiny bells were still tinkling. The sound, by some mysterious process, seemed to fill the entire hall. Oily smoke was snaking up from the incense burners.

The air was thick with the unfamiliar, pungent smell of the stuff.

Onstage, the crocodile priests were moving about.

The audience looked on, a little nervously. They weren't *quite* sure what was going on. Or what to expect. As they gawped, the sooty drapes at the back of the stage began to move. Rusty machinery creaked. Golden light streamed out.

"*Aaaaahhh...*" the onlookers gasped.

A monstrous effigy of Queen Mbembé took shape as the curtains parted. It had been there all along, hidden from view. Its red eyes glowed through the drifting smoke. The sun-disc on its head blazed, in the eerie light from above.

"*Lord, save us!*" Septimus whispered.

He felt ill, suddenly. He closed his eyes and moaned. The golden statue on the stage was identical – *in every last detail* – to the one that he and Billy Moon had chopped to pieces, out at Egypt Point. It was as though someone had found the smashed pieces and reassembled them. Though this was clearly impossible. The broken bits of *their* statue were in Deptford. Hidden away. On the *Sabrina Louise*.

Nobody could have put them back together.

How many of these damned things have they got? he asked himself.

He breathed deep. Gradually his heartbeat slowed. His fear subsided. The gang had assumed that the statue they'd come into possession of was unique. But this was clearly not the case. There were at *least* two of them. Possibly more.

Dozens of the bloody things could have been produced. From the same moulds and drawings. In the efficient Paris workshops of *Beliau Frères*.

It was a liberating realisation. It lessened the seriousness of their crime. No great harm had been done. The horrible thing had already been replaced.

There it was. In front of his eyes. Shining through the smoke.

"*Behold, Her Perfect Majesty!*" the Grand High Pontieff thundered, in a voice that shook the old walls. "*Queen Mbembé! The Queen of the Heavens! The Devourer of the Dead! The Keeper of the Book of Names!*"

He fell to his knees and pressed his mad head to the floorboards.

The crocodile priests, meanwhile, were moving things around. Tables and chairs were being brought out. A wooden cabinet with numerous small drawers was dragged into place, at one side of the stage. The audience watched, interestedly.

This, they guessed, was what they'd really been waiting for.

The payment they'd been promised, for bothering to come.

Blackthorpe got back to his feet.

"Step forward, citizens!" he rasped. *"Your destiny awaits!* Your names will be entered into the Great Book! The book of Record! The blessings of Her Celestial Majesty Queen Mbembé will be showered upon you! From this day forth and for evermore! *Come!* Step up! *Cast aside all fear!* Join us! *In the mystic light!"*

There were stairs at both sides of the stage but the crocodile priests had arranged things so that people went up at the left-hand side and down at the right.

Immediately, the crowd began pushing forward.

Septimus joined them. Despite his qualms.

A hooded priest sat behind the Great Book, quill in hand.

"Your name, brother?" he asked Septimus.

"*Uh...* Solomon."

"And your family name?"

"Solomon, *uh...* Smith."

"Are you ready to enter the light, Solomon?"

"Why would I not be?" Septimus sneered.

In the time it had taken him to climb the steps to

the stage Septimus had gone from being half-terrified to being in the mood for a fight. It was the story of his life.

"Very well!"

That, it seemed, was all there was to it. He could have told them that he was the Man in the Moon and nobody would have batted an eyelid. The hooded priest put the name in the book, without even looking up. The quill squeaked as he wrote.

Septimus crossed the stage. Through the swirling smoke. The Grand High Pontieff was back on his knees. At the statue's feet. He was banging his head on the stage-boards and jabbering weird nonsense. Like an escaped Bedlamite.

The statue raised its arms as Septimus went past. Its red eyes flashed.

A woman nearby screamed and fainted. Her friends came to her aid and dragged her away. For a horrible moment, Septimus thought that she was dead. But then, a moment later, she was back on her feet, and giggling.

Another of the hooded priests was dispensing the *Eau Sacré*. He had a greasy bottle of the stuff, and a filthy spoon. Septimus hesitated. The spoon had already been in numerous other people's mouths. Half of them would have had the pox.

But then... *there was the question of the money.*

"Open your mouth, good sir," the priest hissed.

"*Uuugh...*" Septimus grunted.

He sucked the ghastly stuff from the spoon and pretended to swallow.

The crocodile priest appeared satisfied. He extracted

a package from the tall wooden cabinet behind him. A brown envelope with an official-looking red seal.

"*Your reward,* sir!" he spat, as he handed the packet over. "*Twenty shillings in coin!* As promised. *The Crocodile Queen is generous!* Further payments may be had at the Temple of Dreams, in Southwark. Along with further instruction – should you wish to know more. Services are held each evening. From sunset onwards."

"*Gurub, urub...*"

Septimus grabbed the money and ran.

He was trying his best to hold the *Eau Sacré* in his cheeks. It wasn't easy.

The obnoxious taste of the stuff didn't help. He took a last look around as he left. A chaotic scene met his gaze. The crowd were getting restless. The golden statue was hideously aglow. *It looked almost alive!* The Grand High Pontieff was ranting in strange tongues at its feet. With his face pressed to the floor.

An argument had broken out at the other side of the stage. A drunken woman was refusing to reveal her name. She was unfastening her blouse, with the apparent intention of baring her breasts and dancing a little jig. Men with loaded pistols in their belts were hurrying towards her, through the eddying purple incense smoke.

Septimus groaned and headed for the door.

In the foggy quiet of the street he spat out the *Eau Sacré* and wiped his mouth on the back of his hand. As far he could tell he hadn't swallowed any. He stopped outside a well-lit tavern and counted the money they'd given him. It was a shilling short, in actual fact, but he could hardly go back and complain.

He washed his mouth out. As a precaution. At a pump in the tavern yard. Lachlan was convinced that the stuff was harmless but Septimus wasn't so sure.

The people who drank it seemed to mostly end up dead.

It was a strange business. The so-called *ceremony* had made no sense at all. It had been like one of the old Gaiety entertainments. All they'd wanted, as far as he could see, was to spoon the disgusting *Eau Sacré* into as many mouths as possible.

To what end? he asked himself as he walked.

But – try as he might – he couldn't think of an answer.

He took several wrong turns, in the foggy alleyways of the waterfront, and ended up quite lost. It was past midnight when he finally got back to Limehouse.

Thieves' Street was unusually busy. Ghostly figures were lurking in doorways.

The front door of the Rose Tavern was wide open. Light and warmth were seeping out into the fog. People were hanging about in the street, despite the cold.

Septimus pushed past them and went inside.

The downstairs room was empty. There were coats and hats on chairs and candles on some of the tables. The place had obviously *been* busy. Madam O'Reilly was pouring herself a drink, at the bar. She glanced up as Septimus wandered in.

"Septimus! *Praise the Lord!* I was hoping that you'd come!"

"What is it? What on earth is going on?"

"It's Lachlan. He's in the kitchen. The girls are looking after him."

"Looking after him? Why? Is he unwell?"

"He's *worse* than unwell. He's been *attacked.*"

"Oh, *please,* no! Attacked by... *what?* Not the ..."

"We don't know. He isn't really talking sense. He was *extremely* drunk when he came in, about half an hour ago. I've never seen him in such a state. Lachlan usually takes his drink well. He's half-Irish, after all. Half bloody French. For some reason he wandered through into the kitchen. After he'd knocked a table over. Then, just moments later, we heard him screaming. Enough to chill your blood."

"But, uh..."

"That's all I can tell you, Septimus. I've been shaking like a leaf! It was like the night of Susie's murder! All over again! *It's the same bloody thing!* The thing that killed Susie! *What else?* This time it came for Lachlan. Don't look so horrified. He's not dead. Far from it. He's been raving like a lunatic. He was even *singing.* In Irish! At one point. *Sad old songs.* I was almost in tears."

With trembling hands, Madam O'Reilly poured herself another brandy. As an afterthought, she found another glass and poured one for Septimus, too.

"Go through and see him. He's been asking after you."

18

THE HORROR AT GRAYSONS' YARD

Septimus hurried through to the kitchen. Some of the girls were at the door, peering in, with worried looks on their faces. They drew aside to let Septimus pass.

Lachlan was flat on his back in the middle of the floor. He was whimpering. Miserably. Through his teeth. Harriet and another woman were ripping off his clothes and using the torn cloth to bandage his wounds. It had clearly been a violent attack. Blood was still trickling down the greasy walls. For Septimus, the scene was *eerily* reminiscent of the scene in Susie's chamber on the night she'd died.

But Lachlan had somehow – by some miracle – survived.

He screamed as Harriet splashed vinegar into his wounds.

"Bhaaaa!"

"We *have* to do this!" Harriet told him, sternly. "It's for your own good! We don't know *anything* about this creature! We don't know what it is. We don't know where it's come from. It could be *diseased*. It could be afflicted with things we've never even *heard* of. This stuff stings, I know, but... *it might just save your life.*"

"*Bhaaaa!*" he screamed, again, as she splashed more of it on.

"Get some brandy," Septimus told one of the girls. "I've got money. I can pay for it. Bring a couple of bottles and some glasses. One for everybody."

Lachlan raised his head.

"*Septimus? Is it really you?*"

"Of course it's me, you idiot. Don't move! Lie still! Harriet knows what she's doing. You're in good hands. You're going to live. That's the important thing."

Harriet had been a prize-fighter in her youth. She'd travelled the length and breadth of the land, taking on all-comers at country fairs. Men and women alike. She'd been quite famous. Cuts and bruises didn't frighten her.

Lachlan was still trying to push himself up.

"Septimus! *Thank God you're here!* I was worried about you. We need to talk. *In private.* There are things you need to know! *Important things!* The bastards are after us! *They know who we are!* Terrible things are happening! *The worms!* I've *seen* the bloody things. *At close quarters.* One of them came for me. I'm lucky to be alive. *Jesus!* We've got to get out! *Before it's too late!*"

He pointed to the wall.

"*That's where it came from! That weird hole!*"

There was a rough opening in the wall. Just below the ceiling. The coal-cellar steps were on the other side. The hole had been boarded-up, at some point, but the rotten old planks had been smashed to smithereens by the force of whatever had come through. The fragments that remained were still smoking, slightly.

The brandy arrived. Lachlan guzzled half a pint of it and immediately passed out. With a defeated moan, he gave up struggling and fell back against the floor.

Harriet prised the bottle from his grasp and took a drink herself.

"What was he doing in the kitchen?" Septimus asked her.

"Heaven knows. We'd been *extremely* busy. The place was full of foreign sailors. Spaniards. Russians. Lascars. It was that kind of night. I'd seen him come in. Drunk as a lord. Somebody had to help him as he crossed the room. I was surprised to see him in such a state. It crossed my mind that something was wrong. I thought it might be to do with this new woman of his. The one who's moved in with him. The horse thief. He disappeared into the kitchen and then, just a moment later, a *bloodcurdling* scream came out. Everything just stopped."

"When did all this happen?"

"Half an hour ago. He'll survive. It's not as bad as it looks. He's lost blood but most of his wounds are quite shallow. Scratches, almost. *As though he was clawed.* By something. Heaven knows what. The deeper cuts look more like bites. You can see the teeth-marks. There's a nasty gash on his thigh that might need attention. We'll get him looked at tomorrow. The local barber is quite good. I'm not too worried. Give him a week and he'll be back on his feet."

"*Rash... ash... dash...*" Lachlan gurgled.

His limbs were twitching, as though he was still trying to fight the thing off. Blood was dribbling from his nose. Harriet wiped it with a vinegar-soaked rag.

The shock seemed to revive him.

"Septimus?"

"I'm still here. Don't worry."

"We need to talk," he whispered again. "I've *seen* things, tonight, Septimus. *Terrible things!* Things you wouldn't believe. *I've seen the bloody worms!* First in Deptford. In the damnable fog. And then here. Of all places. *Dear God!* I'm a little inebriated, it's true. *But I'm not stupid.* I know what I saw. I was going out to the yard. To pass water. But then I came in here. I'm not sure why. To collect my thoughts. It was quiet. *That's when the bloody thing came for me!"*

"You survived. That's the important thing."

"I was drunk. I could hardly stand up."

"It might have helped. At least you didn't die of terror."

Septimus took a closer look at the hole in the wall. It didn't look big enough for any sort of *creature* to have crawled through. A chimney-sweep's apprentice would have had difficulty wriggling through it. There was a grimy old earthenware sink directly below. Both the sink and the wall around it were splattered with Lachlan's blood. As though that's where he'd been when the attack had happened.

"Is that wall, uh... *solid?*" Lachlan asked.

Septimus thumped it.

"Solid as a rock. As far as I can tell."

"It came straight for me. *It was breathing fire!* Its teeth were dripping. I screamed blue murder. It almost had me. But then these lovely ladies appeared. *Out of nowhere.* They saved my life, I swear. The bloody thing just...

vanished. Like a ghost at cock-crow. I think I fainted. At that point. My legs gave way."

"You were lucky to survive."

"But... *Mr Serocoal...*" Lachlan whispered. *"He's..."*

"He's what?" Septimus asked, bewilderedly.

Lachlan sobbed. He seemed unable to explain.

Madam O'Reilly brought another bottle. On the house, this time. Harriet found some fresh apparel for Lachlan. The Rose Tavern had an ample supply of men's clothing. Customers frequently left things behind. The cupboard in the back was stuffed to bursting with shoes, shirts, breeches, waistcoats, wigs and hats.

"He can stay the night," Madam O'Reilly proposed, as Harriet struggled to reclothe the recalcitrant Lachlan. "We can't send him home in this state. The poor devil. He's at death's door. He needs to rest. There'll be an empty bed upstairs."

"I'll take him home in the morning," Harriet offered. "When he's sobered-up. This new woman of his will be getting worried. She'll be wondering where he is."

"Mulu?" Septimus spluttered. *"She'll be hoping he's gone to hell."*

"That's not what I've heard," Harriet hinted, with a wink. "I know the Irish girls. The ones he rents rooms to. I've heard the story from them. This young woman has got Lachlan well and truly hooked. Believe me! He's promised to take her to New York. She's told the Irish girls that she's thinking about it. She's a bloody horse-thief. So I'm told. They were *made* for each other, the pair of 'em."

Septimus shook his head in disbelief.

"Are we talking about the same person?"

As gently as they could, they got Lachlan to his feet. Madam O'Reilly had given him a fairly large dose of laudanum, to help with the pain. He moaned and groaned as they dragged him upstairs. The chamber had an old iron bed with a straw mattress, some well-used sheets and a tattered blanket. Lachlan grumbled, drowsily, as they tipped him onto the bed and pulled the blanket up over him.

Little else could be done until morning, when the local barber-surgeon could be summoned. Harriet went back downstairs. Septimus was on the point of leaving when Lachlan reached out, suddenly, and grabbed his wrist.

"Don't go, Septimus... we have to talk. About Mr Serocoal..."

"Don't worry about Mr Serocoal," Septimus told him. "He's the *least* of our worries. It's *you* we're concerned about. You need to rest. Harriet will keep an eye on you. I'll go down to Deptford at first light and explain things. We can still deliver the gold. *As planned.* Get some sleep! I'll see you in the morning. We'll get that leg of yours looked at. It's just a gash! Don't worry! You'll live!"

"No, no, no... you don't understand."

Lachlan tried to raise himself but failed. He fell back against his pillow.

"Mr Serocoal is..."

He sobbed and sniffed.

"Mr Serocoal is... gone."

"Of course he's not gone! He's in Deptford! As far as I know."

"No, no. *It's the truth!* It's what I've been trying to tell you. I couldn't talk in front of the women. *He's gone.* I found his mortal remains. Down by the river. In Greenwich. It's the reason I got so drunk. You know it's not like me. I can handle my drink. As well as any man. *Normally.* But the shock was too much for me. Serocoal was one of my dearest friends. *I should never have got him involved with this business.* He was a good man. A decent man. I'll burn in hell!"

Septimus pulled a chair over to the bed and sat down.

"What are you talking about?"

"I hardly know where to begin. I'm still a little befuddled. We were on the ship. Earlier. After we'd dropped you off. Just passing the time. Discussing our plans. How we were going to spend the money. That sort of thing. Serocoal went up on deck to relieve himself and didn't come back. After a while I went up to see where he was. It was foggy. As usual. I called his name but there was no response. The dog was behaving quite oddly. That's when I started getting worried."

"Of course. Understandably."

"We left Smalt and the dog on board and went out to look for him. Me and Billy. Around the creek. The local paths. The waterside taverns. Nobody had seen him. Nobody knew anything. In the end I left Billy on the Southwark side and went over the bridge into Greenwich. That's when I found him. On the foreshore."

"Dead?"

"Worse than dead. If such a thing is possible. *Bloodless. Mutilated.* It was a worm attack. I just knew it. He was lying near Graysons' Yard. That big timber yard at the mouth of the creek. The body was half-submerged in the foreshore mud. I hardly recognised him, at first. In the dark and the damnable bloody fog. Then I saw those tattooed stars on the back of his hands and I knew beyond doubt that it was him. My old friend John Serocoal. How am I ever going to tell his wife?"

Tears welled in Lachlan's eyes.

"What is she going to think of me?"

"You can't blame yourself, Lachlan. It's these damnable... *creatures.*"

"It's *them,* Septimus! *The Sign!* They're behind all of this! They want us dead! *They know who we are.* They're picking us off! One by one! *Capitaine Clézio.* Then Mr Serocoal. And then...*they came for me!* By some miracle, I survived. *But for how long?* They're out there! *In the fog!* Watching our every move! We have to get away! Out of London. *As soon as we've got the money!* We could leave on a late coach. If there is one. To Falmouth. How long would it take us to get there? Do you know? A couple of days? A week?"

"Two or three days, I suppose. But... you're not *entirely* talking sense. These worms are not... *supernatural.* They're just... *murderous, flesh-eating creatures.* Brought here quite by chance, I would imagine. From Africa. Or India. Or who-knows-where. On some foreign vessel. Hidden in the cargo."

Lachlan moaned and shook his head.

"I've *seen* the bloody things! I'm a *little* inebriated, I know. I drank a lot of rough brandy. Enough to kill a bloody horse. At some *vile* bloody tavern in Greenwich. A lively sort of place. Somebody emptied my pockets while I was there. God knows how I ever got back to Limehouse. I have no recollection. Do you think they'd make me some coffee? It might help to clear my head."

"I don't see why not. I'll go down and ask."

Septimus went downstairs and asked at the bar. The establishment was busy again. A fiddle-player was entertaining a noisy crowd. The attack in the kitchen was all but forgotten. Nobody had died. Things had quickly returned to normal.

Lachlan was sitting up, shivering, wrapped in his blanket, when Septimus got back. One of the friendly kitchen-wenches had warmed-up some coffee. It was far from fresh, but Lachlan didn't seem to care. He gulped it down. Septimus wasn't sure whether to stay or go. The Irishman was in an odd state of mind. He'd had a huge dose of laudanum, on top of the brandy he'd drunk earlier.

"I need to tell you what happened," he breathed, as he finished the coffee. "In case they come for me again. It's important that you know! I sat by Mr Serocoal's body for a long time. In that godless, lonely place. With the fog swirling around me and the Thames lapping at my feet. I promised him that I'd look after his wife. That I'd make sure she was provided for. It all sounded so... *horribly empty.*"

"Are you quite certain that it *was* Mr Serocoal?"

"Of course! I've known him all my life!"

"Where is he now? It will be high water. We can't just leave him there. He'll get washed away. I could go down there myself, I suppose. Even at this hour."

"He's *gone,* Septimus. That's the worst part of it. While I was sitting there talking to him – about this and that – a Sign of the Crocodile Queen hearse rattled up. Out of the bloody fog. For a moment I thought I was dreaming. It drew to a halt. On the riverside road. Barely twenty feet away from me. A pair of those ghastly priests were up on the box, peering down at me. That's when I knew, *beyond all doubt,* that they were responsible for his death. How else could they have found him! They'd come from *miles* away! From Barnaby Street! In the middle of the bloody night! They were *looking* for Mr Serocoal. *They knew where to find him!* It was as plain as daylight. *They'd come to collect him!"*

"Did you let them take him?"

"We had quite a set-to, believe me. One of them climbed down from the hearse and paddled out through the mud to where I was squatting. A faceless fiend in a pointed hood. My blood ran cold. If I'd had a pistol with me I would have shot him dead. Right there and then. Mr Serocoal had *no connection at all* with the Crocodile Queen. They tried to tell me that he did but it was an outright lie. He was an atheist. A *Jacobin,* you could almost say. The only thing Mr Serocoal believed in, besides his loved ones, was the revolution. *Freedom for the common man!"*

"But they took him, uh?"

"In the end. The hooded bastard insisted that I was mistaken. When I threatened to walk into Greenwich and raise the constables he said he could prove it. He loosened Mr Serocoal's collar and pulled out that gold chain he used to wear. His lucky chain. He'd worn it for years. Dangling at the bottom was a Crocodile Queen pendant. Shiny gold. Beautifully-made. Strangely luminous. It was a devilish trick, no doubt. Serocoal would never have fallen for such appalling nonsense. But all the fight had gone out of me, somehow. It didn't seem to matter what happened to the poor sod, now that he was dead. I regret it now, but..."

Lachlan wiped away a tear. He looked pale and ill, in the candlelight.

"Does Billy know?"

"Nobody knows. You're the first person I've spoken to. Billy might still be out there. Still looking. He might have met some girl and started drinking. It's hard to tell with Billy. You know what he's like. I'd given him some money. Earlier in the evening. A few guineas. I just hope he's safe. Somebody will have to inform Captain Smalt. He'll be wondering where on earth we all are. There's *more* to this story though, Septimus. *Much more.* I haven't got to the strangest part yet."

"With regard to Mr Serocoal?"

"With regard to... *just about everything.* I walked away and left Mr Serocoal to his fate. What else could I do? The tide was coming in. The crocodile priests had brought a box. They were trying to pull Serocoal's remains up out of the mud. I couldn't bear to watch. The fog was getting worse. I just wandered off. Along the foreshore. I needed a drink. I ended up at the Red Lion. Further up the Greenwich waterside. Do you know it? By King's Stairs. It's popular with sailors."

"I know the place. Vaguely."

"It was still open. There were lights in the windows. I could hear music and laughter. I was about to go in, but then, as I climbed the steps, something caught my eye. Out on the river. As the fog shifted. It looked like the upturned hull of an old wreck, except that... *it seemed to be moving.* Like something *alive."*

"*Uh?*"

"That's the way it looked. I couldn't see it so well. In the dark. I was still reeling from the shock of finding Mr Serocoal. I'd already had a drink or two. On the *Sabrina Louise,* earlier. In Deptford Creek. A bottle or two. I retraced my steps. Went back down to the foreshore. I thought it might be a stranded whale. They come up-river, sometimes, and get stuck when the tide goes out. As I got closer though, I could clearly see what the thing was. There was no mistaking it. From the descriptions I'd heard. I could see its teeth and its diabolical, blood-red eyes. It was a *worm,* Septimus! *A hundred feet long and in its death throes.* So it appeared."

"You're jesting. I hope."

"It's the truth, I swear. I nearly dropped dead on the spot."

"It could have been a... *sea-monster.* Of some sort. *A kraken."*

Lachlan shook his head.

"It was a worm. *A dying bloody worm!* I froze with fear. My heart was pounding. I hardly dared breathe. It was *exactly* what that unfortunate Italian girl described to Madam O'Reilly. A huge mouth. Slimy, pointed teeth. *Tendrils* at the back of the head. Hideous red eyes. Even as it lay there, dying, in the Thames mud, its eyes were slightly aglow. It was *watching* me! Through the fog."

"*Dear God!* Could it have been the one that killed Mr Serocoal?"

"Quite possibly. It wasn't so far away. A few minutes' walk. No more. I stood and watched it for a while. It was jerking and shuddering. Then, as I tried to creep away... *the ghastly thing burst open.* Stinking bits of flesh exploded out of it. I pulled my coat up over my head to protect myself. It was all I could do. The stuff was splattering down all around me. When I looked again the dead worm was still twitching. Horrible... *slurping* sounds were coming from the remains."

"*Lord above...*"

"It gets worse," Lachlan went on. "Something was *emerging.* From what was left of the worm. The head slithered out first. *Then the rest of it.* Pushing its way out. *Dripping with slime.* I stared in horror. It was a *serpent.* Of some kind. With thin, black, leathery wings. Weird, cold light was flickering around it."

"*Heaven protect us!* How *big* was this thing?"

"Big enough. It could have swallowed me whole. Almost. Fortunately for me, it seemed to have more important business in mind. It just sort of *stood there,* for a long time. Squawking and preening itself. Trying its new wings."

"*Jesus!*"

"Then, in the blink of an eye, it was gone. It pulled itself up, extended its wings and took off. Towards the city. *As though it knew where to go.* I could hear the uncanny sound of it as it circled up into the fog. The steady beat of its wings."

"And then what?"

"I stood there, in the foreshore mud, shitting myself, for another ten minutes. I didn't know if the bloody thing was going to come back. The tide was coming up around me. Eventually I had to move. To save myself from drowning."

"Was it anything like that other creature we saw? At Egypt Point?"

"Exactly the same. Smaller, but otherwise identical. The one at Egypt Point must have been fully grown. This one was just a baby. It's an *infestation,* Septimus. Just as you've kept telling us. The worms and the flying creatures are of the same flesh and blood. First the maggot... then the fly. That's the way it looks."

Septimus stared, thoughtfully, into the candlelight.

"And then... the crocodile priests."

"*Exactly...*" Lachlan agreed. "They're in this up to their evil bloody necks. Every time there's a killing, one of those ghastly black hearses turns up. Before the corpse is even cold, in most cases. *As though they have prior information.*"

"Uh, huh."

The pair sat in silence for a moment. Septimus was remembering the stories he'd heard from the goat-man. Ebenezer Withers. About the mysterious tunnels under the Necropolis – and the legion of lost souls he'd seen down there.

The candle was guttering out. A doomed moth was circling around it. With a sigh, Septimus got to his feet.

"Get some sleep, my friend," he said. "Harriet will keep a watchful eye on you. I could go down to Deptford right now, I suppose. I'm thinking about the captain. He needs to be told. He'll have no bloody idea of what's happened."

"Leave it till tomorrow, Septimus. It's late. You don't want to be out on the river at this time of night. I couldn't bear to lose another friend. Smalt is probably snoring in his bunk. I'm more worried about Billy. He's got a new girl in his life. A brewer's daughter. From Bethnal Green. A lively piece. He introduced her to me. I'm scared that she'll lead him astray. I shouldn't have given him all that money. *Five guineas!* It was a bit stupid of me. He has a fondness for the drink."

"He *earned* it. Billy's a good lad."

"Of course! It's just that... women and money tend to go to Billy's head. I've known him long enough. You might have to take charge of things, Septimus. Just for the next day or two. Until I'm back on my feet. I'll come with you, obviously, when we deliver the gold. Most of it is already in boxes. It won't take long to load it. Onto a carrier's cart. Mr Orzinga will have to be told. About his old friend."

"Don't worry. The worst is over. You need to rest."

Septimus extinguished the candle as he left. Lachlan grunted a sleepy 'goodnight' and closed his eyes. Septimus crept away, as Lachlan drifted off.

He stumbled downstairs. Like Billy, he had money to spend. The tavern was still busy. Septimus thought he'd stay a while longer. He was in need of a drink.

Unlike Billy, he had no-one to share his good fortune with.

But female company was easily come by, in the Limehouse night.

19

MISCHIEF AT THE CROW HOTEL

Septimus was back in his own familiar, dingy chamber when he woke, the next day. It was early morning, he guessed. Going by the light and the sounds from outside. He felt slightly ill. As he often did at that hour. He couldn't immediately remember where he'd been, the night before. What he'd drunk. Or how he'd got home.

He lay in bed for a while, staring up at the decayed ceiling-beams, the cobwebs and the sooty, cracked plaster. Little by little, things came back to him.

Mr Serocoal was dead, he recalled, with a shiver.

Lachlan *himself* had been murderously attacked.

"Oh, Jesus..."

Things were going from bad to worse. *Three* of their comrades-in-arms were now dead. Clézio, Spiker and Mr Serocoal. Lachlan had almost been the fourth.

But all was not lost. Lachlan had survived, with no more than a few cuts and bruises. And they still had the gold. All they had to do was deliver it.

Everything was arranged.

At some point in the night Septimus had brought a woman back to the Crow Hotel. He had no recollection at all of where he'd met her, or what her name had been. She'd had long, dark hair. Rouged cheeks. A soft voice and sad eyes.

His old leather coat was draped over the end of the bed but he was otherwise fully-clothed. He even had his boots on. It was the way things went, sometimes.

The woman had left without a word. She'd not woken him. Septimus glanced around to see if she'd left anything behind, but there was nothing. No sign that she'd been there at all. It seemed a little odd. A little puzzling.

"*Oh, no...*" he groaned. "*No, no, no...*"

His money had been in one of the inside pockets of his coat. There'd been the change from the five pounds he'd given Madam O'Reilly, at the start of the day, *plus* the nineteen shillings he'd got from the Sign of the Crocodile Queen, and some other money, too, he thought. He'd had *at least* three pounds on his person when he'd parted company with Lachlan. Possibly more. Even allowing for what he'd spent.

He pulled his coat off the bed-post and rummaged through the pockets. They were all empty. Frantically, he searched them all again. To no avail. His nocturnal companion had been thorough. She'd taken every penny he had.

"*Fuck!*" he screamed. "*The devious, thieving bitch!*"

She'd even left the door open. He went over and slammed it shut. Whoever the woman had been, she was long gone. He cursed and sobbed. There were a few coins in his breeches' pocket that she'd missed, he realised, as he paced about the room, remonstrating with himself. He pulled them out and counted them.

Five shillings and few loose coppers.

"For God's sake!" he moaned.

He examined his yellowing eyes in the wash-stand mirror.

"What is the bloody world coming to?" he asked his reflection. *"Are there no decent people left? I'd have given her the bloody money. If she'd just asked."*

Slowly, he calmed down. His breathing slowed.

It was hardly the end of the world.

There was only a day to go. If all went well. Septimus was concerned that the goldsmith might be less accommodating, now that his old friend Mr Serocoal was gone. Serocoal had been the gang's ambassador – and chief negotiator.

His sudden demise was going to take a lot of explaining.

It was almost *beyond* explaining. All they could do, Septimus reasoned, was to tell the truth. As far as possible. As much of it as they dared.

He fished a drowned spider out of his washing-bowl, splashed a handful of dirty water onto his face and tidied himself up. As best he could. The worst was over, he told himself. The gold was safe. The light-fingered lady he'd brought home had at least left him the price of a drink, and some breakfast.

He donned his old leather coat and trudged downstairs.

There were strangers in the entrance hall. New arrivals. A rather fine-looking fellow in a powdered wig and his female companion. The pair had a pile of trunks and cases with them. As though they'd just returned from foreign parts. Mrs Lusardi was offering them one of the grand rooms on the first floor. She was talking in the high-pitched voice she used when addressing people of *quality*.

Septimus hurried past.

Zeelandia Street was cold and quiet. It was still misty, down by the river. Coal was being discharged from lighters. Horse-drawn wagons were queuing up to haul the stuff away. Septimus patted the horses' sweating flanks as he ambled past. He felt some sympathy for the great, gentle beasts. All that lay in store for them, after their years of toil, was to end up as dinner for old ladies' cats.

The Rose Tavern was closed when he reached Thieves' Street. Disappointedly, he turned away. He guessed that the place had been open all night. Normally one of the girls would take charge in the morning if Madam O'Reilly was still abed. But it didn't always work out. Occasionally, after a long night, they *all* slept late.

He remembered a little pie-shop in Ratcliffe. He'd eaten there once or twice. In the early days. Before he'd discovered the Rose Tavern. The shop was on Narrow Street. A few minutes' walk away. On the western side of the Limehouse Cut.

It was a coal-heavers' haunt, down a grimy passageway, but they served good coffee, along with pies and puddings. Fresh bread, too. If you got there early enough. You could even get a drop of brandy, in the back room, though the shop wasn't actually licensed to sell the stuff. The bottle just *happened* to be there.

The pie-man glanced up from his *Gazette* as Septimus

came in. He grunted as he recognised Septimus's face. Unusually, for the time of day, there was no-one else in the place. Just an old brown dog. Half-asleep by the stove.

"I'll take a coffee," Septimus said. "And some breakfast. Whatever you've got, really. A morsel of bread. Some butter and cheese, perhaps. If you have it. I'm not feeling so well. I had a rough night. *Drinking*. It's the story of my life."

The man put his paper aside and kicked the dog out of the way.

"Where is everybody?" Septimus asked him. "Is it a public holiday?"

"You haven't heard? The *revolution* has begun, my friend. It started early this morning. Battles are going on. All over the city. The army has been called in. Troops from the Tower. The militias. The artillery. Blood has been shed."

"*Dear God!* I had no idea. I've only just risen from my bed."

"You're a gentleman, of sorts, then? I wouldn't have guessed. If you'll forgive the observation. Hopefully, it will be all over by nightfall. I couldn't endure another day like this. I've barely taken tuppence since I opened the doors. At dawn."

He poured Septimus a coffee.

"Announcements about new taxes were pasted-up during the night. That's what it's all about. *Money*. Funding for the bloody war. The trouble is, not everybody can read. It takes a while for new ideas to catch on. Things have to be... *properly explained*. But then, first thing this morning, gangs of excise-men and constables started arresting people and dragging 'em off. To who-knows-where. *Dozens of 'em.* So I've heard. *Poor bastards.* Penniless street traders, mostly. They were charged with *not having a licence*. That's what sparked things off."

He brought Septimus's breakfast over as he rambled.

"*No licence?*" he went on. "What are we to make of that? *Eh?* Are we no longer free men? *Nobody* has a licence. Nobody in these parts had even *heard* of such a thing. A hawker of old clothes was shot dead, on Periwinkle Street, after he refused to hand his stock-in-trade over to some drunken soldiers. Shortly after that, a furious mob attacked the excise-men. Dragoons from the Tower opened fire on the crowd. Several people were killed. After that, all hell broke loose."

"*Jesus!* I was at my lodgings. I didn't hear a thing."

"It hasn't been so bad around here. The worst of the fighting seems to have been on Cable Street. The crowd put barricades up. My wife was briefly caught-up in the chaos. Mercifully, she wasn't hurt, though she was considerably distressed. Where will it all end? *What's the bloody point?* We can't pay taxes if we're dead."

Septimus couldn't help but agree.

The dog watched, hungrily, from a safe distance, while Septimus breakfasted. The cheese was excellent. The bread was fresh. It was pleasantly warm.

He rounded off his repast with a measure of cheap brandy. It was already late morning. Almost midday. A respectable time to take a first drink, he told himself.

The proprietor had gone back to his newspaper. Septimus threw a handful of coins onto the table as he left, without asking how much he owed.

"Come again!" the man shouted after him.

Septimus waved but didn't look back. He wasn't thinking of being in London much longer. Things were clearly going from bad to worse. As he walked homeward along Narrow Street he heard the unmistakable rattle of musket-fire. Volley-fire. From well-trained soldiers. He stopped to listen. The sound was coming from the direction of Limehouse Bridge Dock. Not *so* far away from the Crow Hotel.

The revolution had spread to Limehouse, it seemed. Septimus thought it best to disappear. For the rest of the day, at least. Until things had returned to normal. He made his way up to Shipping Stairs with the intention of taking a boat to Deptford, but when he reached the stairs there were no boats to be had.

The boatmen had vanished. There wasn't a soul in sight.

Unsure of what to do, he wandered into the nearby street-market.

A chaotic scene confronted him. The market-traders, too, had fled, leaving their overturned carts and stalls behind. The pavements were strewn with discarded produce. French onions and Spanish oranges. Broken eggs and wriggling eels.

Enterprising locals were salving what they could from the wreckage.

"What happened?" Septimus asked a woman with a babe-in-arms and a rotten cabbage stuck, a little incongruously, between her breasts. "Where is everybody?"

She shrugged.

"Don't arsk me. The soldiers started shootin'. Everybody ran for it!"

"Where are they now? The soldiers?"

"Zeelandia Street. That's where orl the racket is comin' from. They've cornered *a foreign agitator.* So I've 'eard. At the filthy old Crow 'otel."

"Oh, no..."

Septimus left the market and dashed off in the direction of his lodgings. It wasn't very far. A small crowd had gathered, at the bottom end of Zeelandia Street. There was a strong smell of spent gunpowder in the air. The Crow Hotel was barely visible, through the dust and smoke. Septimus pushed his way through the gawping throng, to a spot a little further up the street, where he had a better view.

"What's going on?" he asked a toothless old woman.

She moved a little, to let Septimus squeeze in beside her.

"Gord knows who 'e is," she told Septimus. "The *army* chased 'im darn 'ere. From Bluegate Fields. That's what we've 'eard. He shot a parish constable. *Shot 'im dead.* The body's still lyin' there. Up the street. Up by that old 'ouse."

She pointed, vaguely, towards the top end of the street.

"He shot a constable?"

"That's what they're sayin'. I only just got 'ere."

The crumbling facade of the Crow Hotel was just about visible through the smoke. A window had been thrown open, high up, on one of the top floors. It was the same floor that Septimus lived on, though his own room was round at the back, overlooking the yard. The man at the window had a musket. He was waving it around, somewhat erratically, as he looked for another target in the street below.

Is it one of my neighbours? Septimus wondered.

He rarely saw anything of his fellow lodgers. They kept themselves to themselves. Mostly. One or two of them took breakfast in the downstairs dining-room but Septimus had never joined them. He'd never felt *entirely* welcome at the Crow Hotel. Even in the early days when he'd been solvent, and mostly sober.

The soldiers – dragoons from the Tower by the look of them – were sheltering behind a low wall, directly opposite the hotel. A red-coated officer raised his head to take stock of the situation. Immediately, another shot rang out. The ball hit the wall-top brickwork and whistled off, harmlessly.

While the revolutionist reloaded, the soldiers returned fire.

The reports echoed back from the surrounding streets.

Broken glass tinkled down from the front of the hotel. The soldiers peered up, nervously, then ducked again as another shot came from the high window.

The bastard has got somebody reloading for him, Septimus realised.

There were at least two of them up there. A man and a woman, perhaps. But things weren't looking so good for them. They were hopelessly outnumbered.

The soldiers were getting ready to storm the building.

I need to get into my chamber, Septimus thought.

Everything he owned was in there. His clothes. His haversack. His paper and pens. His memoirs, too – the few pages he'd already written.

While he watched and fretted a Sign of the Crocodile Queen hearse clattered into view. It rolled along to where the murdered constable was lying and juddered to a halt. The black horses snorted, impatiently, while the hooded ghoul at the reins climbed down and examined the constable's slumped body.

The doleful vehicles had become an everyday sight on the streets of London. The crocodile priests had a curious *instinct* for death. *Violent* death, especially. In some cases, as Lachlan had pointed out, the hearses appeared to have been on their way *before the fatal crime had even been committed.*

As though they'd known in advance.

As though Queen Mbembé was *hungry* for the blood of the dead. For the lost souls of the city.

Is it like this in Paris? Septimus wondered, suddenly. *Is this happening all over the world? In New York? In Calcutta? In Cairo? In Constantinople?*

He shivered at the thought.

Another vehicle was approaching. Through the dust and smoke. The soldiers cheered as a horse-drawn artillery-piece thundered into the street. The horses were quickly uncoupled and led off. Uniformed artillerymen dragged the ten pounder into a covered alleyway. Across the street from the hotel. The dragoons provided covering fire while the heavy piece was positioned and made ready.

More windows were smashed. More broken glass rained down.

Septimus wondered where Mrs Lusardi was. She was going to be furious about the damage. It was possible that she didn't even know what was going on. She was often out, at this time of day. Visiting her relatives in Ratcliffe, or walking her ill-tempered little dog. Out in the fields, or down by the river.

The first round from the ten-pounder went high and toppled one of the hotel's big chimneys. Brick-dust and tiles rained down. The onlookers gasped as a huge chimney-pot dropped and shattered. The second shot was more accurate. The ball hit the front wall, just below the open window, and went straight through.

It was the *coup de grâce*. A collective moan rose from the crowd as the wall disintegrated. In front of their very eyes. A dusty avalanche of bricks and mortar thundered down into the street. The spectators screamed and backed away.

As the dust cleared, the full extent of the damage became apparent. Most of the building's frontage had gone. Floors hung out at strange angles. Chairs and chamber-pots were still tumbling. The onlookers stared, open-mouthed, as a carved mahogany wardrobe toppled out. It hit the ground with a crash and broke apart.

Did I lock my room? Septimus wondered.

He couldn't remember.

It wasn't clear what had happened to the foreign agitators.

They were quite possibly buried in the rubble.

The Crow Hotel still stood – *just about* – but its days as a flea-pit hostelry were clearly done. What was left was beyond repair. Half the building had gone.

All that was left was a smoking ruin.

While the soldiers probed the debris for anything worth stealing, Septimus picked his way across to the half-buried front porch. Nobody challenged him as he went up the steps. The shattered door creaked in protest as he forced it open.

He took a deep breath and went in.

The entrance hall was thick with dust. Parts of the ceiling had collapsed. It was weirdly quiet. Bewildered rats were scuttling about. Watched by a committee of equally puzzled cats. The main stairs appeared undamaged. Septimus crept up.

An apocalyptic scene confronted him. Up at the top. Most of the rooms on his floor had disappeared. The remains of the corridor dangled out into empty space. High above the street. Pigeons were already flying in and out.

He opened the door to his own chamber and peered in. It was just as he'd left it. As far as he could tell. There wasn't even much dust. His belongings were still there. He stuffed what he could into his haversack and hurried back downstairs.

Other faces had now appeared. In the rubble-strewn hall. The elderly night-watchman, Mr Podo, had emerged from wherever he spent his daytime hours. He was sitting at his desk with a confused, sleepy look on his face. As though the noise had woken him but nobody had yet told him what had happened.

Dust was still floating down.

The *émigré* countess, half-dressed in a revealing silk undergarment, was shouting outrageous insults at Mr Podo. In racy Parisian French. She was dressing herself while she ranted. Mr Podo was trying his best not to look. Or listen.

"*Another room?*" she screamed. In English. "*Putain!* You really *theenk* I want to spend *one more moment* of my life in zees...*'ell 'ole?* What about my *clozes?* My *toiletries?* It eez all out in the *street.* Buried in the... *feelth!* You theenk I am going to go out there *naked* and poke around under zer... *ordure...* looking for my most private... *theengs,* in front of all zese disgusting... *common people?*"

She was quite plump, in the flesh, Septimus couldn't help but notice. There were goose-pimples on her pink arms. Despite her layers of fat, she was clearly feeling the cold. She whirled round and glared furiously at Septimus.

"*Merde!* What are *you* staring at? *I 'ave never in my 'ole life been so...*" She struggled to find a word. "*...'umiliated!* Where are my fucking *intimacies?*"

She'd managed to wriggle into a rather elegant, dusty dress while she'd been shouting. Her coat was hanging on the back of a chair. Septimus picked it up and held it while she slipped her arms into it. She pulled it on without thanking him and buttoned it up. It was a modish, dark, woollen topcoat with a grey fur collar. The fur looked as though it had come from some kind of wolf.

"Speak to *him* if you want your money back," Mr Podo suggested, pointing a quill-pen threateningly at

Septimus. "*He's* the cause of all this trouble! We could have the place rebuilt, from *the ground up,* with the money he owes us, and *still* have enough in hand to feed the poor of the parish for a twelve-month!"

"He's exaggerating, my dear lady," Septimus assured the countess. "I paid them every penny I owed, just yesterday. *With interest!* I'm an old soldier. A man of honour! I even fought for the French Republic! I still bear the scars."

The countess regarded him with a puzzled, frightened look.

Septimus fumbled in his pockets and pulled out a few small coins. All he had left in the world – after the adventures of the previous evening. Altogether it came to about two and sixpence ha'penny. Gently, he took the countess's hand and dropped the coins into it. Mr Podo's eyes widened. He leaned over the desk and stared at the little heap of coins, as though he thought he might be dreaming.

"*Monsieur...*" the countess murmured. She bit her lip.

"Take it, *madame,*" Septimus told her. "It will get you a room for the night, at the very least. You can't stay here. The whole bloody place could collapse."

He picked up his haversack and made for the door.

"Can I accompany you?" the countess called after him. "I 'ave no-one."

Her fury had subsided. Septimus hesitated. He studied her anxious, pale, aristocratic, Gallic face, with its odd wrapping of ancient wolf-fur.

"*Madame...* you mistake me, I fear. I'm no gentleman. Far from it. My advice would be to try the French community around Golden Square. Take a hackney-coach. It should only cost you a shilling, at this time of day. *Adieu.*"

"*But, sir...*" she pleaded.

Septimus hurried off. He had problems enough of his own. He wasn't sure why he'd given the countess his money. Something touching in her face, perhaps. Or the odd thrill of seeing her *déshabillé*. He could have invited her to join him at Lachlan's house. Along with Mulu and the Irish girls. Lachlan himself was half French. But the place was already crowded, by the sound of things, and Lachlan had no great fondness for the titled classes. Wherever they happened to be from.

In Lachlan's eyes, they were all criminals.

The ten-pounder was being hauled away when Septimus got outside. The artillerymen were strutting about looking pleased with themselves. It had been a good day's work. The building was a *magnificent* mess. It would almost certainly need to be pulled down. Barefooted urchins were picking through the rubble in the street. Looking for anything the soldiers might have missed.

Septimus set off for the Rose Tavern.

He was in need of a drink, and some civilised company.

As he walked, he remembered that he'd also promised to go to Deptford, at some point. What with one thing and another, it had slipped his mind.

It had been a confusing day.

Captain Smalt would be getting worried.

20

BILLY FALLS FOUL OF THE LAW

Septimus was hoping that somebody would be able to lend him a few shillings. For a day or two. The sun was already going down when he reached the Rose Tavern.

He'd spent most of the day in Zeelandia Street. Watching the world fall apart.

Harriet Wildfire rushed across the busy room to greet him.

"Septimus! *Praise the Lord!* Where have you *been?* We've been worried about you! You were quite drunk when you left last night. Such *awful* things are happening! Lachlan told me about Mr Serocoal. He didn't want to talk about it. I had to almost beat it out of him. I took him home in a hackney-coach. Early this morning. Eventually, over in Poplar, he told me the whole, dreadful story."

"Does anyone else know?"

"Only Madam O'Reilly. I had to tell her. Out of common decency. She and Mr Serocoal were old friends. They'd been lovers, I think. *Long ago.* In their younger years. I spared her the worst of it, but even so... she took it quite badly. I gave her some laudanum and put her to bed. The poor woman. Lachlan was asking after you, by the way. He wants to see you. Where have you been all day?"

"*Oh...*" Septimus grunted. "Here and there. There was some trouble on Zeelandia Street. A local constable was shot dead. The culprits took refuge in the Crow Hotel. Of all places! It's where I've been living. This past six months."

"I know the place. There's been trouble everywhere. Barricades were erected on Cable Street. The army opened fire on the crowd. People were killed. After that, things went from bad to worse. What happened on Zeelandia Street?"

"Soldiers from the Tower had been chasing some unlucky bastard. He'd run all the way from Bluegate Fields, apparently. He was shooting from a window. Up at the top of the Crow Hotel. There were two of them, I think. Him and his woman, perhaps. The artillery turned up, while I was there. They managed to hit the place with their second round and that was it. The whole bloody building came down."

"All of it?"

"Most of it. I need to find some new lodgings."

"Lachlan will take you in. He'll be happy to see you."

"How is he?"

"He'll live. The local barber stitched the worst of his wounds this morning. He can still walk. Just about. This new woman of his is looking after him."

"*Mulu?* Are you sure she's not putting poison in his food?"

"That's not the way it looked to me. Lachlan has met his match in that young woman. She was *furious* with him for staying out all night. *Without telling her.* They were screaming stupid insults at each other like an old married couple."

"*Really?*"

Harriet winked and leaned closer.

"Why not? Lachlan has *money.* Or, at least, he soon will have. He's a good catch for a girl who's got nothing. They *like* each other, secretly, if you ask me. They just don't want to admit it. They were almost *made* for each other."

"*Do you think so?*"

"*It's fate,* Septimus. I know about these things."

"Did Lachlan mention our, uh... *other business?*"

"There was news," Harriet confided. She lowered her voice. "*A very handsome black footman turned up. Earlier today. In a private carriage. Quite the gentleman, he was. Very nicely dressed. The girls were all aflutter. He'd brought a sealed letter for Lachlan. One of the girls took it round to the house. It was a confirmation that everything is arranged. The money will be ready. As promised. Lachlan sent me a message. He asked me to let you know.*"

"Thank God! At least *something* is going right."

"The cargo is safe," she said. "I've been over to Deptford."

"Was Billy there?"

"He wasn't on the ship. Captain Smalt was there alone. I had to tell him about Mr Serocoal. He was devastated. Like the rest of us, I suppose. At least Lachlan survived. It could have been worse. We could have lost them both."

"What about Billy? Has anybody seen him?"

"One of the Irish girls saw him. Late last night. At the Crown and Anchor in Ratcliffe. He's been *drinking*. Throwing money around. She said 'hello' but he didn't recognise her. He was in such a state. She was worried about him."

"He'll sober up soon enough. Money doesn't go far when you start drinking like that. Not in Sailor Town. I speak from experience. He's probably sleeping it off somewhere. At this very moment. With a sweet lady at his side, no doubt."

"Billy's young."

"As long as he keeps his mouth shut. Tomorrow is the day, then?"

"That's the way it looks. Do you want a drink?"

"A brandy would go down well. Can I pay later?"

Harriet laughed.

"Sit down, you fool. I'll get us a bottle."

While Harriet went to the bar Septimus found a seat near the fire and dropped into it. The coals were blazing. The big room was crowded and warm. He glanced around. Some Chinese sailors were drinking at a nearby table. A couple of Madam O'Reilly's regular girls were trying to strike up a conversation with them. Despite the problems of language, things seemed to be going quite well.

An interpreter wasn't needed.

Harriet returned with a pint of brandy and two glasses.

"I'll join you, Septimus. I'm in need of a drink myself. These past days have been a bloody nightmare. First Susie! Now Mr Serocoal! Not to mention all the other deaths. Every day we hear more bad news. French troops are massing on the other side of the Channel, so they say. But tomorrow we'll have the money, eh? We'll be starting our new lives. I still don't know *exactly* what you gentlemen have been up to. Smalt has refused to tell me. He says it's best that I don't know."

"He's probably right. Don't take it amiss."

She shrugged as she uncorked the brandy.

"I'll find out soon enough, I suppose. What bothers me more is this *dreadful* business of the worms. What *are* they, Septimus? Where have they *come* from? Lachlan was rambling on like a man possessed when I took him home this morning. He was in a *very* odd state of mind. The worms are... *fiends from hell,* he told me! *Satanic servants of the Crocodile Queen!* I thought it was the laudanum speaking. As much as anything. We'd given him another huge dose. To help with the pain."

"Lachlan is one of the few people who've *seen* one... and *lived.*"

"But... *what are they?*"

"I'm as wise as you are, Harriet. They do seem to be connected, in some mysterious way, with the French cult. They first appeared in Paris. According to Lachlan. He'd heard mention of them when he was over there. He thought it was just stupid talk. But now they're *here.* Suddenly. In London. *Killing people!*"

"Might it be part of some *dastardly* French plot?"

"Possibly. Some *very* strange ideas have taken hold in France. Since the storming of the Bastille. Paris is a huge city. The poorer folk are squeezed together, shoulder to shoulder, in the narrow streets. Ideas can spread very quickly. I was in France last winter – by chance – though I kept well away from Paris. I'd heard some *shocking* stories. *Satanic rituals were being performed!* In Parisian churches! A sort of...*fascination with evil* had taken hold of people. In certain circles."

"Lachlan told me about the *Temple des Rêves*. Around the corner from his mother's place. In Montparnasse. It has its own, vast, ghostly, cemetery, he says. Like the one they're creating here. In Southwark. The black hearses are as busy in Paris as they are over here. It's a terrifying thought. *Where will it all end?*"

"I wish I knew."

"Susie was *happy,*" Harriet continued, "until she became involved with those bastards! She attended a ceremony in Wapping. *Two days later she was dead!* She'd drunk that *potion* they go on about. The *Eau Sacré*. They gave her twenty shillings! *Pah!* She could easily have earned it elsewhere. A pretty girl like her."

Septimus poured himself another brandy.

"I also drank the *Eau Sacré,*" he confessed. "Though it may not have been authentic. Lachlan had bought it in Paris. When he went over to visit his mother. Some local rogue had sold him the stuff. Real or not, though, it has affected me, I can't deny. I've been having the *strangest bloody dreams*. About Susie! She's been appearing in my chamber. *Night after night.* Like a wandering ghost."

"That's understandable."

"Is it? I'm not so sure. The Susie who appears in my chamber is not the sweet girl we knew. She's more beautiful, if anything, but... *colder*. She wants me to join her in the afterlife. What kind of woman would expect that of a man?"

"It doesn't sound like the Susie we knew," Harriet agreed.

The brandy was nearly finished. A pint didn't go far.

"Another bottle?" Septimus suggested. "I can pay tomorrow."

"I'll get you one, don't worry," she told him, with a wink. "But I have to work. I'm going to perform. I'm not really in the mood, but... I owe it to Madam O'Reilly. This will be my final night. After all these years. We're upping anchor. Smalt and I. Heading south. As soon as we've got the money. Why don't you join us?"

"I wish I could. I've got, uh... *things to do.* Here in London."

"We could find you a berth, if you change your mind. Think about it! We'll all meet up tomorrow. In Deptford. To divide the money and celebrate. It will be quite an occasion! Lachlan wants to see you, by the way. He's worried about Billy, and the matter of moving the goods, in the morning. He needs reassuring."

"I'll talk to him."

Harriet gave Septimus a friendly kiss on the cheek and hurried off. Septimus bolted the last of the brandy. He didn't know *exactly* where Lachlan lived. It was in Poplar, he knew, but for one reason or another he'd never actually been there.

He'd meant to ask Harriet.

The tavern was filling up. More candles were being lit. Septimus poked the fire while he waited for Harriet to return. He found the coal-tongs and dropped a few more lumps into the flames. Up until now he hadn't been *at all sure* that things were going to work out. So *many* things could have gone wrong.

So many things *had* gone wrong.

But the worst was over.

By this time the next day, they'd be sharing out the money.

Septimus wasn't sure what he was going to do with his own share. Most of his thoughts involved Lady Constance. In one way or another. His desire to see her was growing stronger by the day. *Somehow,* he had to get into Ermine House.

The first thing I'll do is visit a bathhouse, he promised himself.

An outbreak of noise and shouting interrupted his thoughts. A drunken foreign sailor was trying to push his way in through the front door. One of the Rose Tavern girls was trying to kick him back out into the street. Septimus glimpsed a weather-beaten face and mass of tangled hair. It was hard to tell what language the fellow was speaking. He was *insanely* drunk. The noises he was making didn't sound like language at all. Peace returned when a pair of public-spirited coal-heavers stepped forward and smashed a heavy brass spittoon into the sailor's face.

Defeated and bloody-nosed, he staggered off into the night.

A scruffy street-urchin had slipped in, almost unnoticed, while this altercation was going on. Nobody paid him much attention as he crept from table to table, studying faces, as though he was looking for someone. Someone in particular.

With his hat in his hand, he approached Septimus.

"Would you be Mr Slim, sir?"

"I might be. It depends. Who wants to know?"

"Mr Lachlan, sir. I'm to take you to him. I'll carry your bag."

"I'd prefer to carry it myself. Where is he?"

"Two minutes' walk, sir. Just follow me."

"Two minutes?"

The lad picked up the haversack. Septimus swayed, a little groggily, as he got to his feet. He looked around for Harriet but she was nowhere to be seen.

He tightened his coat as he followed the lad out into the night. It was *cold*. The fog was thickening. He trudged along, following his ragamuffin guide as best he could. Nothing looked familiar, in the dark. Occasional patches of light glowed through the murk. From tavern windows and the odd, smoky street-light.

The walk took considerably longer than two minutes.

"Where are we actually going?"

"Poplar, sir. We're nearly there."

Lachlan had moved to Polly Lane, Poplar, when he'd first started making a little money from the coal business. His wife had left him, for some reason, at around the same time, and he'd started renting out rooms. On a fairly casual basis.

The Irish girls had been there for a month or two.

"This is it, sir. This is the place."

It was a gloomy passage, lined on both sides with tumbledown wood and brick houses. Rusty iron bars covered most of the windows. The overhanging upper stories almost met in the middle. A few miserable lights showed through the fog.

A malodorous kennel gurgled down the middle of the alley. Rats were busying about, bold as brass, among the wet stones and the heaps of waste.

Septimus had expected something a little more... *salubrious.* The lad rapped on a low door.

"He said you'd give me thruppence for my trouble, sir."

"I haven't *got* thruppence. Come back tomorrow and I'll give you sixpence. That's a promise. We can perhaps do some more business together."

The kid grinned and ran off. The arrangement seemed acceptable.

Lachlan's ghostly face appeared as the door creaked open.

"Septimus! *Thank God you're alive!* Nobody seemed to know where you were. Young Jack found you, eh? He's a good lad. I told him to look for an evil-looking bastard in a filthy old leather coat. *Ha, ha!* Come on in!"

He held the door while Septimus stepped through.

The room beyond was smoky and warm. The house was quite small. Smaller than Septimus had imagined, when Lachlan had spoken of it. It had been a tavern, of some sort, at one time, so Lachlan claimed, though it could never have held many people. Coals were burning in the fireplace. Candles were lit on the mantle above. A huge mirror, in a splendid, gilded frame, stood in one corner. A lady's mirror. It looked out of place in the shabby room. As though it really belonged elsewhere.

A half-open door led through to a grimy scullery.

With a well-stocked coal cellar down below, Septimus didn't doubt.

Mulu appeared from the rooms above while Lachlan was re-bolting the front door. Septimus stared in astonishment as she sauntered down the flimsy stairs. He hardly recognised her. The dirty-faced *gamine* from Egypt Point was no more. A swaggering young madam had taken her place. She was attired in a low-cut, modish black dress. A diamond pendant hung from a silver chain at her neck.

A love-token. By all appearances.

I'll be damned, Septimus thought. *Is it really the same woman?*

He bowed. Graciously. A flicker of a smile crossed her face.

"We don't have much to offer," Lachlan apologised. "A drop of rum?"

Mulu dragged a little table over to the fire. She found a dusty bottle and banged it down. Along with three glasses. Lachlan prised the cork out.

"It's all we've got, Septimus. I hope it's to your taste."

"Rum suits me fine. They say it's good for your health. What about you, my friend? Are you recovering? Did you sleep? Are your wounds healing?"

"*Slowly!* You know how it goes. I'm taking laudanum. For the pain. This *damnable* gash in my leg is the worst thing! *Dear God!* It had to be sewed-up! I can walk. *Just about!* But you will have to take charge tomorrow, Septimus. *Nothing else has changed!* We can deliver the goods. *Exactly as agreed!* Anytime after midday. The money will be there. I got a letter. From Mr Orzinga."

"Harriet mentioned it."

"It was a *most* courteous letter. Addressed to Mr Serocoal. Orzinga's footman delivered it. He turned up earlier. In a rather splendid private carriage, apparently. It caused a bit of excitement. On Thieves' Street. As you'd expect! The neighbours were all peeping out of their bloody casements. Wondering who in the world it might be, and what his business was. *Nosy bastards!*"

Septimus chuckled at the thought.

"But it was brought round here, uh?"

"Harriet sent it round. She'd realised that it could be important. She hadn't dared tell the footman that Mr Serocoal was dead. Understandably, but... *what are we going to say when we get there?* How are we going to explain things? Mr Serocoal's sudden disappearance is going to seem *extremely* odd. *To say the least!* After he'd introduced us, and argued over the price. It won't look good. We'll just have to tell the truth, I suppose. As best we can. And pray that he believes us!"

"We can't lie to him. It would just make things worse."

"He must have heard talk. About the worms. *Everyone* has."

"What about transport? Has that been arranged?"

"Smalt has arranged something. We just have to get there. In the morning. As early as possible! I'll meet you at the ship. I've got some crutches. You and the captain will have to do the serious work, I'm afraid. The lifting and loading. Then we'll go to Poland Street. Just you and me, I think. And the wagoner, of course."

"What about Billy? Where is he?"

Lachlan moaned and shook his head.

"That's *another* problem! Billy's been locked-up! He's in Newgate!"

"In *Newgate?* What on earth for?"

"Disorderly behaviour. *He broke a window.*"

"And they've *jailed* him? Just for that?"

"So it seems. He's been charged with disturbing the peace, and *possibly* with attempted theft. After all the bloody windows Billy has broken, with his damned explosions! His girl came round here in the small hours, weeping and howling. It was an *accident,* she says. Billy was drunk. *Stupidly* drunk and playing the fool. Somehow he broke the window of a clockmaker's shop. On Cheapside. It was only one pane of glass, she says, but it was three o'clock in the morning and the noise woke up the whole street. The clockmaker came down in his night-clothes, waving a loaded blunderbuss around and shouting for the night-watch."

"Heaven save us! Are you sure he's in Newgate?"

"So his girl says. He'll go before the magistrates tomorrow. Billy just laughed, she says, at the sight of this old man in his night-shirt, with his rusty old blunderbuss. He laughed till he was blue in the face. Till he could hardly stand. Tears were pouring down his cheeks. He was still laughing when the constables turned up and took him away. We have to get him out, somehow."

"Disturbing the peace is not so serious."

"It's not a hanging offence, but the clockmaker is trying to have the charge increased. To attempted theft. That's more serious. *Transportation* would be the best that

Billy could hope for, if he was convicted. Botany Bay! We'd never see the poor lad again. I'm hoping that Harriet will be able to help. She *knows* people. Magistrates. Lawyers. Bishops. People with power. Harriet's famous arse has elevated her into those kind of circles. I'll speak to her tomorrow."

"She's well-connected, it's true," Septimus agreed. "We'll have *money,* too, don't forget. Enough to pay for a good lawyer. We could have Billy out by the end of the day. Money works miracles. The clockmaker could be paid to drop the case. That would be the end of it. We'll need to have words with Billy though. When the time comes. You're going to have to talk to him, Lachlan. Give him some fatherly advice. Set him on the right road. Before he drinks himself to death. Or ends up on the bloody gallows. Mulu, too. What is she going to *do* with all the money we've promised her? It could go to her head. She could get into *all kinds* of trouble. An innocent young woman. Alone. In London. With money to throw around."

Mulu had left, while the men had been talking. She'd gone back upstairs, taking her drink with her. They could hear her shuffling about, in the room above.

"A good point," Lachlan sighed. "Though I don't think Mulu will be a problem. She's not *exactly* innocent, if the truth be told. Or even so young. We talked a bit. Finally. Earlier today. Seeing me in bandages seemed to soften her heart. Just a little. I got her some new clothes, too. That helped."

"Where is she from?"

"Some village on the Norfolk coast. I forget the

name. Her father was a farrier. She's good with horses. She can ride. She went into service, at some big house in Hertfordshire, when she was no more than a child. But it turned sour. She was abused. One of her employer's sons took a fancy to her. The bastard tried to force himself on her. In the kitchens, at night, when nobody was around."

"*Oh, fuck...*"

"Mulu decided to get out of the place and find herself a better position. One moonlit night, when everybody in the house was fast asleep, she dressed herself in men's clothing and stole a horse from the stables. A pedigree beast, as it turned out, but she didn't know that. She rode it down to London, through the night, and tried to sell it at Smithfield Market, early the next morning. Unfortunately for her, the hue and cry had already gone up. The news had travelled faster than she had. Somebody recognised the horse and she was arrested."

"What happened?"

"Horse-stealing is a hanging offence, of course, even for a woman," Lachlan went on. "Sadly! She was facing the rope. At least as a possibility. But then, *astonishingly*, the young bastard who'd tried to rape her turned up in court and spoke in her favour. She escaped the noose. All she got was a year in Newgate."

"The lucky bitch," Septimus murmured.

"Indeed. But... it changed her life forever. She was penniless and homeless when she got out of prison. Her only friends were the thieves and whores she'd met inside. She went back into the horse-stealing business, but before the year was out she was arrested again. This time she claimed to be with child. Whether it was true or not, it saved her skin. She was sentenced to Transportation for Life. Court bailiffs took her down to Portsmouth and put her on a ship with fifty other women. Mulu thought they were going to America. She wasn't *entirely* displeased. She only found out the truth on the morning they sailed. They were on their way to New South Wales – on the other side of the bloody world."

"So... how did she ever get back? It's supposed to be impossible."

"She never left our shores. As things turned out. She didn't even get as far as the Isle of Wight. They'd erected some sort of cookhouse on the ship's main deck, and Mulu was put to work in it. Her and a couple of other women. The prisoners had to be fed. She'd told them that she was a professional cook. Trained in a big house. It was half-true. She'd been some sort of kitchen-maid. The great advantage was that her ankle chains were taken off. As they sailed out of Portsmouth harbour, she took her chances and jumped overboard."

"*Ha, ha!* What a woman!"

"It was a stupid thing to do. They were in deep water. The currents could easily have dragged her down. She'd learned to swim as a child but they were half a mile off-shore when she jumped. The marines on board opened fire but didn't hit her. Mulu thinks they deliberately aimed wide, but I'm not so sure. The bastards were probably just bad shots. The ship would have been rolling. There would have been other vessels close by. It's a busy waterway.

Generally speaking, everything was in her favour. As long as she kept her head and kept going."

"She got ashore, obviously. Where did she go from there?"

"I don't exactly know. She's had some hard times."

"And then she met Spiker."

"That came later. They hadn't known each other all that long. She's been wandering around for years. Stealing horses. Selling cures for the pox. Trying to stay out of trouble. A bit like yourself, Septimus. Like so many of us. And now – after all that – she's going to be rich. The strange workings of fate, eh?"

Lachlan noticed Septimus's haversack.

"Have you left your lodgings?"

"I had no choice. The bloody place has fallen down. I was hoping that you could put me up. Just for a night or two. Until I get organised."

"Come to America, Septimus! With me and Mulu."

"*You and Mulu?* Are my ears deceiving me?"

"Well... you know how it is. Once people get to know each other."

"I need to think. I might even go back to India. It's a *splendid* country, Lachlan. Once you get used to the heat. I could buy myself a mansion in Calcutta and set up house. With a hundred servants and a native mistress! That's the way they live. The bloody British. In their palaces. With punkah-wallahs fanning their heads. In the hot season. I've seen it with my own eyes. It's a mightily tempting thought. But first I have to get into Ermine House. *Somehow.* To see Lady Constance. I need to know what *she* wants. Before I decide."

"Your best bet will be the drains. In the middle of the night."

"I can't do that. It's out of the question. *I'd stink.* She'd take me for a fool. There must be a better way. I could just turn up, I suppose. Early one morning. Bold as brass. With a fake calling-card. Who is going to recognise me, after all these years? My own mother wouldn't recognise me. I could claim to be anybody. A distant relative. A foreign tourist, come to admire the house. I'll think of something. It will take me a day or two, in any case, to get some new clothes."

"It will take you a bloody week to get cleaned up. A few hours at a bath-house wouldn't go at all amiss. Get a shave, while you're there. Keep the moustache, eh? As a disguise. They're quite fashionable, these days. Among the moneyed classes."

The rum was almost gone. Lachlan rooted out another bottle. Mulu was still upstairs. The Irish girls were absent. Lachlan talked, lazily, about his plans.

His dreams of a new life. In the New World.

"*America...*" he breathed. "It's a *republic,* Septimus! *A land of the people!* We could sail together. *All of us!* You and me. Mulu. Lady Constance. If you could persuade her to come. A couple of servants. *Why not?* Billy and his girl, if we can get the silly bastard out of prison. Then there's..."

A sudden racket from the alley outside distracted him. The dull thump of something heavy dropping to the ground. Followed by some noisy hammering.

And a woman's scream. Muted by the fog.

"What the...?"

Lachlan put his glass down. He took a pistol from a shelf above the fire and stepped across to the window. A tattered curtain hung over it. He pulled the rag aside and peered out. Through the grimy panes. Nothing much was visible. The fog had worsened, considerably, while they'd been talking. The alley was poorly-lit.

"It's probably nothing," he said. "Foot-pads. Perhaps. Or house-breakers. *Evil bastards!* We do have a few problems of that sort. In this neck of the woods. It's a bloody disgrace. Why don't they pick on the rich? Like normal people. What are they thinking of? People around here can't feed their own children."

Cautiously, he unbolted the door and leaned out.

Yellow fog flooded in from the world outside.

Mulu reappeared, at the top of the stairs.

"What is it?" she asked.

"I don't know," he called back. "I can't see a bloody thing."

Clutching the pistol, he stepped out into the cold.

21

DASTARDLY DEEDS

Dim lights glowed through the murk. Doors and windows were opening. Worried voices could be heard, as people crept out. Looking for the woman who'd screamed.

"She's here!" someone shouted. *"Bring a lantern!"*

The woman had fallen to the ground, not far from Lachlan's front door. She was still shaking. Something had clearly terrified her. She seemed unable to speak. She whimpered, like a frightened child, as the neighbours gathered around.

She was pointing. Into the dark. At *what,* exactly, was unclear.

Septimus had followed Lachlan out into the night. He ventured a little way up the lane and listened. In case the evil-doers were still lurking. All he could hear were scurrying rats, and the gurgle of sewage in the central kennel. Water was dripping from the overhanging roofs. Nothing much was visible. In the fog.

Whatever had taken place, the perpetrators were long gone.

The local watchman turned up. With a lantern on a pole.

Nervously, he swung it about. Casting light here and there. Something in the grisly shadows caught his eye. With the lamp held high, he edged towards it.

A faded shop-sign came into view. *'Jos. Merryfield & Sons'*, it proclaimed. *'Purveyors of Ironmongery & Household Goods'*. Wooden shutters covered the large windows below. A bloodstained bundle of old rags hung from the boards.

For a horrible moment, nobody moved.

"For the love of God!" somebody murmured. *"What is it?"*

Septimus knew what it was. He'd seen the like of it before. In Susie Kettle's chamber. At the Rose Tavern.

Mulu appeared, with a candle she'd brought from the house. Septimus took it from her and stepped closer to the hideous remains. All that was left of a man. A tarnished silver trinket in the shape of a dolphin dangled, raffishly, from his left ear.

It was Captain Smalt.

"Oh, fuck..." Septimus groaned.

Lachlan approached. He stared in horror.

The manner of the captain's death was plain to see. To anyone who knew the facts. He'd been fed upon. By a worm. Persons unknown had then nailed the barely recognisable remains to the wooden shutters of the shop.

Directly opposite Lachlan's front door.

Something else caught Septimus's eye. He lowered the candle. Several golden guineas, splashed with blood, lay in the dirt below. It was impossible to tell whether they'd slipped from the captain's pockets, or had been scattered there.

As a potent warning to the rest of the gang.

The way the coins lay, in plain view, suggested the latter.

"For God's sake!" Lachlan screamed. *"Those heathen bastards!* They'll pay for this! I swear! *Get him down! Someone! Please!* The poor innocent soul! And if one of those bloody hearses turns up – *tell them to go to hell!"*

He was waving the pistol about wildly. Mulu took it from him.

"Who would do such a thing?" he wailed. "Nailing the poor devil up like that? Like a dead rat! *Not the worms.* Obviously. You need *hands,* to hold a hammer and bang nails in. *Human beings* committed this outrage! They must have dragged him here. From wherever he was killed. To my front door!"

"There may be worse to come," Septimus suggested. "This is the third attack we've suffered! *In just two days.* First Mr Serocoal. Then you. Now the captain. It can hardly be coincidence. *They know who we are!* It's plain to see. This is Blackthorpe's doing! He's *taunting* us! He *wants* us to suffer. Before the final end, when we, too, get ripped to shreds. By one of these *ghastly creatures."*

"No, no, no!"

Lachlan looked horrified. He shook his head.

"I see your point, Septimus, but... *it makes no sense.* We covered our tracks well. No-one on the *Helga* survived. The entire crew went to the bottom. We burned the ship. Clézio *dissolved.* Who could have talked? *It's not possible!"*

Septimus shrugged.

"Let's just hope you're right."

A local carpenter levered the nails out of Smalt's body.

It was a gruesome spectacle, in the fog and the ghostly lamplight. The captain's bloodless remains slumped to the ground, like a bag of old bones, as the final nail was drawn out.

Lachlan muttered a quiet prayer and crossed himself.

"What a *terrible* business! Another funeral to be arranged, uh? *Dear Lord!* I don't even know which faith he followed. Harriet might know. They were close. She'll be heartbroken. We could throw a blanket over him, just for now, I suppose. Until morning. What else can we do? It's the middle of the bloody night."

"The crocodile priests will turn up. Before dawn."

"Let them come! I've got guns in the house. I'm ready."

Most of the neighbours had left. The excitement was over. The watchman promised to make a full report to the Parish Officers, though it didn't seem to matter much whether he did or he didn't. Nothing was going to bring Smalt back.

In the house, Lachlan refilled their glasses. Mulu took a sooty saucepan off the fire. Whatever she'd been cooking had burned to ashes. She cursed, like a whore from hell, as she carried the smoking pan out into the scullery.

The men sat silently. In the unhappy candlelight. Septimus was the first to speak. He picked Lachlan's pistol up from the table and examined it.

"You've got other guns in the house, you say?"

"Two or three. There's another one in the privy. Outside. I've been keeping them handy. It seemed wise. In the circumstances. I've also got a *very* nice pair of gentleman's travelling-pistols. Upstairs. *Lovely guns.* Beautifully-made. Billy lifted them off some drunken cove in Smithfield Market. A couple of weeks ago."

He made a face. To show that he didn't *entirely* approve.

"I'd passed them on to a pawnbroker friend of mine. For a valuation. He sent them back. Just this morning. With an apologetic note. He didn't want to handle them. *Too unusual*, he said. *Too distinctive.* Too much of a risk."

"Can I take a look?"

"You want to see them?"

"I'd be interested."

Lachlan hobbled upstairs. His wounds were bothering him. He returned with an expensive-looking rosewood carrying-case that he passed to Septimus. The box shone prettily in the candlelight. There was a brass makers'-plate on the lid.

'Etherington & Lime, Gunsmiths – London – 1782', it boasted. Septimus opened the case and took out one of the guns. He whistled.

"Your friend is no fool. These are *splendid* weapons. They must have cost a bloody fortune! They're just what I need. Can I borrow them?"

"I don't see why not. What do you have in mind?"

"I'm going to put an end to this madness. Right now. Tonight."

"What are you proposing?"

"I'm going to find the evil bastard responsible. *Lord Blackthorpe.* I'm going to blow his brains out. With one of these rather lovely pistols. It's something I should have done years ago. Better late than never, eh? Is this good powder, would you say? Here in the box? With the guns? It looks good. Has anyone tried it?"

"It should be good but... *don't be too hasty,* Septimus! Let's talk this over. We're all shocked! It's been a *terrible* day. How are you going to find him? He'll have people around him. *Dangerous fanatics!* You won't get anywhere near him."

"I'll take my chances."

"What would it achieve? In any case? If you shot him? The *worms* are the real problem. We *know* that. Poor Captain Smalt was slain by a *worm.* Down in Deptford. Very likely. *I know!* I've *seen* the bloody things! At close quarters! I was attacked myself, don't forget! I'm lucky to be alive! *Dammed lucky!"*

Septimus was busy loading the pistols.

"Blackthorpe is behind all of this," he muttered. "The crocodile priests. The worms. The death-carts. *They're preserving the damned corpses!* Did you know that? In those tunnels they've been digging. Under the Necropolis. A friend of mine has actually *seen* them! Down in the dark! A ghostly army of the dead. Grey shades with claws and yellow eyes! Standing in neat rows. *Waiting for orders!"*

"Heaven save us!"

"This is what we're up against! Blackthorpe is *channelling* something. Some *evil spirit* has taken possession of him. Out there in the sugar islands, perhaps. I saw things myself. *In Saint-Domingue.* In the back-streets of Port-au-Prince. The weird little shrines. Dedicated to gods and demons that we Europeans know nothing of. We'd hear the ceremonies, at night. My old lover, Rozalita, would sometimes attend. But they're *here* now. In London. Those selfsame demons. And *Lord Blackthorpe* is their obedient servant. I have to do this. Wish me luck."

"How are you going to find him?"

"I know *exactly* where he'll be. At the Temple of Dreams. In Southwark. Where else? That's his London address, nowadays. He'll be there. Ranting and chanting in front of his cowed followers. I'll just walk in, say hello, wish him a pleasant evening and put a bullet into his head. *For Smalt!* And all the others."

"They won't let you in! You won't get past the gates!"

"I've been *initiated*. They'll be *expecting* me! My name is in the Great Book! A false name, actually, but I doubt that anybody really cares. It's all horse-shit."

"But, Septimus... let's, uh..."

"Don't worry about the guns. I'll return them in the morning."

"It's not the *guns* I'm worried about! It's you! I don't want to lose *another* friend. You don't *have* to do this. We've still got the gold! As far as we know. By this time tomorrow we could be on our way to America! You and me. Billy and his girl. Mulu and Lady Constance. We'll take a coach to Falmouth. We could almost *buy* a bloody coach! Mulu could take care of the horses. There are regular sailings from Falmouth to New York. We'll be safe. Once we're out at sea."

Septimus was no longer listening.

"I'll be back before dawn. God willing. This is my *destiny,* Lachlan. For once in my life, I'm going to do the right thing. *Somebody* has to do it. We can't just sit here and let the mad bastard pick us off, one by one. Pray for me, uh?"

He pushed the pistols into his belt and stuffed everything else he needed into his coat pockets. Lachlan watched, worriedly, from the fireside.

"How are you going to get out of the place, afterwards?"

"There'll be a moment of panic. Nobody will know quite what to do. They'll just stand there with their stupid mouths hanging open. By the time they recover, I'll be long gone. Give me that other pistol as well, eh? If you don't mind. I'll take all three. It pays to be well-armed. Hopefully, I'll only need one shot."

Lachlan passed it over. He followed Septimus out into the fog.

"Septimus!" he shouted after him. *"Wait! I've got a better idea!"*

But Septimus had already vanished.

He was trudging through the cold fog. Heading west. Trying his best to remember the unfamiliar paths his young guide had led him down. His plan was to walk the several miles to Southwark, by way of London Bridge. It would take an hour or two, but it would at least give him time to think. Despite what he'd told Lachlan, he had no idea of how he was going to get into the Temple of Dreams.

There would be guards on the gate. Almost certainly. They *might* let him in. They might not. His best course of action, he decided as he walked, would be to throttle one of the unsuspecting crocodile priests and steal his garments.

The hooded robe would be a perfect disguise.

The hour before dawn would be the time to strike, he thought.

It was a lesson he'd learned in his pirate days.

Despite the fog, he eventually found his way back to Narrow Street. From there on, he knew where he was. He crossed into Ratcliffe, where the taverns and alehouses were largely still open for business. Drunken whores pestered him as he walked. They took him for a sailor ashore, in need of female company. At any other time Septimus would have stopped and talked, but this was no ordinary night.

He hurried past, with no more than a friendly nod.

Ghostly tenements loomed around him, in the fog. Some dilapidated houses were being demolished, on Denmark Street. Homeless families were sleeping in the ruins. Fires were burning, here and there. Ragged figures could be seen. Huddled around the flames. They glanced in Septimus's direction as he went by.

Hailstones started falling. Septimus shoved his hands into his coat pockets and trudged on. The fall got heavier, and noisier, as he stumbled along. The stones were clattering down. He could hardly see where he was going.

Grunting and cursing, he pulled his old coat up over his head.

He leaned down and picked up a handful of the tiny stones. They were cold and hard, with jagged edges. Like marble chippings. From a mason's yard.

They weren't *hailstones* at all. Just little stones. Falling from the sky.

"Heaven save us!" he groaned.

A miserable-looking dog slunk past with its tail between its legs. Except for the dog, and Septimus himself, the streets were empty. Even the rats had gone.

The tumbling ended, as suddenly and mysteriously as it had begun. An eerie silence ensued. Other things began floating down. *Living things.* Obnoxious little whispering creatures that fluttered their slimy wings and *wriggled* as they fell.

He caught one as it floated by and immediately dropped it in disgust.

"Cockroaches! Dear Lord! It's raining cockroaches!"

The abominations were spinning in the night air as they came down. They appeared to be of the same species as the ones that already infested most of the local taverns, pie-shops and lodging-houses. They had the same dull, dark carapace. The same vile, thin legs and the bright little red eyes that seemed full of cunning.

Septimus spat and cursed and pulled his coat tighter.

He was somewhere in the vicinity of East Smithfield, not far from the Tower, though he couldn't yet see that august edifice, through the fog and the swarming cockroaches. They squashed under his feet as he walked. He shook himself, like a wet dog, to get the awful things off his clothes and out of his hair.

The evil bastard has read my mind! he thought. *Blackthorpe! That's why he's picked on cockroaches! He knows how much I hate the bloody things!*

The notion that Blackthorpe could read his mind was almost as disturbing as the living swamp he was paddling through. The black beetles were still falling.

An eerie shriek stopped him in his tracks as he neared

the Tower. It had come from somewhere above. Out of the unholy dark.

He pulled out one of the pistols.

"You'll pay for this, you bastard!" he yelled into the night. "I'll find you! I promise! Wherever you are! You're not invincible! Whatever you might think!"

The tumbling stopped. As though this particular jest had run its course.

Septimus shivered. He was half-expecting something worse, but, for the moment, nothing came. One of the old toll-booths at the end of the bridge caught his eye. The booths hadn't been used for years. They were derelict and decayed.

He slipped inside. The interior stank but he felt safer. He could hear the river splashing up against the piers of the bridge, far below. Then, as the fog shifted, he caught sight of the dome of St. Paul's, half a mile away. Over the roofs.

"Oh, no..." he groaned.

Grotesque flying creatures were circling in the moonlight above Wren's great dome. The sky was full of them. Septimus recognised them. He knew exactly what they were. He'd seen one at close quarters. Out in the estuary. At Egypt Point.

Lachlan had seen one emerging. In the Greenwich midnight.

From the body of a dying worm.

Septimus stared out. Through the rotted doorway. He scarcely dared breathe. The awful scene disappeared as the fog moved again. He shrank back into the malodorous dark. It was cold. He was shaking. From his hiding-place he could hear the *swish... swish* of the creatures' wings, and their chilling, unearthly calls.

"*Oh, Jesus...*" he muttered.

Other sounds reached his ears. Screams and shouts. The clamour of a great commotion. A fire-bell was jangling. *Clang, clang, clang!* The screams were coming from the nearby streets. Night-watchmen had raised the alarm, he realised. Terrified citizens were fleeing their homes and running for their lives.

The metropolis was under attack.

From the heavens above.

Church bells began tolling. Warning of the peril. The streets would soon be full of soldiers, Septimus assumed. Dragoons from the Tower would arrive first, followed by troops from the various camps that had been set up around the city. The generals had been preparing for a French attack. Along the lines of 1066. No-one had anticipated a plague of blood-sucking serpents, but Septimus suspected that the soldiery would take it in their stride. Once the initial shock had worn off.

Fearful souls were soon streaming past. White-haired old men clutching money-boxes. Bewildered children. Servants. Women in their night-clothes.

Illogically, the crowds were all fleeing south. *Towards trouble.*

It seemed to Septimus that the flying creatures were *driving* people in that direction. Over the bridge. Towards Southwark... and the Temple of Dreams.

"*It's the bloody French!*" a fat woman in a nightdress screamed as she ran past Septimus. "*French magicians have created these terrible things! The French army has landed in Kent! They'll be here by morning! Heads will roll in the streets!"*

She was carrying a battered old brass candlestick with a stub of candle in it. The candle had blown out but the woman was gripping the precious object as though her life depended on it. As though it was all she had left in the world.

Septimus hardly knew what to do. The creatures were circling in the foggy darkness overhead. He could hear their shrieks, and the hiss of their wings. There was nothing particularly *French* about them. As far as he could tell. If *anyone* had created the ghastly things, he told himself, it was his old foe – *Lord Blackthorpe*.

What he couldn't quite see, as yet, was... *why?*

While he pondered the question, one of them appeared. Out of the vile fog. Directly above his head.

By the look of it, the thing had been *feeding*. On human flesh. Bloody red slime was dribbling from its rows of teeth. Its red eyes glowed through the murk.

When it came for him, he was ready.

He dragged out one of the purloined pistols and fired at the creature's eyes as it closed in, gripping the stock with both hands to be sure of his aim.

BA-DOOOM!!! The blast echoed back from nearby buildings. The thing was so close he could smell its foul breath. The ball went in through its ugly mouth and out through the back of its head. It shrieked as it tumbled away.

Pieces of its brain flew out in every direction.

Astonishingly, it didn't die immediately. It beat its way back up into the fog and disappeared. As though it hadn't even noticed that most of its head was gone.

Septimus could still hear the slapping of its wings, up above. He was half-expecting the odious thing to sprout a new head and return to the fray, but then – with a final defeated gurgle – it gave up the struggle and plummeted to earth.

It hit the river with a huge splash. Stinking Thames water rained down. Septimus retreated into the safety of the old toll-booth. He could hear people screaming outside. *Thousands of people.* From where he was hiding, inside the booth, it sounded as though the entire population of the city was on the move.

Carts and carriages were rattling southwards across the bridge. Septimus peered out, worriedly, from his hiding-place. They were going the wrong way, he just *knew*. Towards some even greater peril. He wanted to rush out into the road and warn them. Before it was too late! But some instinct held him back.

He knew they wouldn't listen.

There was no reason why they should. That was the truth of it. He had no more idea of what was going on than they did. None of it made any sense.

Is Blackthorpe in league with the French? he asked himself.

It seemed unlikely. Though by no means impossible.

His resolve to assassinate the Grand High Pontieff was weakening. He hadn't expected such chaotic scenes, when he'd borrowed the guns. He left the bridge and wandered off. Along Thames Street. Heading west. Towards the Strand.

He was thinking of Lady Constance. If the invasion really had begun, he reasoned, the French would be in

London by daybreak. It was only seventy miles or so, from the coast. The overnight coaches could do the journey in twelve hours.

A well-trained army, fresh to the field, might halve that time.

Lady Constance, with her grand house and her noble French heritage, would be in the gravest of danger. The *sansculottes* would have little sympathy for her.

There were already corpses in the streets. The pavements were strewn with human remains. The stench was atrocious. Septimus held his nose as he walked.

Buildings were ablaze. On almost every street.

Lamps had been knocked over, he guessed. In the rush to get away.

On several occasions he was forced to take refuge from the flying creatures. In derelict buildings, back-alleys, unlit porches and stinking public privies.

The Strand, when he finally got there, was foggy and quiet.

He crept past St. Mary le Strand church. In the haunted shadows of the graveyard walls. There were overturned carriages, and dead horses, in the road.

The horses, too, appeared to have been killed by the creatures.

Ermine House looked abandoned. Candles were lit, in one or two of the attic rooms, but there were no other signs of life. The porters' lodge was boarded-up.

The front gates were chained shut. Septimus could easily have climbed over, but he was scared of being shot. By a petrified watchman.

A lane at one side of the building led to the stables

and the extensive rear gardens. The surrounding walls were intimidatingly high, though an intruder had once got in that way, Septimus recalled. One winter's night. Long ago.

An ambitious young rogue had managed to scale the riverside wall. He'd got into one of the basement pantries and stolen a box of silver spoons. With the distinctive Blackthorpe family crest on the handles. By some miracle he'd got away without being caught, but things hadn't gone *quite* so well for him afterwards.

The spoons had been recovered fairly quickly.

The lad had been hung. Barely a fortnight later. At Tyburn.

Beyond the fortress-like rear gates, an overgrown path led down to the river. Septimus picked his way along it. The great walls loomed above him, in the fog.

The spoon thief, he recalled, had brought his own ladder.

In Septimus's day the walls and outbuildings had been well looked-after. Things had clearly changed. The masonry was crumbling. Weeds of all kinds were growing out of it. The riverside walls were completely overgrown. He pushed his way through a patch of nettles and tugged at some thick ivy. It felt safe enough.

Any fool could get up there, he thought.

His heart pounded as he climbed. He'd not eaten since breakfast. *And* he'd been drinking. He cursed his own stupidity as he dragged himself up the wall.

Mercifully, the ivy held. He reached the top and peered over.

Nobody challenged him. Despite all the noise he'd

made. As far as he could tell there wasn't a living soul around. Dim light from one of the basement kitchens was visible, through the fog. Most of the house was as dark as midnight in hell.

A moving candle caught his eye. Up in one of the attics.

Someone was still in the place. One of the servants, he guessed.

Wooden scaffolding obscured the outlines of the East Tower.

The tower had been added to the house, against the original architect's wishes, when Lord Blackthorpe had decided that he needed an *observatory*. They'd been fashionable, at the time. The King had had one installed, at Buckingham House.

The observatory was still there, Septimus noticed. He could just about make it out. Up in the gloom. The scaffolding ended some way below it.

Repairs were being done to the adjoining roofs, it seemed.

The safest way into the house, he decided, would be through the attics. If he could climb the scaffolding. Once he was up there, he could smash a window.

He crawled along the wall to the stables, clambered over the slippery roofs and dropped, as quietly as he could, into the deserted gardens. Decades had gone by since he'd last walked that way. Nothing much had changed. Strangely.

Two huge bronze elephants still guarded the steps of the south terrace. They'd been a gift, he recalled. From an Indian Nawab. They'd been brought up the Thames and dragged ashore by a hundred men. Into the secluded rear courtyard, where they'd stood, incongruously, in the grey English cold, ever since.

Septimus shivered. In sympathy.

He could hear the flying creatures. In the darkness above.

The scaffolding, when he reached it, looked desperately unsafe. The poles were wet and slimy. They weren't even well-fixed. The ropes had worked loose.

But he'd come too far to turn back.

He wished himself luck and started climbing.

He had to stop, half-way, to catch his breath. A snarling stone lion's head glared down at him from the parapet. Septimus vaguely remembered the thing.

He clung on. Panting and cursing.

I'll start eating better, he told himself. *Once we've sold the gold.*

An area of flat roof caught his eye. A large iron water-tank had once stood there, he remembered. For some reason it had been removed. In its day the tank had supplied the whole house. Water had been pumped up to it from a well in the grounds. All that was left was the rotten roof, and some bits of ancient lead pipe.

Cautiously, he reached out and tried the old planks. They felt solid enough. He let go of the scaffolding and jumped across. Instantly... the roof gave way.

He screamed as he plummeted through. For a horrible moment, he thought he was done for. But fate wasn't finished with him. *Not yet.* He crashed, head first, into the space below. What was left of the roof came down on top of him.

"*Fuck!*" he screamed, as the wreckage poured down.

The pile he'd fallen into had probably saved his life. He wasn't seriously hurt. No bones were broken, as far as he could tell. Though he was covered from head to toe in sooty filth and he'd made enough noise to waken the dead. The occupants of the house, if there were any, could hardly have failed to notice his grand entrance.

He pulled out one of the pistols, and cocked it.

Stagnant water was dripping all around. As though the old lead pipes in the roof had never been properly drained. The air was full of dust and wriggling spiders. He'd landed in what appeared to be a... *storage chamber.* Of some sort.

The door was wide open. Candlelight was flooding in. A pair of startled women were standing outside. They were staring, wide-eyed, at Septimus.

One of them was Lady Constance!

This was the moment Septimus had dreamed of. Though it wasn't at all the way he'd imagined it would be. He was half-buried in filth, and waving a stolen pistol, shakily, at the world. Blood was dribbling down the side of his head.

Lady Constance didn't look pleased to see him.

She looked – *terrified.*

22

THE HOUR OF THE
CROCODILE QUEEN

Septimus composed himself. As best he could. He struggled to his feet and stood, blinking, in the light. The fact that Lady Constance hadn't recognised him had confused him. Just a little. Though it had been a while since they'd last met. His hair was longer. He was thinner, too, and he hadn't shaved for nearly a month.

He hardly recognised himself, sometimes.

"*Captain Slim,* your ladyship..." he mumbled. "*Septimus...*"

He felt like an impostor. A lying rogue. A pathetic sneak-thief who'd fallen through a hole in the roof. There was no such person as *Captain Slim* anymore.

He'd come to a bad end. Decades ago. Murdered by a jealous husband. Everybody knew that. He'd dipped his spoon in Lady Constance's honey-pot and got caught. *The stupid bastard.* Nobody had seen him since. *Served him bloody right.*

"*Septimus?*"

She took a cautious step forward and looked him up

and down. Her well-bred nose twitched at the back-street smell of him. Septimus wiped the muck off his face.

Lady Constance stared. She glanced around, worriedly. As though she was about to call for help. Septimus's heart sank. The way things were looking, he was heading for the dungeons. Again. Atoning for his sins. It was the story of his life.

Then, unexpectedly, she put her hand to her mouth and giggled.

"Bring the candles closer, Marianne," she told the girl at her side.

A candleholder, with two or three wax candles, stood on an elegant little table behind the two women. The younger woman was a servant, it seemed. Lady Constance's personal maid, Septimus guessed. While Marianne attended to the candles, Lady Constance took a closer look at the sorry figure in front of her.

"Dear God!" she murmured. *"Septimus!* Am I dreaming? Is it really you? Where on earth have you *been?* For all these years? I thought you were dead."

"I've been back six months. Not from the dead, obviously. From the Spanish Main. And thereabouts. That's where they took me. Your husband's lackeys. After that fateful night. They beat me half to death and then, for some reason I've never fathomed, took me down to the Pool and put me on a ship to the bloody Americas. *In chains.* Why they didn't just cut my throat and throw me in the damned river, I've never quite worked out. It would have been so much simpler."

"They told me you were dead."

"It was half-true. I should have written. I meant to.

But then... *you know how it is*. The years have just flown by. I was in Venezuela. Then Saint-Domingue. *For years.* Good times and bad. It could have been worse. I'm still alive. *Just about.* But we have *urgent problems,* my lady. The French army has landed in Kent. So rumour has it. Flying creatures are attacking the city. *Murderous creatures!*"

"We've seen them. One of the watchmen was carried off."

"But you didn't leave the house, thank God."

"We hardly knew what to do. The servants have disappeared. We heard screams. Out in the night. I was in my bedchamber, reading, when it all started. I called Marianne and we tiptoed downstairs. *That's when we saw them.* Through the high windows. Those... *things.* Out in the fog. What *are* they?"

"Fiends from hell. Is there no-one else in the house?"

"It seems not. They've all fled. The place has been half-empty for years. My bullying husband is long-gone. There's been talk of a divorce. I've had letters from his lawyers. Accusing me of harlotry. What were you doing on the roof?"

"Playing the fool," Septimus muttered. "As usual. I was trying to get in without being seen. I got over the riverside wall and up the side of the tower."

"Did no-one challenge you?"

"There was nobody around. Not a living soul! It's like a *graveyard* out there, my lady. Whole streets are empty! People have run for their lives. You can hardly blame them. These creatures are *eating* people! They're *carnivorous!*"

"We saw them at work. The poor watchman."

"I've also lost friends."

"What are we to do?"

"Are there still guns in the house?"

"In the armoury, of course, but... I don't have a key. The house steward will have it. Wherever he is. We could break the door down, I suppose."

Septimus shook his head.

"We don't have time. We need to leave. Before things get any worse! We could take one of your carriages and drive north. To the Scottish borders! If the horses are still there, that is. The French army could be here before dawn. Can we get into the observatory? Does that old telescope still work?"

"Of course. What are you thinking of?"

"It might give us a better idea of what is going on."

The door was close by. Lady Constance led him over to it. Marianne hung back. Her mistress stopped, and sighed.

"Do what you need to do, Marianne. *But be careful!* I couldn't bear to lose you. *Hurry!* Take the candles. Just leave me one of them."

"She has a sweetheart on her mind," Lady Constance explained as the maidservant hurried away. "Some lad she met in church. They've been *seeing* each other. She's convinced that he wouldn't have left without her. I pray to God that he hasn't been taken. By one of these ghastly... *creatures*. It would break her heart."

Septimus followed his one-time lover up the steps of the tower. To the observatory. The candle-flame hissed and fluttered as she led him in. The domed chamber, with its immense copper canopy, was dusty and dark. It was *icily* cold.

Lady Constance moved from place to place, lighting more candles.

She smiled at Septimus.

"Does it bring back memories?"

"Indeed. We spent many an afternoon up here."

She laughed.

"We were younger, then. I'd given up hope of ever seeing you again. But... here you are. Fallen from heaven! At this fateful hour. I hardly dare think what would happen if the French were to get their hands on me. My forbears were of the old nobility. It's no great secret. Everybody knows it. *I could lose my head.* We all know what's been happening in Paris. *Dear God!* How have they managed to take us unawares like this? Don't we have *spies* anymore? Across the Channel?"

"I'm sure we do, my lady, but... *demonic* forces are at work here."

She wiped away a sudden tear.

"My vile husband wouldn't give a *damn* if my head were to roll. He's living a blissful life overseas. *In Jamaica.* So I'm told. With a *hareem* of unhappy slave-women he's taken as brides. Every gossiping fish-wife in Billingsgate knows it! *Disgraceful* cartoons have been published! In the ha'penny scandal-sheets. *And* elsewhere. I rarely leave the house. People point and titter. I feel such a fool. The Duchess of Devonshire is the only person of any account who still speaks to me."

Septimus looked puzzled.

"I fear I must correct you, my lady. On one point, at least. Your despicable husband is not in Jamaica. He's back here. *In London.* Leading an even stranger life than the one you've heard report of. He appears to have gone quite mad. In the tropical heat, perhaps. *It happens.* I saw similar cases. In India."

"But, Septimus..."

"It's a lot to take in, I know. But it's the truth, I swear. Lord Blackthorpe is here in London. I've seen him with my own eyes. He's peddling some ghastly potion. *Eau Sacré,* they call it. He's actually *paying* people to drink the stuff."

"I've, uh... tried it myself. Marianne had been given some."

"Oh, Lord! Can we open the roof?"

She crossed the chamber and tugged at a lever. Chains clanked. Cold light filtered in as the moving panels of the dome slid open. It was almost dawn.

"Is the telescope in good order?"

"It's been oiled and cleaned. Once or twice. Nobody really uses it anymore. Nobody ever did. Isaiah had become obsessed with the idea that there were people living on the moon. That's the reason he had all this built. Not long after our marriage. He came up here night after night. For months on end. And then, quite suddenly, he seemed to lose all interest. It was a complete waste of money."

She found a piece of cloth and dusted-off the lenses.

"I still come up here, occasionally. To pass the time and take a look at the world outside. You can see for miles, in the daytime. Even without the telescope. You can see as far as Greenwich, on a clear day. I watch the boats going by. The people in the streets. Carts and carriages. Dogs and cats. The gypsy camps on the other side of the river. I've seen them dancing. Late at night. Around their fires. Sometimes I wish I'd been born a gypsy. To have that freedom."

"*Uh, huh...*"

Septimus's mind was on more pressing matters. He cranked the heavy wheel that rotated the apparatus. Turning the telescope this way and that.

Without really knowing what he expected to find.

He put his eye to the glass.

The night-fog was lifting. He could see for a mile or two, already, in the pre-dawn light. Buildings were burning, across the city. The Thames bridges were still thronged. A million terrified citizens were fleeing for their lives.

There was no sign, as yet, of an approaching French army, but the danger was by no means over. The flying creatures were still circling, in the gloom above.

"Where did you see my husband?" Lady Constance asked, suddenly.

"At the old Gaiety Theatre. In Wapping. He's fallen in with a heathenish Parisian cult. *The Sign of the Crocodile Queen.* He was buying souls. For his new mistress. At twenty shillings a head. I came out tonight with the avowed intention of shooting him dead. For the sake of humanity. But then... these *creatures* appeared and I thought of you, my lady. I was concerned for your safety. I'd heard that you were here alone. The whole of London seems to know your story."

"How long have you been back in England?"

"Six months. I didn't have the courage to come and see you."

She studied him, thoughtfully.

"You've *changed,* Septimus. I hardly recognised you."

"I haven't been eating well. You know how it is. Sometimes. One thing and another. We should leave, now, I think. It's become strangely quiet. I don't like the sound of it. We'll take one of your carriages. If the horses are still there."

"I can't leave without Marianne. She's my dearest love."

"We can't wait much longer. She could be *anywhere.*"

He took another look through the telescope.

It was getting lighter. The fog was clearing. A few dense patches remained. In the riverside streets. The river itself seemed unusually flat and still.

Septimus studied the motionless, glinting surface.

"Dear Lord..." he muttered.

Astonishingly, the Thames had frozen over.

This is Blackthorpe's doing, he told himself. *Meddling with the weather seems to be one of his favourite party-tricks. He's trying to spread fear.*

Lady Constance was shivering.

"It's so *cold,* Septimus," she whispered. "I can't travel dressed like this. In my night clothes. I'd freeze to death. Before we reached Islington. I don't even know where my winter clothes are. Marianne will know, I suppose, when she gets back. Where is that silly girl, for heaven's sakes? Where can she be?"

Septimus took his old leather coat off and passed it over.

"Put this on, my lady. It's a rough old thing, I know, but it will help to keep you warm. There'll be travelling-blankets, all being well, in the coach-house. We're going to need them. The temperature is *plummeting*. The river has iced-over."

Her nose wrinkled as she pulled the heavy coat around herself.

"It *stinks*, Septimus! *Good God!* Where on earth did you find it?"

"I bought it at a plague sale. In Maracaibo. Half a lifetime ago. It's perfectly safe. Don't worry. I've been wearing it for years. I've grown quite fond of it."

"You should get a new one. Sometimes... you have to let things go."

Septimus didn't respond. He was studying the frozen landscapes on the far side of the river. They were strangely deserted. Nothing whatsoever was moving. The fleeing crowds he'd witnessed earlier had vanished. It hardly made sense.

Unless...

A terrifying thought occurred to him.

Once again, he cranked the wheel. The Temple of Dreams swam into view. The scaffolding had gone. The finished structure was eerily aglow, in the fog.

Hundreds, perhaps thousands, of the flying creatures were streaming around the great dome that topped the building. Dark holes were opening, as if by magic, in the base of the dome. The blood-splattered, bloated creatures were wriggling into the holes. With their wings folded. Like foraging wasps, returning to a nest.

Have they been consuming human flesh? Septimus wondered.

Horribly, it looked as though they had.

The Necropolis came into view, as he moved the telescope.

Ghostly shades were flitting along the foggy paths between the tombs.

Inexplicably...the graves were opening!

Septimus groaned.

"*Uuuugh...*"

He adjusted the lens and looked again.

"*Oh, my God!*"

"What is it?" Lady Constance asked.

Septimus hardly knew. He recalled the dreadful tales that Ebenezer Withers had told him. At the Swan Inn. *Of the grey men with yellow eyes.* He'd only half-believed the old man, at the time. He hadn't *wanted* to believe him.

But the grey men were real... and they were on the move.

The Great Necropolis of Queen Mbembé was giving up its dead.

A ghostly army was rising from the underworld. From the very depths of hell. The tombs were opening. Thousands of the grey shades had already emerged.

They were swarming along the twisted paths of the Necropolis. Towards the Temple of Dreams...

"*Lord, help us!*" Septimus whispered, as he looked on.

He backed away from the telescope. As though he'd seen enough. Lady Constance stepped forward and put her own eye to the lens. She shuddered.

"*Good God! What are they? Ghosts?*"

"I've got no bloody idea," Septimus confessed. *"The risen dead.* By the look of it. We need to get out of here.

Right now. Out of London! As far away as possible! We'll take one of the smaller carriages. If the horses are still there."

She looked uncertain.

"Let's just hope there is one. We don't keep many, these days. The stables are half-empty. There's a little gig in the coach-house. We could take that. If there's a pony to pull it. The larger carriages are in poor condition. They've hardly been used for years. I don't go out much. The house has become my prison."

"We'll take the gig. If the horses are gone we'll just have to walk. There may even be horses running loose. Out in the streets. It's by no means impossible. Perhaps even the odd hackney-coach. Still touting for business. Though they'll be charging ten times the legal rate. *At the very least.* Do you have, uh... *money*, my lady? We're going to need a bob or two. I haven't got a farthing to my name."

"How have you been living?"

"Heaven knows. I was close to becoming as rich as a bloody lord when this madness started. The proceeds of a robbery. *We won't need much.* Just enough."

"I've got a few guineas in my chamber. And some jewellery."

"That will do. I'll pay you back. I promise."

"What about Marianne? We need to find her!"

"It may be too late. Let's hope not."

He took a last look through the telescope. Luminous, eerie mists were gathering around the Temple of Dreams. The ghastly flying creatures were still coming and going overhead. Their struggling victims were still being dragged, half-dead, half-alive, into the hideous black holes at the base of the dome.

It was a terrible thing to behold.

Septimus cursed, but... *there was nothing whatsoever he could do.*

Wave after wave of the walking dead from the Necropolis were tramping up to the temple's front entrance and disappearing. Into the umbrageous beyond.

Like the ghouls of Septimus's recent nightmares, the ghostly figures all looked the same. They had scaly grey skin, yellow eyes and ugly little wings.

Crocodile priests with whips were lashing the backs of any malingerers.

Septimus was about to turn away when something else caught his eye.

The great dome, high above it all, had begun to glow.

A whirlpool of eldritch fire was forming, in the darkness around it. Ghostly lights were flickering *inside* the dome. Shadowy, shifting shapes could be seen.

Almost as though... something was being born!

A weird silence had fallen over the city.

"Oh, no..." Septimus murmured. "Please... no..."

He shook himself to be sure that he wasn't imagining things. The Temple of Dreams was... *transforming.* It was spinning, soundlessly, and *rising,* into the dark sky, as it turned. Thunder rumbled, in the blackness beyond.

The great dome was *melting.* It was *swelling.* And *cracking...*

Like a monstrous cosmic egg.

"Blackthorpe!" Septimus whispered. *"What have you done?"*

Lady Constance was waiting, by the door.

"What is it?" she asked, worriedly.

"*It's...the Temple of Dreams!*" he stammered. "The bloody thing is... *alive! It's... moving! It's breathing!* Dear God! We need to leave! *Let's go!*"

Ashen-faced, he pushed the telescope aside.

"This is your mad husband's doing! Heaven knows what he's thinking of! I saw him, last night. At the old Gaiety. Muttering weird nonsense, at the feet of a monstrous golden statue. I thought it was an act! Some foolery. To impress his deluded followers! I should have known better. I could have throttled him. Right there and then. It would have been so damned easy!"

"But, Septimus..." Lady Constance began.

An explosion, somewhere close by, cut her off in mid-sentence.

It was hard to tell where the blast had come from.

Broken glass tinkled from a thousand shattered windows as the pair fled the observatory. Filthy smoke flooded in from the world outside. It was dark, once again. Inexplicably dark. As though something had *consumed* the early dawn light.

Lady Constance grabbed a candle as they rushed out.

"*Which way?*" Septimus asked. His ears were still ringing.

"*The main stairs!*"

Septimus's memories of the great house had dimmed, over the years. There were miles of corridors, and several staircases, including one or two that were only ever used by the servants. He followed Lady Constance through the dusty gloom.

Everywhere he looked there were things he'd forgotten.

A wretchedly-decayed alligator in a glass case distracted him for a moment as he hurried past it. The beast had been shipped from the Americas, he recalled. It had survived for almost a year, in a specially-dug pond at the back of the house, but then, for some reason, Blackthorpe had had it shot, and stuffed.

The glass eyes of a moth-eaten Bengal tiger glimmered through the murk. Portraits of Lord Blackthorpe's ancestors peered down from the walls.

Like disapproving ghosts.

The grand staircase at the front of the house swept down into a huge, high-ceilinged entrance hall. All of it fashioned in *exquisite* Italian marble.

Semi-naked goddesses gazed down from the heights.

Septimus followed Lady Constance down the sweeping stairs.

Except for the goddesses, the great hall was deserted. A candelabrum with a few fluttering candles had been left, by persons unknown, on a stand at the foot of the stairs. It was the only source of light. Lady Constance's candle had blown out.

Weird sounds were coming in from the streets outside. Strange, wild howls. It could *almost* have been the wind.

As a precaution, Septimus stopped and reloaded the pistol he'd discharged earlier, at London Bridge. He glanced around as he worked. The fabulous gilded ceilings – executed by Mr Orzinga and never paid for – were dimly visible, up above. Visions of the house as it had once been flooded his mind. For a brief moment.

A sudden commotion brought him back to his senses.

Someone was hammering at the front doors.

"Marianne!" Lady Constance cried.

She rushed towards the doors, but then... before she was even halfway there, she stopped and froze. In terror! *Luminous yellow eyes were peering in at her.*

A contingent of the grey men had found their way to Ermine House!

They were trying to smash their way in.

"*Septimus!*" she screamed.

"Move away!" he shouted. "They won't get through! Not easily! Those doors are a foot thick. The windows are barred. Even so, we need to get out of here! *To the stables!* Which way do we go? I hardly remember! It's been so long!"

"*The South Terrace!*"

She led the way, through echoing, empty corridors, to a morning-room at the back of the house. Septimus remembered it. Vaguely. Though he hardly recognised it. Nothing looked familiar. In the hellish, smoky dark.

The doors were all open. As though others had fled that way.

The stone columns outside were wreathed in fog. The rear terrace overlooked the gardens. There was a small courtyard below. Twisting steps led down.

Septimus followed Lady Constance out. Into the haunted night.

Little could be seen, in the ghastly blackness that had

fallen over the city. A puzzling, fiery glow was visible. Over to the south-east. Above Southwark.

Nightmarish shrieks and howls were coming from all sides.

"Marianne!" Lady Constance called.

But, once again, there was no answering cry.

"Do you have a *boat*, my lady?" Septimus asked her, suddenly. "You had several, at one time, as I recall. There was a boathouse. Down by the river. Partly underground, if I remember rightly. Is it still there? If we could just get to *Deptford,* all our troubles would be over! I've got friends in those parts. Friends and money! *A fortune in gold!* A ton of the bloody stuff! On a vessel in Deptford Creek. Our intention was to sail to America. I was hoping – *hoping and praying* – that you would consent to accompany me."

"To America?"

"You're unprepared, I realise, but... *what have we got to lose?"*

Lady Constance was no longer listening. She was staring. Past Septimus's pleading, anxious face. At something in the night sky. Septimus hadn't yet seen it.

She touched his arm, softly.

"Look!"

He turned to look.

"Oh... God!"

A monstrous, flaming apparition was rising over the city. A molten fireball that filled half the sky. It was the Temple of Dreams. *Transformed.* The heathen shrine was *changing shape* as it rose. The magnificent dome had gone. The walls and towers were no more. All that remained was a blazing, blood-red sphere.

In the dreadful night.

It was *spinning*. Silently. Strange lights were floating around it.

"*Heaven, save us...*" Septimus whispered.

The ground was shaking. Shattered slates and bits of stone were rattling down from the roofs above. The Corinthian columns were swaying, dangerously.

"*Move!*" Septimus shouted. "*Away from the house!*"

Lady Constance seemed unable to move. He took her hand.

At the same moment – the spinning vision exploded.

There was a blinding flash, and a distant, dread rumble.

Queen Mbembé emerged. Her shimmering form filled the heavens and lit up the shattered landscapes below. Her jewels glittered. Like a storm of stars.

Beneath her bejewelled toes, the city groaned.

This was the end, it seemed. *The dénouement.* The terrible reward for mortal sin that Septimus's father had thundered about from his pulpit.

On a thousand inebriated Sundays.

Ermine House was collapsing. Debris was tumbling down.

Purple flames were licking around Queen Mbembé's oiled limbs.

She was *melting*, Septimus realised. As though for her, too, this was the end. She laughed and danced as the flames consumed her. And then – in the final moments, as her temporal body dissolved – *a new horror burst from within her!*

A ghastly abomination. A hundred miles high. With

innumerable, slimy, spiderlike, wriggling legs, and a monstrous, bloated, blood-red abdomen.

Its evil eyes glimmered. Like the embers of dead suns.

Its wing-cases opened as Septimus watched. Immense wings emerged.

"*Uuuuuugh...*" Septimus moaned.

He swayed, dizzily, as the ground under his feet shook.

Cold fire streamed from the creature's pitiless eyes.

Lord Blackthorpe's eyes... Septimus realised, as he stared.

This was the fiend that had taken possession of Blackthorpe's soul.

Buildings exploded, across the city, as the apparition directed its fiery gaze this way and that. Within moments, entire districts were ablaze. Ermine House was already on fire. Smoke and flames were pouring from the high windows.

Septimus had lost sight of Lady Constance, in the confusion. He was about to call her name when a sudden, powerful tremor threw him to the ground.

Worse was to come...

As he struggled to his feet, a two-ton block of soot-blackened Portland stone crashed through the terrace roof – directly overhead. It was the snarling stone lion he'd come face-to-face with earlier. On his way up the scaffolding.

It shattered as it hit the solid paving below.

Pieces of it flew out in every direction.

A fragment the size of a cannonball hit Septimus in the side of the head. Weirdly enough, he hardly felt a thing. It was no worse, really, than being punched in the face by a drunken coal-heaver, in the course of a late-night tavern brawl.

The sound of his own blood throbbed in his ears as he dropped.

Tzz...tzz...tzz... tzz...tzz... tzz... tzz...

Dust filled the air around him. He felt curiously weightless and at peace. Despite the hole in his head. Ermine House was tumbling down around him. The whole city was in ruins. Strange dark figures were flitting about in the shadows.

People he'd never seen before. He had no idea who they were. Lanterns were being lit, by silent servants.

A court had been convened. In the gilded banqueting hall. The Grand High Pontieff was in the judge's chair, looking down at the assembled multitude.

A mask of mud and feathers, smeared with blood, concealed his face.

Septimus blinked as he peered about. Everyone he'd ever known was there, it seemed. Friends and enemies. Kitchen maids and rent collectors. People from the distant past that he still owed money to. He spotted his stern-faced father. In amongst the crowd. His mother, too, with several of his siblings. People from around the world were appearing. The Venezuelan pirates. The beautiful Rozalita. His Calcutta lover, Zaira, who he'd sworn he would marry... one day.

The Chief Prosecutor adjusted his wig and pointed at Septimus.

"Adulterer! Thief! Fool! Betrayer of dreams!"

"STRING THE BASTARD UP!" the drunken jurors shouted, with one voice.

Tzz...tzz...tzz...tzz... tzz...tzz...tzz...tzz...

"*Make way for the Great Cockroach!*" an attendant shouted.

Trumpets sounded. The doors of the courtroom burst open.

The creature stood about four feet high. Its antennae fluttered as it probed Septimus's aura. It was walking on its hind legs with its head thrown back in a most arrogant manner. The rest of its hands and feet were pushed into the pockets of an expensive evening suit. The blue silk sash across its chest bore the Masonic insignia of '*Le Grand Orient de Saint-Domingue*'. Its black beak was twitching.

"*Grobfunch!*" it spat.

Septimus tried to make the horrible thing disappear, but he couldn't quite summon the willpower. He closed his eyes and covered his ears. He could feel the earth shaking, beneath him. Susie Kettle floated by. As though in a dream.

The air filled with the sweet smell of her perfume.

The courtroom had evaporated when he opened his eyes again. The Great Cockroach had vanished. The howling and screaming had faded away.

Familiar, cold, brown, London fog was drifting around him. Water was lapping up against the ruins of the terrace.

The Thames had burst its banks, he realised. The mysterious ice had melted. Grey dawn light was filtering through the fog. Another day was beginning.

A golden boat came into view.

It appeared to be one of the splendid ceremonial vessels that Guildsmen and Freemasons used for their annual progresses upriver. Billy was at the helm. With his girl. Lachlan and Mulu were aboard. Lady Constance was on the foredeck.

She was beckoning.

"Septimus! Come!"

Septimus rose, dazedly, to his feet. He wondered where on earth they'd found the boat. He guessed that some old friend of Lachlan's had arranged things.

His spirits rose as the craft bobbed ever closer

Luminous pink mist was gathering around it.

Everything is going to be alright, he told himself. Their efforts and sacrifices had not been wasted! The golden boat would take them all to the New World!

He sighed. Contentedly.

As the ghostly mist closed in.

This book is printed on paper from sustainable sources managed under the Forest Stewardship Council (FSC) scheme.

It has been printed in the UK to reduce transportation miles and their impact upon the environment.

For every new title that Troubador publishes, we plant a tree to offset CO_2, partnering with the More Trees scheme.

For more about how Troubador offsets its environmental impact, see www.troubador.co.uk/sustainability-and-community